Also by Susan Rebecca White

A Soft Place to Land
Bound South

A Place at the Table

SUSAN REBECCA WHITE

A Touchstone Book
Published by Simon & Schuster
New York London Toronto Sydney New Delhi

Touchstone
A Division of Simon & Schuster, Inc.
1230 Avenue of the Americas
New York, NY 10020

This book is a work of fiction. Any references to historical events, real people, or real places are used fictitiously. Other names, characters, places, and events are products of the author's imagination, and any resemblance to actual events or places or persons, living or dead, is entirely coincidental.

First Touchstone hardcover edition June 2013

Designed by Aline C. Pace

Manufactured in the United States of America

10 9 8 7 6 5 4 3 2 1

Library of Congress Cataloging-in-Publication Data

White, Susan Rebecca.
A place at the table / Susan Rebecca White. — First Touchstone hardcover edition.
pages cm
"A Touchstone book."
I. Title.
PS3623.H57896P58 2013
813'.6—dc23
2012049547

ISBN 978-1-4516-0887-8
ISBN 978-1-4516-0894-6 (ebook)

To Teagan and Olivia: *you, you, you, you, you*

Gather up the fragments left over, so that nothing may be lost.
John 6:12

CONTENTS

Prologue

Alice and James in North Carolina

Wild Sow

(Emancipation Township, North Carolina, 1929)

For Alice, looking at James was like looking back at herself, only a washed-out, lighter version, and with short wavy hair instead of plaits held in place with pieces of torn-up muslin. Alice had been looking at James all twelve years of her life, she who entered the world exactly fifteen months after her brother. From a young age they would have staring contests; first one to blink lost. They were constantly engaging in these battles of will, though Alice was always the loser. James could stare through the tears building up in his eyes, while Alice couldn't bear the sting.

Saturday nights, after supper, nighttime chores, and the weekly bath, the extended family would gather in Granddaddy and Granny's house, where Alice and James also lived, their mother having moved them all there after their father died. They would read Bible verses, sing songs, recite poetry. Sometimes the elder adults told stories of slave days while the children sat at their feet, listening or playing with cornhusk dolls or the treasured set of marbles Granddaddy kept in a black velvet bag and stored on the top shelf of the pie safe. During one such time Alice and James retreated to the corner of the main room. They sat across from each other, knees bent, the flats of their feet touching, so they were connected. In their laps they each held a small chalkboard from school and a stub of chalk. They had an idea. They were going to transmit their thoughts to each other through the air.

They were always saying the same thing, always laughing at each other's private jokes, though no one else understood what was so funny. And so James thought they should test it, see if there really was something strange going on. He told Alice to think of an image—an ear of corn, a candle, a squirrel—and write the word for it on her chalkboard. Then James would concentrate real hard and draw whatever image he saw in his mind. Again and again he drew the right word, missing only occasionally.

"Cat."

"Raccoon."

"Tomato."

"Pig."

"Flower."

"Mother."

They called their mother over to them, tried to show her the amazing thing they were doing, but as soon as she heard the word "magic" she told them to quit fooling with spirits and get back with everyone else before she whipped them for blasphemy. They obeyed but continued playing their mind-reading game anytime they could, lying to Mother about why they needed the chalkboards, pretending they were busy memorizing math equations for school.

Mother often threatened to whip them, but she rarely did. For large crimes, she would hand them over to Granddaddy to discipline, and while he had never whipped Alice he had once whipped her brother, a beating so severe it had laid James up for days. But usually Granddaddy would come up with other punishments, punishments that involved extra chores or no dessert or even the silent treatment for a week, and not just from him but from everybody in the community of Emancipation Township. Granddaddy confessed that while he'd whip a child if he had to—and that one time there had been no choice but to beat James into submission—it turned his stomach to lash black skin. As a boy he had seen what had happened to the slave who had tried to run away from Hortican Stone's farm. He had seen a back lashed to bone.

Alice and James were down by the creek, checking on one of their rabbit traps. James looked puzzled. The trap was missing its bait but contained no rabbit, and both he and Alice knew this should not happen, because he always placed the lettuce far enough back so that the door would bang closed before the rabbit even got a nibble. Even if some other animal had taken the food, it should be trapped inside the box for James to find and release. Often when this occurred the freed animal would try to follow James around afterward. There was just something about James that drew animals to him. The year their father died James turned one of their chickens into his pet. Or rather, the chick claimed James, following him everywhere. Pretty soon she was riding high on James's shoulder anytime he wasn't doing farmwork or playing stickball with the other boys.

Suddenly there was a thunderous drumming and a surge of heat and the earthy smell of animal and *swoosh!* A wild pig almost nicked them in her passing, splashing their bare feet with cold creek water as she crossed to the other side, out of Emancipation Township and into the woods that separated their land from the town of Cutler, North Carolina, where they had to bow their heads and pretend not to be so free anytime they needed to do business at Sam Hicks's General Store.

For a moment Alice and James remained silent, in awe.

"She got herself a litter," James finally said. "See those tits?"

Their granddaddy would scold James if he heard him talk this way. Crude and unsophisticated. True, Granddaddy himself stumbled over the written word and he sometimes slipped into country speech, but the children of his children were given opportunities he never had, including a schoolhouse run by a steady rotation of college graduates, lured to Emancipation to experience the pride that comes from working in a community owned and run by Negroes. Alice's grandmother Rachel, Spelman degree in hand, had been the first of these young people to come. Other Spelman graduates followed, along with male teachers from Morehouse and Howard, where James was expected to go the following year when he turned fifteen, just as two of his uncles had gone before him, one now a doctor in Washington, D.C., the other back on the farm, raising his own family.

Alice had not noticed the animal's tits. She had been too mesmerized by how fast the sow ran. How ugly she was, with her thick coat of dirty, pointy hair, her elongated snout, her tiny black eyes. The sow was a beast, fierce and ferocious, while the pigs they raised on the farm were almost comic, oinking with excitement when Alice walked toward their pen carrying the slop bucket. And when their diet shifted from slop to acorns—finishing the pigs on acorns was the secret to the sweet succulence of the Stone family hams, which Sam Hicks sold fast as he could get them at the General Store—they became even more frenzied at feeding time, as Alice approached with buckets of acorns, taken from the supply she and James and the other cousins gathered every fall and kept stored in the barn. Mother said the pigs liked those acorns as much as Alice liked pecan pie.

"We find her piglets, we eat high all winter," said James.

While Alice craved sweets, her brother loved meat. Chops and ribs and butt and bacon. Sausage sizzling in its own fat, the key ingredient in the white gravy Mother fixed, which she poured over biscuits, made tender and flaky by a lacing of lard through the flour. You would think that with the number of pigs their family slaughtered each fall James would have as much meat as he desired. But crop prices were down and the tax bill was high and last year they'd sold every pig they raised just to get through the winter. "Thank God Almighty for swine," Granddaddy said.

James and Alice stared into the distance, following the blurry path of the racing sow. They saw her go over a hill on the other side of the woods. She disappeared for a moment before reappearing on the top of another hill. And then they saw her turn and disappear again, this time for good. As if she vanished into the earth, though probably she had just entered a cove.

"C'mon," said James. "Let's get her."

He was carrying a loaded rifle. He took it every time they went trapping, in case there was an injured animal in need of a mercy killing or they spotted a raccoon high up in the trees. But the sky was a pale lavender, soon to be swallowed by dark. They were expected home before this happened, home for a supper of fall vegetables and Mother's good yeast bread, and maybe some meat—squirrel most likely. And for dessert they could eat as many crunchy apples, the first of the fall season, as they wanted.

"We're not gonna find that thing," she said.

"Granddaddy says wild pigs are the devil on crops. You know he'd want us to kill it."

Alice did not know this at all. She imagined their granddaddy would want them to come home, right away. But she also knew what James was thinking, that if he could bring home a slain pig and her piglets, his granddaddy couldn't help but show pride in him. Alice knew he was imagining Granddaddy's expression when he saw the kill.

Imagining Granddaddy clapping him on the shoulder, calling him son. Like he did to the other boys who made Granddaddy proud.

Granddaddy *was* proud of James, surely. Alice had seen Granddaddy cheer on the sidelines when James hit a home run during a stickball game. Alice had seen the glint in Granddaddy's eyes when James brought back eight rabbits from the woods, all trapped during one day. But Granddaddy's pride in his oldest grandson was never directly expressed. The old man was forever swallowing what gentle thing he might say to his headstrong boy.

Mother claimed that James and her daddy were too much alike to get along well. She must have been talking about their temperaments, because appearance-wise, James was tall and thin while Granddaddy was short and stocky. And Granddaddy's skin was the color of roasted coffee beans, while James's always reminded Alice of peanut shells.

James knew the woods the way Alice knew Mother's recipes. He was a quiet walker, each step deliberate. The children were barefoot, as they would be until the first frost. The ground was mostly soft beneath Alice's feet, though occasionally she would step on something sharp and pointed and have to stop and dig the stickler out. Her feet were so callused she hardly even noticed the sting.

About twenty minutes into the hunt, as they ventured deeper and deeper into the land outside Emancipation, James stopped short, motioning Alice to him. He pointed to a menacing contraption on the ground, a thick chain attached to a giant mouth with sharp rusty teeth, ready to spring should you step inside it. When she saw the jagged metal teeth, stained with dried blood, Alice yelped. James hushed her, saying it was only a bear trap, but that she should keep her eyes on the ground in case there were others.

They walked on, their footfalls forming a rhythm as they padded along the ground, strewn with fallen leaves, many already turned the colors of autumn. Off in the distance Alice heard the distressed cries of an animal. The scant hairs on her arms popped up.

"What was that?" she asked.

"I don't know."

Alice yearned to be inside her granddaddy's house, beside the fire, safe and warm.

"Let's go up here," James said, turning left, making his way up an unmarked hill and through a growth of thin, young trees. The hill-side was slippery with fallen leaves, and Alice had to grab onto the tree branches to support herself. But the one she grabbed snapped in two, and Alice, off balance, fell backward.

"You okay?" James asked.

Alice nodded. She was. She stood up, looking around for a moment while she got her bearings. She stared in the direction of an oak tree off to the side. She thought she saw an owl perched on one of its branches. She had heard the calls of a barred owl earlier that evening: *woot, woot, woot, woo; woot, woot, woot, woooh!*

"Ready?" James asked. He was waiting for her on top of the little hill. He told her which trees to grab, and she followed his direction. When she was just below him he extended his arm and she grabbed onto it tightly. He helped her up, and they were safe and on another cleared trail, higher.

"Where are we going?" she asked. It was darker now, and she was cold.

"There's a cove up here," he said. "Maybe she's nested in it."

"I thought they rooted in mud piles."

James turned and put his finger on his lips. "Shhhh."

"Why are you shushing me? They do."

James held his finger in front of his lips and glared at her.

And then she heard it. A rustle. A low hum. More rustling, more crunching. Someone or something was making its way through these woods. She heard talking, but she could not yet make out what was being said. And then she saw them, down below, on the path they had walked on, three white men. Three guns by three sides, a lantern with a flickering flame lighting the way. One of the men had beautiful red hair, illuminated by the lantern's glow, the hair the color of the skins of the apples she was supposed to have eaten for dessert that night. One man had something besides his rifle tucked beneath his arm, something round and coiled, which looked to Alice like a snake. Two bluetick hounds loped behind the men. Hunters, thought Alice. Looking for the sow, too.

"The look on that boy's face," said one of the men, chuckling, shaking his head.

They were closer now, in hearing range.

"'Please, suh, I didn't take no chickens!'"

"Lying nigger."

"He's eatin chicken now, boys. He's eatin chicken now."

An explosion of laughter.

Alice did not fully understand what these men were talking about, but she knew she needed to change into something other than a girl. She needed to become one of the trees, to plant her feet into the ground, to be unmoved, even if someone walked right up to her and stared her in the face. *Don't blink.* Granddaddy was always saying that the trees had borne witness to all of human misery. The trees were here when Jesus Christ walked the earth, when he was hung on a cross made from one of them.

The men were directly below them now. When the sow had charged by at dusk, Alice had felt heat, smelled something feral and of the earth. There was a stench to these men, too, a musky mix of sweat and adrenaline. Alice closed her eyes. Relied on childhood logic: *If I can't see you, you can't see me.*

Beside her James had turned not to tree but to stone. Like their namesake.

The men kept walking. Eventually Alice lost sight of them, though she could still catch snippets of what they said. Something about coming back the next day to show him off to the other boys. Something about maybe they ought to tree a coon while they were out there, but nah, they'd already done that. Laughing again, low and hollow.

Alice smelled something new, a whiff of ammonia. She turned her head toward the smell and by the moon's white glow saw a darkened line down James's pants.

They saw the rope first, illuminated by the nearly full moon, hanging from the branch of a pecan tree a good fifty yards away. They made their way down the hill toward it, picking up speed as they went. They slowed when they saw the boy, the boy hanging from the rope. His head was tilted back, his chin pointed toward the sky, as if he were looking for God. His hands were bound behind him with more of the thick rope. His once white shirt hung around his waist, the empty arms dangling. There were diagonal stripes across his back, the skin around the lashes puffed, swollen. How skinny he was, skinny enough that Alice could see his ribs. He was as skinny as James. He was a boy like James, maybe even the same age. This could not have happened to a boy like James, a boy who also had long, delicate fingers.

There was something white coming out of his mouth. Alice got closer, covering her face with her hand to block the terrible smell that was all around, a smell of shit and fear and mud and bile. Chicken feathers. They had stuffed chicken feathers into his mouth. There were so many feathers, some wet with vomit. They must have stuffed the feathers in his mouth before they hung him. They must have held him down. He must have been so scared. The feathers would have been dry and soft, but the quills would have poked him. They would have poked the back of his throat, making him choke. He would have been gasping to breathe, but he could not breathe because the feathers were in his mouth. He would have gagged, then vomited, and the force of the vomit would have sent some of the feathers out of his mouth and onto the ground below. The men would have laughed. And then stuffed more feathers back in.

James put his gun down on the ground, hugged the trunk of the tree, and shimmied up it, swinging his body onto the branch the rope was tied to. James took his knife out of the back pocket of his overalls and started sawing away at the rope, sawing and sawing until finally it was down to its last threads. "Move," he said to Alice before cutting the remaining tie. The body landed on the ground with a thump, still dead, as it had been the moment before, but no longer swinging, no longer on display for white men to gloat over.

"We gotta get Granddaddy," James said. "Granddaddy will know what to do."

By the time they reached their house, the rounded moon was high in the sky. They were so late. They were supposed to have been home hours before. Mother, Granddaddy, and Grandma Rachel were all waiting in the living room, their mouths straight lines across their faces, a child's drawing of angry adults.

"Praise Jesus," whispered their mother when they walked in the door. She was already out of her seat, running toward her children. She knelt before them, embraced them together, one in each arm. She must have fried something for dinner, for she smelled of peanut oil and, just beneath, lavender, which she dried and poured into sachets to bury beneath her undergarments. Her embrace lasted only a moment. She put her nose first to Alice's head and then to James's. She inhaled, as if checking to make sure these really were her kids, fleshy and alive.

She was crying, but her words were angry. "You my only babies, you know that? Alone in those woods, at this time of night."

Their granddaddy had risen from his chair. He stood behind their mother, a thick leather belt wrapped around his hand. When he spoke his voice was more somber than Alice had ever heard it. "You have anything you want to say for yourself?"

He was talking to James.

"We found a boy," said James, speaking quickly, as if he could stop what had happened in the woods if he got the words out fast enough. "A colored boy. Hung by a rope. We saw the men who did it, too. Three white men with two bluetick hounds. I don't know their names, but I could point em out if I was looking at em."

The muscles in Granddaddy's face froze. He loosened his grip on the leather belt. It uncoiled and fell to the floor, the metal buckle hitting the wood with a clang.

"You know who this boy was?"

"No, sir."

"The men who did this—they see you? They know you was there?"

James shook his head. "No, sir. We was high up on a trail and they passed under us, coming back from it. I had my rifle. If I had known what they had done, I would have shot em all dead."

Granddaddy was in James's face, grabbing the boy's cheeks with his hand. "Don't even joke about that."

"I ain't joking."

Granddaddy didn't flinch at the word "ain't."

"You sure they didn't see you?"

"I'm sure. We waited till they was way off before we cut down the body."

"You did what?" This came out a roar. Alice felt something seize up in her, and she worried she might go to the bathroom, right there.

"We cut him down. Weren't gonna leave him hanging there. I cut him down with my knife."

Granddaddy let loose James's face. Backed up and sat back down in his rocker, made from a felled pine tree. The old man sat and stared straight ahead.

"Anyone see you cut down that boy?"

"No, sir. Was just Alice and me there."

"Thank God. Thank God Almighty. He was watching out for you, that's for sure."

"I was only doing what was right."

"I know, son."

Alice glanced at James, but her brother did not seem to notice what Granddaddy had just called him.

"But you can't go messing with a white man's killing. Hurts my heart to tell you, but it's the truth."

"You didn't see what they did."

"You think I don't know? You think I ain't seen things? You think I wasn't born into life under the mercy of a white man?"

"But that was back in slave days. Now they call you mayor. Now Hicks sells your hams."

Granddaddy shook his head. "Hicks sells my hams cause he makes money doing so. Simple as that. And you can bet he don't go advertising a colored man raised them, neither."

"But we're the Stones. That's how we got this land in the first place. Cause we proved our worth."

James and Alice, along with all of the other children in the community, had long ago memorized the story of the founding of Emancipation Township, same as they memorized Bible verses for Sunday school. How after the War Hortican Stone gave Granddaddy's parents twenty-five acres of land in North Carolina, just across the state line, not forty miles from Hortican's own farm near Danville, Virginia, where William and Nellie had been stalwart and loyal servants.

How Granddaddy and his family moved onto the land in 1869, when Granddaddy was only fourteen. How young as he was, Granddaddy already had a vision of what the land could become, a refuge for all freed men, where colored families lived, worked, played, and prayed together.

"Son, we got that land cause Hortican Stone started messing with my mother since before I was born and didn't let up till his mind was so addled he couldn't bother her no more. Got to thinking she was his wife once his own wife died of smallpox, right after the War, and neither Mama nor Daddy did anything to convince him otherwise."

Alice looked at her brother. He was staring at Granddaddy and Granddaddy was staring at him and an electric understanding buzzed between the two of them. No words were spoken, but Alice understood what was being said.

White blood could hide inside dark skin for only so long.

There was a reason James was so light.

"You saying we didn't earn this land?"

"We earned it all right."

"You saying even though we kin to Hortican Stone, a group of white men could lynch any one of us, anytime, and there ain't a thing we can do about it?"

"I'm saying nothing of the sort. I'm saying we got to be careful, that's all. I'm saying we can never forget what a blessing it is we own this land. Don't matter how we got it. Matters that it's ours. Matters that we keep it ours. We got a precious, precious life here, son. You know that. Yeah, it's dangerous out there, and nothing in this world is pure. But inside Emancipation, we doing bout as good as we can. We just have to be careful when we step outside, that's all. We just have to know it's another world out there. You've always known that. We all have."

Except James hadn't. This Alice knew for sure, as sure as she knew he was thinking of a chicken the other night, then an apple, then a horse.

"It's just how it is, son. It's just something you got to learn to live around."

Three times that night Granddaddy called him son, but for James it no longer seemed to matter.

The next week, when they went into town to buy supplies, James stood by his mother at Sam Hicks's counter and pointed to the bolt of blue fabric with the little red flowers scattered across it like a loosened bouquet, the fabric Alice admired every time she went to the store, thinking how pretty she would look in a dress made from it.

Of course James knew it was the fabric Alice had always wanted.

"Five yards, please," he said, winking at Alice, as if he were doing something nice for her, as if he were doing something kind.

"Cain't sell you that one, boy," said Hicks jovially. "But I got a pretty red one I can cut for you. Real similar pattern, as a matter of fact. A mouse or some critter chewed up on its edges, so I moved it over here to the colored shelf, and now, lucky you, looks like it's got your name on it."

He pointed to a bolt of dusty red fabric lying beside the burlap and the muslin.

"Didn't know my money was a different color, too," said James, enunciating every word, just as their teacher Miss Robinson had taught them to do.

Alice wanted to point out that her brother was lying, that he didn't have any money to buy the fabric with in the first place.

Hicks sucked on his teeth and stared hard at Alice's mother.

"He been sick, suh," she said. "Real feverish. He outta his mind. I so sorry. We gonna get him home. Get him home and into bed and when he all healed up you better bet his granddaddy gonna make it so he never say nothin like that again."

Alice had never heard her mother speak so country.

"He needs to check himself and do it quick," said Hicks, nothing friendly about his tone.

Alice heard someone walk into the store. She looked up front and saw a man with a shock of red hair, vibrant as the skin on a crisp fall apple.

When Granddaddy learned what happened at the store, he did not steer James out to the barn to try to beat sense into him, as Alice thought he would do, but instead ordered him into the cellar to wait until they figured out a plan. James had to be hidden. He had to be hidden until they could get the details worked out. James was no longer safe on the farm. He had to go away. They had relatives in New York City. James would go live with them. There was no other choice. The boy was out of control. He didn't realize the danger he was in. It was like that time two years before, the only time Granddaddy ever whipped him, when James had walked through the front door of Hicks's store, on a dare from one of his cousins, even though colored people had to enter from the back. Once inside you could walk all the way to the front if you wanted, but you had to enter through the back.

If Hicks noticed James walking through the front door, he hadn't recognized the transgression, hadn't recognized that James was colored, that he belonged with the Stones. But back at the farm, after Granddaddy learned what happened, he started shaking he was so mad. He had used the horsewhip on his grandson. He had torn James up.

But James still hadn't learned.

And now he had to be hidden and hidden well, because who knew what might happen? Who knew what James might do next if left unchecked and on his own? Even if James were to change his behavior, recognize the gravity of the situation, who knew what damage had already been done? Somebody might come looking for the boy who attempted to buy white fabric at the store, the boy who dared to give lip to Sam Hicks, the boy who had the audacity to suggest his money was as valuable as a white man's.

The cellar beneath Granddaddy's house was cool and dank and lined with packed dirt. They kept turnips and rutabagas and parsnips in there, and big burlap sacks full of potatoes. That evening Granddaddy went down to where James was waiting, bringing his grandson a tin of biscuits, each stuffed with precious bits of ham trim and butter. Granddaddy told James to eat them all. While James ate, Granddaddy emptied one of the giant burlap bags of potatoes, cutting a small hole at the bottom with his knife. He instructed James to climb into the bag, lining up his face with the hole so he could breathe, tucking his legs up under him so nothing stuck out. Granddaddy told James that someone would come check on him as often as possible, to let him out so he could relieve himself, to bring him something to eat, but there might be long stretches in between. James protested, but Granddaddy was stony and unmoved. James acquiesced, crawling into the bag. Granddaddy rolled the potatoes back into it, surrounding his grandson in grit and starch. And then he left James down there while he rode his horse to relatives who lived more than fifty miles away, asking them to send a telegram to New York saying James was coming. If Granddaddy were to send it from Cutler, someone in town might inform Hicks, who might inform the men who had lynched the boy, who might be waiting for James when he arrived at the station to board the train.

Alice was so lonely in bed at night, without James curled up on his cot in the corner of her room. She lay next to Mother, silent and rigid, biting her fist, trying not to think of anything, because there was nothing she could think of that was okay. Nothing was safe. All of this time living in Emancipation, and nothing had ever been safe.

She lay like that for a long time. So stiff, so scared, she did not know how she would ever feel calm again. How she would ever again sleep. But then she must have fallen asleep, because she was dreaming, and in the dream she found the sow. On her own, walking through the woods, she came upon the animal, rooting in mud. She was even bigger and nastier and uglier than Alice had remembered. The sow looked at Alice with her mean black eyes and snorted. And then she was charging toward Alice. She was going to knock Alice down. Alice put her hands out. Alice put her hands out and her nails, sharp as the spikes on a bear trap, sank into the sow's hair-covered flesh. And then the sow disappeared and it was the hung boy Alice was embracing, the hung boy Alice couldn't release, the hung boy whose mouth was still stuffed with feathers. And suddenly Alice knew the awful truth. The hung boy was James. It was James who had been whipped and hung from a tree. It was James who was dead.

Every night they listened in fear for the sounds of men riding onto their property, looking for the boy who had dared to claim his worth equal to theirs. But the men never showed up. Still, James stayed hidden in the cellar for three days, until his exodus was fully arranged. When he finally emerged one early, early morning, with only a moment to say good-bye to Alice, James appeared even paler than before. Alice had been staring at her brother since before she could remember, but during that first brief absence—followed by a longer, final one—she must have forgotten how light he really was. So light was he that for a moment Alice believed she was looking at a white boy.

Part One

Bobby in Georgia

I

Royal Ambassador

(Decatur, Georgia, 1970)

Some people think being a Royal Ambassador is just like being a Scout, but boy, are they wrong. It's better! Cause everything we RAs do, all of the games and craft projects and circle shares and stuff, is in the name of Christ. And as our RA leader Mr. Morgan says, nothing is as sweet as Jesus, not even Coca-Cola. Mr. Morgan even has a T-shirt that has "Jesus" spelled out in fancy letters like it is on the Coke bottle, and beneath that it reads, "Is it!"

Once I drank a whole one-liter bottle of Coke by myself and I got so fidgety my hands were vibrating like our seventy-two-year-old neighbor down the street, Mr. McDade, who Mama says has the shakes. Mama made me run around the house ten times just to get out some of my energy. At least she didn't hook me up to the zip line, which is what she used to do with my brother Hunter, who's wild.

Daddy built the zip line a long time ago, as a sort of a combo

Christmas present for all three of us Banks boys. It runs through the backyard, just before the land turns to woods, where all sorts of squirrels and rabbits and frogs live. What the zip line is, really, is just a long wire stretched tight between two trees. And there's a handle on wheels that runs along the wire. You walk up the hill to the starting post, grab the handle, lift your knees, and whoa! There you go. Sometimes Daddy will give me a big push to start, and that's the best because then I go *flying* through the air, the wheels squeaking and screaming on the wire. When I'm just about to smack into the other tree either I touch the ground with my legs, sort of bumping to a stop, or my brother Troy—he's the oldest—will grab me, stopping the flight.

But what Mama used to do to make Hunter calm down was attach him to the zip line using a bungee rope and two carabiners, which are these big clips, one that would hook on to the handle and one that would hook on to the belt loop on the back of Hunter's pants. Course, he could have reached back and unclipped the carabiner, but he knew if he did he'd be in real trouble when Daddy got home. So Hunter would go along with whatever Mama told him to do. Usually she'd make him sprint up and down the length of that wire for half an hour or so. Mama said that way he could get out some of his energy without getting into any real mischief.

Hunter is also an RA, but he doesn't take it seriously. He's only in it for the M&M's. The other day he got in trouble for not listening during Mr. Morgan's talk about the Wayne and Evelyn Marshall Truth Tellers Foundation, which is the missionary group we help sponsor. The third time Mr. Morgan caught Hunter goofing off he made Hunter pull his chair right next to his. Then he kept on telling us about our missionaries. He said that Mr. and Mrs. Marshall are originally from Kansas, but they moved all the way to Calcutta to help run an orphanage for children living on the streets. "And sure," said Mr. Morgan, "the orphanage provides food and shelter, and that is wonderful, but more importantly, it introduces the poor orphaned children to Jesus. Can you imagine," Mr. Morgan asked, "growing up without parents *or* Jesus? And I'm not just talking about children in India," he said. "There are poor, godless orphans living *right here* in Decatur, Georgia, too."

Then Mr. Morgan showed us the picture of the special boy we are sponsoring, a boy who lives at the Marshalls' orphanage in Calcutta. He's my age—nine years old—and his name is Amit Patel. He is dark brown and real skinny, even skinnier than me. The funny thing is, when I looked at his picture, even knowing he doesn't have a mama and daddy, I didn't feel sorry for him. That's cause he's got a smile like he's holding onto a wonderful secret. It's a smile that makes me want to meet him, that makes me think he and I could be good friends.

I want a good friend, a best friend. There are boys in the neighborhood I play with sometimes, but Hunter's always with us and that makes it not as fun. Hunter says I act like a sissy and then he starts pretending to talk with a lisp, and it's not fair cause that's not how I talk! It's just that sometimes when I get really excited the words get jumbled up in my mouth and they don't come out good. It's cause I've got too much to say and I don't slow down enough to say it clearly. Least that's what Mama says, and she should know; she majored in child development at the University of Georgia, where she also earned her MRS. (That's a joke Daddy likes to tell, and whenever he does Mama will sort of slap him on the arm and tell him to hush, she was a very good student.)

There is a picture book Mama used to read to me called *Little Black Sambo.* It's about a boy who lived in the jungles of India. Even though I'm in the advanced reading group at school—Miss Lisa says I read at the eighth-grade level—I still like to flip through the pages of that old book. I wonder if Amit Patel is smart like Little Black Sambo. Little Black Sambo is so smart he tricked four tigers out of eating him. What happened was, Sambo was taking a walk through the jungle and he ran into four hungry tigers who thought Sambo would make a good breakfast. But instead of letting them eat him, Sambo tricks the tigers into chasing their own tails round and round a tree until they run so fast they turn into butter, which *Sambo* then eats, melted on top of a tall stack of hot pancakes.

If I ever meet Amit Patel I'm going to ask him if he's ever heard of a tiger running so fast it turned into butter. I don't *think* that could really happen, but then again, there are mysterious and wonderful things that occur every single day. Least that's what Mr. Morgan says. And I sure don't think a tiger turning into butter is any stranger than Jonah living inside the belly of a whale.

Everyone has a best friend but me. Even Mama. Daddy says that Mama and Betsy Meadows are "glued at the hip." They are so close that we boys call her Aunt Betsy, even though she's not kin. Aunt Betsy lives down the street, but she and Mama met long before they were neighbors. They knew each other even before they were married. They were both at the University of Georgia together, where they were members of Alpha Delta Pi sorority, which Daddy said had all of the prettiest girls. Aunt Betsy has two boys, identical twins, a year younger than Troy. She says they are double trouble, but they've never given me any. And I guess Aunt Betsy's going to have another baby soon; at least that's what she was talking about the other day.

It was midafternoon and Mama had finished all her chores, so she telephoned Aunt Betsy and told her to come visit. Aunt Betsy was there in a flash and a minute later the two of them were relaxing on the screened-in back porch, each lounging on one of the two white wicker chairs made extra comfortable by thick pillows covered in a pretty fabric with big flowers all over it, their feet propped up on matching ottomans. Mama had put two Tabs in the freezer before calling Aunt Betsy, so they'd be good and cold. Aunt Betsy sipped from hers while Mama's rested by her side. I could see Mama's handprint in the bottle's condensation.

I stood behind Mama, scratching her head while she and Aunt Betsy talked. Mama is not a fan of the new "wash-and-wear" hairstyles. She says at five foot two she needs all the lift she can get. The puffed hair on top of Mama's head is hard from all the hairspray she uses, but you just push through and you can get to her scalp.

"All I'm saying is, after what those boys put me through, I'm praying for a girl. I'm serious, Edie; you pray for me, too."

"You think you had it bad? You don't remember Hunter? Mercy! I was on my knees each night praying the next one would be a girl."

"You were?" I asked.

Mama reached her soft hand around to pat me on the arm. "But I was wrong, sweetheart. The only reason I prayed for a girl was I thought a girl would be easier. But you were an angel, weren't you, doll? Slept through the night almost as soon as you arrived, only fussed when you were hungry or had a dirty diaper, didn't mind sitting on the kitchen floor and just playing with Play-Doh all morning, while I did my work."

"I remember," said Betsy. "I was jealous. You were a dream baby for sure, sweetheart. While Hunter was wild."

"Was?"

"Is," said Betsy.

"He just came out that way. Fast and fearless. Once when he was three or four I left him alone in the living room for half a second, and next thing you know there was Hunter on top of the Mission bookshelf. To this day I don't know how he got up there. It's got a glass-fronted case. He must have scaled the sides."

"Good Lord," said Betsy.

"Well, he's on top of that thing and he's got his little red cape on around his neck and he's holding his arms out in front of him like he was at the pool and about to dive off the board. I heard myself saying the three words I said most often to him, 'Hunter, no sir!' but I was too late. He was already plummeting toward me. I managed to catch him, but I twisted my ankle doing so."

"Mercy."

"But honestly, Betsy, don't worry too much about this next one. The surprise babies are a gift from God. That's what everyone says. Certainly was the case for Bobby. Not that I love any of you better than the rest, you hear, son? But you *were* an easy baby."

Mama is always checking her words, trying to make sure she doesn't play favorites, but I know she loves me best. Probably has something to do with how much I love her, too. She just smells so good, on account of how often she rubs her hands with Jergens lotion, which is scented with almonds and cherries. She is prettier than most other mothers, too, so pretty she was runner-up in the Miss Georgia contest back before she married Daddy, and she flat-out won a contest for her face to be on the side of the Greenfield Pralines N' Cream ice-cream box. She almost always wears a skirt and heels—except when she is doing her "fitness walks" or gardening or deep cleaning the house—so she just clicks along the kitchen floor like a dancer. And she is the best cook in the world, well, except for Meemaw, whose pound cakes are so good ladies buy them straight out of her kitchen. Meemaw sells them for five dollars a cake, taking a maximum of ten orders a week, which always get filled. She says the steady baking is no problem now that she no longer has her job working in the lingerie department at Davison's Department Store.

I love to help Meemaw and Mama cook. By the time I was two I could crack an egg without getting any shell in the bowl. Mama swears to this, even though Christians aren't supposed to swear. Most afternoons I'm in the kitchen with Mama, snapping beans or peeling potatoes or husking corn or mixing meat loaf, while Troy studies in his room or is off meeting with the Fellowship of Christian Athletes and Hunter plays sports outside.

There are two rules Hunter has to follow when he goes outside to play. He has to always have a friend with him, and he has to wear a whistle on a string around his neck. If a bee stings him, he's supposed to blow and blow and blow on that whistle until an adult comes running. Or have his friend blow the whistle for him, depending on how bad off he is. He's only been stung once in his life, but he swelled up all over. It was during the annual Fourth of July church picnic supper at Clairmont Avenue Baptist. We all ate on the lawn, on blankets. After the desserts were served, but before the fireworks began, the kids started playing Red Light, Green Light. Hunter was the caller, so I stayed with Meemaw on the blanket, who brought one of her pound cakes to the potluck even though she goes to her own church and not ours. The reason I stayed with Meemaw was because Hunter didn't play fair. He always said I moved even when I didn't, and he would send me back to the starting line.

Plus, I just love spending time with my meemaw.

Suddenly Hunter threw his arms up in the air like someone being saved on television, then fell to the ground. And before I could even wonder what had happened Daddy was rushing toward him like a football player charging the goalpost. Daddy scooped Hunter up in his arms and raced to the parking lot where our station wagon was parked. Mama followed, yelling along the way for someone to tell Meemaw that Troy and I were to go home with her and wait for them to call. Later Mama told us that Daddy drove pell-mell to the hospital, breaking about a dozen traffic laws along the way. Turned out Hunter fell over on the field cause he got stung by a bee and was allergic. At the hospital they shot Hunter up with this stuff called epinephrine and Benadryl, and sent him home with a bunch of it, that and a boxful of needles. And they gave Hunter a pair of dog tags like Mr. Morgan has from Vietnam, only Hunter's tags say that he is allergic to bees.

It probably doesn't even matter whether or not Hunter wears those dog tags; everyone at church and school knows about his allergy, and every grown-up is prepared. There is epinephrine and a needle in the nurse's office at school, put aside especially for Hunter, and there is some in the RAs' meeting room, and in Mama and Daddy's bedroom at our house, and at Meemaw's house, and at the home of Hunter's best friend, Dixon, who doesn't seem to be so much a friend as he is a person for Hunter to trade punches in the arm with.

Still, it bothers me that Hunter has a best friend and I do not.

I guess he doesn't count as an actual friend, but I love spending time with Mr. Morgan. Unlike the other RA leaders, Mr. Morgan has all of his hair and he wears jeans to meetings instead of pleated khakis or Sansabelt slacks. And Mr. Morgan has green eyes and a dimple in each cheek when he smiles. He was in ROTC in college, just like my daddy. Later, Mr. Morgan served two tours of duty in Vietnam. He still does push-ups and sit-ups each morning. When he flexes his biceps it looks like there's a tennis ball beneath his skin. He tells us it is important to remember that our bodies are our temples and we are to honor them by doing stuff like eating our vegetables, brushing our teeth, hugging our mamas, and exercising every single day.

I always try to stand next to him during the closing prayer, when we gather in a circle. Sometimes I can't help but grab his hand if it happens to be hanging by his side, idle. He'll give my hand a little squeeze, but then he'll pull away. But he never pulls away meanly. It's just that his hands are busy: He has to clap to get our attention, or point to one of our craft projects hanging on the wall, or dig a Certs out of his pocket. Once Hunter noticed me reaching for Mr. Morgan's hand and he started pointing and laughing all wild like a hyena. "Look at the little girl!" Hunter said, and I dropped Mr. Morgan's hand, fast. But Mr. Morgan scolded Hunter, not me. "I'm ashamed of you," he said. "Bobby is not only your brother by blood; he's your brother in Christ. And we don't make fun of our brothers in Christ, not here and not anywhere. Now who's up for a game of Go Fish?"

He wasn't talking about Go Fish the card game. We were fishing for Bible verses. In the center of the room Mr. Morgan put a kiddie pool filled with water. In the pool were a bunch of sealed plastic Baggies, each with a Bible verse typed on a sheet of paper and a weight inside. On the outside of each Baggie was a bunch of metal paper clips. We took turns with a fishing pole made of bamboo with a magnet attached to the end of the line. We'd dip our line in the water, and whichever Baggie it pulled up, that was the verse we were to memorize for the week. Everybody was always hoping to get "Jesus wept," but no one ever did. I figured Mr. Morgan didn't even put that one in there—it was just too easy.

To join the RAs you have to memorize 2 Corinthians 5:20: "We are Ambassadors for Christ." And that is just the start of all the scripture you have to learn. Each year we get medals depending on how many Bible verses we memorize: Twenty-five gets you a bronze medal, fifty gets you silver, and seventy-five gets you gold. Troy received a gold medal and the RA Bible Award during his final year, when he was not only a Crusader but also a Knight. I am a good memorizer, like Troy, but Hunter is terrible at it. He can't see his letters right. He'll just stare and stare at the little slip of white paper until Mr. Morgan comes over and reads it for him. Then Hunter tries to repeat whatever Mr. Morgan said. Usually he gets the words wrong. Like the time his quote was "Iron sharpens iron, and one man sharpens another." Hunter said, "Iron sharpens man and one man irons another." Everybody got a good laugh out of that and Hunter's face turned red, but

Mr. Morgan gave him his M&M anyway and said weren't we lucky that we all had mamas at home to do the ironing for us.

My favorite part of RAs is making craft projects for Christ. Today we are making testimonial license plates for our bikes. Mr. Morgan gives us all rectangles made out of plywood with two holes punched out of the top. On the crafts table, covered in old newspapers, he spreads out smelly markers and little cups of paint and paintbrushes and glue and glitter. Then he passes around a sheet of animal stickers and tells us we can each choose two. I choose a giraffe and a zebra. Mama has a zebra print top that she wore on her anniversary date with Daddy, which made Daddy widen his eyes and say Mama looked wild! Mr. Morgan tells us to mark "JLMTIK" on our pieces of plywood. Once our tags are decorated, we'll attach them to the fronts of our bikes with two pipe cleaners each. Then when our unsaved friends ask, "What do those letters on your bike stand for?" we can witness just by answering their question. "Why, they stand for 'Jesus Loves Me This I Know.'"

The official colors of the RAs are gold and blue. I paint my tag all over with the darkest blue I can find. Hunter glances at it and snorts. "How you gonna write on top of that?" he asks. I don't tell him, but I have a plan. Instead of writing my letters with markers, I form them with Elmer's glue, then shake glitter all over them so that the letters sparkle and shine. I figure this will attract attention from miles away, plus I just love the way those sparkly letters look, all gold and glittery. When I finish, Mr. Morgan is so impressed he holds my tag up for everyone to see. He wants to know where on the tag I am planning to put the animal stickers and I tell him I think I might save them for something else, cause I don't want to mess up the color scheme. Mr. Morgan says he guesses that will be okay.

After we clean up everything, Mr. Morgan gives us a "straight talk" about witnessing. When witnessing, he says, you have to make sure not to act all superior and know-it-all-y. "God loves every single one of us," Mr. Morgan says. "Even the lost. Especially the lost. And it is our job to coax lost souls to us, so they too can know God's love. Think about the smell that comes out of the kitchen when your mama is baking cookies. Makes you want to go in there, doesn't it? Well, that's exactly how we need to present God's love, as something warm and sweet and inviting. So when your friends ask about your license tag, tell them what it stands for, yes, but also make sure to tell them that you made it at this really neat club where you get to build race cars and have turkey shoots and play Go Fish and eat M&M's.

"Now, if you are talking to a friend and he asks specifically about Jesus, by all means keep talking. Let him know that Jesus loves you and will never let you down. Let him know that with Jesus in your life, you don't ever have to be afraid, because even when you're scared—especially when you're scared!—the Lord is right there with you. But if he doesn't ask about the Lord, just invite him to come to a meeting. Once he's here, he'll see what it means to be part of a Christian community, and he'll want to keep coming back for more!"

Mr. Morgan tells us that our challenge for the next week is to talk with three unsaved friends about our relationship with Christ. The problem is everyone I know goes to Clairmont Avenue Baptist and is already a Christian.

I determine to cast my net far and wide and find someone new.

And then I realize just what I need to do: take my bike over to Meemaw's this upcoming Friday when I go to her house for a spend-the-night. I spend the night with her once a month, so the two of us can have some QT—which means "quality time." This Friday is going to be especially fun, because not only will we do the usual stuff—watch animal shows, decorate a cake, pull out the box from her closet that holds the pair of chopped-off braids from when she was a little girl—Meemaw has a new kitten named Moses and I am going to meet him and maybe even hold him if I am extra careful.

Meemaw lives on the other side of the railroad tracks from us, kind of near Agnes Scott College, where Mama went for two years before transferring to the University of Georgia. In Meemaw's neighborhood, the houses are older and more run-down and there are a lot of colored families living there. Daddy says the neighborhood was nicer when he was growing up, but times they are a-changing! He just hopes his mama doesn't lose all the money in her house as the whites move out and the Negroes move in. But Meemaw says there is no way she is moving. No sir. She raised her babies and buried a husband while living in that house and she isn't about to move away from her memories just because some of her white neighbors aren't able to see that we are all precious children of God.

I bring my bike, freshly christened with the JLMTIK license tag, to my spend-the-night at Meemaw's. She is waiting on the front porch swing, dressed in a pair of pink shorts and the T-shirt I gave her last year for her birthday, which says: "World's Best Grandma." Her legs are crisscrossed with purple and blue veins.

"You planning on riding away from me?" she asks as I walk my bike up to the house.

"I wanted to show you the license tag I made."

She makes her way down the front porch steps to get close enough to examine it. "Well, if that ain't the prettiest thing! What's it mean, though, I wonder?"

I have a feeling she knows, but I answer anyway. "Jesus Loves Me This I Know."

"For the Bible tells me so! That's wonderful, precious. I just love it. And I love the way it glitters! Weren't you smart to make it all shiny like that so people would take notice. Now why don't you leave your bike on the porch for now and you can come in and meet my new kitty. And later I've got a chocolate cake for us to decorate. I'd already fixed a pound cake, but then I got this fierce hankering for a slice of chocolate cake with milk."

Meemaw always ices her chocolate cake with cream cheese frosting. It's my favorite kind because Meemaw and me can dye it whatever color we want. I like pink, but I can only color it that way if it's just Meemaw and me eating it. One time I brought home a batch of pink cupcakes for my family. Hunter asked, "Why'd you choose that sissy color?" Daddy said he bet I'd tried to make them red for the Georgia Bulldogs but just hadn't added enough food coloring. "Isn't that right, son?" Daddy asked, and I answered, "Yes, sir," knowing that was what he wanted to hear.

Meemaw's house is a lot smaller than ours. You walk right into the living room, where there is an old-fashioned fireplace where we sometimes roast marshmallows for s'mores during the winter. You can't even see the wall over the mantel, it is so covered in pictures of family, including every school picture Troy, Hunter, and me have ever taken and a picture of Meemaw's husband, Daddy Banks, in uniform. He died a hero, but Daddy always said Meemaw was a hero, too, the way she raised him and his sister, June, all by herself. Meemaw always corrects Daddy when he says that. She says she *didn't* do it all by herself, she did it with the help of her church family at Second Avenue Baptist, where Meemaw still goes. Meemaw told Daddy she was mighty proud of him for being senior preacher at Clairmont, but she'd been going to Second Avenue for forty-something years and quitting them now would be like quitting her beloved husband. Daddy pretends to understand, but I know it hurts him that his own mama isn't a member at our church.

I ask Meemaw where that new kitten is and she says probably hiding under the bed somewhere. So we tiptoe into Meemaw's room and peek beneath the bed skirt. I see a shiny set of yellow eyes but can't really make out the cat's body. It's awfully dark under there, and

Meemaw says Moses is jet-black. I reach out my hand to see if he will come to it, but he backs away.

"He's shy," says Meemaw. "He'll probably come out later if we just leave him be."

"Maybe we should frost that cake," I say.

She says that's a fine idea, but the cake layers are still a little warm so why don't I take a bike ride while they cool down? I say, "Yes, ma'am," and go outside where I left my bike on the front porch. The license plate, attached to the handlebars with pipe cleaners, looks good. Real good. "JLMTIK" glitters like the golden treasure it stands for. I walk the bike down the porch steps and then I get on it and start riding down the street. I don't see anyone out in their yards until I get to the house at the end of the road, where Jefferson Place dead-ends into Ansley. There is a Negro family out front. Two women sit on folding chairs on the porch while the kids run all over. Off to the side a man wearing shorts and a Braves T-shirt is moving hot dogs around a hibachi grill.

I wave when I ride past and the fat woman sitting on the porch lifts her hand to wave back. I turn around on Ansley so I can ride by them again, only it's uphill, so I have to stand to pedal.

"Hey!" I yell.

"Hay's for horses!" yells one of the girls from the yard. She is tall and thin and dark. She wears a bun on the very tippy top of her head with a bright pink ribbon tied around it.

I try to slow down so someone will ask about my license tag, but it's nearly impossible to do that when you are pedaling uphill. You're pushing hard against gravity as it is; any less speed and you might start wobbling.

I figure I ought to look for other new kids around the neighborhood to show my tag to, since no one but Pink Ribbon has paid any attention to me and all she did was tease. I ride past several houses, passing Meemaw's little brick bungalow, but the front yards are deserted, which is strange considering it's a perfect spring night, warm enough to sit outside but too cool for mosquitoes. But then I smell meat cooking and I realize most folks are probably having a real barbecue out back, not just cooking wieners on a hibachi grill. Meemaw said we might even grill up some hamburgers for our supper and put chili on them like they do at The Varsity.

I decide to try the colored family once more. I turn around and head their way. Maybe they haven't seen my license tag. Because if they did, wouldn't they ask about it or at least say it's nice looking? Smack in front of their house, I turn my handles toward them so they can see the glittery letters. But I turn too fast and run into the fence. Pink Ribbon says, "That fool cain't ride within an inch of his life," and everyone laughs, though the fat woman on the porch tells Pink Ribbon to quit acting ugly.

"I can ride. I can ride real good. I just wanted y'all to see my license tag."

"Well, come on over here and show it to us, then," says the fat woman. She wears a sleeveless top with little strings that tie at her shoulders. Her arms are the biggest I've ever seen. They are bigger even than Daddy's thighs, and Daddy was a football player in high school.

I hop off my bike and walk it up the path that cuts through the middle of their yard. Pink Ribbon comes over and studies the letters. She stands with her legs apart and her hands on her hips. "So? Jesus love me too," she says. "I was baptized in holy waters when I was a baby."

"How'd you know that's what it says?" I ask.

She taps her finger against the side of her head. "Cause I got a big ol' brain in here."

"Keisha, you stop showing off," says the woman on the porch.

"Ain't showing off when it true," she says.

"I got a big ol' hand that can knock some manners into you," the woman says, but she's settled so deep into her folding chair, it doesn't look like she is going to get up to knock anything into anyone anytime soon.

I know I should be happy that Keisha is saved, but I can't help but be disappointed. I wanted to bring a heathen to Jesus. "You know the ABCs of salvation and all that?" I ask.

"I'm in the third grade. You think I cain't read?"

"That's not what I mean! I mean, *A*) accept that you are a sinner. *B*) believe that Christ died for your sins. *C*) confess that you need Christ Jesus."

"I like that, smart boy. I'm gonna tell it to my daddy next time he come visit. He a preacher at Emmanuel Missionary Church in Birmingham, Alabama."

"There she go telling lies again," says one of the other boys.

"You shut up. He too a preacher."

"Maybe so, but he ain't visiting you."

Keisha pounces on the boy, knocking him to the ground and pounding on his arms and shoulders with her fists.

The big woman stands up faster than you would have believed possible and charges over to Keisha, plucking her off the boy by the back of her shirt and then turning Keisha around to face her. "Girl, you better watch yourself! Cain't go knocking down everyone that hurt your feelings. Now you better start acting like a lady, or I'm gonna whup you till you do. You hear?"

"Yes," mutters Keisha.

"Yes what?"

"Yes, ma'am."

"Now you sit yourself on the porch with me and behave."

Keisha's head is bent as she trudges over to the porch and sits down on its top step. I follow, sitting next to her.

"You sure you're saved?" I ask.

Her eyes are wet. She looks away. I have the sudden urge to touch her, to pet her arm and tell her things are going to be okay. But I keep still. After a minute she turns and looks at me. "They just jealous cause I'm a prophet," she whispers. "I got a secret church to show you. Don't you tell no one. You stay in that red house three doors up?"

"It's my grandma's house. It's not where I live all the time."

"You gonna be there tomorrow morning?"

I nod.

"Good. I'll meet you out front at six a.m. Don't be late."

"I don't think my meemaw gets up that early."

"Smart boy don't know how to open the front door?"

After supper, the Billy Graham hour, a big slice of chocolate cake with milk, a bath, stories, songs, and prayers, I lie in bed, unable to sleep. I can't stop thinking about Keisha, so tall and lean with that bright pink ribbon in her hair. I wonder if she really is a prophet, like Elijah or John the Baptist. Except I don't know of any girl prophets. Girls aren't even allowed to be in the Royal Ambassadors. They have their own group, the GAs, which stands for "Girls in Action." But they aren't like the RAs at all. They don't participate in the turkey shoot or build race cars or go on overnight camping trips or learn how to tie eight different kinds of knots or do any of those things. From what I can tell, mostly they just have bake sales and pray for the missionaries.

But maybe it's different if you are colored. Maybe colored people have women prophets. Meemaw says that there are more and more Negro families joining her church at Second Avenue Baptist and that the choir has started switching off each week between singing white hymns and colored ones. Meemaw says you would not believe how much livelier the music is during the weeks when they sing the colored hymns, that Negroes just have something whites do not when it comes to song. So maybe Keisha is a prophet. And if she is maybe God loves her especially, the way God loved Joseph especially, even though his brothers sold him into slavery. Maybe I could get Keisha to say a special prayer for me. Maybe I could ask her to pray to God that I might be more like the other boys. That I might find a way to make friends easier, and for people to like me more and not tease me so much.

But then I think maybe God's already heard my prayer. And maybe God is answering it. Maybe God sent Keisha to be my new best friend.

I wake in the morning to find Moses curled up in my arm. I stroke his soft fur with my finger and listen to him purr. And then I hear a tapping noise. I look up to see the shadow of a head through the window shade. I try to sit up slowly, not wanting to disturb the kitten, but as soon as I move Moses jumps off the bed. I walk over to the window and pull up the shade. Sure enough, there is Keisha, her hair in the same bun as the day before, only today there is a yellow ribbon wrapped around it. I hold up a finger to let her know I'll be there in a minute; then I pull the shade back down. Slipping out of my pj's, I change into the clothes I wore yesterday. This is not like me. I like my shirts to be so clean they still smell of laundry detergent. But I am in a hurry to get to Keisha before she knocks again and wakes up Meemaw. I tiptoe out of my room and down the hall, walking right past Meemaw's bedroom. Her door is cracked open, and even from the hallway I can hear her snoring. I find a notepad in the kitchen and write: "Gone on a bike ride with Keisha from down the street." Then I unlock the front door and let myself out.

Keisha is waiting by the edge of the yard, and she has a bike with her, a bright yellow one that matches the ribbon in her hair. In fact, almost everything she is wearing is yellow, from her T-shirt to her

Keds to her bobby socks. Only things not yellow are her white shorts and her black skin.

"Morning, smart boy. You ready for church?"

"You preaching?"

"Um-hmm."

She hops on her bike and starts pedaling up Jefferson Place toward College Avenue, which is a busy street that I am not allowed to cross on my own. I have to pedal fast to keep up with her. I hope she will turn off somewhere, but no, we turn at College and start riding down it, toward Agnes Scott.

"My daddy would tan my hide if he knew I was riding on College," I say.

"My daddy's in Birmingham, so he cain't do nothing to me," Keisha says.

"Yeah, but your mama would. I heard what she said yesterday."

"She ain't my mama! She my auntie. And she cain't beat me. I'd kill her if she tried."

We keep yelling back and forth as we pedal down the street.

"Where we going?" I finally ask.

"Smart boy, that is for me to know and for you to find out," she says.

We turn right on South Candler, passing Agnes Scott, then take a right at a little stump of a street. Keisha stops in front of a two-story farmhouse that needs to be painted. The lawn in front is scraggly and overgrown. Mama would never stand for such a lawn in our neighborhood. She would send Troy over with the mower, figuring that whoever lived there was either sick or an invalid, because otherwise why on earth would you let your front yard get into such sorry shape?

Keisha hops off her bike, dropping it into the tall grass. I do the same thing, then follow her as she walks around to the back of the farmhouse. "What are you doing?" I ask.

She turns and glares at me. "Hush!" she says.

She keeps walking, so I keep following, making our way down a stone path that leads to a set of tiered gardens. It is magical back here, garden after garden, the first filled with herbs like Mama grows, rosemary and lavender and mint and sage. Beyond that is a rose garden. There must be fifty rosebushes in it, all with different-colored blooms. We keep walking, down to the third tier, where there are tended beds like Daddy's vegetable patch in our backyard.

"Look at this," Keisha says. She stands beside row upon row of little green plants with thick green leaves. She kneels beside one of them and pulls back a leaf. There are small red strawberries growing underneath. She picks one and hands it to me. I've never eaten a strawberry that tastes like this before. It's so rich, with juice like honey. It's nothing like the ones Mama buys at Kroger.

I kneel beside Keisha, feel beneath another of the green plants, and find another berry, just as delicious as the first one I ate. "We allowed to do this?" I ask.

"I ain't never seen no one go in or out of that house," she says. "And I ride my bike by here almost every single day when I go to my auntie's. It's a haunted garden. That or God put it here for us to find. Like the Garden of Eden."

She's talking crazy, but I don't care. Keisha is lively and she is brave and there is nothing more I want to do than to sit here with her looking for berries beneath the green leaves.

"If we really were in Eden," Keisha says, "we'd take off our clothes."

"Well, we're not," I say. "We're in Decatur, Georgia."

"I'm gonna pretend," she says, and she pulls off her shirt. Her chest is flat as mine.

"You take off your clothes, too," she says. "We pretending we Adam and Eve."

"Someone might see us."

"Who gonna see us?"

"Let's pick some of these berries and bring them back to my meemaw and we can eat them for breakfast with pound cake."

"Where we gonna put em?"

"We could put them in your T-shirt."

"I ain't riding back home with no shirt on."

"Fine. We'll use mine. I'm not playing Adam and Eve, but I guess I don't mind biking shirtless."

She shrugs and starts picking strawberries. I take my shirt off and place it down on the ground. We lay our strawberries on top of it. When it is full I tie the ends around it and make it into a little satchel, which Keisha carries as we leave the garden. Once again she motions for me to shush as we walk by the old farmhouse. There is a plastic basket on the handlebars of her bike. She puts the T-shirt full of strawberries into that. Then we hop back on and start riding home, the early-morning air slapping gently against my bare chest.

When we arrive home, Meemaw is out front, fertilizing her hydrangea bushes.

"Well, I am sure happy to see you!" she says. "Though I really ought to switch you for running off like that."

Meemaw never switched me in my life.

"We just went on a little ride," I say.

Keisha jumps off her bike and holds it steady while she gets the satchel of berries out of the basket. Then she lets the bike drop to the ground. "We brought you a present," she says. "They wild strawberries."

"Wild strawberries?" Meemaw takes the satchel, opens it, and frowns. "These don't look like no wild strawberries to me. You took them out of someone's garden, didn't you?"

"Yes, ma'am," I say, before Keisha can make up another lie.

"But it was a really big garden. They won't even know these are missing."

"Lord have mercy, Bobby, you just cain't do that! You hear me? Whoever grew those berries could have come running after you with a gun! People are protective of their crops, specially something hard to grow as a strawberry."

"Yes, ma'am," I say. I had started to feel bad about taking the berries during our ride home. Now I feel awful. I wonder if God will punish me for stealing.

"And you too, young lady," says Meemaw.

"Yes, ma'am," says Keisha, though she does not sound sorry.

"All-right then. Why don't y'all go inside, wash up, and let me fix you some breakfast. These strawberries would taste right perfect on a slice of pound cake, but I think that might be sending you two rascals the wrong message, so how about scrambled eggs and bacon instead?"

"Yes, ma'am," I say.

"Miss Keisha, you want to run tell your aunt that you are over here?"

"Aw, she won't mind."

"Well, why don't I just phone over there and make sure. You know your number?"

Keisha nods.

"And no more sneaking off, you hear? You and Bobby can play together all you want; you just make sure a grown-up knows. And Bobby, you go put on a shirt. Your daddy is coming to pick you up at nine. I don't want him to think I'm turning you into a wild Indian."

Meemaw follows us inside. I go to my bedroom to get a clean shirt. I can hear Meemaw speaking in gentle tones on the phone. She keeps saying, "No bother, no bother at all. Those two are getting on like gangbusters. Oh no, don't you worry."

After Meemaw hangs up she fixes us our breakfast, then goes back outside to keep gardening, saying she already had a bowl of oatmeal. While we eat, Keisha and I play a game where we pretend that each sip we take of orange juice gives us the power to transform into anyone—or anything—we like. Keisha pretends she is a banana split from Dairy Queen, because that way she will always have its taste on her tongue because her tongue is part of the split. I pretend I am a bullhorn so everyone will listen to what I have to say.

"You just need to speak up, smart boy," says Keisha. "You kind of sort of whisper your words. Who gonna listen if you do that?"

I shrug, then bend over and lick her arm. "Yum," I say. "I got the part with strawberry syrup."

"You crazy," she says, but she is smiling.

There is a loud knocking on the door. Keisha's auntie, probably. I hear Meemaw answering it. "Well, hey there, sweetheart! Didn't expect to see you this morning, but I'm sure glad I get to! Where's your daddy?"

"In the car. Listening to the Braves game. Is Bobby ready?"

It's Hunter.

"Should be. I've got a pound cake for y'all. Come on in the kitchen and I'll get it for you. Bobby's in there."

Hunter and Meemaw walk into the kitchen, where I stand by the sink, rinsing off my dish. Keisha is still at the table, finishing her juice.

"Keisha, this is Bobby's brother Hunter. Hunter, this is my neighbor and Bobby's friend, Keisha."

"Hi," Hunter mutters.

"Hey," she says.

If Hunter weren't standing there I would remind her that "hay is for horses."

"Our church is having a picnic next week if you wanna come."

"Where do y'all go to church, sugar?" asks Meemaw.

"Zion Baptist."

"That's a nice place. Nearby, too. I'm sure Bobby would love to go with you, wouldn't you, son?"

"Yes, ma'am. Is it a potluck? Should I get my mama to fix something?"

"We're bringing soda. You don't have to bring nothing."

"Daddy said to hurry," says Hunter.

I glare at him but follow his order, going to the bedroom to get my bag. Keisha, Hunter, and me all walk out the door together. Meemaw's phone rings just as we are leaving, so she waves good-bye instead of hugging and kissing me and watching me walk to the car like she usually does. Outside the house I wave bye to Keisha and tell her I'll see her next week for the picnic. She tells me not to go strawberry picking without her, and then she picks up her bike from the front lawn, straddles it, and starts riding home.

She isn't ten feet away when Hunter asks, real loud, "Why are you playing with that nigger girl?"

I know Keisha heard because I see her back jerk as she pedals toward her house, but she doesn't stop or turn around or anything. I want to say something. To stand up for her. To tell Hunter he is a bully and a jerk. To tell Hunter no one likes him anyway. And I try. But I can't make the words come out. And now she is farther down the street and I know that if I want her to hear me I'll have to yell, and what if she didn't actually hear Hunter? What if what I thought was her back jerking at his bad word was actually just her sneezing or something?

Daddy has popped open the trunk of the wagon so I can shove my bike in there. By the time I get it situated Hunter has already taken the front seat. I get into the back and, without meaning to, start crying, crying like the time I got separated from Mama at Davison's Department Store downtown.

"What in the world is the matter?" Daddy asks, switching off the game and turning to look at me.

"He called my new friend a nigger," I say, pointing at Hunter.

First time in my life I have ever tattled on my brother.

"You mean that little colored girl y'all came out with?" Daddy asks.

I nod.

"Is that true, son?" asks Daddy, turning his attention to Hunter.

Hunter just looks down at his lap, not saying anything.

"Tell me the truth, son. Did you call her that name?"

"Yes, sir, but she didn't hear me. I said it soft, and she was already walking away."

"Doesn't matter if you whispered or shouted it, it's unacceptable language and I will not have it. When we get home you and I are going to discuss this further in private, you hear?"

Oh boy. Hunter is getting the belt. Daddy doesn't spank all that often, but when he does, he makes sure you remember it.

Hunter mumbles, "Yes, sir." And then he shoots a backward glance at me that is so full of evil the hairs on my arms pop up, as if they are soldiers standing at attention.

2

Gracious Servings

(Decatur, Georgia, 1975)

How, Mama asks, could she say no when Mrs. Lacy Lovehart herself asked Mama to host a luncheon for The SERVERS (*S*weet *E*arnest *R*everent *V*essels *E*njoy *R*espect and *S*alvation)? This is *Lacy Lovehart,* for goodness' sakes: confirmed Christian, former Miss America, and current spokeswoman for the Central Georgia Peach Growers Association. Still, the upcoming event has Mama nervous as a cat in a carrying case. Sure, Mama says, she herself did publish *Gracious Servings,* a book on Joyful Christian Entertaining, and sure, she has both hosted a thousand luncheons and instructed other women on how to do so, but still. Mrs. Lovehart is famous and a legendary beauty, and there's going to be a photographer from the *Atlanta Journal* covering the event, which means Mama's homemaking skills will be on display for *everyone who gets the paper.*

But Mama knows how to cope. "The best way out is through," she says at breakfast, the top of her hair covered in a blue and white bandana. Hunter, Daddy, and I all know what this means—Troy would know, too, but he's gone, a sophomore at Duke.

Cleaning Lady has arrived.

"Cleaning Lady" is an official term that Daddy came up with, way back during the early years of his and Mama's marriage, before any of us were born. Daddy loves to tell the story of first "meeting" Cleaning Lady, after six months of wedded bliss. Usually, he says, Edie was sweet and fun, easy to be around, albeit mighty energetic. But when Mama's parents called from LaGrange to say they were coming to stay in Mama and Daddy's new house in Decatur for a week, boy howdy did Cleaning Lady arrive. Daddy said Cleaning Lady was *beyond* energetic, manic even, pulling everything out of every closet, every cabinet, every drawer: cleaning, sorting, and rearranging. And Cleaning Lady did *not* dress to impress. Usually Mama changed her blouse and applied fresh lipstick each night before Daddy came home, but Cleaning Lady met Daddy at the door with a bandana still tied around her head. She did not even stop her cleaning to eat dinner with Daddy but instead fixed him a peanut butter sandwich—not even taking the time to spread on jelly!—and a glass of milk.

Daddy says that after each of Cleaning Lady's first few appearances he and Mama would argue and be cross with each other. But, Daddy later realized, Cleaning Lady was a part of Mama, and when he married Edie he agreed to love her, warts and all. Cleaning Lady even became a topic in the seminar he hosts each year for married couples, called Keeping the Spark Alive!

Hunter *hates* Cleaning Lady. Maybe I should, too. And I do hate how snappy and irritable she makes Mama. But I love how the house sparkles after a good deep clean, and I don't mind helping out. After breakfast I ask if Mama needs help scrubbing the kitchen. Mama chews on her lip for a minute but then quickly takes me up on the offer, as if it might go away if she doesn't say yes real fast.

• • •

"Have you decided on what you're wearing?" I ask, spraying Fantastik on an emptied shelf of the refrigerator.

"I'm half-tempted to wear that Diane von Furstenberg wrap dress I got on sale at Davison's," she says, dumping a Tupperware container of old tuna noodle casserole into the garbage disposal. "Though I have a feeling Lacy Lovehart might disapprove. Not of the dress so much, but the message behind it."

"That a woman can easily slip out of it?" I ask.

Mama laughs but then cuts a suspicious look at me. "How you come up with these things. . . ."

"Wear your St. John suit," I say.

Daddy gave her that suit for Christmas, and it is her pride and joy.

"You don't think it's too much?" Mama asks.

"Too much of everything is exactly enough," I say, stealing a line I heard on a soap opera.

Mama lets out a little laugh. "Yes, but the St. John is so severe. Lacy Lovehart always looks so sunny and colorful when she's photographed."

"Well, sure. She's trying to look like a peach."

Mama laughs again and I feel myself inflate with the air she releases.

"Should I toss these hotdogs, or are they still good?" I hold up a leaky plastic package with two remaining Oscar Mayer wieners in it.

Hunter walks in from the living room, where he was watching *Hollywood Squares.* "I'll take em," he says.

"No, sir, you will not," says Mama. "I'm using them for pork and beans tonight."

Hunter grunts, then disappears into the walk-in pantry. "Did someone eat all the potato chips?" he calls.

I ignore him and keep talking to Mama. "What about that pink suit you bought at Mark Shale? With the little linen jacket with the bone buttons?"

"Potato chips?" yells Hunter.

"Excuse me?" says Mama, though she heard him perfectly.

"Please, Mama, where are the potato chips?"

"They're in the bread box!" she calls. "And put them back when you're finished. I don't want them going stale."

I hear thrashing around in the pantry, and then Hunter comes out, holding a bright yellow bag of Lay's in one hand, stuffing them into his mouth with the other. Mama glances at him and frowns.

"I'll tell you what the problem with that suit is: If I get hot and want to take off the jacket, the little silk blouse that goes with it is practically see-through. It absolutely requires a camisole."

"So wear a camisole," I say.

Hunter squints his eyes. "What's a camisole?" he asks, pronouncing it "cam-saw."

"Nothing you need to worry about," answers Mama.

She turns her attention back to me. "I can certainly do that. The problem is, I don't have an undergarment that works well beneath it, and I absolutely cannot host Lacy Lovehart . . ." She pauses, then whispers, *"While not wearing a brassiere."*

"Wear the Mark Shale suit. And the camisole. And go buy a bra that works. Is it that the cups are too big?"

Hunter makes a noise of disgust and stomps out of the room.

Mama reaches out, rests her hand gently on my cheek. "Darling, how do you know about such things?"

Because I love looking at the pictures in your Vogue *magazines, Mama. Because I notice anytime a woman's slip shows. Because I know pink is a good color on you while yellow makes you look sickly. Because I'm me, Mama, and I've always been this way.*

I smile, shrug my shoulders. "I dunno," I say.

For parties, Mama always has everything ready in advance. "Ladies," she warns in *Gracious Servings,* "when it comes to entertaining, take a lesson from the Boy Scouts: Be Prepared."

The day of the Lacy Lovehart luncheon, Mama is nothing if not prepared. The crab dip, which will be served hot with Club Crackers, waits in the refrigerator, a sheet of plastic wrap adhered to the dip itself, so it won't dry out. The toast cups—buttered pieces of crustless white bread, baked in muffin tins so they hold the shape—are stored in a large Ziploc bag. The chicken salad—all white meat, with fresh tarragon and peeled white grapes—is piled high into a pretty yellow bowl in the refrigerator, the sides wiped down so no signs of mixing remained. The Jell-O salad with bing cherries and pecans quivers in its mold. The crudités are cut and chilling in cold water to keep them crisp; the curry dipping sauce is mixed. And dessert, a fluffy, frozen, lemon thing made with Cool Whip and condensed milk, waits in the freezer atop its graham cracker crust.

I am in the living room watching *The Price Is Right* when I hear a loud gasp coming from Mama's bedroom. And then she appears before me, her natural prettiness exaggerated with extra blush and mascara, her hair stiff with Aqua Net, her panty hose and one-inch white pumps visible beneath her terry-cloth housecoat that zips up the front.

"Where is Sofie?" she demands.

Sofie, our sweet and slobbery eleven-year-old yellow Labrador retriever whose hips are as bad as her breath, was once full of energy. Sofie and I used to spend hours playing fetch in the backyard, or tug-of-war, or ride the doggie-horsey. But now all Sofie does is dig holes in the backyard, lie on the patch of monkey grass she's claimed as her own, and sit under Daddy's chair on the nights he is home for dinner, knowing that he has the most tender heart of all of us when it comes to animals and will often feed her scraps.

I shrug, not taking my eyes off the screen. An older lady with blue-white hair is trying to figure out how much a matching washer and dryer would go for retail.

"One hundred eighty five," I say.

Mama walks to the television set and mashes the power button with her finger. The picture dissolves into silver and black static, which fades and then disappears.

"Robert Banks, *listen* to me. Where is Sofie?"

"She's outside, I think."

I must have given Mama a wounded look, because she sighs and her tone softens.

"I don't mean to be short with you. Today is a big day. You know that. And everything is ready, everything is prepared, but I can't find the undergarment I bought that works with the camisole. I know it was in my lingerie drawer last night, because I checked. It was curled up right beside the camisole, its price tag still on. But now it's not there. I feel like I'm losing my mind. The only explanation I can come up with is that I somehow took it out of the drawer this morning when I woke up early to make coffee for your father and Sofie got hold of it."

Sofie is famous for stealing underwear from the dirty-clothes basket. Over the years she has eaten through countless pairs of Mama's panties and our briefs. But Mama has never complained of Sofie stealing bras.

"It probably got shoved into the back of your drawer somehow," I say. "You just can't find it because you're nervous."

"I've turned that drawer inside out. And I can't find it because it's not there. I don't have anything else to wear besides the Mark Shale suit. My nails are painted to match. I bought a lipstick especially for it when I went to Davison's for the bra. And I haven't checked my other clothes for wrinkles or stains. Lord knows what shape they are in."

Mama's clothes are never wrinkled or stained.

"I need you to go outside and see if Sofie has dropped it in any of those holes she's dug up. If she has maybe I'll have time to wash it quick in the sink with Woolite and put it in the dryer on Delicate."

I hoist myself from the plaid couch and walk through the kitchen to get to the back door. At the little breakfast nook in the corner, where two benches and a table are built into the wall, sits Hunter, wearing swimming trunks and a white Fruit of the Loom undershirt, stuffing a heaping spoonful of Cap'n Crunch and milk into his mouth.

I don't say a word to him and he doesn't say a word to me, either; instead he just stares ahead as if we aren't even in the same room. That's just what we do—ignore each other. But then out of the blue, he'll attack. Like at the beginning of the school year when I opened my science book and discovered an index card, planted between the pages, that read, "FAG." My brother hadn't even bothered to disguise his handwriting, a small, slanted print I'd recognize anywhere. Soon after I made him a batch of brownies with two squares of chocolate Ex-Lax melted into the batter. Hunter pretty much ate the whole tray, which I left out on the counter, knowing Mama wouldn't touch the brownies for fear of the calories and Daddy wouldn't be home to eat them. All night Hunter kept getting up to run to the bathroom while I just smiled in the dark.

We have nearly an acre of land in our backyard, starting with grass that eventually leads to woods, which a creek runs through. Between the grass and the woods is a border of high monkey grass. This is where I find Sofie, in her special patch, where the blades lie flat, pushed down by her weight day after day. I walk to her, kneel beside her. Man, does she stink. Like mud mixed with dead animal. But her eyes, her almond-shaped eyes—they are human. Daddy swears she's a person trapped inside a dog suit.

"Hey, girl, have you been a little thief?" I ask, using the stubs of my nails to scratch beneath her collar. I push up on her where her chest hits the grass, making her stand. There's nothing underneath her, no bra cup or chewed-up elastic strap. I put my hands on her mouth, forcing it open so I can look inside. It's possible that she ate the bra, but there's no sign of it in her mouth. All I see are the brown stubs of what once were sharp, white teeth.

I guess she could have buried it. She follows me as I walk to the old swing set to look around, peering into the little holes she has dug in the ground, when I hear my full name being called. I look and there is Mama, standing in the frame of the back door, still in her heels and housedress, her hair covered in the silk scarf.

"Now! Get in here now!" she barks.

It is official. The stress of throwing the luncheon for Mrs. Lovehart has driven Mama plumb crazy.

"I'm coming, I'm coming," I mutter. I walk but do not run to the house.

At the door Mama grabs my arm, not even loosening her grip once she yanks me inside. She's hurting me and I start to tell her so, but I can't speak in the face of the awful look she is giving me. In her left hand is the bra.

"You found it," I say, as if the fact that she found the bra has not yet caught up with her mind. As if the moment she realizes the bra is no longer missing she will loosen her grip on my arm and stop looking at me funny.

Only then do I notice Hunter, standing behind Mama, still in his swim trunks and T-shirt. His hip is cocked against the side of the avocado-colored refrigerator. His arms are folded across his chest.

"It was Hunter who found it. But I believe you can tell me exactly where it was."

"I have no earthly idea," I say, wincing as soon as the words come out of my mouth. Even I can hear how prissy I sound.

Mama starts crying, her tears messing up her eye makeup.

"Oh, Bobby," she says. "Why would you hide my underwear in the back of your dresser drawer? And not just my bra. Hunter said there was also a pair of panties in there, a pair I lost months ago and had just assumed Sofie had gotten. And Hunter said he found this—"

Mama lets go of my arm and pulls a wrinkled, glossy page from a magazine out of the pocket of her housedress. She holds it out for me to see. Even wrinkled, I recognize the picture of the skinny, naked man, grinning as he holds his erect penis in his hands. I found the picture blown up against a curb in the parking lot behind the 7-Eleven. Ripped out of some porn magazine, I guess. I stuffed it into my pant pocket, bicycled home, and hid it in the space between the dresser and the drawer, taking it out only when I am sure no one else is home.

Hunter must have found it when he was planting Mama's underwear. Or maybe he found it beforehand and planned this whole thing in response.

Seeing it in Mama's brightly lit kitchen makes me turn all wobbly, like I need to grab onto something or my knees might buckle. No one was supposed to see that picture but me.

"It's not mine," I say, my mouth so dry it's hard to get out the words. "Why would I want to look at that? And I didn't take your underwear. Hunter did. He must have stolen it from your drawer and put it in mine. That's what you did, isn't it?"

Mama and I both look at Hunter. He speaks as if it is painful to do so. "I walked in on him, Mama. I should have told you after I did, but it was just so weird I didn't know what to do. It was a couple of weeks ago. He must have thought he was alone in the house. He was standing in front of the mirror on our closet door, wearing your stuff—your bra and underwear. Not this one, a different one. I think he's been doing this for a long time, Mama. I think he's really sick."

I spring, like a dog attacking an intruder. Mama holds her arm out to the side, blocking the path, and I think of the many times she has made that exact same motion while driving, when she comes to a sudden stop and worries I'll go flying through the window. Except this time she isn't protecting me. This time she's protecting Hunter from me.

"Don't," she says, her voice gritty. She is looking at me in a way she never has before. It's as if behind each eye someone has switched off a lamp.

She believes him.

Yes, the dirty picture is mine, but the rest of what Hunter said is a lie. I have never dressed in my mama's underthings. I would never dream of doing such a thing. I don't want to do such a thing. And yet I know I'm guilty. That picture from the magazine. I cannot believe I am standing in the kitchen with Mama, that picture between us.

Mama looks exhausted. The corners of Hunter's mouth show the faintest smile. He is loving this.

"He's lying," I say meekly.

"Son," she says. "Please don't make things worse."

We stand there for a moment, looking at each other sadly. And then she straightens her shoulders, glances at the clock above the stove, sees that it is 10:30 a.m., stuffs the picture into one pocket, the bra into the other, and rotates her body so that she can address us both.

"My guests arrive in an hour," she says. "Bobby, you are to put the breakfast dishes in the dishwasher, and then make sure there's a clean monogrammed towel in the guest bathroom. Yes, I have checked twice already, but for my peace of mind I need you to do it again. After that, I want you to shower and put on khakis and a polo shirt. I don't care how hot it is, I want you boys in long pants for Mrs. Lovehart.

"Hunter, you shower now, and both of you, make sure to wipe up any water that gets on the sink and on the floor. I expect you boys to be seated in the living room, shirts tucked in, by eleven-twenty sharp, ready to greet my guests. When they arrive, Bobby, you are to offer lemonade, and Hunter, you are to pass around the hot crab dip. And then I want you two to say good-bye and I want you out of the house. And I swear to my sweet Lord Jesus, if you come home having so much as touched each other I will have your daddy tear you apart. I don't care how old you are. And if he doesn't do it to my satisfaction I will do it myself, and don't think I don't mean it. And don't even think about showing up at this house again until six-thirty p.m., at which point you better be here sharp for dinner with Daddy, during which none of us will say a word about what Hunter found in Bobby's drawer until I figure out what to do."

"But *Mom,*" Hunter protests. "He's sick."

"You don't think I know that?" she asks.

I am dutiful, doing everything Mama asked of me. I shower, dress in long pants, check to make sure there is a clean hand towel in the guest bedroom. I sit on the couch in the living room with Hunter, waiting for her guests to arrive, two polished silver trays on the coffee table before us, one filled with glasses of lemonade, the other with crab dip, Club Crackers, and Mama's monogrammed linen napkins. Sitting next to Hunter is pure h-e-l-l. My throat hurts just being near him, aches and tightens so that breathing feels like work. Which is helpful, in a way, because it keeps my mind off the tears pushing at my eyes, tears that I will not let fall. *Will not.* But then they do. Pool over and run down my face, landing on my khaki pants. Hunter glances at me, his eyes showing disgust. But he does not say a word. He's as scared of Mama as I am.

The doorbell rings and Mama strides out of the kitchen, stopping short of the door to take a breath and say a quick prayer. In *Gracious Servings* this is something she advises all hostesses to do in that second before greeting their guests. Ask the Lord to calm your nerves and open your heart to the festivities ahead.

After her pause, Mama throws open the door. "Well, hello! Welcome! I am so delighted to have y'all!"

And in spill the ladies, along with a scent of mixed floral perfumes. The last one to enter is Mrs. Lacy Lovehart herself, so luminous I stand as if at attention. I have seen her on television before, but in person she is brighter, magnetic. And tall—at least five foot ten in flats, which I recognize from *Vogue* as Jack Rogers Navajo sandals, the ones Jackie O made famous when she wore them in Palm Beach.

Lacy's hairstyle is much more modern than Mama's, falling in loose waves around her shoulders. She wears a sleeveless shift in her signature color of peach, her arms toned and tanned as if she plays a lot of tennis. She wears a necklace of big, round silver beads, and on her arm is a silver bracelet weighted with charms. But it is her face, her glowing skin, her wide eyes, that suck me right in.

Mama turns and smiles at Hunter and me. Her smile means it is time for us to come forward with our offerings for the ladies. I lift the tray of lemonade off the coffee table; Hunter hoists the tray with the crab dip and crackers.

I make my way to the buzzing hive of pastels and perfume, offering them the lemonade, which Mama has poured over cubes of frozen lemonade, so when the ice melts it won't weaken the drink. For the occasion she has pulled out her crystal tumblers, "EBM" etched into the glass. Hunter follows behind, offering the dip and a napkin to each lady. He doesn't speak so much as he grunts, but they get the message and ooh and ahh as they put the dip in their mouths.

Lacy does not take a lemonade off the tray. "Aren't you precious," she says. "But might you happen to have a peach iced tea?"

I glance at Mama, worried.

"Oh, Lacy, I'm so sorry. I have Coca-Cola, sweet tea, and coffee, but I don't have any peaches. Man ate the last one this morning."

Well, that's a flat-out lie. Mama hasn't bought any peaches at all this summer. She says none of the ones at the grocery store have looked any good.

Mrs. Lovehart lifts a glass of lemonade off of my tray. "This will suit me just fine," she says. "Though you *should* try peach iced tea one day. It's simply wonderful!"

It is as if Mrs. Lovehart is in a commercial. I glance at Mama to see her reaction. She looks irritated.

"I could run over and see if they have any peaches at the Seven-Eleven," I volunteer.

"A boy with initiative will become a man with leadership skills!" says Mrs. Lovehart, touching my forearm with her manicured hand. "Very impressive."

She winks at me, a wink I've seen her give before on television.

"Thank you, Bobby, but I think we'll be fine," says Mama, her lips tight. "Now please, ladies, have more crab dip and lemonade, and then these boys are going to say their good-byes so we can get down to business before we enjoy our lunch."

A moment later and we are dismissed.

Hunter takes off down the driveway, probably on his way to Dixon's. I make my way into the woods behind our house. The air is softer here. Walking beneath tree limbs, bright with green leaves, I am able to distract myself, a little, by listening to the noises of the birds and the tree frogs. I breathe slowly, trying to slow down my heart. I inhale and smell the dirt. Know that it smells loamy, which is one of the words we learned in *Wordly Wise* and which I immediately matched with this soft place of greens and browns. I make my way down to the creek, sit on a rock beside the running water. I dip my hand in. The water is cold and a little dirty. I think of my mama's dimming eyes, the crumpled picture she threw on the kitchen table, my secret brought to light. I'd rather be dead than for Mama to have seen that picture.

Maybe I *could* die.

Maybe I could just take off my shoes and walk down the middle of the creek, balancing myself on the rocks until I step on a slippery one. Fall face forward and drown in six inches of water. It could happen. It *did* happen last year, to a kid from Decatur High. He was on a camping trip with his family, and he left the campsite early in the morning, probably just to hike around, and ended up falling and drowning in shallow water.

I imagine a boy's body lying face-first in the water. I try to picture my own body, found by Mama and Daddy. I try to imagine the grief they would feel. But all I can see is Hunter, Hunter drowned.

Hunter dead.

3

The Firefly Jar

(Decatur, Georgia, 1975)

At night I dream of killing my brother. I dream I choke the life out of him, my thumbs wrapped around his neck. I dream I hold one of Daddy's rifles, only a few feet away from Hunter's heart, while he teases me, tells me I am too much of a fag to pull the trigger, until I feel my pointer finger bend at the joint and I see the look of surprise on his face just before his expression shifts from shock to pain. I dream I straddle him, a brick in one hand, bringing it down upon his head until what once was stubborn and hard becomes soft and broken.

During the day I ignore him. Try to pretend he doesn't exist. Summer stretches long and hot. After I finish whatever chores Mama asks me to do, I go to the woods behind the house. The woods are my only place of peace. I stand beneath a white oak and scratch a line on my arm with the point of the pocketknife Daddy gave me on my fourteenth birthday, along with his twice-rehearsed speech (first given to Troy, then to Hunter) about how every man ought to carry a good, sharp knife. The clean sting of the blade distracts me temporarily from the tangled knots that twist in my stomach, knots of shame and fear, guilt and rage. Blood springs to the surface of the cut and I lean against the textured bark of the tree, exhaling.

It is so green in these woods, the light from the sun cutting through the trees' leaves, casting speckled shadows all around. The birds call to each other from branch to branch. Overhead I spot a bright blue bird. I lose myself for a moment watching its quick, nervous movements.

One thing I know: Mama has not told Daddy about the underwear Hunter hid in my drawer, because Daddy continues to act jolly around me as always. But Mama herself treats me with more and more distance, like I'm an injured cat found under the front porch, history unknown, possibly diseased. An animal she feels obligated to feed, though is afraid to pick up.

A bee buzzes near my ear, and without thinking I capture it, cupping it in my hand. I open my hand quickly, and the bee shoots out without stinging me. Ears alert, I listen. Just a little ways off I hear a low hum, a steady buzz. Energy. I walk toward the hum. It grows louder. Another bee flies by, and I know what I have found even before I see the hive in a hollowed-out space in the trunk of the tree. I am looking at the buzzing hive, but I am seeing Hunter, years before, on the ground at the church picnic, red faced and choking. I am seeing the firefly jar Daddy made for me when I was a kid, nothing more than a Bell canning jar with ventilation holes punched into its metal lid. There was a net, too, with a long pole. I would capture the fireflies and deposit them in the jar, transforming it into a handmade night-light, a temporary wonder.

I head toward the house with purpose.

• • •

There's a chance the net and jar have been lost or given away, but if they are still around they are in one of two places, the basement or the garage. I check the garage first, since I can get to it without anyone else even knowing I'm home. Daddy keeps the garage, which is his domain, shipshape. Our bikes hang in descending order of size on hooks from the ceiling. The space where Daddy parks his car is empty and spotless, swept clean. Mama's wood-paneled wagon is parked in a precisely determined spot, the front fender aligned with a Ping-Pong ball suspended on fishing wire from a hook in the ceiling. Daddy constructed the Ping-Pong ball plumb line for her so she would know exactly where to stop. If she pulls up any farther, it's hard to get around the car, any farther back and she can't shut the garage door. Stored against the side of the garage is a lawn mower, with a cover on it. Hanging from nails on the wall are several different sizes of saws. Near those are shelving units, the highest two shelves storing cans of WD-40, a couple of toolboxes, a handsaw, and a drill. The only thing on the next shelf down is a box of mousetraps, left over from an infestation that occurred in the kitchen last spring.

The remaining shelves are empty, no firefly jar or net stored on them. Maybe they're in the basement. Entering the house through the back door, I am relieved to see that no one is in the kitchen. I hear the sound of a hair dryer coming from Mama and Daddy's room. Hunter isn't in the den watching television, and the door to our room is closed, meaning he must be in there. Probably flexing in front of the mirror above his dresser. That or jacking off, which I have heard him do in the middle of the night, when he thinks I am asleep.

I open the door leading to the basement, flicking on the light as I go down the stairs. It's not a scary basement, not a dungeon. Daddy painted the concrete floor barn red and finished it with a glaze that keeps the paint from chipping. It's chilly down here and as well organized as the garage, only there's a lot more stuff. Lots of boxes. There is my Little People Kentucky Fried Chicken restaurant and my Little People castle. I used to love making the Little People fall through its trapdoor. There are a bunch of cardboard boxes with my name marked on them in black marker. I open one. It contains all of the G.I. Joe figures Daddy and Troy gave me, plus a stuffed dog—Ruff Ruff—that was a Christmas gift from Meemaw. I don't want to say how old I was when I finally stopped sleeping with Ruff Ruff. Even now, at fourteen, I feel guilty leaving Ruff Ruff in the box with the G.I. Joe men. It's stupid, I know, but I worry his feelings are hurt that he's stored with toys I care nothing about. Still, I close the box with him in it and open another. Inside are books, dozens of Golden Books, an illustrated Children's Bible, *Where the Wild Things Are*, *Goodnight Moon*, *The Runaway Bunny*. I put the lid back on. In another box is an old baby blanket of mine, yellow with alphabet blocks stitched onto it. Aunt Betsy gave it to Mama when Mama was pregnant with me, before anyone knew whether I'd be a boy or a girl, because yellow could go either way.

Seeing that blanket takes me back. I remember how the other side was made of satin and how cool it felt to the touch. It's dumb, I know, but I want to feel it against my cheek again. I lift it from the box, and there, underneath, is the firefly jar, along with a Fisher-Price doctor's kit and an old, old bottle of blowing bubbles.

Here it is, not even dusty.

I continue looking for the net, but I can't find it anywhere. I decide this is okay. It might actually be easier to catch the bees in my hands. Except for the worry of getting stung. I already cupped one without getting hurt, but that was just dumb luck. If I'm going to catch a bunch of them without a net, I need protection. I think of the rubber gloves Mama wears when she washes dishes by hand, so she won't mess up her nails. She keeps a whole box of them underneath the sink in the kitchen.

I put the firefly jar down on the floor and return everything else to its original box, its original space. I pick up the jar and walk back upstairs, turning off the light before I close the door at the top of the stairwell. I can still hear the sound of Mama's hair dryer coming from the bedroom. I walk into the kitchen. Draped over the faucet is a pair of rubber gloves, drying from their last use.

I snatch the gloves, but then pause, putting them back. Mama might notice if they're missing. I look under the sink and find a box of them. I pull a pair out. As I stand I hear someone enter the kitchen. Startled, I turn around, holding the rubber gloves in my hand.

It's Hunter. He looks me up and down. "Planning to stick your hand up your ass?" he asks.

I ignore him. The only other choice is to fight, to become a ball of bodies whirling around, blood and hair flinging from the fury. Mama would hear the commotion, and she would come and break us up, and this I will not allow. Never again will I let Mama get between us, now that I know whose side she is on.

I carry the gloves and jar out of the kitchen, glancing back at Hunter to see if he's still watching me. He's at the refrigerator, pulling out bologna and mayonnaise, fixing himself a sandwich, I guess, though it's five o'clock in the afternoon, only an hour before dinner. Hunter's appetite is the butt of many Banks family jokes. Mama swears he has a tapeworm.

I know there's something nasty inside of him.

This is what I tell myself: that if I trip over a branch on my way out to the woods, or I cannot find the hive again, or I get stung—even once—while trying to steal the bees, I will know that God does not want me to do this. But I complete my bee-gathering mission easily and without any fuss. I return to the hive, put on the gloves, pull out one, then another, and finally a third, and deposit each into the jar. An arsenal for the war I've been fighting with my brother for years.

I have been lying in bed for over an hour, needing to know for certain that Hunter is asleep. He's been snoring lightly for the last half hour. Before I rise, I say a silent prayer: *God, if this is wrong, let the bees have died in their jar. Let one of them sting me when I try to release it. Do something to show me that this is not your way.*

I lean over and retrieve the flashlight hidden under my bunk. I tiptoe to the bedroom door, making sure it is soundly closed. I walk to the closet, pull the blanket off the jar, and shine the flashlight on it. The bees rest still and motionless on its bottom. My chest tightens at the realization that they are dead, at the realization that God has intervened, that he does not want me to do this.

But when I pick the jar up they start buzzing again, angry, very much alive.

I walk to the foot of our beds and, balancing the jar in one hand, climb up the railing of our bunks. The wooden railing creaks from the pressure of my weight. Really, we outgrew these bunks years ago. We outgrew sharing a room, too, but Mama insisted on turning Troy's room into her sewing room after he moved out. Hunter groans and shifts but doesn't wake up. My feet on the railing, I stand above his sleeping form. With my free hand, I untuck the sheet and the blanket from the foot of the bed. Slowly, slowly, I unscrew the jar until the lid is loose, ready to come off as soon as I lift it. I slide my hand, holding the jar, beneath the sheet.

"Hunter," I command. "Wake up."

He stirs but does not say anything. With my free hand I grab his foot, shake it hard. "Hunter."

"Huh?" His body jerks and he opens his eyes, but he still doesn't seem to see me.

"Don't move."

He turns over angrily and puts the pillow on top of his head. I slap at his leg through the blanket. He better not think he can ignore me tonight.

"I'm holding a jar full of bees. If you take the pillow off your head you can hear them buzzing. The jar is in my hand, under the sheet, and the lid is loose on top. I can release them right now. If you move I'll release them, and maybe they'll sting you, and maybe they won't. And if they do, maybe I'll run and get Daddy, or maybe I'll wait until it's too late."

"What the fuck?" He takes the pillow off his head.

"Shut up. I want you to shut up and listen to me. Maybe you'll get stung tonight or maybe you won't. But know this: The woods behind our house are filled with bees and I know how to catch them. And I will. I'm a regular bee charmer. I will catch them again and again. I will bring a jar full of bees into our room every night and I will release them in your bed while you are sleeping and you will be stung and you will die. Do you hear me?"

He sits up suddenly, jerking the covers off his body. The motion knocks the jar out of my hand. I hear it break on the hardwood floor below. The bees fly straight up, buzzing loudly, by the side of his top bunk.

Hunter squeezes himself into the corner of the wall, like a kid in a horror film. I remain standing on the bunk bed railing, still taller than him.

"I want you to leave me alone," I say.

"Just open the window, okay?" Hunter asks. "Get them out of here."

I climb down the railing, then walk to the head of his bed, where he is crouched in the corner. The bees buzz around me, but I am not afraid.

"No more notes in my textbooks, no more calling me a fag in

front of your friends, no more hiding things of Mama's in my drawers, none of it."

"Get them out of here."

"First promise. Promise that you will leave me the fuck alone."

First time I've ever said that word aloud.

"I promise. I promise. Please get them out."

"Why should I believe you?"

He screws up his face into a pained expression, then starts to cry. My brother Hunter is crying. "Please. Please open the window and get them out."

His tears are a gift, revealing the power I now have.

I walk to the bedroom window, turn the lock, and push the window up as far as it will go. As if summoned, the bees fly out, and it is done.

4

I Never . . .

(Decatur, Georgia, 1977)

Every afternoon during track practice I try to outrun Pete Arnold, who is a miler like me. I can't. He can't beat me either. We are matched, sprinting side by side, each motivating the other. The first time Coach Latham had us do time trials I shaved ten seconds off my personal best, which is nuts, considering it wasn't even a real race. Pete acts all serious and "in the zone" during practice, but afterward, when the team gathers on the bleachers for Coach Latham to go over his "Daily Nuggets" (Coach's term), Pete sits beside me, making commentary, his Yankee accent noticeable even at a whisper.

"C'mon, man, the boys can't breathe. Go up a size, will ya?" Pete laments while Coach Latham, sausaged into his shiny gym shorts, holds forth on the necessity of wearing a jockstrap. I have to stare at the ground and squeeze my wrist with my hand during Pete's comedy routine, to keep myself from laughing out loud.

It's hard not to lose it around Pete.

• • •

My parents are almost always at our meets. Track is the only sport I'm any good at, and Mama and Daddy, taking whatever athleticism they can get, fall all over themselves to encourage me to Keep Running! Sometimes Pete's mom comes to our meets, too, though she's always late. She's a secretary at a law firm downtown and doesn't get off work until after 5:00. She's beautiful in a trashy sort of way, her bleach blond hair feathered back on the sides like Farrah Fawcett's. She wears lots and lots of mascara and plunging V-neck tops. She sure doesn't look like Mama or any of Mama's friends. She looks out of place is how she looks. Which she is. She moved Pete down here from Boston last summer, after she and Pete's dad split up.

Even though he's a Yankee, the white girls at Decatur High like Pete a lot. (Who knows, the black girls might like him, too, but everyone keeps pretty separated.) Despite how goofy he is and the funny T-shirts he wears, he carries himself elegantly, his limbs almost liquid, his fingers so long they border on odd. He has perfectly square teeth that look like white Chiclets all lined up in a row. His hair is blond like his mama's, worn a little shaggy and grown out on the sides, same as mine.

Ever since Daddy mentioned to Mrs. Arnold that she ought to come check out Clairmont Avenue Baptist, quietly letting her know that she wouldn't be judged for being a divorcee, Pete and his mom are at church most Sundays, his mom dressed for a cocktail party, Pete with his button-down oxford half tucked into his khakis. Our family always sits up front. Pete and his mom always arrive late and sit near the entrance. I try not to glance back at Pete during the services, but I can't help myself. I like knowing he is there. Once I saw Pete with his head tilted back, looking up at the ceiling as if he were counting the tiles. I asked him about it afterward. He said there was a watermark on the ceiling that looked like the state of Massachusetts and he wondered if it was a sign.

"Of what?"

"That Ma will wise up and move us back to Boston."

"How can you believe in signs left on the church ceiling but not believe in God?"

God's existence is an ongoing debate between the two of us. Pete claims he's an atheist, but I don't really think he is. I think he's just trying to annoy me. I kind of like our discussions, though. We get into long arguments about the human nature of Christ (Pete says that if Jesus was a man then he got erections), and the shame of Jimmy Carter pardoning the draft dodgers (which Pete thinks was a good thing and not shameful at all), and Watergate (actually, we don't really disagree on that; we both think Nixon was a creep). When I debate Pete I try to show absolute faith in my convictions. But lying in bed at night I will sometimes allow myself to imagine, for a moment, the possibility that Pete's way of seeing the world might be as valid as my own. And then I have to shake my head fast, as if shaking the crumbs off a place mat, because I don't want the scariest of Pete's convictions—that there is no God who cares about our lives—to settle.

Sometimes after practice Pete and I hang out at his house. It isn't actually a house at all but half of a run-down duplex on a dead-end street off East Ponce. Today we sit Indian-style on the floor of his bedroom, the green shag carpet soft beneath our legs. Pete has the slide projector going. Images of his family's long-ago camping trip to the Arizona desert flash against the wall while Fleetwood Mac's *Rumours,* which Pete is obsessed with, spins on the turntable. The images of the desert are strange and otherworldly: barren mountains striped with gradations of pink. Pete, gap-toothed, is grinning in every single picture, his dad's arm wrapped around his shoulder. Pete couldn't have been older than eight. Back then his hair was so blond it looked almost white.

Pete says *Rumours* sounds even better when you're high, but his mom found his bag of pot and threw it away. I am relieved he doesn't have any to offer. Relieved I don't have to say no again. I am forever refusing Pete's offers of beers, stolen from his mom's endless supply in the fridge. I use my dad as an excuse, but the truth is, I am less afraid of Daddy than I am of altering my mind around Pete. The truth is, even cold sober it is all I can do not to reach over and touch him.

But I never let myself touch Pete, not even casually, not to flick a piece of lint off his shirt or to slap him on the back or anything. While Hunter, who is a running back on the football team just like Daddy was, will come barreling down the hall at school and tackle one of his teammates to the ground. Straddle him and pretend to hawk a loogie in his face.

When "Songbird" comes on, Christine McVie's declaration of love so clear and true, I pretend I have to pee just so I can leave the room.

Besides me, Pete's other friend at Decatur High is a girl named Shawna Pringle. Shawna has always been weird. She is not like the other white girls at Decatur High, with their curling-iron bangs and their bright blue eyeliner. Shawna has long dark hair, so dark it is almost black, which she wears in a single braid down her back. Her preferred outfit is a Fruit of the Loom V-neck undershirt worn with a faded pair of Levi's jeans. Occasionally she switches things up and wears overalls. And she always wears Birkenstocks, which we call her Jesus sandals. She bought them at some hippie store in Little Five Points.

Shawna can get to places like Little Five Points because she has a car or, rather, a pickup truck, powder blue with an open bed. It belongs to her granddaddy, but he can no longer drive. His diabetes got so bad he had to have his legs removed. He gave the truck to Shawna on the condition that she keep it in pristine condition, requiring her not only to wash it once a week, but also not to remove the Confederate flag bumper sticker that reads, "I Don't Care How You Do It Up North!"

Shawna and I weren't friends before Pete, but now we are. We didn't really have a choice; it was just part of the deal of getting to hang out with Pete. Anyway, it's fine. We like each other. Last weekend Shawna drove Pete and me to Midtown Atlanta. We rented roller skates from some place on 10th Street, then made our way inside Piedmont Park. I was a wobbly skater. Pete was okay, but Shawna was really good. She could leap down stairs and over trash cans and do twists in the air. At one point she even had a small crowd gathered around her. Pete and I just looked at each other and shook our heads, like proud but confused parents, wondering *How did we have this child?*

Later we waited for her outside the public restrooms. She had already been in there ten minutes, but Pete said that was nothing, she had kept him waiting for over half an hour before. "She'll tell you all about her blockages if you really want to hear," he said.

"I don't," I said,

A trim man with a thin mustache walked up to us. He wore flip-flops, tight jeans, and a sleeveless shirt with armholes so loose I could spy his smooth chest through it. His exposed feet looked tender and new, each toenail filed into a perfect half-moon. His feet looked like they belonged to an overgrown baby.

"Waiting for someone?" he asked, placing his manicured hand against the stone façade of the restroom.

"Yep," said Pete, not exactly unfriendly but certainly not inviting.

"Why don't you and your friend come wait at my apartment? We could smoke a joint."

"I doubt my girlfriend would be into that," Pete said.

As if on cue Shawna walked out of the bathroom, slapping her hands together vigorously, as if she just completed some difficult task.

"Maybe next time," the man said archly, walking away as fast as he had appeared.

"Oh my God, which one of you did that fairy try to pick up?" asked Shawna.

"Why, he just wanted to show us his apartment, sugah," said Pete, all mock innocence with his fake *Gone with the Wind* accent.

"Sick!" said Shawna.

"I know," I said. "It really is."

During homeroom, Shawna announces that we are going to go to the Laser Show Extravaganza tonight.

"The Granite Rock laser show? Are you kidding me?" asks Pete. "I saw an ad for it on TV. It looks awful."

"Shut up; it's awesome," says Shawna. "There's bad music and lasers and you eat Kentucky Fried Chicken and bask in the glory of southern craziness."

I've never thought of the laser show as crazy—just fun. My family and I went last summer, when it first opened out at Granite Rock, which Daddy calls the poor man's Stone Mountain. We arrived at dusk with a picnic and spread a blanket out on the flat field beneath the face of the granite mountain, which is carved with the image of Robert E. Lee on horseback. The show didn't start until it got dark. Then they projected a bunch of laser images—cartoons really—against the rock face, accompanied by music. It was really neat, like something out of the future. Plus, Mama packed a good picnic. That night she brought us plenty of ham sandwiches and Lay's potato chips, plus orange slices and Oatmeal Caramelitas, a salty, buttery layer of oats topped with chocolate chips, walnuts, and melted Kraft caramels. And for some reason Mama brought a big jug of sun tea instead of her usual so-sweet-it-hurts-your-teeth stuff.

I am waiting in the living room with Mama and Daddy for Shawna to pick me up. I keep glancing at my Timex, nervous. Shawna was supposed to be here by 5:00, but it is already 5:18. Mama is methodically licking stamps and placing them on addressed envelopes for yet another SERVERS fund-raiser she is hosting for Lacy Lovehart. Watching Mama lick those stamps makes my throat tighten. Mama hasn't acted the same toward me since that first luncheon she hosted for Mrs. Lovehart, over two years ago. It isn't that she's mean, just cool. Almost formal. Daddy acts just the same as always, which means Mama never said a word to him about that afternoon.

Daddy is watching the Braves on television. I pretend to watch, too, but the moment I hear Shawna's horn beep I leap off the sofa.

"Bobby, your friends need to come in and say a proper hello," says Mama, her eyes meeting mine while her tongue dabs a stamp.

"Oh, Edie, this isn't the cotillion. Just a group of young people going to a casual event." Daddy winks at me, jovial and self-assured.

"Yes, sir, that's right," I say, and I head fast for the door before Mama argues back. Mama *says* that Daddy is the head of our household while she is its heart, but the truth is she doesn't often get overruled on anything.

Once outside I slow jog to the truck and open the door to the cab. It fits three, tightly, though it's a little awkward if you are in the middle, because the gearshift gets in the way of your leg. But Pete is already squeezed in the center seat, so I don't have to worry about that. Still, I am a little scrunched on account of the red Igloo cooler on the floor at my feet.

Shawna and Pete are awfully giggly as we wind our way through my neighborhood of sturdy ranches and Cape Cods, the lawns rolling from the houses down to the sidewalk like green skirts over the bellies of pregnant women. Once onto the busier Clairmont, Pete tells me to get him a Miller Lite out of the cooler. Shawna says she wants one, too.

"Compliments of Roselyn?" I ask Pete as I open the cooler and pull out two cold cans.

"If she notices any missing I'll just say Ricky drank them."

Ricky, a beefy guy with a thick head of hair and an air of arrogance so potent it could be bottled, is the latest of Pete's mom's boyfriends. Although really "boyfriend" is too grand a title, as these men stick around about as long as a thunderstorm on a hot summer afternoon.

Pete hands a can to Shawna, then pops the tab on his own and takes a long sip.

"Want some?" he asks, handing the can to me. He always asks, and I always refuse.

"Wait—are we being filmed for an *Afterschool Special* or something?" I say, deadpan. Pete and I love watching the terrible acting on the ABC *Afterschool Specials,* with their dramatic plots and their high-stakes endings.

"Yep," says Shawna. "Now bottoms up, young man. I want you to do something crazy and learn a lesson."

I know she's just joking, but hearing Shawna call me young man immediately brings Mama to mind. Her tongue darting in and out of her mouth as she licked the envelopes for the SERVERS fundraiser. The fact that she didn't say good-bye when I walked out the door. Mama's love for me has become so restrained. It's not that she withholds her love completely, but rather that she measures it out, teaspoon by teaspoon, as if giving me too much at once would be unwise. As if she might oversalt.

"Oh, what the heck," I say, fake jolly, though I am thinking of Mama's furrowed brow. I take the can from Pete's hand.

"Oh my God, we've finally corrupted him!" says Pete.

"PTL!" Shawna says, which is short for "Praise The Lord."

I roll my eyes and take a sip. From the way Mama and Daddy talked about alcohol, I imagined beer would taste like sewage or cat pee or something equally disgusting. But the Lite Beer from Miller tastes okay. Not great. Not like a Coke or a Grape Fanta or something like that, but fine. Just kind of watery and flat.

Pete and I trade the can back and forth. His mouth touches it, then my mouth touches it, then his mouth touches it, then my mouth touches it again. We finish the one and I pop open another. All the while Shawna drives, taking Scott Boulevard to Highway 78, then merging onto 285 N, toward Tucker, where Granite Rock is located.

"Good thing we're driving 'I Don't Care,'" remarks Pete.

"Why, cause it's so cool?" asks Shawna.

"That and we're getting deeper and deeper into Dixie. That red truck up there is the fourth I've seen with a Confederate flag bumper sticker."

"Maybe there's a redneck convention going on," says Shawna.

"Yeah, it's called the Granite Rock Laser Show Extravaganza," says Pete.

"You're such a Yankee snob," I say.

"Go, Sherman," says Pete, pumping his fist in the air.

I slap him on the thigh. First time I've ever deliberately touched him.

Just before we drive up to the entry booth, Shawna grabs a blanket out of the narrow space behind the front seat and drapes it over the cooler. Clearly she is used to sneaking alcohol into places it's not allowed. She is cool as can be while paying our entry fee, calling the man in the booth "sir." Once inside we drive and drive until we finally get to the parking lot for the laser show. It's nearly filled. There are families all over, moms and dads carrying picnic baskets and blankets and yelling threats at the children running wild in front of them. All I can think about is settling down on our blanket and eating a piece of chicken. I've been smelling it in the car ever since we left KFC, but Shawna wouldn't let me eat in her truck.

"Have some respect," she said.

We make our way onto the field, along with the rest of the crowd. Immediately a kid selling fluorescent glow sticks approaches us. Pete buys us each one, stubby yellow things you have to snap in the middle to activate. Shawna and I break ours open like normal people, while Pete tries to activate his by karate chopping it against his leg.

"Anyone ever tell you you're kind of an idiot?" I say, smiling.

"Guess that explains why we're such good friends," he says, punching me on the shoulder.

Pete Arnold and I are good friends.

Shawna and Pete argue over where to put the blanket. Pete wants to get as close to the rock face as possible, while Shawna says we should search for the flattest ground. I don't care where we sit as long as I get to eat my chicken while it's still hot. Finally they agree on a place off to the side of the field that's still pretty close to the mountain. We spread out our plaid blanket and plunk down.

"Gimme some of that bird!" I say.

"Hold it," says Pete. He tucks a white paper napkin into the collar of his T-shirt and hands Shawna and me napkins, too. "First we say grace."

I punch him in the arm. Second time I've touched him tonight. "Forgive him, Father," I say. "He knows not what he does."

I'm joking, kind of, but I really do wish Pete wasn't so flippant about God.

"What's wrong with being grateful for this chicken? Now let us hold hands and thank God for it."

Shawna grabs one of my hands and Pete grabs the other. His hand feels cool and dry in mine. I hope mine doesn't feel clammy.

"Thank you, Father," says Pete, "for this fried bird and these good friends. And thank you for the invention of lasers, which shall entertain us on this fine May evening."

"Amen," says Shawna.

"Sorry, God," I mutter under my breath.

"What did you just say?" asks Pete. He has this thing where he smiles at you with only one side of his mouth.

"I was apologizing to God for our disrespect."

"I don't understand. Preachers' kids are supposed to be really bad. What is wrong with you?"

"I drank a Miller Lite! What more do you want?"

"You girls stop bickering and hand me the plates," says Shawna.

I shoot her a look. Pete shoots her the bird. But then he tosses a plastic bag full of paper plates and napkins to her. She serves us, pouring the iced tea into red plastic cups, piling chicken, mashed potatoes, gravy, and a couple of biscuits each onto our plates. It's an almost entirely brown meal. Mama would say it needs a colorful vegetable to complete it, but brown or not, it tastes good. Salty and hot, except for the tea of course, which is cold and sweet.

"Let's play 'I never,'" says Shawna.

"What's that?" I ask.

"A game. It goes like this: If I say, 'I never brush my teeth,' everyone has to drink, assuming, of course, that everyone here actually does brush their teeth."

"You know what happens when you assume," says Pete in a singsong voice.

"You make an a-s-s out of 'u' and me," says Shawna.

She and Pete do this bit all of the time.

"Why do you say you never do something you actually do?" I ask.

"It's an opposites thing. The point is you say 'I never' about things you've actually done. Like, you could say, 'I never go to track practice,' and you and Pete would both have to drink. Or you could say, 'I never miss an episode of *Laverne and Shirley*,' and you would have to drink."

"I don't watch *Laverne and Shirley*, you dork."

"We need drink-drinks in order to actually play," says Shawna, ignoring me.

"Let's just play with sweet tea," I say.

Pete starts wiggling his eyebrows. He reaches into the front pocket of his shorts and pulls out a small leather-bound flask.

"Clearly someone was a Boy Scout," says Shawna.

"Cause a distraction while I take care of this," Pete says.

Shawna farts, loudly. A bearded guy sitting on a blanket about ten feet away gives us a look like he isn't really sure he just heard what he heard.

"That's disgusting," I say, fanning the air around me. "And I don't think causing a guy to look over here counts as a distraction. At all."

"And we're good," says Pete, putting the cap on the newly spiked gallon of tea and shaking it furiously. He dumps his cup of virgin tea into the grass and refills it from the doctored batch. He dumps mine out, too, and pours me a new cup, then does the same thing with Shawna's.

"Bobby, you go first," she says.

"Hmm. Okay. I never put chocolate ex-lax into a batch of brownies I made for my brother."

Neither Pete nor Shawna drink, but I do. The bourbon tea goes down surprisingly easy. Mainly it just tastes really sweet, like KFC tea always does.

Shawna bites her lip for a minute, thinking. "I never walked in on my parents having sex."

She and I both drink. I hadn't known what I was seeing at the time. I was only five or six. But thinking back on it later, I figured it out. Especially when I thought of how my dad, covering Mama with his body, yelled at me to get out, get out, *right now*.

"I've never watched porn," says Pete. I figure looking at a magazine isn't the same thing as *watching*, so I don't drink, and neither does Shawna.

"How?" I ask after Pete finishes his sip.

"There was an X-rated theater in Boston. A friend and I went. You were supposed to be eighteen to get in, but no one asked for our IDs or anything. It was pretty gnarly. There were guys jacking off in their seats."

"Gross," says Shawna. She swats at a mosquito that lands on Pete's thigh.

"I've never gotten hard at school," I say, and then immediately regret my words. They are going to think I'm so weird.

"Ew!" says Shawna, but she looks delighted as both Pete and I drink.

"Are you kidding?" she asks him. "When? How? Oh my God. Sick!"

"It happens," says Pete, shrugging.

"Admit it," says Shawna. "It was the first time you saw me walk into math class, wasn't it?"

"Yeah, right," I say, the bourbon tea making me looser and looser.

"Well, it's happened more than once," says Pete. "But one time was pretty funny. Weird funny."

"Tell! Tell! Tell!" demands Shawna.

"It was the day we were dissecting frogs in Dr. Floyd's class. And

I really didn't want to do it. I know it sounds dumb, but I had a pet frog when I was a kid and I just did not want to go slicing into a dead one. But I couldn't figure out how to get out of it.

"I couldn't object on moral grounds because Leslie Kaplan had already tried doing that and Dr. Floyd told her to 'shut her mouth or get an F.' I thought about trying to pass out but decided I couldn't because A) I might actually hurt myself and B) I'd look like a total pussy. I wondered if maybe I could throw up, blame it on a bad burrito or something, and get sent to the nurse's office during dissection time. All of those thoughts were churning through my mind when, *bam*! Dr. Floyd plops a dead frog onto the little plastic cutting board in front of me and just like that, I've got a boner."

"For Dr. Floyd?" asks Shawna, incredulous.

"No, for the frog! I mean, not for the frog, but because of the frog."

Shawna laughs from some deep place inside her. "You are going to so regret having told me that story, Monsieur Froggie Boner."

"We can't help it," I say. "They just pop up."

"Literally," says Pete, giving me an exaggerated, yuck-yuck wink.

"Do you have one right now?" asks Shawna. Her cheeks are red, probably from the alcohol, but she looks prettier than I've ever seen her.

"Are you kidding? No," says Pete.

"I never went to the Granite Rock Laser Show Extravaganza," I say.

We all three drink.

"Nice retreat," Shawna says.

Pete slaps at a mosquito. When he lifts his hand there is a spot of bright blood on his forearm.

"I'm not retreating. I'm just playing the game. Oh, what I would give for an Oatmeal Caramelita right now!"

Shawna and Pete look at each other and start laughing hysterically. "I'm sorry, an oatmeal-caramel what-the-fuck?" asks Pete.

"Shut up. They're good. Buttery and a little salty with chocolate chips and a layer of gooey caramel. You're really missing out if you've never had one."

"I've never had an Oatmeal Caramelita," says Shawna.

"I thought you couldn't say 'I never' if you really never have," I say.

"My mom makes them," she says.

She and I both drink.

"Then why'd you make fun of me for bringing them up?"

"Because you sounded like Gomer Pyle."

Two purple lasers flash, indicating that the show is about to begin.

"Oh, goody, goody gumdrops!" says Pete. He kicks off his shoes and lies on his back in the middle of the blanket. I lie on one side of him, Shawna on the other. "Classical Gas" comes on over the speakers. I guess they're starting mellow.

With "Classical Gas" the lasers just sort of swirl around, but when it ends and "Spirit in the Sky" comes on the lasers make illustrations of the lyrics, including one of Jesus holding open his arms to welcome all to heaven when they die. Seeing it through Pete and Shawna's smart-ass perspectives, I can understand that it's dorky, but I'm sorry, it's also neat. Pete's yellow glow stick lies on the blanket between the two of us. It illuminates how close our hands are to touching. They are too close, but I don't move. If I were to move my hand, to rest it on my stomach or behind my head, Pete might sense that I am trying to pull away from him, and that would be strange, because why would I pull away unless I was *trying* not to touch his hand?

I try to relax. It's a perfect May night, not too hot, with a little bit of a breeze. And here I am, lying on a blanket with two friends, hanging out. Isn't this what I always wanted? What I have wished for since I was a little kid? No. What I want, what I wish for, is to reach out and touch Pete's hand, lying so close to mine. What I want is to be alone on the blanket with him, snuggling into his shoulder as we watch the face of Granite Rock light up with lasers. What I want is to hold him, to kiss him, to press my body against his. To be here as a couple, not a threesome.

Except such desires aren't real. Aren't true. They come from messed-up wiring in my brain that I need to ignore. Messed-up wiring that I will one day learn to fix.

When "Georgia on My Mind" comes on, Shawna sits up and announces that she has to go to the bathroom.

"Should we just meet you at the car at the end of the show?" asks Pete.

"You're *so* hilarious. And for the record, I'm going to be quick. I don't even have to poop."

"Boy, am I thrilled to know that," says Pete.

Shawna walks off. It's just the two of us. This is what I wanted, and yet I feel jittery, nervous. I feel a pebble, just below my shoulder, but I don't dare move to adjust. A breeze passes over us and with it I smell the remnants of our fried chicken, plus Irish Spring soap and, underneath that, Pete's sweat. Not dirty sweat, like the smell of Hunter's football uniform after a game, but clean sweat, the sweat that comes naturally just from being a guy and being alive. Pete is wearing a Mr. Bubble T-shirt that fits close to his chest. I want to roll over on my side so I can look at him more closely. I want to study him.

"Did I ever tell you about my dad's mistress?" he asks.

"What?"

Pete has never really talked about his dad at all, besides showing me those slides from Arizona and saying he was a big Red Sox fan.

"Everyone knew about her. He kept her in a suite at this fancy hotel in Boston for something like five years. She was his secretary."

The fact that his dad could afford a suite at a fancy hotel for five years surprises me more than the fact that he had a mistress. Pete and his mom's place is such a dump.

"Did you ever meet her?"

"Yeah. When I was younger Dad would sometimes take me to the restaurant at the hotel. It was this really swank place called the Oak Room. Carla, Dad, and I would all get steaks."

Now I do turn on my side; I'm so intrigued.

"Oh my gosh. What was that like for you?"

"The thing I remember most was all of the deer heads mounted on the wall. That and how crazy good the steak was. I guess I was pretty clueless about everything else."

"But your mom's so pretty. I mean, why would your dad need to have another woman holed away at a hotel?"

"Mom says he did it because he could. Correction. She says 'that bastard' did it because he could."

I try to imagine my father keeping a spare woman at a hotel in Atlanta. It's impossible. Mama's will is just too strong. She simply would not allow him to do that. I imagine Mama starting a prayer chain, calling on the women in SERVERS to pray the harlot out of Daddy's life. I imagine them circling the parking lot of the hotel, holding hands, praying and chanting until the other woman was driven out and away forever.

I wonder why Pete and his mom don't have any money. It seems like his mother should get a lot if his dad is rich enough to keep his mistress in a hotel suite for five years. I wonder what it would feel like to live in a cheap duplex with just your mom, your dad so far away and never coming to visit. I suddenly feel so sad for Pete that without thinking I reach out, put my hand on his forearm.

"That really sucks," I say.

"Oh, don't feel sorry for me," says Pete, all breezy and nonchalant. "Were I still in Massachusetts I wouldn't be enjoying this delightful little ditty."

I hadn't even noticed, but the song has switched again, and now

"Sweet Home Alabama" is playing at full force, the lasers creating the shape of a billowing Confederate flag. I settle on my back again. It seems the serious talk is over.

"You're aware they're referring to George Wallace, right?" asks Pete.

"Huh?"

"In the song. That bit about how much they love the governor in Birmingham.'"

"Who's George Wallace?" I ask.

"You're kidding, right?"

"Where the heck is Shawna?" I ask, trying to change the subject. Sometimes I get tired of talking with Pete about how backward the South is.

"I keep telling her she should go see a doctor about how long it takes her."

"I think she dawdles just to annoy you."

"What kind of a word is 'dawdles'?"

I shrug. It's a word my mom uses every Sunday. *We have* got *to get to church on time, so don't you boys dawdle over breakfast. You hear?*

"You know what we were talking about earlier?" Pete asks.

"About your dad?"

"No. Unexpected pop-ups."

I don't say a word. I can't.

"I've got one. I just can't help myself. I get all fired up thinking about Dixie."

As I roll my eyes, my gaze lands on the bulge against his shorts. And just like that, I get one, too. I can't help it. He looks down at me and starts laughing.

"We've got to get these under control before Shawna comes back," he says. "Or she'll insist we have a threesome or something."

"Sick," I say.

"Think about Latham's gym shorts," says Pete.

"Shut up, shut up, shut up," I say.

At that moment Shawna appears, standing over us on the blanket, her upside-down face looming large. "What are you crazy kids doing?" she asks.

"Just enjoying this fine cultural event," says Pete.

I laugh wildly, inappropriately.

Shawna settles back on the blanket and starts digging through her backpack, pulling out a bag of Fig Newtons. "You want one?" she asks me.

"Sure," I say. She tosses me a cookie, which lands on my chest. Still lying down, I bring it to my mouth and bite into it, the fig seeds popping beneath my teeth. Hunter used to tell me the crunch in a Fig Newton was little dead flies that got caught inside the fig. I feel my erection start to go down.

While Shawna was gone, Pete's and my blanket became a float, slipping over the rope that marked protected waters, drifting beyond the lifeguard's range. Though I wanted to be alone with Pete, I am suddenly grateful for Shawna's presence. She makes it okay for Pete and me to be together on this blanket at all. She has pulled us back to where it is safe.

The show ends with "Southern Nights," which the lasers illustrate with a picture of a man in overalls casting a fishing line into a pond. As soon as the song ends, a refrain from "Dixie" comes on over the speakers. A chorus of rebel yells rises from everyone around us.

Pete leans toward me and whispers, "Uh-oh. The natives are getting frisky."

"What did you say?" asks Shawna, but Pete waves away her question.

The lasers outline the carving of General Lee on horseback, and then they animate the legs of his horse so that the General is first walking, then trotting, then galloping toward some destination other than defeat.

"How much would you pay me to yell, 'God bless Sherman!' at the end of this song?" asks Pete.

"Don't," says Shawna. "I'm serious. You'll get the crap beat out of you."

"Aw, let em try," says Pete, all punchy and confident. "I'm small, but I'm slow."

"Well, there's a ringing endorsement," I say.

"Wait. I mean I'm small, but I'm fast."

"You are fast. My track times are so much better this year with you on the team. I've never pushed myself this hard."

"You inspire me!" gushes Shawna. Shawna rarely goes a moment without being sarcastic. But neither, really, does Pete.

"I do it for Latham," says Pete.

"And his big, sweaty balls," says Shawna.

"Sick," I say.

The show ends with fireworks. As soon as the last spark fades into the sky, Pete jumps up and starts gathering up our blanket and our trash. Shawna tells him that it doesn't matter how fast we get to the car, we'll still be stuck behind a thousand others trying to get out of the lot. Pete says not if we race. He is all hyped up. As we rush to the parking lot he keeps putting his hands on my shoulders and jumping, using me like a bench vault.

I can't stop smiling. Everything is beautiful. Pete is beautiful, all lean and defined. Shawna is beautiful in her baggy overalls and her long braid. The night air is beautiful. Even life at home is okay. So much better than it had been. Tolerable. After what I did to Hunter, my brother keeps his distance, an easier thing once Mama finally allowed Hunter to take over Troy's old room. Hunter is scared of me, and so Hunter leaves me alone. And when it comes to my brother, I can't ask for much more.

Mama mostly leaves me alone, too, but that is only painful and not a relief. Still, I have gotten used to it, am able to forget about it much of the time, like at this moment, the soft night air blowing through the open windows as we wait behind a line of cars to get out of the parking lot, the three of us squeezed together in the cab of Shawna's truck.

Back in Decatur, we stop for snacks at the 7-Eleven. I get Dip-N-Sticks, while Pete gets an Almond Joy and Shawna gets Big League Chew bubble gum. We tease her about it, ask her if she's going to join the softball team with all of the other lesbians, and she tells us to shut up, but then she glances at her watch and gasps, "Oh shit!" saying that she has to get us home right away because it's already 11:40 and her curfew, which her parents are really strict about, is midnight.

"Don't worry about taking me home," says Pete. "I'll just sleep over at Bobby's."

When Shawna pulls up to my house all of the lights are off but the one in my parents' bedroom. Hunter is probably sleeping at his friend Rocky's house, where he spends most weekends. Rocky is the youngest of six kids and his folks have lost all interest in being parents, so they let Rocky throw parties and do whatever he wants. I am surprised Mama and Daddy let Hunter go over there. Surely they've heard rumors. But maybe not. Maybe because Rocky is the quarterback of the football team they just assume he's well reared.

I let us in with the key. It takes me a few times to get it inside the lock, but eventually I manage. Once inside Pete goes to my room while I go to the bathroom and rinse my mouth out with Scope. Then I walk to my parents' room, knocking on their closed door.

"Come in," calls Mama.

She and Daddy are both sitting up in bed, reading. Mama wears a white nightgown with lacy shoulder straps. Daddy has on his old blue-and-white-striped pajamas from Brooks Brothers. Mama looks so pretty that for a moment I feel like a child again and I imagine myself rushing to bury my head in her chest, which would smell of Jergens Lotion and Laura Ashley Number I perfume.

"Is it okay if Pete sleeps over?" I ask, praying that there is nothing funny or slurred about my speech.

"Did he check with his mother?" asks Daddy. He is reading a book that his men's group is discussing at church, titled *Dare to Discipline.*

"She's fine with it," I say, knowing she'll probably be happy to have the apartment to herself for a night. Still, I'll remind Pete to call her from the extension in the kitchen, farthest away from Mama and Daddy's hearing range, so they won't know we waited to ask for Mrs. Arnold's permission until after they gave us theirs.

"All right then," says Daddy. "Now tell me, how was the show?"

"Neat. Same as last year."

"Do you need help setting up the trundle bed?" asks Mama.

"I've seen you do it. I can figure it out."

"Son, those are words a father likes to here," says Daddy.

"Yes, sir. Well, good night."

"Good night, son," says Daddy.

"G'night," murmurs Mama, her eyes having already returned to *All Things Wise and Wonderful.*

Pete waits in my room, shoes off, sprawled on his back on the bed, lying smack below the overhead fan, which whirls at full speed. "Do those still work?" Pete asks, pointing to the fluorescent glow-in-the-dark stars dotted on the ceiling that Mama stuck on years ago.

"Yeah," I say. "But they're pretty old. They glow for about two minutes, then fade."

"Do you have any more booze in the house?"

"Hello?" I say, taking my house keys out of my pocket and putting them on the plate on my dresser. "Have you met my dad, Pastor Banks?"

"They don't even drink behind closed doors?"

"Nope."

"That's bizarre."

"If you say so."

"Hey," says Pete. He looks at me. "Turn off the light. Let's see the stars."

"They're kind of lame."

"Let me see."

I flip off the light. Suddenly my room is all shadows. Pete looks like a bump across the bed, lit only by the stars' fluorescent glow.

Pete thumps the bedspread. "Come here. I want to show you something."

My heart.

Pete thumps the bedspread again. It is the same one I've had for years, red with white sailboats printed on it.

I sit on the bed's very edge. Pete, still lying down, rolls toward me and puts his head in my lap.

I say nothing. To speak would be to confirm what is happening.

"Hi," he says, turning his head so he is looking up at me.

Silent, I put my hand on his chest, pressing down on his T-shirt so I can feel the hard spot of bone between his pecs. He sits up, swings his legs over the edge of the bed so that he is sitting beside me, our thighs touching. And then his face is coming toward me. His mouth smells of bourbon. I feel his lips, which are soft and warm and full, pressing. He puts his hand on my cheek as he kisses me, his tongue going into my mouth as if he has done this a million times before. I cannot fight this. I do not want to fight this.

I kiss him back softly. Trying not to think of how much I want him. Instead I tell myself that we are just practicing, for our future girlfriends, our future wives. We are drunk and we are practicing. We are such good friends. Such good friends that it is hard to find a way to show our affection. This is not a homosexual thing; this is a really-good-friends thing, like Jonathan and David in the Bible.

The overhead fan cranks and whirls, stirring the air around us. This delicious, cool air.

And then Pete pushes me back onto the bed, suddenly and with force, and I let him, let him straddle me with both legs, pressing his crotch against mine. I feel his erection. He must be able to feel mine. I don't say a word. To say a word would make it real and this is not real. This is not real. This is the best I have ever felt in my whole life. Except it can't be happening. For it to be happening would mean we are like that skinny man with the mustache at Piedmont Park. And we aren't like that, we aren't like him, we can't be. We are just two really good friends. We are just really, really good friends who love each other, who are finding a way to show how much we love each other.

Pete is lifting up my shirt and pulling it over my head, the way Mama would when I was little and she would help me into my pajamas, only Pete's motion is urgent. He is kissing my chest, letting his lips linger and tug on my nipple, and it feels so good I cannot say *stop.* I cannot say anything except to let out a little moan because nothing has ever felt as good as what Pete is doing right now, unbuttoning my fly and pressing his hand against me. And oh God, oh God, this cannot be happening, it isn't happening, because it is so wrong, wrong, wrong; I know it is wrong even as I am bucking my pelvis up toward Pete. I want him. I know it is wrong, but I cannot say a word about the wrongness of what we are doing because if I do he might stop, and right now, with the fan spinning above me and him touching me, nothing is worth more. Nothing. Not Mama, not Daddy, not God. Pete slides two fingers inside the elastic band of my underwear and I am thinking, *Don't stop, don't stop, don't stop.* And then something does stop, though it takes me a moment to recognize what it is.

The fan. The overhead fan has stopped spinning. There is a noticeable silence in place of its whirl. A light shines in from the hallway. Pete jumps off me. Mama, so pretty in her white nightgown with its lacy straps, stands in the doorway, the door open, and she is saying something, but I can't understand because language makes no sense. I am dizzy. I might pass out. Pete looks at me and there is fear in his eyes and, weirdly, this calms me because I want to be strong for him. Daddy must have been just a few steps behind Mama, because I see him in the doorway now, too. I see him scan the scene and I see his self-assurance, so much a part of him, just fizzle right out. He is a balloon, punctured in the air, deflating as it lowers to the ground. And still I do not say a word, even though Daddy has asked me to do just that, to explain to him, please, what in the name of God we think we are doing.

I had forgotten to tell Pete to call his mom, and she had called instead, wild with worry when her son didn't come home. We never heard the phone ring. The whirl of the fan must have been too loud. And so Mama made her way to my room, telling Daddy that she could handle it (did she know what she might find?), but Daddy followed her, angry at me for lying, planning to give both Pete and me a good talking-to. If Mama knocked on the closed door we did not hear it over the fan. Or maybe it was our excitement for each other that plugged our ears. That made me forget to tell Pete to call his mom in the first place. But none of that matters. What matters is that we are exposed. Exposed doing something that once caused God to destroy an entire city. Doing something that puts our eternal souls—our *eternal* souls—in peril.

This Daddy says again and again, pacing back and forth in front of the bed where Pete and I sit, as far apart from each other as we can, our heads bowed.

When the doorbell rings we all move downstairs, as if we are one. Pete's mom looks haggard and exhausted, the circles under her eyes like small change purses. She is telling Daddy how sorry she is. She is wiping away tears. On his way out Pete glances at me, gives me a small, worried smile, but doesn't say anything, just follows behind his mother.

I sit on the sofa in the living room while Mama and Daddy discuss the terrible thing they came upon, speaking of me as if I weren't there. Mama says, "It's clear he wants to hurt us." I stop listening. A softness, like cotton, settles around my brain. I can no longer be here. Mama and Daddy could not have witnessed Pete and me doing what we were doing. I have to disappear. At some point Daddy says this is too big of a problem for them to handle on their own. At this I tune in. There is talk of Riverside Military Academy; there is talk of a rehabilitation center in Virginia, a place that is known for turning wayward teens around. I know that Daddy recommends it only to desperate parents with especially destructive children. The type who chop off the cat's tail and set the drapes on fire. "It's not an easy place," Daddy once told Mama after encouraging a congregant to send his troubled child there, "but better to suffer some temporary discomfort here on earth than to burn for eternity."

At last I am told to try and get some sleep, that there will be lots to figure out the next day, that Daddy has some calls to make, to seek wise counsel, but bottom line is they love me and they are going to help me fight whatever sickness has gotten inside of me.

Back in my room I sit on the edge of the bed, where Pete and I first started kissing. I am so very tired. All I want is to lie down and sleep. But I know I cannot. I know I am fighting for my life and I must stay awake. I know that by morning my fate will be outside of my control. Daddy will have contacted his oldest friend, Colonel Higgins, who will probably suggest military school, while Mama will probably push for that place in Virginia.

This I know: I will not survive either. And so I open my window to the cool night air and push myself through, landing on the soft dirt below. I don't take anything with me. I walk slowly around our house, afraid of setting off any lights. But once on the street, though the way is lit only by streetlights, I run pell-mell, faster than I have ever run in a race, faster even than if Pete were beside me, up Lamont and then down Clairmont, which is such a busy street during the day, but in the middle of the night is ghostly, empty. I could easily trip, smack my face against the pavement, break my nose or my front teeth or even an arm. Be stranded in the middle of the road, for someone to find or someone to run over. But I can't; I won't. Falling is not an option.

I run, arms pumping, through downtown Decatur, passing the courthouse, then, later, the high school. I run until I cross the railroad tracks, until I am in Meemaw's neighborhood, on Ansley. I run down Ansley until it intersects with Jefferson Place, passing the house where Keisha's auntie still lives. I do not stop until I am in front of Meemaw's bungalow. Her porch light is on. I knock, and my grandmother comes to the door right away, wearing her pink velour housecoat that zips up the front.

"I've been thinking about you all night," she says, leading me inside. "I got out of bed hours ago, so worried I couldn't sleep. I kept picturing your precious little face and I knew something was wrong. Are you hurt, sugar? I think Jesus was trying to tell me you'd been hurt. I almost called y'alls house, but I decided to wait till morning. I didn't want your mama to think me an old fool. But something has happened, hasn't it?"

I nod. I am staring at one of the photos hanging above the mantel. It's one of Hunter, Troy, and me, taken years ago. I couldn't have been older than six. In the picture I am curtseying for the camera; Troy and Hunter stand solid and stoic behind. We all three wear navy Izod shirts and khaki shorts, picked out by Mama.

"Sit down, sweetheart; I'm going to get you something to drink."

I make my way to Meemaw's ancient sofa, covered in a floral print that has faded over the years, the once red roses now the palest pink.

Meemaw returns from the kitchen carrying a mug. She hands it to me, and I got teary after taking a sip. It is warmed milk, darkened with vanilla and sweetened with sugar. The drink she would always fix when I was staying over and could not sleep.

"Sweetheart, are you in some kind of trouble?" she asks.

"Yes, ma'am," I whisper. "Yes, ma'am, I am."

"Does it have something to do with that new friend of yours? That Yankee boy from your track team?"

I look at her, stunned. I nod, too embarrassed to answer her question out loud. I am so ashamed. My face is hot and I am so exhausted and I want to weep, but I fight the urge because I know if I do I will lose all my strength. I will crumble.

"I don't understand what's happening between you and that boy, Bobby. I've seen the two of you together, and, well, I just don't understand."

I hold my breath. If Meemaw says she can't love me it won't matter whether or not I'm going to hell. I will already be in it.

She picks up my hand, holds it in her soft, wrinkled one. "What I do understand is that you are a beloved child of God."

She looks up to the ceiling. "Do you hear that, Jesus? He is still your beloved child."

"They're going to send me away," I say. "To military school or some place for juvenile delinquents. I won't make it at either place, Meemaw. I won't."

She is quiet for a moment, as if waiting for an answer. And then a look of certainty passes over her face and she presses her lips together and nods. Picks up my hand again. "You are *not* a delinquent, and you are not a child who should go to military school. If your mama and daddy want to send you away, they can send you to me. You can come live here. I'm slowing down. I need help. Man's always saying that."

"I don't think they'll let me. It's bad, Meemaw. They caught me doing something really bad."

"Now listen, I don't want you to worry. I know how to get Mannie to do the right thing. Edie might fuss, but that's all she's going to do. Your meemaw is not going to let anyone throw you to the wolves. Your meemaw is going to keep you loved and safe. You hear me?"

Something loosens in my chest, a rock pushed aside, and the trapped air expels itself in sobs and there is my meemaw, pulling me into her embrace, patting my back and whispering soft words both to Jesus and to me, trying to convince the two of us that I am worthy of love.

Part Two

Bobby in New York

5

LETTER HOME

May 15, 1981

Dear Meemaw,

Money goes fast in New York City. There's no way around it. The other day I was walking around my neighborhood—the neighborhood where the residence hotel is—and I passed what you would have called a precious little bakery. French. There were tiny cakes in the display (petit fours), each about a square inch in size, dipped in white glaze and topped with a rose made of pink frosting. Well, I ordered two. (One for me, one for you . . .) You won't believe how much they cost. Two dollars and fifty cents! For two little bits of cake! The worst part was, I didn't say anything at all. I was too scared of looking unsophisticated, like a yokel.

I'm sure I do come across as a yokel. One of the front desk guys at the hotel calls me Mr. Deliverance (ha ha ha) because of my accent. Apparently I have a thick one. Who knew? Pete Arnold used to tease me about having one, but I always thought that was because I made fun of the Yankee way he talked.

Everyone dresses differently up here. And not like how they used to dress, not how you described, back when you and Granddaddy Banks visited Manhattan before he shipped off for the war and you were intimidated by all of the ladies with their white gloves and fox stoles. No. Things are grittier now. Ripped jeans, spiked hair, torn shirts. Like the other day when I stopped by my friend Mike's room to see if he wanted to go get a drink. (Sorry!) I was just standing in his doorway, waiting for him to respond, when he walked right over to me, grabbed my shirt by the collar, and ripped it halfway down the front. "There," he said. "Now you're ready to be seen."

Mike is from Providence, Rhode Island. He has a terrible accent, the opposite of soothing. Which is okay, I guess, for a guy. But I can't imagine somebody's mama talking that way. The only southerners I've met are this little band of evangelicals who are also staying at the residence hotel. They are from somewhere in Tennessee. Half of them have guitars and they are always sitting around the lobby, singing folk songs about Christ. I'm not sure what they do during the day, maybe distribute tracts to apartment buildings, but every night there they are singing their songs. I know some of the lyrics from having been an RA, but I've never asked to join in. To tell the truth, Meemaw, this merry band of evangelicals seems pretty naïve to me, like they think they can change this whole city just by strumming their guitars.

The truth is, I don't think this city changes all that much. I think it changes people. I've only been here three months, and it's already changing me.

I wish you were here. I wish I could phone you. I wouldn't be able to afford to talk for long, but at least I could hear your voice. The truth is, I'm lonely. You don't know how alone you are until you move by yourself to New York City. Here's the thing about this place: No one cares. No one cares about Bobby Banks up here, no, ma'am. To be honest, that realization can be exciting sometimes, freeing, like no one knows you and no one cares, so you can do whatever the heck you want. That's when I might go to a bar or go to the clubs or walk through the Ramble at Central Park at dusk, observing all of the forbidden things happening around me. Compared to Mike, who is forever sharing details of his sexual exploits, I'm pretty inexperienced. But I can't claim innocence. I suppose it's been a long time since I could do that.

Daddy always said that God knows each and every one of our hearts. It's hard to imagine that here. That night I was out with Mike, after he ripped my shirt, we were on the Upper West Side, walking on Broadway, and some guy turns a corner and nearly walks into us. I start apologizing, even though it was actually his fault, and the guy reaches out and grabs the St. Christopher medal I wear—wore—on a silver chain around my neck and just rips it off. Just rips it off and runs with it. As if it's worth any money, when in fact I purchased it for five dollars at a little secondhand shop in the East Village.

Don't worry, Meemaw, I haven't turned Catholic or anything; it just made me feel safe to wear the Patron Saint of Travelers around my neck. Actually, I don't imagine you would mind if I did go Catholic. I can just imagine you saying, "As long as you've got God in your heart." Lord, you were a good person, Meemaw. I don't think they make many like you.

I have a roommate at the hotel. It's hard to get a single here, and besides, it's so much cheaper if you double up. My roommate's name is Alex Marcus, and the only times I see him are late, late at night when he comes into the room and starts jumping up and down on his bed, chanting, "Oh my God, I'm so coked up! I'm so coked up!" He's not talking about Coca-Cola, Meemaw.

Can you see me from where you are? Is any of what I'm writing down news to you? Are you witnessing my life? Truth is, I don't always *want* you looking at what I'm doing. I certainly didn't want you looking the other night at the Anvil. Just turn away when I'm at a club, okay, Meemaw? Just turn your head and know I'm still your Bobby, just a little roughed up.

I try to avoid the bars and the baths. I really do. I'll tell myself I'm not going to go, and I don't, not for a long time, not for a month, and then I'll get this hungry feeling and without telling myself where I'm headed I'll leave the hotel and find myself there.

But that's not how I spend most of my time. Most days I'm looking for a job, and if not that, I'm exploring the city, trying to do something both cultural and cheap. I went to the main branch of the New York Public Library the other day. Boy, does it beat the heck out of any library I've ever been to, even the big one in downtown Atlanta. I sat in the reading room among the rows and rows of tables with little banker's lamps positioned every few feet, a pile of magazines beside me. I had been job searching earlier that morning, literally pounding the pavement, and I was discouraged and exhausted. And so I read *GQ* and *Esquire* and *Vogue* cover to cover while college students studied around me and a wild-haired man wearing a brown sweater scribbled away at what must have been a novel. It was nice to be in such a beautiful space. There's sure nothing beautiful about the residence hotel. Not that I'm complaining, Meemaw. It serves its purpose. I just aspire to a life more lovely. I guess I've still got some of Mama in me after all.

Lord, am I worried about money. I have got to get a job soon, because I know that once the money you left me runs out, that's it. I cannot expect any from Mama or Daddy. Sometimes I get so scared it's like my heart clenches up in my chest. I imagine myself having to move back home, having to take the train because I can't afford the plane ticket, arriving at the Amtrak station on Peachtree, calling Daddy to come pick me up. I imagine being driven back to

Decatur, my duffel bag in the back of Daddy's car, and Daddy and me walking in the back door to greet Mama, who would be chilly but resigned.

Sometimes I imagine being homeless in New York. Wandering the streets looking in old trash cans for leftovers to eat. It could happen, Meemaw. I have no college degree, no safety net.

But I sound ungrateful. That's the last way I want to come across. It still makes me teary to think of you sliding that envelope filled with cash across the table at The Colonnade, after I had finished my turkey dinner and you your chicken livers. That was the night you told me about the time you left Daddy and June with your mama and took the train to New York City to spend the week with Granddaddy Banks before he was shipped off to Europe from Jersey City. You told me about being intimidated by the fancy ladies, and eating at Schrafft's and being served a butterscotch sundae that was the most delicious thing you ever put in your mouth. You told me that all those years later you could still remember how exciting it was to be in Manhattan, how tall the buildings, how elegant the people: the men in their hats, the women in their white gloves. You told me that not only did New Yorkers impress you with their elegance, but they seemed to have a shared sense of adventure. And then you told me that while you would miss me "like the dickens," you thought New York City might be the perfect place for a "special, creative boy" like me. Then you slid that envelope across the table, and I opened it, and it was filled with cash.

Five thousand dollars. Five thousand dollars is a lot of pound cakes sold. A thousand pound cakes, except no, more than that, because that doesn't account for the money you put into each one, the money for butter and eggs, sugar and flour, pure vanilla extract. And then you tithed, didn't you, Meemaw? Gave ten percent of your profits to the church. So really, Lord knows how many pound cakes you had to bake to earn five thousand dollars of profit. Two thousand?

Two thousand pound cakes slid raw into the oven, and pulled out golden and fragrant?

When you gave me that money, did you realize how soon after I would go? Did you think I might first finish up my degree at Georgia State? I bet you knew I would leave as fast as I could. I bet you knew that I was bored with school, that I was lonely, that I needed a change, something drastic. Your intuition was always so good, Meemaw. Like how you knew I was in trouble that night I got caught with Pete Arnold. (He didn't even show up for your funeral, Meemaw. I thought he might.) Maybe your intuition let you know you didn't have long left in this world and so you slid that cash over to me while you were still here to see my reaction. Which was to cry. Just break down and cry because you slid my freedom to me. Much as I loved living with you, I guess we both knew I couldn't keep doing it forever.

The next day I called a travel agent and booked a one-way ticket to LaGuardia Airport, and you told me that a lady at your church knew of a residence hotel where young men new to the city could stay, at least temporarily, and I phoned up there and booked a room for the first two weeks, thinking surely that was long enough to find an apartment. (Ha.) And then the week before my flight was to take off, you died. Died while planting petunias, getting ready for spring. Your heart just stopped, they said, and you fell over sideways onto the ground. You had been sitting on that little stool you used to wheel around while you gardened, to soften the impact on your knees. Mrs. Reid from next door said she looked out the window and there was Miss Millie mounding dirt around her flowers, and then she blinked, and there was Miss Millie, fallen to the ground.

Meemaw, did you plan it? Did you plan to die right before I left so I would be forced to see Mama and Daddy one more time? Lord. You always got your way, didn't you? That's what Mama always said, that you were all sweet and soft on top but a master manipulator underneath.

I know Daddy would have liked for your funeral to have been at his church, but of course it was held at Second Avenue Baptist. And the place was packed. I hope you know that. So many people rose to speak in your honor. Lord knows how many people you touched during your lifetime. Small gestures adding up to a lifetime of service. That's how your pastor described it. So many gestures were recalled: how you would bring a tuna noodle casserole to anyone in your neighborhood or your church who had a hospitalized family member, or a death in the family, or a new baby. How you always offered to feed a neighbor's cat or water a neighbor's plants when they were away on vacation. How you brought cut flowers all summer long to the elderly black lady who lived down the street from you, who was isolated and alone in her house, whose only company, often, was yours. How you baked your pound cakes with such love and care, and didn't charge your regular customers for their cake during their birthday week. How you kept account of people's birthdays.

I had my own story of appreciation to tell, Meemaw. But I remained quiet. Sat silently with my brothers, a Banks boy again. Hunter had driven down from Athens and Troy had driven up from the Medical College in Augusta. After the funeral service Mama opened the house up to anyone who wanted to come by. She served several of your pound cakes, pulled from the freezer and defrosted. She served the cakes with berries sweetened with sugar and Cool Whip. Eating my slice made me think of communion, Meemaw. Because you were in the sweetness of that cake. Because I could taste your love when I ate it.

My flight to New York was only three days later. I was so afraid of chickening out, of not going, that I didn't change my ticket. I went to your house and packed up my belongings, as well as a few things of yours that I wanted for sentimental reasons, including your old metal tube pan and a picture of the two of us from when I was five years old or so, sitting on your lap on your front porch swing. I left the rest for Mama and Daddy to deal with. Maybe that was wrong. Maybe I should have stayed and made sure nothing important was thrown away. But I knew if I stayed I might not ever leave. I might be too weighted down by grief. So I took that flight on Eastern Air Lines to LaGuardia, ate my little bag of peanuts and drank my Coca-Cola while looking out the tiny window at the clouds below. And then we descended, and I saw the city's skyline, and all of a sudden I realized, I had moved. I had left my home and moved here. I gathered my possessions from the baggage claim, slinging my duffel bag from the Army-Navy store over one shoulder and holding your old burgundy Samsonite suitcase in my opposite hand, shivering already though I wasn't even outside yet. I took a shuttle to Grand Central Station, where I joined the crowds, alone. Hoping—at that moment, at least—that you were watching.

6

Pounding the Pavement

(New York City, Summer 1981)

Today I filled out an application at Bloomingdale's, dreaming of working in their gourmet shop, though willing to work in any of their departments. I'm not, however, holding my breath for an offer considering that the woman who took my application barked, "Who do ya think I am, your grandma?" after I called her ma'am.

Leaving Bloomingdale's with no prospect of employment, I vowed not to obsess over what might happen if I can't find a job, if I spend all of Meemaw's money and have nothing to fall back on. I will not think of how vulnerable I am, of how many jobs I've been turned down for so far. Instead I will relax my clenched heart by looking for other men, men like me. It's easy to tell who they are. For starters, they have bodies shaped by hours at the gym and they wear their shirts a little tighter to show off their muscles, an extra button undone at the collar. They wear their jeans tighter, too, the fabric around the crotch a little worn, a little frayed, the result of taking a wire brush to them, just to rough them up in the right places, a trick my friend Mike showed me my second night at the hotel.

Mike taught me other things to look for, too: an earring in the right lobe, a wallet attached to the belt with a chain, a leather jacket or vest—not that many would brave leather in the New York summer heat. I have heard that there are handkerchief codes, too, different colors of handkerchiefs worn in the back pocket indicating different turn-ons. That's a little more advanced skill set than I have, but I can sure recognize a fag when I see one. If I spot an especially attractive man, sometimes I will follow him, see where he goes. Make a mental note of the place, vowing to return later.

I head south on Third Avenue, deciding I'll check out Beekman Place, which runs between 51st and 49th Streets. I want to see if I can find the town house where Auntie Mame lived. I'll never forget watching that movie with Meemaw. It came on *The Late, Late Show,* and while Meemaw did mutter a few "oh my's" and "mercies!" during Mame's more drunken moments, she and I both loved it. Once I moved up to the city, I realized that practically *every* gay boy worshiped Auntie Mame and the actress who played her, Rosalind Russell.

Walking, I am reminded for the thousandth time of how much I love this city, despite its crime, its expense, its hardness. In tandem with the trials are daily jolts of inspiration: the Chrysler Building coming into sudden view; the fruit vendor I frequent who always gives me extra grapes or an apple; the way the setting light hits pink against the Hudson River at dusk. Just as I reach 51st Street, a young woman with cheekbones like cut glass and Mia Farrow's pixie haircut—the one she wore in *Rosemary's Baby*—swishes by, heading west. I turn to stare as she walks away. Could she *be* Mia Farrow? It's certainly possible. On impulse, I follow the woman, trying to figure out if she really is the famous actress. She turns the corner at Second Avenue, and I, realizing I'm an idiot to trot after a (maybe) famous person as if I'm some slack-jawed tourist, turn and head back toward my destination.

That's right, Bobby, don't be an idiot chasing after Mia Farrow. Instead stalk the home of a fictitious character from an over-the-top movie. Lord.

So wrapped up am I in my self-chiding that I almost walk past the "Help Wanted" sign hung from a hook on the front door of one of the town houses on Fifty-first. But then I backtrack, realizing what it is I have seen. *Café Andres* is embossed on the wooden door, above the sign.

This is not a home but a restaurant.

I run my fingers through my hair. It feels just like Daddy's used to, thick and rough and curly. I dab my pointer finger with a little spit and smooth down each eyebrow, first the left, then the right, then slide my nail sideways through the space between my front teeth, hoping to dislodge any food that might have gotten stuck there. Usually I carry mints in my pocket, but when I reach for them I feel only the crumpled remains of a Certs wrapper.

Opening the town house door, I walk down a little flight of stairs and then across a marbled hall that smells of dust and long-enclosed air. At the end of the hall is a swinging door with a smoked-glass mirror. I push it open, finding myself in another world. The whole interior is lush with furnishings; many, like the life-sized marble statues positioned about the place, seem to have no purpose other than to charm. Everywhere you look there is an object taking up space: an upright piano in the corner, cake plates stacked atop each other on the bar, whirling fans overhead, a parrot observing the whole scene from a swing in the corner of the room. Billie Holiday's recorded voice pipes in from hidden speakers. The scene gives me the sudden desire to drink cocktails and lounge. Not that there is anyone to lounge with. At three o'clock in the afternoon, with the exception of a formally dressed woman with a prominent brow seated at a corner table, the place is empty of customers.

As I walk toward the bar the parrot on the swing squawks, "Stella!" As if summoned, an impeccably groomed man shoots out of the kitchen through the swinging door and rushes to greet me. He has a full head of silver hair. He wears a crisp white linen shirt, unbuttoned at the neck, tucked into a pair of light blue trousers, surely a linen and cotton blend. His braided belt, made of white cotton, wraps around his slender-as-a-girl's waist. On his feet are blue Sebagos, just a few shades darker than his pants.

"Hello, hello!" he calls. "Please, sit anywhere you like. Would you like to know our menu or are you simply craving a drink to relieve you from this heat?"

With his tanned skin and dark eyes, he looks Mediterranean. But his accent, faint though it is, sounds Eastern European.

"I'm actually here because of the 'Help Wanted' sign," I say.

He smacks the palm of his hand against his forehead in a theatrical fashion. "Tsk, tsk, I was supposed to remove that, wasn't I? Unfortunately, the position is filled. And anyway, I was looking for an assistant in the kitchen, practically a line cook, and I'm sure you want front-of-the-house work, don't you? Heaven forbid we hide a face like yours in the back."

The fact that there was recently an opening for a chef's assistant is almost too much for me. Five minutes ago I did not know this place existed; suddenly it feels as if my birthright has been snatched away, like Jacob tricking Esau, though I don't even have a bowl of lentils to show for it.

"You're a hundred percent positive it's filled?" I ask. I step just a little closer to him, make eye contact. "Because I have training, as a chef."

Liar, liar, pants on fire. My only training comes from Mama and Meemaw.

"Oh yes, Jose is already hard at work julienning vegetables and prepping chickens to roast for tonight's dinner. But come, sit; there's no reason I can't conduct a little informal interview, get your telephone number, et cetera, et cetera. That way if anything ever does come up I can give you a call."

I have no telephone number save for the front desk at Good Shepherd, but I am nothing if not good at avoiding questions I don't want to answer. I follow him to a small, round table near the entrance where he says he can keep an eye on things.

"May I get you a drink? Coffee, tea, perhaps even a sherry?"

"A drink sounds lovely," I say, patting my pocket with my hand. "But I left my wallet at home."

"Well then," he says, arching his eyebrows, "you shall have to be doubly entertaining."

Except I'm not the entertaining one. Gus Andres, the café's owner and namesake, is. He fills me in on the history of the restaurant as if he were Liz Smith, gossiping about an actual person, assuring me that the restaurant used to cater to a far more bohemian crowd, though "now it's mostly ladies who lunch."

"Everyone loved to sit in the back garden," Gus says, after insisting on bringing me not just a glass of sherry but also a bowl of chocolate mousse topped with softly whipped cream, the dessert, he says, that the café is known for. "Tanaquil said it was her favorite place in the world."

"Who's Tanaquil?" I ask.

Gus slaps my hand in reprimand.

"My dear, are you really telling me you know nothing of Tanaquil LeClercq?"

I shake my head.

"Every member of the board of education in Alabama ought to be shot!"

Not five minutes before, I told Gus I was from Georgia, not

Alabama, but I'm already figuring out that facts seem to mean very little to him.

"Tell me about her," I say.

"Only if you promise to be a good boy and eat your mousse. You haven't touched it."

I take a bite, closing my eyes while I marvel at the dessert's complexity: It tastes deeply, darkly of chocolate, and yet its texture is so light. It is as if you are eating air. Air, butter, and chocolate, that is.

"Is there coffee in this?" I ask.

"Gold star! Espresso. It really intensifies the chocolate flavor."

"That reminds me of how my grandmother always put almond extract into her pound cake. Just a splash. You couldn't really taste the almond, but it really brought out the sweet, nutty taste of the butter."

"Hmm. The young man has a good palate. Well then, that *is* good news. Now. You asked about Tanaquil LeClercq. Tanaquil was quite possibly the finest dancer who ever graced the stage. By the time she was nineteen she was a charter ballerina in Balanchine's New York City Ballet. Balanchine, as you surely know, was a legend, a god, the man who invented modern ballet. Balanchine's marriage to his third wife, also a dancer, was ending, and, inevitably, he found a new muse in Tanaquil. He secured a divorce, and they married."

"When one muse stops delivering, find another?" I ask.

Gus arches a brow at me but continues. "Then tragedy struck. At twenty-seven, Tanaquil contracted polio, and she never walked—let alone danced—again."

"How terrible," I say. "But let me guess. Balanchine found a new muse?"

"Heavens, child. Your cynicism is killing me. And yes, they divorced, but not immediately afterward. They probably would have divorced sooner, actually, if polio hadn't struck. Balanchine was not meant to spend his entire life with one woman, though Tanaquil would be the last woman he actually married."

"He sounds like kind of a jerk," I say.

"Dear boy, please do not speak of such genius with such disrespect."

"Marriage is marriage because it's for life," I say. "You love the person warts and all, for better or for worse."

I am quoting Daddy, which is crazy, to move so far away and start spouting Baptist adages in a Manhattan café.

"Believe me, I'm all for loyalty, but I detest rules. And neither Tanaquil nor Balanchine followed conventional rules in their union. And I say, hoorah to that! Be open to all life has to offer. Eat from the banquet set before us. Ignore what the world determines is 'right' or 'wrong.' Such puritanism only leads to unhappiness, and besides which, the rules change from age to age. What's taboo today won't be tomorrow."

"But you've got to have some rules," I say, once again defending the world I ran from. Next thing you know I'm going to quote Daddy's all-time favorite saying, *You've got to stand for something, or you'll fall for anything.* "I guess it's a matter of figuring out which ones are just niceties and which ones are real."

"Well, damn the niceties! The other day I overheard one of my customers saying that the relationship between Woody Allen and Mariel Hemingway in *Manhattan* was pedophilic. If that particular customer weren't a regular with a taste for expensive wines, I would have shown him the door!"

I have never seen *Manhattan.*

"Why pedophilic?"

"Well, she was seventeen, about to turn eighteen."

"And he was . . . ?"

"Forty-two, and her mentor, something every young person ought to have. How else are they to learn anything? Eventually the ingénue moves on, of course. Blossoms. In the case of this particular Woody Allen film, the young girl leaves for London to conquer the world. But she goes there knowing about sex and art and Chinese food and old black-and-white movies, all things that will bring her much pleasure in life. She received from him an education."

"And he received from her a blow job."

I can't believe I said that. It just popped right out. Probably the result of spending time with Mike, who seems to think it's his job to be crude. Gus looks as shocked as I feel.

"I feel so dreadfully sorry for your generation," he says. "There's no romance to be had, only endless anxiety over equality."

He stands abruptly and goes to check on the woman sitting in the corner. "Darling, darling Lenora," he says. "What else may I get you?"

Gus is wrong. I have no anxiety over equality. What I'm anxious about is money, food, shelter. Heck, had Gus offered, I would probably allow him to educate me in any manner he chose. Except I read him wrong. After his abrupt departure, I decide it's time for me to leave. He meets me at the door, and when he does I step in too close, put the flat of my palm against his shoulder, and ask if there is anything he might like to teach me.

I can't believe I'm saying such a thing, but I'm desperate. And so lonely. Lonely enough that even the company of an old man sounds comforting. And anyway, I like the company of old people. At least, I liked Meemaw's company.

"Subtlety for starters," he answers. "But who am I to criticize a little country mouse let loose in the big city, trying to find a nibble of cheese? The problem, my dear, is that I am not a cheese monger, only the humble owner of this café. But I tell you what: Your palate impressed me. Come back tomorrow and we'll see if that translates to you having skills in the kitchen. Jose can julienne a vegetable, but that's about it. If it looks like you might be able to cook, I'll train you using Alice's cookbook, *Homegrown*. Alice started this place with me, and though she has moved on, most of the recipes we prepare are from her repertoire. I pay minimum wage, plus you get fifteen percent of the waitstaff's gratuities. We'll be closed all of August. We still keep up the old summer schedule, back before there was any air-conditioning in New York and *everybody* went away. I should warn you that it's an unpaid vacation, though if you are very skilled I might be able to get you some catering jobs on Fire Island."

"Oh my gosh, thank you so much. You won't regret it. I'm an excellent cook. I was trained in Paris."

He looks amused. "Paris, Texas, maybe. I would work on your accent a bit before spreading about *that* little fiction. I'll teach you Alice's recipes, but you're also going to need to know some basics of French cooking, how to make the major sauces and all of that. Julia Child is your best bet for that. You can get a cheap copy of *Mastering the Art* at the Strand."

"Where?"

"Oh my, you really are fresh off the boat. Broadway and Twelfth. But before you do anything else, take a look at this." He hands me a glossy magazine titled *Vanities*. "They interviewed me about the café. Impudent reporter, but the piece turned out all right. Read it thoroughly. I might give you a quiz on it when you come into work. It's important you know the history of this place."

I have no idea where to put the magazine. I hold it in my hand until I am well away from Gus Andres and the restaurant, but then I roll it up, stick it in my back pocket, and walk, bounce really, down the street.

7

"Just Don't Call It Elaine's"

An Interview with the Always Entertaining, Sometimes Cantankerous, Gus Andres

In a town where restaurants open and close with the speed of a camera shutter, the fact that Café Andres has remained in business since 1946—albeit with what one could only call irregular hours—is in itself noteworthy. But dig into the history of this outwardly unassuming restaurant on E. 51st Street and you will discover a fascinating past: Seemingly every artist that mattered during that golden era of creativity spanning from the end of World War II to the start of the McCarthy trials not only passed through the café's front door but lingered for hours in its capriciously decorated interior. The most coveted seats: the six tables in the courtyard garden, shaded by a 100-year-old American elm. While past patrons include luminaries from an array of disciplines—the choreographer Balanchine, the actress Katharine Hepburn, the photographer Richard Avedon—it was the young writers who frequented the café in the late 1940s that longtime proprietor Augustin "Gus" Andres alludes to with the most pride. Mr. Andres, who at 72 is almost disconcertingly dapper in his jacket and tie with matching pocket square, recites with relish the names of the writers who once frequented his establishment, many of whom were southerners having fled the stultification of their hometowns for the stimulation of Manhattan. Among them were Truman Capote, Tom—"Tennessee"—Williams, Carson McCullers, James Baldwin, Horton Foote, and Donald Windham. Even Faulkner paid the café a visit, on a trip described by Mr. Andres as "a shakedown of the publishing industry."

In honor of the café's 35th anniversary, we spoke with Gus Andres about his long career and his many encounters with celebrity. We meet at his apartment on Beekman Place, which offers a stunning view of the East River. At the start of the interview Mr. Andres, ever the host, offers chocolate mousse, butter cookies, and mint tea from a Spode pot. Given Mr. Andres's love of both entertaining and writers, is it any wonder the dining room walls are lined with shelves, all holding row after row of hardcover books?

VANITIES MAGAZINE: This is a gem of a place you live in. Pre-war elevator building on a quiet tree-lined street, 11-foot beamed ceilings, parquet floors, gorgeous moldings, killer view. Owning a restaurant is a notoriously risky enterprise, but from looking around this place I would say that Café Andres has done quite well.

GUS ANDRES: Heavens no! I make no money on *that* little folly. No, I came to inhabit this apartment by sheer virtue of staying in Manhattan when so many others were choosing to move out. I bought it ten years ago in the early 70s when all of the tiresome, milquetoast residents were fleeing the city like teenagers running home, afraid of missing curfew. As one who remained, all I could think was good riddance. The modus operandi of New York City has always been opportunity, never safety.

It was my dear friend Randall Jones who led me to this gem. Randy had heard that there was a one-bedroom for sale on Beekman

Place that the owner was positively giving away. Well. *Beekman Place.* Sure, it might be a tad stuffy, but Auntie Mame made her residence here. How could I resist? The apartment for sale had belonged to a widow with a lot of fusty old furniture cluttering up the space and wallpaper in what I suppose was meant to be a yellow floral design, but which most resembled overcooked scrambled eggs. The widow's children lived in Westchester and wanted nothing to do with the apartment, and I suppose potential buyers were scared off by the drab furnishings. But one of my few virtues is that I can see past almost anything. And anyone, for that matter.

VANITIES MAGAZINE: You're referring to the fictitious Auntie Mame, yes? The legendarily eccentric bon vivant played by Rosalind Russell in the movie adaptation of Patrick Dennis's novel?

GUS ANDRES: Yes. I will never forget the moment in the movie when Mame tells her nephew, "I'm going to open doors for you. Doors you never knew existed!" I dreamed of having an influence like her in my life. And I should add, I always hoped Rosalind Russell would walk through the doors of Café Andres, allowing me to spread a banquet before her. But alas, that was not to be.

VANITIES MAGAZINE: The café is known for its cuisine. This mousse we're eating is wonderful. Absolutely sublime. I love how it's so light I can see the air pockets when I spoon into it, and yet the taste is as intense as a cup of espresso. It's a café favorite, is it not?

GUS ANDRES: Indeed. We've had the mousse on the menu since the day we opened. I whipped this one up. It's easy to do. You'll find the recipe in Alice Stone's charming book, *Homegrown,* published nearly 20 years ago now. It's mostly recipes celebrating her childhood on a farm in North Carolina, but she included a final chapter with favorites from the café. The secret to making the mousse is to make sure the melted chocolate and coffee is at the exact right temperature before you beat in the egg yolks. You want to rub the chocolate on your lips to test. If it feels as warm as a lover's body lying in the sun, it's the perfect temperature. If it burns—well, that too is a part of love—let it cool a few more minutes.

VANITIES MAGAZINE: I did not realize Chef Stone had such a sensual approach to her cooking.

GUS ANDRES: I may have elaborated on the metaphor, but the technique is hers. Alice is the best cook I have ever known. I believe it is because she paid such careful attention to the "why" behind her most successful dishes.

VANITIES MAGAZINE: Let's talk more about Alice Stone, with whom you opened Café Andres. By all accounts she was a fascinating individual—a black woman raised in a farming community of freed slaves in North Carolina who moved to New York during the Depression, worked a variety of jobs, including laundress, seamstress, and department store window decorator—something the two of you often did together—and then suddenly, though she had no formal restaurant training, she was the chef at Café Andres. And this was all before she turned 40! In later years she would become known first for the cookbook you mentioned, *Homegrown*, and then for a series of shows she did on PBS, each focusing on a different region of the South and paying especial attention to the contribution of African-American cooks to the cuisine. Tell us more about Alice: Did you two meet through the world of window dressing? How did you come up with the idea of opening the café?

GUS ANDRES: We met in the midthirties, long before our window-dressing days, at a gathering thrown by the Communist Party. A Communist Party party, how do you like that? For a long time I kept my past association with the Bolsheviks—limited though it was—under wraps. The McCarthy trials scared us into silence. But now . . . well . . . let's just say that the singular advantage of old age is you lose your fear of other people's judgments.

Alice became a Communist because it was the only political party that would touch integration. I should add, this was before we found out about Stalin's purges and all of that nastiness. Though honestly, I was never that political. Was never a card-carrying member or anything or that sort. In fact, I was only at that particular event because Randy was hosting it, and you know how it is when you are throwing a party—you're terrified no one will come. So I agreed to be filler—a warm body, if you will—and there I was, bored senseless while these unkempt Bolsheviks spoke to me about which eastside buildings they would like to occupy once the Revolution came, when in walks this stunning black woman, carrying a blackberry pie.

VANITIES MAGAZINE: Wait. It was a *potluck* Communist gathering?

GUS ANDRES: That was what was so delightful about Alice's pie. The spirit of the evening had been so drab, so earnest. The only refreshments provided were beer and hoop cheese. Everyone thought they had to be so austere at those things and here comes Alice with this gorgeous pastry bursting forth with dark, ripe fruit. I was forever telling Randy that the only party I approved of was one that served cocktails, and in walks Alice with a decadent offering for the Bolsheviks. It was perfect. She was perfect.

VANITIES MAGAZINE: Is that when you decided to open the restaurant?

GUS ANDRES: No, no, no. The party was a decade before. *I* actually decided to open the restaurant. Randy is a photographer, as you surely know, and he wanted a place to display some of his work. We had rented the storefront of a little town house on E. 51st, and Randy was trying to convince me to open a frame shop in the space. He would provide the art for the walls; I would do the framing. Which is basically the same thing as he writes the novel, she types it up for him, so you can see why I hesitated. The town house had a marvelous courtyard garden. One day Randy and I were sitting back there having a cocktail and one of us said, "Wouldn't this make a wonderful setting for an intimate little café?" And just then Alice showed up looking for a cigarette. She just happened to stop by. Seeing her standing at the door, I suddenly had a vision. I saw her in the kitchen, fixing blackberry pies for a crowd. And without even considering my words I burst out with, "Alice, darling, we are opening a restaurant and you are going to be the chef!"

VANITIES MAGAZINE: I'm struck by the fact that you rented a storefront without knowing what sort of business you were going to open.

GUS ANDRES: Well, why not? The rent was cheap—$45 a month—which Randy and I split. I knew we would come up with something.

VANITIES MAGAZINE: It was a different city back then, wasn't it?

GUS ANDRES: It was a wonderful time. More innocent. For starters, you simply didn't have ancient people like me toddling around. People dropped dead at a decent age back then, 60 or 65. And there were all of these soldiers coming back from overseas, just spilling into the city. You cannot *comprehend* the level of optimism we felt at that particular moment. The country had been through so much in such a short amount of time: The First World War, then the Depression, then World War II. But in 1946 our future looked bright. We had defeated Fascism. We had saved the Free World. And now the soldiers that survived were home and the economy was good and New York was booming. It was simply a heady, heady time to be alive.

VANITIES MAGAZINE: But you did not serve overseas.

GUS ANDRES: Heart murmur.

VANITIES MAGAZINE: How did you feel about that?

GUS ANDRES: When the U.S. joined the Allied forces, I weighed maybe 95 pounds, wet. I don't think I would have done much good fighting with our boys. What I *was* good at was selling war bonds at the theaters during Intermission. In that way I contributed.

VANITIES MAGAZINE: Back to the restaurant. You told Alice Stone you were opening a restaurant together and she said?

GUS ANDRES: She was a very savvy woman. She said, "Make me part-owner."

VANITIES MAGAZINE: Which you did.

GUS ANDRES: Yes, and then she came and sat in the garden with us and we started dreaming up ideas for the café. It was her notion that we should serve a prix fixe menu. She just thought it would be easier, which it was.

VANITIES MAGAZINE: Did Alice Stone have any culinary training?

GUS ANDRES: A childhood of eating with the seasons on a farm in North Carolina. And the most astute palate of anyone I have ever met. Give Alice a taste of anything and she will immediately tell you what it is missing. I can hear her now: *Grind in some pepper, grate a little orange zest, add a pinch of salt, throw in a splash of vinegar, let the dough rest for five minutes before kneading it again.* Any culinary problem, Alice had a fix. I suppose her official training was the copy of *Escoffier* that we bought her, from which she learned to make all of the French sauces—though of course she never bothered much with *sauce espagnole,* which simply takes hours and hours to prepare.

VANITIES MAGAZINE: Under Chef Alice Stone the restaurant became renowned for its excellent cuisine. What are some of the specialties of the house?

GUS ANDRES: Her mousse of course. She made both a lemon and a bittersweet chocolate mousse, and you could choose one or the other for dessert. When we first opened we served the mousse French-style, in big bowls, passed around the table along with softly whipped cream. You simply scooped out what you wanted. It was divine. I couldn't serve it that way anymore, of course. Either the health department would shut me down or some terribly fat man wearing a T-shirt and sneakers would come in and treat dessert as an all-you-can-eat contest. And then there was Alice's roast duck with green olives. She only served it once the weather turned cold, but come November clients would start calling up, asking if it was duck season yet.

VANITIES MAGAZINE: Miss Stone worked at Café Andres from 1946 to 1965. Why did she leave? Was there any sort of falling-out between the two of you?

GUS ANDRES: Well, goodness, she was at the café for 19 years. That is a long time to remain at a restaurant, if you ask me, especially one with a prix fixe menu. You can imagine how weary she must have grown preparing the same dish again and again, night after night. Working on *Homegrown* gave her some distraction, but it didn't last forever. Plus she had married the most *tiresome* sort of man, an absolute *bore* if you must know, and he was jealous of all the time she spent away from home, and so she decided to dedicate herself to him exclusively. She divested her ownership, and she and her husband moved upstate and began an organic farm.

VANITIES MAGAZINE: She began an organic farm in 1965? It's astounding how ahead of her time she was.

GUS ANDRES: Well, I don't know if she used the term "organic" or not. She was simply working the earth the way her relatives in North Carolina did. She wanted to grow the best vegetables she possibly could. She was forever haunted by how much better food tasted when she was a child. She's an interesting bird, that Alice: a wonderful mélange of New York bohemian and sweet, southern country girl.

VANITIES MAGAZINE: Alice was from the South, and you have already mentioned that the café was a refuge for southern writers, especially during the late 40s and 50s. Why do you think southern expatriates were so drawn to the café?

GUS ANDRES: I think it has something to do with the fact that time moves so slowly at Café Andres. To get to the restaurant you must first walk down a long hall. I like to say that the hall serves as the portal to another time and place, like going through the wardrobe to C. S. Lewis's Narnia. Once you actually step inside you forget the nagging details of your everyday life. I can't tell you how many of my customers, when going through a divorce, ate lunch at the café every single day during their ordeal, claiming that it was the only place where they felt calm. When I hear southerners reminisce about sitting on the front porch, sipping a drink and watching fireflies, I think it must be an experience similar to what we offer. And we pay careful attention to detail at Café Andres, which I think is a southern thing as well. I am always saying to Randy, "Where would we be in life without our garnishes?" Beauty is so crucial. Why glop on the sauce when you can spoon it over the roast chicken just so? Why bruise the basil when you can so easily avoid that by making sure every leaf is dry and using a good sharp knife to cut it into a chiffonade? Why discard the leaves on a stalk of celery you plan to put on a crudités platter when the leaves—though you wouldn't want to eat them—add such an air of whimsy and art?

Shakespeare was right, all of life is a stage, but that is especially true of a restaurant. And I think it's also true of the southern experience. There is a lot of playacting going on in the South. A whole lot of acting indeed. And we all know how deeply eccentric southerners are. As Truman Capote might say, Mama could have shot at Daddy with her pistol over breakfast, but that doesn't mean the two of them won't put on their finest and enjoy dinner out at Galatoire's that night.

VANITIES MAGAZINE: Yet your menu never offered southern food. Why?

GUS ANDRES: I apologize for bringing up Truman again, but it makes me think of how he used to drive Alice mad with his requests for her to make him fried chicken, like his cook at home used to do. She would say to him, "I am not your mammy!" So there was that. And can you blame Alice for being sensitive of the fact that she was cooking for an almost entirely white clientele, with the occasional exception of Jimmy Baldwin? And also, we opened the café in the late 1940s, when "sophisticated food" meant French cuisine. Had we served collard greens and fried chicken, we would have lasted a day. So Alice cooked with a French influence and a southerner's innate sense of seasonality.

She was the first person I ever met who simply refused to serve raw tomatoes anytime but in the dead of summer. Alice made a wonderful Boeuf Bourguignon, a real customer favorite, but she would only prepare it November through the beginning of March, no matter how often people begged for it year-round. Same with her roast duck with green olives. She was very stubborn that way, very particular about how you should eat and why. And perhaps being stubbornly opinionated about how and when food should be consumed is a more southern trait than whether or not you fry green tomatoes or pickle watermelon rind or eat—I don't know—pimento cheese.

VANITIES MAGAZINE: Let's talk about your friend Randall Jones, who you mentioned is a well-known photographer. He photographed several of the more famous artists from the restaurant, didn't he?

GUS ANDRES: His photographs remain my most treasured possessions.

VANITIES MAGAZINE: The two of you own a house together on Fire Island.

GUS ANDRES: Well, neither of us could afford to own on our own.

VANITIES MAGAZINE: But he is your partner in every sense of the word, yes?

GUS ANDRES: I see no reason why this line of questioning has any relevance.

VANITIES MAGAZINE: I apologize if I offended you, but the question *is* relevant. Many from your list of famous clients—Truman Capote, Tennessee Williams, James Baldwin, Carson McCullers—were not only southern but also bisexual or homosexual. Why did they all flock to you?

GUS ANDRES: I don't even know where to begin to address your impudence, but I'll start here. The most important piece of information about an artist is not whom he or she invites into his or her bed! Such thinking drives me mad, as if sex is the single and solitary defining thing about a creative person. Read *Breakfast at Tiffany's,* my dear. Read *In Cold Blood.* The exactitude of Capote's prose, the simplicity of his language that captures the hidden melancholy in all of us . . . this is what is lasting of Truman. This and only this!

VANITIES MAGAZINE: Okay, clearly I've struck a nerve, so let's move on. Who was the most exciting celebrity to walk through the café's door?

GUS ANDRES: Gold star! Excellent question! Well, let's see: It was always such a thrill when Jackie O came, as much to see what she was wearing as anything else. But I will tell you, one of the most charming memories I have is when Madeleine L'Engle arrived at the restaurant with her handsome husband, Hugh Franklin. They were both such tall people. She had a rather imperious way about her, softened by her eyes, which had the innocence of a child. They came for dinner one night shortly after the restaurant had opened. I'd be surprised if she were 30. She stood ramrod straight at the host station. I came up to her chest, mind you, which put me right at the eyes of her black fur stole. The eyes on the stole were almond shaped, seemingly alive, and then they blinked! I admit, I let out a little shriek of fright. And Madeleine stroked her stole and said,

"Oh, Touché, I thought you were a better actor than that!" It turned out Touché was her poodle, draped around her shoulder to look like a wrap, a trick that Madeleine employed when she needed to take the dog on the subway.

Of course I let her bring the dog to the table. I just decided then and there that the health inspector was not going to walk through the door that night. Madeleine said Touché could stay wrapped around her shoulder the whole evening—that the dog truly was a trained actor—but I said, "No, no, let her curl up beneath the table." We were a favorite of the Franklins after that, though they moved a year or two later to some falling-down place out in the country.

VANITIES MAGAZINE: Many people have called Café Andres the Elaine's of its day.

GUS ANDRES: I have heard that comparison made, but it is utterly spurious. For starters, Elaine's is not known for its food, and we are. But more importantly, back when it was a celebrity haunt Café Andres was a secret place for people who knew how to have a good time. It was *not* a place to see and be seen. In fact, it was the opposite of that. There were no cameramen lurking outside to take one's picture, like at the Stork Club. Anytime I got wind that a restaurant reviewer was on the premises I bribed him not to make his review too prominent. We were very selective about who we wanted dining there—though it had nothing to do with one's level of fame. Not like at Elaine's, not at all. At Café Andres a charming imp from the Village could get as good a seat as Diana Vreeland. The café was not a place to do business, not a place to social climb. It was a place to while away a few hours in the company of interesting, entertaining people.

VANITIES MAGAZINE: Well, that certainly sounds lovely.

GUS ANDRES: It was. It was a precious, precious time. A time I yearn for still.

8

Letter Home

January 1, 1982

Dear Meemaw,

It is a new year, and life is changing fast. I am apprenticing to become a chef, and I have an apartment—a studio—about which Mike gives me all kinds of hell (sorry, heck) because I don't have to put up with a roommate like he does. I tell him that it's a dump, that the only thing good about it is that it's near the café, but the truth is it has an incredible kitchen, unheard of for an apartment its size.

The studio is not the sort of place I would have found on my own. It's not the sort of place you find without a connection. Gus Andres, my boss, found it for me. His friend Randy knew someone who knew someone who was moving out, and I was able to slide into the unit without any change in rent. It's a little tricky, because I never actually signed a lease. The super, who lives in the basement, knows

I am here, so I don't have to sneak around or anything, but I do try to fix any small things that need repair, so as to not make unnecessary demands on him. Makes me grateful that Daddy taught me that stuff, actually. Makes me grateful that I know my way around a toolbox.

Speaking of Daddy: He has started phoning me, every few weeks. We speak very briefly. Mostly he just tells me what is happening with Hunter and Troy and Mama. In a nutshell, Troy is doing great (he's engaged), Hunter is doing fine (he's in "real estate development," whatever that means), and Mama is being Mama as always. Apparently she has become even more involved with Lacy Lovehart's Save Our Sons campaign. I told Daddy that I really didn't want to hear about any of that, and he was actually pretty respectful and switched topics, telling me instead about the Mississippi mud cake that Mama made for his birthday. "Lot of candles on that cake," Daddy joked, and I pretended to laugh, but it made me sad. Daddy offered to fly me home for Thanksgiving, but I told him I couldn't get off work. That was a lie, Meemaw, a flat-out lie. Gus is closing the café for a week over the Thanksgiving holiday, and he'll shut down for two weeks over Christmas. It's crazy the schedule he keeps. He says he has a "gypsy" soul and can't be tied down for too long. I told him I could run the place while he went away, but he said no, he believes the café needs a rest just like the rest of us, that "the fields should lie fallow." He and Randy are going to Morocco over Christmas and suggested I come along. Honestly I think they just want me to carry their luggage. They're both really old, though both quite spry. Maybe it was dumb, but I turned him down. Thought I'd just stay in the city over the holidays.

Back to my apartment. It's a fifth-floor walk-up on East 58th between First and Second, right by the entrance to the Queensboro Bridge. The apartment faces the street, meaning traffic roars past my window day and night, which is one of the reasons why the rent is so cheap. That and the landlord hasn't done anything to improve the place in twenty years. Utilities are included in the rent, but the landlord is stingy as Scrooge when it comes to heating the place. (I have never felt as cold in my life as I have this winter.) The first really cold night I spent here my breath condensed into white chilly puffs, even though I was inside, but then I had the bright idea to cook something, and of course that warmed everything right up.

Because that's the thing about this place, the bizarre, wonderful, weird thing: It has a fabulous kitchen, which is, frankly, unheard of for a studio apartment in a run-down old building. In the building's better days, back in the 50s, a family was renting the two-bedroom apartment adjacent to my little studio. According to Gus, the woman living in the two-bedroom started giving cooking lessons out of her own kitchen and this aggravated her husband, who hated coming home from work with a bunch of strange ladies crowding his home, sipping cocktails and making idle chatter. But his wife was a really good cook and a really good teacher and did not want to give up the gig. So as a compromise they rented the neighboring apartment—my studio—and made it into her "cooking school." Now from what I gather, the cooking school was nothing more than a chance for Upper East Side ladies to giggle and gossip while a meal was prepared in front of them. And then they would eat their crepes or their chicken Kiev or whatever and go home drunk and happy. Gus jokes that what those ladies learned besides the lubricating nature of alcohol he will never know, but the end result is that I have a six-burner Wolf oven in my tiny studio.

Also bizarre is *why* the woman left the stove when she moved out and why the landlord allowed her to do so, as it makes the apartment *all* stove, that plus a wooden counter long enough to fit a twin mattress on top of. (Which I swear I considered doing when I first moved in!) But I resisted the urge to sleep in the kitchen, instead using the thin twin mattress already in the sleeping loft, reached by a ladder. Other than that, there's a doll-sized bathroom whose sink has separate faucets for hot and cold—meaning it's a real pain to wash my face—and a shower so tiny I have to squeeze to fit in it.

Were she at all inclined to visit, I believe that Mama would be proud that the kitchen is the absolute center of the apartment. The kitchen was certainly the center of our Decatur home. And just as Mama did—probably still does—I cook pretty much every meal I eat, unless I eat at the café. I don't mind cooking all my meals, but even if I did, there's really not another option. I'm not *as* broke as I was when I first moved to the city, but each month my bank balance gets awfully close to zero. Not that I don't treat myself to a Papaya King hotdog sometimes, or maybe a falafel sandwich from a street vendor. And occasionally Gus will take me somewhere nice to "develop my palate," but that's rare. Though I can't afford anything sold at them, I do love wandering through the fancy gourmet markets, especially the one at Bloomingdale's. That place is so amazing, Meemaw. You have never seen so much good stuff in one place. I looked for Schrafft's when I first got here—wanting to eat a butterscotch sundae like the one you told me about—but I think they've all shut down. Mostly I shop at this really cheap grocery store I found in Spanish Harlem. They sell cheap cuts of meat—oxtail, trotters, and pigs' ears—as well as all varieties of offal. (I always think of you, Meemaw, when eating livers, think of you eating them every Sunday after church at The Colonnade.) I like to poke around the Asian markets, too, bringing home gingerroot, lemongrass, fish sauce, dehydrated shrimp, won-ton wrappers, dozens of different chilies, and soft little candies wrapped in rice paper that dissolves in your mouth. As a special treat I go to the green market in Union Square on the weekends—which is a farmer's market smack-dab in the middle of downtown. Even though I really can't afford the produce, I'll often splurge anyway, arriving home with one or two perfect things—carrots the color of rubies with bright springy tops, or a little bag of fingerling potatoes, their skins delicate and golden.

And here is where life gets really interesting, Meemaw. There's one woman I kept noticing at the green market. I didn't notice her *only* because she's black, though that certainly had something to do with it. It's funny, every time I see a black person up here I tend to smile too much, act too familiar, because I assume the person is also from the South and is also a fellow expat, as Gus calls us. But it wasn't solely this woman's blackness that drew me to her. It was her dignity. I swear, she carried herself like a queen, and she was always wrapped in the most beautiful scarves, her white hair pulled back into an elegant bun. And the concentration she applied in choosing her vegetables! It was as if she could understand the whole world in one little stalk of cauliflower, the way she would hold it up and then turn it slowly in her hand, studying its curds, its few yellowed spots, the tight leaves around its base.

The vendors all recognized her, and it seemed they all had stashed away something special, just for her.

"Gotcha some fresh eggs today, Alice, with nice orange yolks like those country eggs you grew up with."

"Here are some persimmons, good and ripe, like you was looking for last week."

"These are the best of the fingerlings I grow. I know you like a good potato."

She would reward each vendor with a brief but radiant smile, her teeth as white as her skin was dark. And then the smile was gone, replaced by a somber look, as if her smiles had to be carefully rationed.

I began thinking of her as the African Queen of the Green, and I made it a point to look for her every Saturday during my early-morning comb of the place. One morning I spotted her there with a tall white woman, who was neatly dressed in khaki slacks and a button-down navy shirt printed with little white anchors, tucked in at the waist. Around her neck was a bright red scarf, tied rather jauntily. To be honest, she reminded me of Mama, only less done up, less "painted." She wore her straight hair parted down the middle, the tips brushing her shoulders—a girl's haircut, except for the streaks of gray. She had freckles across her cheeks, and if she wore any makeup at all it was just a touch of pink lipstick and perhaps a little mascara.

I liked her right away. She looked sensible and no-nonsense—but kind. I know it sounds pitiful, but I followed those two around like a puppy as they went stall to stall collecting various fruits, vegetables, and herbs. I noticed that neither of them spoke much outside of commenting on produce and they kept a measured distance. And yet there was a real affection between them. Like how they hovered together excitedly over what looked to me like pieces of gingerroot, only yellower and more knobby.

"Mother used to shave these raw into chicken salad," said the black woman. "Tasted almost as if there was a truffle in there."

"How delightful! I believe Jack once made a creamed soup of these, though he nearly sliced off a finger trying to peel them all."

"Mother would just soak them in bowls of hot water to remove the clay and the silt. She'd get them so clean we could eat them with the skins on."

Though I had overlooked the strange roots earlier, suddenly I wanted nothing more than a bag of them, to shave into chicken salad and puree into soup.

The black woman carefully selected a few choice ones, placing them into a brown paper bag she had retrieved from her purse. "I'll make chicken salad and put these in it, just for nostalgia," she said. "We can eat it on our picnic tomorrow."

Oh, Meemaw, I felt like a little boy with his nose pressed against the candy store window. I wanted to go on a picnic with those two!

I wanted to have chicken salad enhanced with shaved roots that taste like truffles! Instead, I waited until they moved onto the next vendor before selecting my own little bag of knobby fingers. "Sunchokes," said the farmer when I asked what they were.

At home in my apartment, I tried soaking the sunchokes in hot water but found that after each bath they still had orange streaks on their flesh, as if they had grown in red clay. I wondered why we had never eaten a sunchoke grown in Georgia, since the red clay looked like it could have come straight from your backyard. (I admit, Meemaw, I had an urge to suck on the root and see if I could taste the land in which it grew. I remember how you used to suck on little bits of clay sometimes, brought to you by an old friend from Alabama. You said you grew up doing that and were teased something awful for being a "dirt eater," but you couldn't help it, sometimes you needed to taste your roots. I remember I tried a little of your Alabama clay, sucking on it like it was a Popsicle. At first it was sort of awful, and then, strangely, not so bad. Comforting almost.)

Finally, I realized I was going to need to peel them, but I had nothing but a paring knife to do it with, which meant I ended up cutting off more than I kept. Still I managed to salvage a little pile of peeled sunchokes, which I roasted in butter at 425 until I could stick the point of a knife through one without any resistance. The peeled exteriors puffed and browned and their insides were creamy and a little sweet, balanced with a few sprinkles of salt and pepper. Which is to say, they were delicious and left me craving more, wondering what other fabulous things were out there that I had not yet tasted.

The next day when I went to work I told Gus about seeing the black woman at the market with her white friend and how they bought sunchokes and so I bought sunchokes and I had cooked them and they were wonderful. "Dear boy, did you happen to catch the black woman's name?" Gus asked me, and I said yes, that the vendors called her Alice.

"Congratulations! You've had an Alice Stone sighting! Don't you know that's whose book we've been cooking from?" He flipped *Homegrown* to the back page and there was Alice's author photo. She was a good twenty years younger in it, but yes, that was the African Queen of the Green. "And I imagine the proper lady you saw her with was none other than the editor of this very book, Kate Wolanski, née Pennington."

Meemaw, I remember how you always put quotation marks around the word "coincidence" because you believed God's hand was in everything. That what seemed like chance was really God sorting through his contacts and seeing who needed to be matched up. Well, the fact that the African Queen of the Green was none other than the woman Gus began the café with certainly points to that theory. After learning who she was, I immediately asked Gus if he might introduce me to her. Gus said that he would ring her up, see if she might come have lunch at the café, let me cook for her, and let her apply her famous palate to my cuisine, help me elevate my craft. Of course I'm all knotted up with anxiety even thinking about it, but I told Gus yes, of course, let's do it.

So that is what I'm doing today and tomorrow—Sunday and Monday—while the restaurant is closed: figuring out exactly what it is I'm going to prepare for Alice's upcoming visit. It's so cold here now that I think I will make some sort of a braise, although it can't be one of her recipes, it can't be duck with green olives or Boeuf Bourgignon. Maybe I'll do short ribs with mashed potatoes, or something even simpler, maybe even your fried chicken. Alice likes things simple; this I know from reading her book. And it must be comforting, and provide her with a little taste of the South. I'm thinking of making banana pudding for dessert, but instead of using Nilla wafers, I'm going to use cut-up cubes of toasted pound cake made from your recipe, layering them with homemade vanilla pudding and ripe bananas, and topping the whole thing with meringue.

Maybe I'll make little individual puddings in ramekins, to honor the mousse Alice Stone made famous at the café. I'll keep thinking on it. You send me some ideas if you can, okay? Just send them to me in a dream.

I think of cooking for you all the time, Meemaw. I can't tell you how much I've learned about cooking since I've been up here. Gus calls all of the little things he teaches me *trucs*, which means "tricks" in French. Like stick your onions in the freezer for twenty minutes before you chop them so your eyes don't water, and wipe down the edges of your plate with a cloth before serving so everything looks perfect. (Mama used to do that, actually, when she would serve dips. Wipe down the edges so it looked as if the dip just grew up from the bottom of the bowl naturally.) And when preparing meat, always let it come to room temperature before cooking. And salt, salt, salt. Before we roast chickens at the restaurant we soak them in a brine of sea salt and water for a day. Sometimes Gus just salts the outside of the bird and leaves it uncovered in the fridge, which dries out the skin and makes it extra crispy when roasted at a high heat. That's another thing Gus has taught me—the beauty of heat. Chickens can be roasted at 500 degrees, if you can believe it, and cooking meat on a hot, hot grill really sears in the flavors. Gus says if you try to turn a piece of cooking meat and it feels stuck, to wait a minute or two longer, that as soon at the outside caramelizes it will release from the pan or the grill or whatever and you can flip it over, no problem.

Gus hasn't yet let me solo chef for customers. Instead I prep things: chop vegetables, salt chickens, make sauces. But it feels as if he's grooming me to take over one day. And maybe he is. After all, he's in his seventies. I'm not sure how long he is planning to keep running the place. Except we really need more customers if that is to happen. To be honest, I think Gus is a little stuck in the past. To anyone who will listen he will go on and on about the famous people who once ate at the café, but the problem is, he needs more people to eat there now.

Still, Meemaw. Sometimes I look at where I was six months ago and I look at where I am now and I just feel really lucky. In this city it makes such a difference to have a place that is your own, to have people counting on you, to have a place you are supposed to be. Of course it hasn't escaped my notice that once again I'm spending most of my time with someone much, much older than me. But maybe I'm an old soul, Meemaw. Do you think that might be it? I still go dance at the clubs; I still hang out with Mike, but that's not where my heart is. My heart is in the kitchen, reading through Alice Stone's book, trying out new recipes, tweaking my mistakes, and trying again.

And I'll end with this, Meemaw, because I know it will make you happy, but also, because it's true. You know I've been mad at God for a long time now. Mad for reasons that surely you can understand. But with this job, and this recognition of my own talent, and this growing passion, it's like a little light has forced its way in. It's like God's knocking at the door of my heart once again. And I can hear him knocking because—against all odds—I am starting to feel at home.

9

Like John the Baptist, Dripping with Honey

(New York City, February 1982)

Granted, I'm the one who suggested inviting Mr. Capote to the luncheon for Alice, but I was being facetious. It was after I found out that Kate's husband, Jack Wolanski—a renowned writer himself—would be attending. "Gee, that's a lot of pressure," I said. "Making me cook for the Manhattan literati. Why don't we just invite Truman Capote while we're at it?" Gus's response to my joke was to telephone the author right then and there at his apartment at the UN Plaza. Surprisingly, Mr. Capote answered and, after hearing the invitation, suggested he "might" stop by. Somehow Gus inferred a resounding yes from that tepid response, and he's hyper with excitement at the possibility of the (now) infamous recluse deigning to grace us with his presence.

I suppose if I thought Mr. Capote were really going to attend I might be more anxious about the possibility, but frankly, I think Gus is delusional, and anyway, my anxiety is reserved for Alice, whom I want to impress. She along with Kate and Jack Wolanski all arrive together, right on time. Gus prepared me for meeting Jack by giving me a stack of old *New Yorkers* that contained some of his articles. My favorites are his profiles of the city's more eccentric residents, which read like short stories. Like the one about an Upper East Side dowager with connections to the Kennedys, known as "Mumsy" not only to her children, but also to the rest of her family and even her friends. Mumsy has tea three times a week at the Carlyle with her adult son, Nipps. Nipps will order a Shirley Temple with a straw, while Mumsy can put back three dry martinis and still appear perfectly sober. Mumsy's typical outfit is a misshapen gray skirt, the waist held in place by a safety pin, topped with a Bryn Mawr sweatshirt. Somehow she gets away with this by always accessorizing the outfit with multiple strands of pearls worn around her neck. I guess I shouldn't say "somehow" she gets away with it; she gets away with it because she's loaded.

Gus makes a big production of Alice, Kate, and Jack's arrival, kissing cheeks and complimenting everyone's outfit. He pops open a bottle of Champagne while I pass around a plate of hush puppies, which are, as Meemaw used to say, fresh off the grease. Still, it is obvious that Gus is distracted, that his focus is on the possibility of Truman Capote's arrival.

Jack Wolanski is remarkably skinny and significantly less refined than his wife. He looks as if, minutes before walking into the restaurant, he ran his fingers wildly through his hair, making it stick up every which way, whereas Kate is preppy and polished, her white silk blouse tucked into pleated navy trousers, a pair of sensible red loafers peeking out below the cuffed hems, giving her whole outfit a subtle aura of patriotism. Despite their difference in style, the two of them seem well matched. They have the easy banter of longtime lovers, and within the first ten minutes of their arrival Jack makes Kate laugh out loud, not once but twice.

Alice does not laugh at all. It seems she does not want to be here. She makes little eye contact, training her eyes instead on her fingernails or on Kate, to whom she keeps giving pained expressions. She eats a single hush puppy but does not take seconds. She turns down Gus's offering of a flute of Champagne, asking instead for a glass of water, no ice. Jack valiantly tries to make conversation, but mostly we stand around awkwardly.

Things loosen up a bit when Randy—Gus's "companion"—arrives, full of good cheer and bustling energy. He makes us cluster together so he can take several photos of "the gang," as if we are old friends reunited. At seventy-something years old and blessed with a full head of thick hair, Randy still exudes boyish charm, right down to the way he absentmindedly brushes his bangs off his forehead, like a little boy bothered by something itchy.

After twenty or so minutes standing around, futilely waiting for Mr. Capote to arrive, Gus finally agrees to let us sit down and eat. This provides a little relief, because at least now we can speak of the food before us. The lunch menu—a fish fry—is a risk, I know. But I had determined that it was foolish to serve Alice anything from her own cookbook and I thought a fish fry would be a fun way of honoring our shared southern roots. To the table Gus and I bring fried catfish with tartar sauce, red beans and rice loaded with andouille sausage (a nod to Meemaw's husband, my Granddaddy Banks, who originally hailed from Louisiana), red cabbage coleslaw, collard greens, and a breadbasket filled with hot biscuits, corn muffins, and more hush puppies. I serve it all family-style, letting everyone help themselves.

Ironically, it is Jack, a Jew born in Brooklyn and possibly the thinnest man I've ever seen, who is the most enthusiastic about this most southern of meals, helping himself to three servings of catfish and countless hush puppies. "My God, the batter on this fish is so light and crisp," he says.

But Alice, eating slowly and deliberately, remains quiet, not even finishing the single catfish filet she put on her plate, making me wonder if something is wrong with it, if her palate is so highly developed that she picked up on some off taste the rest of us aren't sensitive enough to recognize. Or maybe her particular piece of fish was bad. But that can't be. It just can't. I bought the fish fresh this morning, sniffed each piece before dipping it first in flour, then egg, then seasoned cornmeal.

Alice's response, or lack thereof, is so frustrating, so anxiety producing, that my leg starts shaking under the table. It shakes so violently that I have to hold it down with my free hand in order for it to stop.

I picture the dessert I've prepared, homemade vanilla pudding layered with ripe bananas and chunks of Meemaw's pound cake, topped with meringue. I imagine Alice rejecting it, and I feel like crying.

And then the restaurant door flings open and a pretty woman, wet hair hanging in ringlets all around her face, bursts inside, looking around wildly at the nearly empty café. She is dripping wet. A bizarre thought—that she is covered in honey, like John the Baptist—crosses my mind, but then I realize that it is raining outside. I can hear the sound of it landing against the windows, a slushy downpour, somewhere between rain and snow.

Kate stands from the table. "Amelia, dear, are you okay?"

"Oh my God," says the wet woman. "I'm so sorry. I thought you and Jack were just having lunch. I didn't realize you were in the middle of an event."

I glance around at the awkward group of people seated at our table. "Event" seems too festive a word for this dreary little gathering.

"Everyone, this is my darling niece, Amelia," says Kate. Though her tone is upbeat, she looks agitated.

"Sweetie, would you like to join us for lunch? Bobby's food is out of this world."

She glances at her watch. "Shit. The girls are at their art class at the Met, but it ends in about twenty-five minutes. I should head up there to pick them up. I was feeling so nostalgic after I dropped them off earlier today that I went back to your apartment and called Cam. I wanted to reminisce about that first year of our marriage, when we were still living in the city. God, what a mistake. You know, I almost wish I didn't know, that I could have just stayed innocent of all of this. But now that I do know—what should I do? Pack up and return to Connecticut today? Lay claim to my husband? Play like everything is normal and fix dinner for our houseguest?"

"Amelia, you are *not* going to fix that woman dinner," says Kate. "That's insane. You and the girls are going to stay in the city tonight. Let yourself calm down. You can go home tomorrow if you want. Tonight let's do something mindless and easy. Get Chinese food and go to a movie, something like that."

"Can we sneak a flask of vodka in with us?" asks Amelia.

"Yes, dear, we can."

Amelia smiles grimly at her aunt, then hands me the now wet dish towel.

"Please pretend a crazy woman never burst in here," she says. "Just let everything return to its original loveliness."

Kate walks Amelia out and then rejoins us at the table. As soon as she sits down she rolls her eyes toward her husband. "Cam again."

"Poor Amelia," says Jack.

"Yes, well, I apologize to everyone for the interruption. That was certainly unexpected."

"That was your niece?" asks Alice. This is the first time she has really spoken all afternoon.

"Yes. My sister's daughter," says Kate. She presses her lips together as if she wants to say something else but is choosing not to in

Though I revel in Kate's praise, I balk at her extending an invita-tion to this woman. I don't think Amelia is going to make the talk around the table any easier. But then my southern hosting instincts kick in, and I stand, summoning my hardiest enthusiasm. "Yes, join us! Let me get you some towels so you can dry off. You must be freezing! Would you like some coffee? Or something stronger? A glass of Champagne? Some wine?"

"Oh God, I'd love a towel. Thank you. And no, I'm not going to interrupt your lunch any more than I already have. I'll just dry off and be on my way. I'm so sorry for interrupting."

When I return from the kitchen with a couple of clean dish tow-els, Kate and Amelia have moved farther away from our table, toward the corner of the restaurant that houses Gus's startling white statue of Venus de Milo. Kate's hand rests protectively on the arm of her niece, who is crying. I stand a few feet away from them, holding the towels, not wanting to interrupt but not wanting to eavesdrop, either.

"Cam says I'm overreacting, of course. He says she's just an old friend, that it's completely innocent. They went to high school together, at Coventry, and you know how Cam is about that damn place; he's prouder of having gone there than UVA. But I'm justi-fied in being upset, right? I mean, it's not normal to invite a single woman to stay at your house while your wife and daughters are in New York, is it?"

"It would certainly upset me," says Kate.

I step in a bit closer to the two of them, holding the towels in front of me like an offering. I am embarrassed by how much of their conversation I have already overheard.

Amelia glances at me, surprised, as if she had not noticed me hovering on the periphery.

"Oh, thank you," she says, taking a towel and dabbing at her eyes, before methodically squeezing it through her wet ringlets. "I'm so sorry I interrupted your lunch. What a mess I am."

order to honor her niece's privacy, though all of us around the table, whether we overheard Amelia's dilemma or not, recognize that the woman is, as Meemaw would say, "in one hot mess of a situation."

"She's a pretty girl," says Alice.

"She *is* pretty," says Kate, and then everyone is silent for a moment, thinking of how to change the subject.

"I hope folks saved room for dessert," I say. I am eager to show off the banana pudding. I made a tester one for myself the other night and it was even better than I had imagined it would be, the pieces of toasted pound cake having soaked up the rich vanilla custard.

"I'm going to have to pass," says Alice. "I woke up with a headache this morning and it's only gotten worse."

"Stay for dessert," chides Gus. "The sugar might help your head."

"I can't," she says, standing. "But Kate, you and Jack stay. No need to cut your lunch short just because of me. Now, where is my bag?"

Under normal circumstances I would jump up and get it for her, but I feel too dejected, too bitter. Would it kill her to be gracious? Would it kill her to acknowledge the effort that went into putting this meal together?

Gus rises from the table and fetches Alice her weathered brown leather satchel. Alice leaves the restaurant to our mumbled goodbyes. An air of defeat settles over us.

Truman Capote, of course, fails to make an appearance.

10

Hostess Gift

(New York City, 1982)

It was Gus who introduced me to Sebastian, setting us up to meet at The Bow Tie, a fussy place not too far from Café Andres that is filled with men in May-December romances. When Gus first suggested I date someone in his forties, I balked, insisting that I was *not* interested in dating some sort of daddy. But Gus argued that I was an old soul and that dating someone my own age would bore and annoy me. I suppose I was flattered by his evaluation, though I was certainly not flattered when I first saw Sebastian. To be honest, I was insulted.

Which is to say Sebastian is not, on first glance, attractive. His nose is bent at the end as if someone grabbed hold of it and twisted. And he's got bug eyes behind thick glasses. Plus, he's short, just under five-seven. But after spending five minutes with him, I forgot all of that. After five minutes I thought: *I want to talk with this man forever.* Maybe because he gave me all of his attention. Maybe because he's traveled everywhere, met everyone, had a million interesting jobs. Right now he's a curator at the Guggenheim, but he's done so much else, including having produced several off-Broadway shows. With all of his accomplishments, he might be vain, arrogant. But he's not. He's got this great, peppy attitude, kind of like Meemaw. It's as if he wakes up each morning ready to be delighted. And every time he eats something I have prepared for him, he acts as if he has just discovered his sense of taste. "Oh, Bobby," he will murmur, and I will feel myself expand.

And then there's his Medusa hair, which I love: bright, black and silver coils that spring from his head, then flop in different directions. When he becomes animated in conversation he starts running his hand through his curls. Something about that gesture makes me want to get him right into bed.

I admit, our relationship has moved fast. After two months I pretty much moved into his three-bedroom apartment at the Belthorp, a glorious old building on West 88th that is in a state of total disrepair. Sebastian pays six hundred dollars a month for his three-bedroom, two-bath (crumbling) palace. For that privilege he gleefully takes the stairs when the elevator is out and sets mousetraps around the apartment to avoid the pretense of calling the super, who will not respond.

"Never underestimate the tenacity of an Upper West Sider with rent control," Sebastian likes to say.

Despite having mostly moved in with Sebastian, I have kept my studio. I pay the rent there while Sebastian pays the rent at the Belthorp. Sebastian calls the studio my laboratory because I go there to cook and work on recipes. I've become obsessed with translating old southern classics into dishes Upper East Siders can understand, simple tweaks such as topping chicken pot pie with puff pastry or frying grouper the way Meemaw fried catfish, but also more daring variations: a chess pie crème brûlé or a pimento cheese soufflé. I think of this as "stealth" southern cuisine, and I have to say, it's bringing in a surprising number of customers. Or rather, the recent write-up we got in the *Times* is bringing in the customers, which called me "a dazzling young chef, barely out of short pants, who has breathed new life into a fading beauty of a restaurant."

Gus was both thrilled and annoyed by the write-up. "Are they implying that *I* am a fading beauty?" he quipped.

Ironically, it was immediately after our disastrous lunch with Alice that Gus gave me autonomy in the kitchen. Kate, Jack, and Randy had left—having devoured my banana pudding—and I was just sitting at the table, head down, feeling as if I had fallen into a dark hole. Gus stood behind me and put his hands on my shoulders.

"Don't fret over Alice," he said. "I love her, but she's always been mercurial. Once, years and years ago, before Café Andres was even in existence, I slighted her while we were decorating a window at Saks by making the tiniest suggestion about how she could rearrange a mannequin's fox stole. She abruptly claimed some sort of emergency and just walked off the job. Could not handle even the tiniest critique! At least not that day. A month later I forgave her and asked her to help me design a window at Bonwit Teller. It was an important job, and I needed her eye. Because when she's on, nobody is better. But Bobby, darling, she was wrong to walk out today. Your meal was superb. And I'd love to see what else you can come up with. So, shall we make it official? Hand you the toque? Not that I'm ready to abandon my post in the kitchen *entirely*, but I'd love to have you come in and cook two or three nights a week, and take over half the lunches. That way Randy won't be able to complain so *tirelessly* about how much I work."

And so what began as a disaster of a day turned into a triumph.

Or as Sebastian (who has New Age leanings) would say: The universe delivered me a beautiful gift wrapped in hideous packaging.

Despite all of my time spent with Sebastian and all of the friends he has introduced me to, I have yet to meet his parents or to visit his childhood home, a town house on Amsterdam Avenue. But today I will do both. We have been invited over for brunch.

I'm relieved that I'm meeting them over brunch rather than dinner, as brunch has become such a familiar custom for me. Sebastian and I are *always* meeting people for brunch. Sebastian is nothing if not social, which means that I have spent a lot of time meeting his friends, dozens of them, including his oldest friends, with whom he attended Dalton. After six months I am even—finally!—able to catch some of the cultural references perpetually bandied about at their dinner parties, to know who they are talking about when they refer to Chuck Close, or Mapplethorpe, or Jasper Johns.

But it is the gay cancer we speak of most often, the cancer that keeps changing names, the cancer that is seemingly contagious, though nobody knows exactly how it is spread. And while the cause of this disease remains unknown, one thing is certain: We all know someone young and beautiful who has died from it.

Everyone is scared, but nobody wants to admit it. We try to determine how the ones who are dying are different from us. That they have more sex, take more drugs, lift more weights, spend too much time in the sun. Really, we have no idea why some of us are dying and some of us are not. We make jokes that aren't funny to ward off the fear.

"Nervous?" Sebastian asks as he presses the doorbell of the three-story redbrick town house, his childhood home.

"Just get a drink in my hand as soon as possible."

"You're such an adorable WASP," he says.

"I'm really not. My parents took a temperance pledge every year. My reliance on a good cocktail is solely your influence."

He smiles, grabs my hand. I squeeze his back but quickly let go. Sebastian has assured me that his parents are "Upper West Side Jewish intellectuals," which I assume means tolerant. Still, I don't want to be touching when they open the door. To ensure this, I shift the gift bag I am holding into the hand closest to Sebastian. It's a hostess gift, as Mama would call it. Though Sebastian is doing his damnedest to play Henry Higgins to my Eliza Doolittle—case in point, the fact that I now reference *My Fair Lady*!—I can't relinquish some of the rules of my upbringing, one of which is: A guest should never arrive empty-handed.

The front door opens, revealing a striking woman. She has black hair with a long silver streak down the front (à la Susan Sontag, whom I actually met, briefly, at a downtown party with Sebastian), and she wears a silk leopard print blouse tucked into white wool trousers, a tangle of thin gold chains hanging from her neck.

"Dahling," she says, kissing Sebastian first on one cheek, then the other. She is as tall as her son, which isn't really that much of a feat.

"And this must be your new friend, Bobby. Delighted to meet you, sweetheart. I'm Dahlia."

"He's my boyfriend, Mother. Not just my friend."

Dahlia rolls her eyes, but indulgently.

"Sorry, dahling, your *boy*friend. Anyway, Bobby, it's lovely to meet you. Sebastian can't stop talking about you, and we're all just so excited about your write-up in the *Times*!"

I feel myself blush. This is all so new. I've had to become comfortable with so much around Sebastian, around his friends. Last weekend Sebastian took me to a pink party. We were all to dress in some shade of the color—Sebastian and I wore matching pink Brooks Brothers button-downs—but one of his friends was dressed head to toe in pink feathers, a human flamingo. Everyone was complimenting him for being so bold, so brave.

It occurs to me that acknowledging the intimacy I have with Sebastian in front of his mother is a different sort of bravery altogether.

"This is for you," I say, handing her the gift bag.

"How kind," she says.

She leads us through a front hall and into the living room. Everything is very modern, very stark. I look for family photos on the walls, or on the mantel, or framed and placed on occasional tables, but I see none. Dahlia must be a minimalist. There are two sofas that face each other, both made of white leather and chrome. The coffee table between them is chrome and glass and has nothing on it but a tall, rectangular vase holding a single dendrobium orchid. The floors are hardwood and highly polished. On the walls hang carved African masks, which is funny to me because Sebastian has them on his walls, too, and I've seen the same sort of thing hanging on the walls of many of his friends, as common up here as full-sized bridal portraits hanging over the mantel were—and probably still are—in Decatur.

"We need drinks," declares Sebastian.

How I love him for that. How I love him for many things. Though I told Gus I didn't want a daddy, I love how Sebastian takes care of me. Not just by spending money—though he does that—but by paying attention. Like how he bought Cheerios to keep in his pantry, because I once mentioned that I like nothing more than a bowl of them with a cut-up banana each morning. Or how he made me a cassette with a mix of all of the songs he played me that I had especially liked, having kept a running list in his head of the ones I complimented. Or how he brought matzo ball soup and Dr. Brown's cream soda to my studio when we first started dating and I had come down with a cold.

"Your father will be back in a minute. He had to go down to the bodega to get the *Times.* Someone stole ours again. I say 'someone,' but I know who it was. That gonif Harry Palmer. How is it that he doesn't have a newspaper subscription, but every damn week I see the Sunday *Times* in his garbage?"

"He takes yours every Sunday?" I ask. "That's horrible."

"No. He rotates. Steals it from one neighbor one week, then another the next. Us, the Millers, the Teitelbaums—it's musical chairs with that one."

"So confront him," says Sebastian.

Dahlia shrugs. "Then I have to deal with his mishigas face to face."

"We need drinks," Sebastian repeats, taking my hand and leading me to the kitchen, which is the size of my mother's kitchen in Decatur. Sebastian opens the freezer door and pulls out a bottle of vodka. "Thank God. Dahlia always has the ingredients for a Virgin Mary, but doesn't always have the vodka on hand to bloody it up. Want one?"

"Yes, please."

"I'll have a virgin one while you're at it," Dahlia says. "You're sure that's not what you boys want? It's not even noon."

"Mother, I am forty-two years old; I can have a Bloody Mary on a Sunday morning if I damn well want one."

"Bobby, are you this touchy with your mother?"

"No, ma'am," I say. "I am not."

I am, in fact, a little taken aback by Sebastian's rudeness. He's always so affable and good-natured with his friends.

"Bobby is a good southern boy," says Sebastian. "Which means he thinks plenty of mean things but never says them aloud. Open his 'hostess gift.' I'm dying to see what he got you. He wouldn't tell me."

"It's nothing," I say.

"Is this lox shmear?" Dahlia asks, opening the fancy gift bag

I couldn't really afford but purchased anyway and pulling out the Mason jar packed with the pink spread.

"Crawfish spread," I say. "But I imagine it would go very nicely on a bagel, same as lox."

I am underplaying how delicious this stuff is. It's just poached crawfish tails blended in the Cuisinart with lots of butter and garlic, and a little cayenne pepper, but it's become my favorite thing in the world to eat. I serve it at the restaurant as an appetizer with toast points. It's probably the most popular thing on the menu besides the banana custard "trifle." (Gus insisted I fancify the name, not letting me call it what it is—banana pudding.)

Dahlia cuts a knowing look at Sebastian, then smiles. "Lovely! Does it need to be refrigerated?"

"Yes, ma'am," I say.

"Bobby, dahling, you have got to stop calling me ma'am. Makes me feel ancient."

"Gosh, I'm sorry," I say. "It doesn't mean anything about your age. It's just what I was taught to do."

She gives Sebastian another knowing look, and suddenly I feel about fourteen years old instead of twenty-one. And then it occurs to me that the age difference between Dahlia and Sebastian probably isn't any greater than the age difference between Sebastian and me.

I am now feeling desperate for a drink, but Sebastian is slow and deliberate with such things. No Mr and Mrs T Bloody Mary Mix for him. He has the *Silver Palate Cookbook* opened and has pulled out tomato juice, horseradish, Tabasco, Worcestershire sauce, and a lemon from the fridge and is now plucking basil leaves off a plant kept on the windowsill.

"Anyone home?" calls a man's voice.

"We're in the kitchen, dahling."

Sebastian's father enters the room. I'm surprised by how large he is. Fat, to be exact. Sebastian is so lithe, and so is Dahlia. I had just assumed that they would be a family of tiny people. Though it is the weekend, his dad is in a suit. He has a full gray beard growing over his chubby, ruddy face. On his head rests a black yarmulke.

"Dahling, this is Sebastian's friend, Bobby. Bobby, this is my husband, Mel."

I expect Sebastian to once again correct his mother, to insist on her calling me his boyfriend or, Lord help me, his lover, but thankfully he says nothing.

"Pleased to meet you, sir," I say, holding out my hand.

"Was I knighted without knowing about it?" asks Mel.

"Bobby is from *the South*," Sebastian says, using a mock whisper as if he were informing his parents that I am a wee bit on the slow side.

"You get the *Times*?" Dahlia asks her husband.

"The place on the corner was sold out, so I had to walk a couple of blocks to the place right by the shul. They had it."

"Well, thank God for small miracles. Okay, look. We've got bagels, we've got fruit salad, we've got cream cheese, we've got lox, we've got tuna salad, we've got whitefish. I'm just going to put everything on the counter and we can all help ourselves, okay? Sebastian, should I make a pot of coffee?"

"Only if you and Dad want some. Bobby and I are having real drinks."

Sebastian hands me a Bloody Mary, topped with chopped basil. The fresh smell of the herb hits my nose before I even take a sip. Heaven.

"Don't bother with coffee," says Mel. "I'm fine with a Diet Pepsi."

Dahlia begins pulling Zabar's bags out of the refrigerator.

"I don't know why you insist on going there," says Sebastian. "You know the whitefish is better at Barney Greengrass."

"Bobby, have you ever heard the expression 'Opinions are like assholes'?" asks Mel.

"Everybody's got one, and they all stink," deadpans Sebastian.

Mel touches his finger to his nose.

Dahlia is pulling the to-go containers out of the Zabar's bags, placing them directly onto the counter. I can't help but think of how my mother would have transferred the purchased salads and dips into her own Wedgwood china bowls, the ones with apples and pears painted along the sides. Not that she would have purchased prepared foods for a brunch.

"Were you at temple?" I ask Mel, motioning to his yarmulke.

"Bobby, let me give you a pointer," says Mel. "Call it shul. Temple is for the Jews who want to be goyim. And no, I wasn't at shul. Not on Sunday."

"Dad has become observant in his old age," says Sebastian. "He wears the beanie cap all the time."

Mel looks at his son wearily.

"Come, come," says Dahlia. "Grab a plate from the cabinet and let's get this show on the road."

Again I think of Mama, how the china would have already been laid out, a napkin for each guest rolled into a polished silver ring. Although Meemaw might not have put out china, at least not for close friends. Meemaw might have just put out a stack of Dixie plates and some paper napkins for backdoor guests, as she liked to call them. (Meemaw had a needlepoint pillow that read: "Backdoor Guests Are Best." I once reminisced about that with Sebastian, who immediately joked that such a pillow would convey a whole different message were we to put it on our sofa.)

Sebastian reaches into the pantry and takes down four brown ceramic plates. He hands me one. It is surprisingly heavy, slightly misshapen, and feels a little rough to the touch.

"Goys first," he says, motioning to the spread of food on the countertop.

"Sebastian!"

"Relax, Dahlia. Bobby doesn't mind a little teasing."

I take a bagel, some plain cream cheese, a tiny bit of lox, and a huge scoop of fruit salad. I want to suggest that Dahlia set the crawfish spread out as well, that it would go well with everything, but instinct tells me to bite my tongue, to let things unfold as they may.

"Try the whitefish," says Dahlia, eyeing my plate. "Despite what my son says, Zabar's does a nice job with it."

"Just a fair warning," says Sebastian. "Dahlia Dahling is known for pushing food."

"Why such a smart-ass?" asks Dahlia, but she doesn't sound truly despairing, more admiring.

Still, I take a scoop of the whitefish.

We eat in the living room, sitting on the white leather sofas, Sebastian beside me, Mel and Dahlia on the one facing us.

"So tell us all about yourself, Bobby," says Dahlia. "We know you're a famous cook, and we know you're from the South, but we don't know much else. Tell us about your family, where you went to college."

I cannot count the number of times I have been asked where I went to college in the months since I began dating Sebastian. Such credentials are of paramount importance to his crowd.

"What were your SAT scores?" jokes Sebastian.

"Well, my mom is a housewife. But she's sort of a super-housewife—she wrote a book about the art of entertaining."

"*Gracious Servings*," says Sebastian. "A guide for young Baptist brides."

"Are your parents very religious?" asks Dahlia.

There is really no way around this, even though I don't want to talk about my Baptist past with my Jewish boyfriend's parents. "Yes, ma'am. My dad's a Baptist preacher."

"No kidding?" says Mel. "I'm thinking you won't be bringing our son home for the holidays then, will you?"

"For godsakes, Melvin," says Dahlia. "Forgive my husband, Bobby. He can be an ass."

Mel appears unperturbed by his wife's assessment.

"No, Mel's absolutely right," I say. "My parents and I have a hard time with each other. We're not exactly estranged, but we certainly talk on the phone a lot more than we visit."

That's an understatement. I haven't once been back to Decatur, and Mama and Daddy haven't once visited me up here.

Sebastian places his hand protectively on top of mine. It's a sweet gesture, but after a moment I pull my hand away, tucking it into my lap. I just can't touch him around his parents. I know Sebastian would like for me to be more "out," for me to be more defiant in my homosexuality. But I sometimes wish he had more patience. After all, he's got over twenty years on me and he's not from the South. When we first started dating we started tracking our histories, determining that while I was making craft projects with the Royal Ambassadors he was participating in the first Gay Liberation Day march.

I wish he could acknowledge how much further I have to stretch.

"What about siblings?" asks Dahlia.

"I have two brothers, both older. I'm the baby. My oldest brother, Troy, is a pediatrician, living in Atlanta. And my other brother, Hunter, works in commercial real estate."

Dahlia blinks a few times. It looks as if she is going to say something, but then she doesn't. "Well again, we're just thrilled about the *Times* piece. I can't wait to try your cooking."

Then why don't you put out my crawfish spread? I think, but of course I say nothing of the sort.

"He's such a talent," says Sebastian, resting his hand on my thigh. "You two need to go to Café Andres before it gets impossible to get in."

"Are you there every night?" asks Dahlia.

"Gus and I—he's the owner—actually split our time in the kitchen. I'm there Tuesdays through Thursdays for lunch, and then I cook dinner Friday and Saturday nights."

"I'll come to lunch next Tuesday," Dahlia says, decided.

"Bobby keeps adding little southern touches to the menu," says Sebastian, still playing the role of cheerleader. "Sneaking them in. Like the little plate of warm cheddar and chive biscuits you get when you first sit down. Unbelievably delicious."

"Sounds fabulous," says Dahlia. "Have you thought of opening your own place?"

"Forget that," says Mel, waving away the idea with his hand. "Ninety percent of restaurants fail. What was your undergraduate degree in?"

"Um, I studied art history," I say, choosing to omit the fact that I never actually earned a college degree.

"So you're a practical guy, huh?" asks Mel.

For a minute I am confused, because there's absolutely nothing practical about a degree in art history, but then I realize he is teasing.

"Right, right," I say, draining my drink. "Lots of jobs out there for art history majors." I try to smile, joke my way through. And then I remember that his own son has his master's in art history and has a damn good job because of it.

"And where did you say you studied?"

"He didn't," says Sebastian. "He just assumed you read it on the résumé he sent over."

"At GSU," I say.

Mel looks quizzical.

"Georgia State University, Dad."

"I was at Columbia," says Mel. "But I left the city for my PhD. Went to the University of Michigan. That was a strange experience, living outside of New York. Not something I'd want to repeat."

"Now that I'm here, I can't imagine ever leaving," I say. "I just love it."

I am pandering, of course, but it's true, I can't ever see myself leaving the city. New York reminds me of the Belthorp, Sebastian's apartment building. It was once beautiful and proud; now it is crumbling, ruined. But that means people like Sebastian and me can live here. Can live here and live together and not be bothered and be okay.

"What is it you love about New York?" asks Dahlia.

"It's where the interesting people are," I say.

Dahlia smiles. I can tell she likes my answer.

The minute we walk out of the town house I turn to Sebastian. "Why didn't your mother put out my crawfish spread? Does she not trust my cooking?"

"Oh, honey, I'm sorry. I should have told you: My parents don't eat shellfish or pork. At least not in their house. If they go out for Chinese food they'll eat it, but only because it's all chopped up into little bits so no one can tell what's what."

"Oh Lord. I'm such an idiot. Your parents keep kosher and I brought them crawfish."

"They actually don't keep kosher; they just avoid the most obviously traif foods."

I'm pretty sure Sebastian has used that word before, but I can't remember exactly what it means. I don't bother asking for a definition, though. I get the drift. Un-Jewish.

"Your mother must think I'm an idiot."

Sebastian puts his arm around me as we walk west on 81st Street.

"Dahlia thinks you're adorable," he says. "She told me so, when you got up to use the bathroom. I'm sure she thinks you're too young for me, but we all know that."

"What did your dad think?"

"God knows. You can't pay too much attention to Mel. He's a little reactionary. About five years ago he had a heart attack, and afterward he turned very religious, very observant. Before, he was this relatively tolerant guy, and suddenly he was questioning the fact that I'm queer, going so far as to suggest that maybe if I *tried* dating a woman I'd realize I wasn't gay after all. It's been a fucking headache, to be honest. That's probably why I didn't introduce you until now. I just don't like dealing with the stress. But they recently got a new rabbi at their shul, and I think his ideas are more moderate around gays, and Mel seems to be loosening up a bit. Or maybe it's just that Mel puts up with me and I put up with Mel because we both love Dahlia too much not to."

I think of my family, of what they would do if I brought Sebastian home to meet them, insisting my mother refer to him as my boyfriend. Insisting my father have breakfast with him. It's inconceivable, really. It would never, ever happen. And yet even knowing that, I feel a sudden nostalgia for Mama and Daddy. For what Mama would serve were she hosting a brunch: sausage, egg, and cheese casserole, coffeecake swirled with cinnamon, pecans, and brown sugar, grits baked with garlic and cheese. There would be the rich smell of coffee in the air, and the subtle scent of fresh-cut flowers from the garden. Daddy would have been there when we arrived, and in every room there would be framed pictures of the family.

It's been over a year now since I've been in New York, absorbing this city. Going to Woody Allen movies. Shopping at Fairway. Watching Balanchine's toned dancers fly across a stripped-down stage. Walking around the reservoir in Central Park. Listening to Gus Andres reminisce about the late 40s, when everyone was young and artists mingled with commoners. I've been mugged. I've learned the difference between the local and the express. I've learned not to talk to the neighbors in Sebastian's building, because God forbid one of them is crazy and then you have to deal with that person for the rest of your life or give up your good rent.

In short, I am learning how to be a New Yorker, and while I might still bring a hostess gift to a brunch and call my boyfriend's parents sir and ma'am, I am growing further and further away from my Decatur roots. But for the first time this fills me not with satisfaction but with melancholy. Sebastian holds my hand as we head toward Riverside Park, where we will walk off the bagels and the schmear. And though I love this man and though he makes me feel both secure and treasured, I am suddenly so homesick I can hardly stand it. I am thinking of Dahlia's stark white walls, and I am thinking of my meemaw, of how you couldn't even tell the color of her living room walls, they were so covered by pictures of our family. I am thinking of her pulling a pound cake out of the oven, how that nutty smell of baked butter filled the air. I am thinking of her soft, doughy skin, how easy it was to hug her, how she smelled always of good things: vanilla, cinnamon, buttered toast. And now my mind is stretching back to when I was a boy, safe and happy with Mama and Daddy: flying through the air on the zip wire, lounging on the Pawleys Island hammock stretched between two tall, skinny trees, catching fireflies at dusk. I am thinking of Daddy's vegetable garden planted in neat rows and I am thinking of rolling lawns and I am thinking of spring flowers, hydrangeas and peonies and irises. I am thinking of all that is beautiful about where I come from. I am thinking of Mama and I am thinking of Daddy, and I am missing them; I am missing them terribly.

But it's an impotent nostalgia. Mama and Daddy are in my past. They would not take me as I am now, not really. Yes, they call to check in, but they don't really want to know me. They only want superficial details that will allow them to create a tidy narrative of who I am—a footloose bachelor, not quite ready to settle down. They were so excited about the mention in the *Times,* like suddenly they had good news about their son to tell their friends, when so many other good things have happened to me, most importantly that I fell in love.

But that is information they would never want to know or share. That I fell in love with a man.

A sadness like hunger spreads through my chest, and I try to distract myself from it by focusing instead on what I might prepare for Tuesday's lunch special at the café. If I could find grits somewhere I could make Mama's casserole with cheese and garlic. Serve shrimp on top. Dress it up with some basil cut in a chiffonade, maybe give it a fancy name—call it corn and *crevettes*—and serve it forth to the New Yorkers who will have no idea what they are eating, who will have no idea they are eating my loneliness transformed.

II

THE MONSTER UNDER THE BED

(New York City, 1985)

Sunday afternoon and we are in bed, my head tucked into Sebastian's arm, my finger tracing his chest, pushing through the hair that grows there so abundantly.

"What's this, a third nipple?" I tease, in the half second before reality catches up with me.

"Hmm?" he asks, drowsy and content.

"Oh my God," I say, circling the bump with my finger. I am no longer drowsy and satisfied but alert, on edge. I pick up his right hand, place it on the spot. "Feel this."

He is silent for a moment; then wordlessly he stands and walks to the closet, opening the door to look in the full-length mirror on the other side. He parts his chest hair with his fingers and examines the growth. It is purple, about the size of a quarter. He turns to face me, fully naked, his legs slightly bowed, his abdomen ropy, the hair on his chest obscuring his toned pecs. "This looks just like what Michael found."

Every few weeks there is another funeral to attend. Michael was Sebastian's best friend from Princeton. They were in an a cappella group together. "All of us trying to be somebody we weren't," Sebastian would say, "And me double. I wanted to be straight *and* a WASP."

They sang in archways, wearing tuxedos on football weekends. The harmony of their clear, young voices lulled the visiting mothers and fathers into believing that the universe was a good and orderly place, that all was as it should be.

It is a rush to get our clothes on, to find our physician's number—a personal friend, he has come to our home for dinner before—to call and beg for him to see Sebastian right away. As it is Sunday, Dr. Wilson's offices are closed, but he is a compassionate man and he tells us to come to his apartment. He lives nearby, at Central Park West and 78th. It is November, cold, and we wear long black coats as we rush to see him. The coats you might wear to a funeral. It starts to snow during the walk over, the first snowfall of the year. Each winter Sebastian welcomes the first snow with boyish excitement. But today he makes no comment, just grabs my arm tighter so neither of us will slip. The white flakes land on his black coat, and I think of the lesions that might overtake his body. The first lesion Michael found was on his ankle, noticeable only if he pulled down his sock and showed it to you. Two months later, his body was covered with them.

Michael was dead within four months; the last month of his life he had stopped making sense, could only speak in gibberish, sometimes had to be tied to the bed to stop him from pulling out the hair on his brows, which he thought were baby snakes, come to eat his brain. This the fate of a renowned painter whose impressionistic "splash" portraits hang in museums. In one of his lucid moments, Michael told us that he wished to paint a self-portrait with all of his lesions, to paint it against the side of a building, to say to New York, to the country, to the president, to the world: *This is really happening.*

It is happening. But all around us, life bustles on. As if the deaths of gay men are irrelevant.

I try to imagine what else Sebastian's mark might be. Poison ivy, a wart, a rash, something, anything besides Kaposi's sarcoma. We are monogamous. And I had such little experience before Sebastian. A hand job in a bathhouse, a kiss on a dance floor. I was such a good Baptist boy when I first landed in the city. What I thought was sinning was nothing more than licking a vanilla ice cream cone.

But think, Bobby. Think. Sebastian has been around so much longer. He and his friends speak of how wild the 70s were, the Wild West of gay sex, of any sex. Back then contracting an STD meant popping an antibiotic or shaving off your pubic hair. *Think, Bobby.* Of how he speaks of those carefree days before he met you, when his favorite way to spend a Sunday afternoon was going to the baths and coming home afterward to listen to the opera.

And then it occurs to me: If Sebastian has AIDS, do I have it, too?

We enter the lobby of Dr. Wilson's building, checking in with the doorman, who calls up to make sure we are expected. I wonder how many other panicked men have visited Dr. Wilson at home, have made this inverse house call to find out, as soon as possible, whether or not they have received a death sentence.

When the elevator stops on the eleventh floor, the color drains from Sebastian's face and his knees buckle. He grabs my arm.

"Oh my God, Bobby. Oh my God. I can't breathe."

We stand in the elevator for so long that the door starts to close, but I push the button to keep it open. "Come on, sweetheart, one step at a time. One step at a time. We don't know yet. Just take one step, good, now another. We're just going to walk down this hall. That's all we're doing right now."

He lets me guide him, step by step, down the hall and to the door where Dr. Wilson is waiting.

"It's going to be okay, sweetheart. It's going to be okay," I murmur, having no idea if I am speaking the truth.

"Let's do the examination in the back bedroom," says Dr. Wilson, leading us through his apartment. "It's more private."

I walk with them to the back room, but at the door Sebastian turns and asks me to wait outside.

"I'm sorry," he says. "I need to do this alone."

Stung, I make my way to the leather sofa in Dr. Wilson's graciously appointed living room, slide into it. Soon I hear a keening, followed by the low murmurs of Dr. Wilson. I hear Sebastian gasp, "Oh God, oh God, oh God." And I realize why Sebastian left me here: so he does not have to face my dismay at the same time that he faces his own. For a moment I am frozen. As long as I remain here, on the other side of the closed door, I can still live in the time before. To go to Sebastian, to push open the closed door, to offer comfort, is to make it real. Yes, Sebastian is keening, but as long as I stay here, life has not permanently changed.

I sit paralyzed on the sofa, while in the other room my lover weeps. And then I see a vision of my meemaw wearing her pink velour housecoat that zips up the front, looking just as she did the night I ran to her house after being caught with Pete Arnold. *Son,* she says, *go to him. Go to him now. He needs you.* I stand and walk to the closed door. I start to knock, but instead I simply turn the handle, entering the room, crossing to him. Sebastian sits slumped over, shirtless, on the edge of Dr. Wilson's bed. His eyes are rimmed with red, as if outlined with a crayon. He looks momentarily surprised to see me, and then he looks grateful.

I sit beside him on the bed, and he leans the full weight of his body against me.

"Oh, Bobby," he says. "When you were little were you scared of the monster under the bed?"

"Yes," I say, though in truth my kid fear had been that when I flushed the toilet a witch would rise from the bowl, grab me around the waist, and pull me down into the sewer with her. For a while, until Mama caught me, I peed in the sink to avoid having to flush.

"Well, the monster is real and he has come to get me."

12

Communion

(New York City, Winter 1988)

Sebastian's death shows itself on Dahlia's face. Whereas before she looked remarkably young for her age and was sometimes even mistaken for Sebastian's sister, the word "crone" now comes to mind whenever I observe the heavy black circles under her weary eyes, the set of three parallel indentations on her forehead, the shallow stream of lines running off from the sad red river of her mouth. Yet, while her son's death aged her, it also gave her the melancholic beauty of a survivor. The beauty that comes from waking up every day resolved to meet the worst that life has to offer with compassion and grace: bringing fresh flowers to the apartment, massaging her dying son's feet with peppermint lotion from The Body Shop, singing lullabies to him from his nursery days, her voice pure and clear, like the ringing of a crystal goblet as a wet finger is run round its lip. There was one song she sang again and again, at Sebastian's insistence, even though it was haunting and sad. "Um umm, I'd like to linger here, um umm, a little longer here, um umm, a little longer here with you."

Whereas Sebastian's father, Mel, turned away. Mel turned away from his dying son, visited only twice during Sebastian's final months, called only a handful of times. Ate and ate and ate, gaining ten, then twenty, then thirty pounds, his petulant refusal to engage in his son's death reflected in his swollen face, which kept expanding, until it was as wide and useless as a Mylar balloon, until he was a balloon man with hapless eyes, a man who could not face what life delivered and so allowed himself to drift away from all that mattered. What more can I say of Mel? To rail against him is to complain of the cold in February, to wish a dip in the ocean didn't leave salt in your hair, to be startled when a two-year-old wants a sugar cookie before eating his broccoli.

He is of little substance. He is little more than a knot and stale air.

As for me, I remain at the Belthorp. It is what Sebastian would have wanted, though not for sentimental reasons, but so that he could retain some sort of hold on his rent-controlled apartment, even after death. Yes, I have become a living punchline to a tired old joke about New York real estate. And Lord knows I need the cheap rent. But that is not why I stay. I stay because at the Belthorp I can remain with Sebastian. I sleep on sheets he picked out; I use his brand of laundry detergent, his brand of dryer sheets, his brand of toothpaste. When the bathroom sink backs up and I pull out the drain, I still find pieces of his hair stuck in it. Not willing to throw them away, I store them in a Ziploc baggie, placing it on a high shelf in the back of the closet, where Sebastian kept his collection of porn videos, which I sometimes watch in an attempt at communion, wanting to link into his specific fantasies and desires so I may be with him again.

Funny: Those videos used to embarrass me; they were low-budget and hard-core. The fact that Sebastian enjoyed them—relished them—revealed something about him I felt was unpleasant, unsavory. Had I been given the choice to wipe out that proclivity, along with a few of his more abrasive personality traits, I would have. (He drove me crazy by arguing the other side, any side, just for the hell of it, just to be a provocateur, once going so far as to defend Lacy Lovehart by saying her Save Our Sons campaign was well within her First Amendment rights. To which I answered, "Baby, that might be, but I just need you on my side with this one.") But now that he is gone I miss his edges, his extremes, the more difficult parts of his personality. Those edges made him Sebastian. It occurs to me that I loved Sebastian the way my father preached you should love your spouse: warts and all.

At night I study Sebastian's art: the Chuck Close print, the Rosenquist lithograph. I listen to the long-playing jazz albums on his record player, try on the African masks hanging on the wall. I wanted to mark Hanukkah by lighting candles in the brass menorah he kept on the mantelpiece in the living room, but early in December Dahlia asked if she might have it and I willingly handed it over. Dahlia also wanted the photo albums of Sebastian as a child. It pained me to part with them, but I told her to, of course, take whatever she needs.

Though I often see Gus at the café and I occasionally have dinner with Mike, my old friend from the residence hotel, who, like me, is perplexed by his HIV-negative status, the only person I allow to come to the Belthorp is Dahlia. She stops by every few weeks for a cup of tea and a little something sweet to eat. When we are together we do not speak of Sebastian's death. We do not speak of our choking grief or our gaping yearning. Instead we speak as if Sebastian is still alive but simply not around, as if he were traveling, like Holly Golightly, whose calling card read just that in *Breakfast at Tiffany's*. We act as if Sebastian has taken a trip to a distant but knowable place—Paris, perhaps, or somewhere even farther, Sydney or Hong Kong.

It would make sense to assume that Dahlia has become a mother figure for me and I her replacement son. But ours is not a relationship of transference. I remember hearing Mr. Morgan, my RA leader from so long ago, speak with fierce loyalty about a friend he made while fighting in Vietnam. Side by side, they survived the war, then both returned to the States to resume normal lives among people who had no idea what they had been through. I imagine my feelings toward Dahlia are similar to those Mr. Morgan had for his friend. We walked through something unfathomable together. We came out on the other side, changed, only to find that much of the world remained the same, callous and indifferent.

While I see Dahlia every few weeks, I rarely speak to my own parents. They do not even know that Sebastian is gone. I never told them much about Sebastian when he was alive, saying, simply, that I was moving in with a friend to a very nice apartment. They did not ask many questions. They remain hesitant to know any but the most general details of my life. Were I to tell them who Sebastian really was to me and that he is now gone, died of AIDS, I fear they might say that Sebastian's death was fitting punishment for a decadent lifestyle. I have no capability to handle such condemnation. If faced with it I imagine I might fly down to Georgia, arrive at their door, and show them the meaning of Old Testament vengeance.

I am sane enough to recognize that I have gone a little crazy.

I never venture to bars or clubs. God forbid I meet a man, bring him home. Even though I have been spared (for now at least), I cannot separate sex from death, no Larry Kramer dramatics needed to convince me of that. I know some gay men who are still fucking their way to oblivion, just to escape the constant pressure AIDS exerts on our lives as we do the hospital-to-memorial-service shuffle, again and again. But losing myself in suicidal sex is not the way through. Instead, I become a hermit, a monk, a ghost. Wryly, I think of myself as the phantom of the Belthorp, an apparition haunting my six-room flat. I cook only at the restaurant, never at home, but instead stock the freezer with Stouffer's frozen entrées: macaroni and cheese, spinach soufflé, lasagna. I watch television religiously but live for Thursday night comedies, for *The Cosby Show* and *A Different World*, relishing the escape into the loving antics of an intact family, followed by the adventures of happy undergraduates coming into their own. I drink too much red wine on too many nights, grow accustomed to a low-grade hangover for much of the next day. I cling to ritual, to coffee made in the stovetop espresso pot each morning, to my jog through Riverside Park, to showing up at Café Andres each night ready to methodically prepare the meals ordered, no longer itching to transform southern classics into haute cuisine, happy now to stick to the standbys demanded of me: my cheddar biscuits, my crawfish spread on toast points, my fried flounder, my potpie. And always the banana pudding made with pound cake instead of vanilla wafers.

The dazzling young chef is no longer dazzling and certainly no longer feels young. At twenty-eight, I am exhausted. At twenty-eight, I have lost everyone I have ever deeply loved.

Early Sunday, mid-December, one of those New York winter mornings that make you consider moving back south after all. When you are exposed to such biting, pervasive cold, the South's mean prejudices seem superficial, nothing a dry martini and a good sense of humor can't conquer. Certainly I am not the same freezing boy I was my first winter in the city—I know now to wear long underwear, thick socks, a down coat that falls past my knees. Still, on this morning I underestimate the weather and walk all the way to Zabar's for a bag of coffee beans and some half-and-half. I stop at the café on the way out, order a cup of coffee to go, along with a still warm ham and cheese croissant, which I eat quickly, ravenously, finishing by the time I walk out of the store.

It is shocking to step outside again. The frigid air numbs all exposed flesh, my cheeks, my nose, the lobes of my ears. I slurp at my paper cup of coffee, trying to keep warm, but it is nearly impossible to walk and drink at the same time and I keep dribbling down the front of my coat. It makes me think of the *Airplane!*-inspired quip Sebastian and I used to trade when either of us would spill: "I think you might have a drinking problem."

One more spill and I decide I've had enough. I look for a trash can, spying one on the sidewalk ahead. I throw my cup away, pausing for a moment to listen to the melodic sounds emanating from the stone church to my right. A sign framed in Plexiglas proclaims this diminutive fortress to be Our Lady of Sorrows.

I have been to too many churches over the years, wearing the same black suit to attend funeral after funeral of gay men, mostly young. I am so tired of memorial services. So weary of the eulogies and the dirges. Which is why I should turn away from Our Lady of Sorrows. And yet I inch closer toward the church, the choir's plaintive hymns matching my own raw grief, its collective voice a swath of densely woven fabric, ripped from the bolt, the edges ragged, unraveling. The door is closed but not locked. I push my way in, look around the empty vestibule, at the stone fountain by the door, at the garish red carpeting, bright as fresh blood. I do not know much about Catholicism, but I know the water in the fountain is supposed to be holy. I dip my finger in it, press a drop against my forehead, figuring what could it hurt? There is a poster board, displayed on a long wooden table, showing photos of a youth mission trip to Guatemala, brown and white kids linking arms and mugging for the camera. I think of my days as a Royal Ambassador, how I wanted to befriend Anjan, the orphan we sponsored in India.

Life runs in circles, I suppose. I was lonely then; I am lonely now.

I keep walking, through the swinging doors that lead into the sanctuary. The choir, taking their seats in the stalls in the nave, consists of only four people, a much smaller group than I imagined, given how powerfully their voices carry. There are not many in the pews, maybe twenty-five people, a few black, mostly white. Almost all have gray hair. One woman turns to glance at me as I make my way down the aisle, but everyone else keeps their eyes facing front, toward the preacher—priest—who is beginning a sermon.

The first thing I notice about the priest is that he is hooked to oxygen, clear tubes running into his nose. His voice is kind and lilting, marked by the effeminate cadence of certain gay men. I wonder if he is HIV positive, if that is the reason for the oxygen. But I notice no lesions, no wasting of the cheeks, no other signs of disintegration. Maybe he is just old. What a blessing in the middle of the AIDS epidemic: to be a gay man who simply grows old.

There is another priest behind him, a broad-shouldered black man with closely shorn hair, his body thick and substantial, his massive chest pushed out in front of him like a football player. I slide into a pew, taking note of the kneeler in front. Kneelers are not the Baptist way.

The priest on oxygen speaks of comfort, of how it is the job of Christians to offer comfort to the suffering world. "Mother comforted us when we were little, but she's not always around to do that now," he says. "So it is up to us to provide comfort and nurturance to each other."

Well, that's the damn truth, I think. I sigh deeply, then inhale, incense filling my nostrils, that exotic musky smell of the Catholic Church.

The remainder of the homily is brief, kind, and unarousing. No one claps their hands in agreement, or murmurs amen, or follows along in their Bibles like Mama used to do, her painted fingernail trailing below the verse. Everything is very staid, very orderly. It is nice, actually. To the priest's point: comforting. Like the rituals I have grown to depend on, the morning espresso, the long runs through the park, watching sitcoms on network television. We kneel at certain points, recite the Nicene Creed—which I, unlike the other congregants, do not know by heart. A collection is taken. I slip a five-dollar bill into the straw basket that floats in front of me, attached to a long wooden pole, wielded by an usher who stands at the end of the aisle. We say the Lord's Prayer. And then it is time for communion, something we only took occasionally at Clairmont Avenue Baptist, and with grape juice instead of wine.

I have long stopped believing in the ABCs of salvation. I have long stopped thinking of Jesus as my Very Best Friend. Still, through much of my life, I have been comforted by the presence of God. It wasn't that I felt protected exactly, but rather accompanied by something holy when I should have felt most alone.

But after Sebastian's death, my sense of God's presence evaporated. AIDS destroyed God for me, the same as it destroyed an entire community of those who create beauty and art, the dazzlers among us, reflecting God's creative spark. But the dazzlers died, again and again, and the response of so many—in and out of the church—was to say that their deaths were deserved. So what were we left with? A tortured male body hanging on the cross. But not resurrection.

Directed by the ushers, aisle by aisle members stand and approach the altar to receive communion. Again I compare this to the Baptist rite of my youth, to the stainless-steel trays passed down the aisle, tiny plastic cups of Welch's nestled inside each indentation. Here the black priest holds an ornate silver chalice, filled, I presume, with actual wine. The usher comes to our aisle and I stand with everyone else, suddenly aching to take of the body, the blood. As I walk to the altar I allow myself this sliver of hope: that God died along with the sufferers so he could be with them fully. That one day a shoot of green might emerge.

Because here is the truth: I want to return. I miss being a part of a church.

It is the priest on oxygen who hands me the round wafer, which looks like a small Carr's cracker. I almost put it in my mouth but hesitate, unsure whether I am to dip it first in the wine. The black priest, holding the chalice, motions me toward him with his eyes, a shepherd collecting a lost lamb.

I stand before him, hungry.

"Are you Catholic?" he asks.

"No," I say, noticing that he immediately looks angry.

He plucks the wafer out of my hand as if it were a cookie stolen from the jar by a naughty child.

He then murmurs some words over me, a blessing, I imagine, though I hear none of it. My head is roaring. I am no longer Bobby Banks, twenty-eight years old, head chef at a once-storied café that has had a second life under my influence, New York City dweller, sophisticated gay man. I am nine, watching Keisha's shoulders jerk when Hunter calls her a nigger. I am fourteen, opening my science book in class to find an index card that reads "FAG" tucked between its pages. I am sixteen, staring at my parents in the doorway of my room as Pete, not yet aware that we have been caught, presses against me, my father's eyes filling with grief as he is forced to recognize his own son as an abomination.

I walk down the aisle of Our Lady of Sorrows, chastened, no bread and wine in my mouth, no Jesus working his way through me. *Idiot, idiot, idiot,* I think, so ashamed at having tried to partake in a ritual that is not mine. I walk past the pew where I was sitting, then keep walking, exiting the sanctuary into the empty vestibule, then pushing through the front door of the church to find myself outside once again. The cold air hits me hard.

Halfway down the block, I remember that I left the coffee beans and half-and-half in the church, on the pew. On instinct I turn to retrieve them, then stop. No. I will not venture back there. I will not prostrate myself before an authority that will not have me. As I turn back toward home I see Alice Stone, heading my way down Columbus, her posture as erect as a dancer's.

Another authority who would not have me.

Alice wears a heavy green wool coat and a scarf wrapped around her neck. The bottom half of her slacks, a coppery red, is visible below the hem of her coat. Her hair, as always, is pulled into a high bun on top of her head, the exact same style Keisha wore as a girl, Keisha, whose image flashes through my head often, which is crazy considering I only really spent that one morning with her and then was never able to get her to play with me again, not after what Hunter said.

Alice doesn't seem to recognize me, at least not at first, but after a moment she smiles and lifts a gloved hand in greeting. I walk toward her briskly.

"Well, hello," I say. Oddly, I feel compelled to hug her, she who has distracted my thoughts from the aborted communion. But I hold back. I do not want to assume an intimacy we do not have when, in fact, we don't know each other at all. Before Sebastian's death I would have told you that I *did* know Alice, that she was prickly and imperious and rude. But now it occurs to me that I only really met her that one time and maybe she behaved the way she did because she was going through a trial of her own. Something that had nothing to do with me or the lunch I prepared.

One thing Sebastian's death has taught me: You never know what private grief others are going through. And in any event, that difficult lunch was years ago. Many things have changed. Surely we both have changed.

"Hello," she says, not offering anything else, smiling enigmatically.

"Can you believe how cold it is?"

"Winter has indeed arrived," she says, just as placid and calm as a yogi.

We stand for a moment, blinking and smiling politely. Were it warmer, we might blink and smile at each other all morning, but it is too cold a day to do that for very long. "Well, I should let you get off to wherever you're going," I say.

"Returning, actually. Headed back to my apartment. I was just at Fairway, buying supplies for my Christmas cooking."

She carries no shopping bags. She must be having her groceries delivered.

"Which way is home?"

"West," she says, pointing. "Riverside Drive."

"Oh good. I'm headed west, too. Shall we walk together?"

She gives me a slight smile, which I take as a yes.

"What do you cook for the holidays?" I ask as we begin walking.

Sebastian trained me to say "the holidays" instead of Christmas. He was always touchy around this time of year. He resented all of the goyim decorations taking over his city, because *after all,* he insisted, *New York really belongs to the Jews.*

"Oh, everything: fruitcake, stollen, mincemeat pies, butter pecan balls, toffee, fudge, peanut brittle."

"Are the butter pecan balls very short and a little salty?" I ask.

"Yes, indeed."

"Those are my favorite. And the mincemeat? Is it real?"

"It's made with meat if that's what you're asking. Bound with suet."

"How big is your kitchen?"

"Small, but it suits me. I take everything one step at a time. Write down a plan before I get started, figure out when I'm going to prepare what, which cookie goes into the oven at which time. Already I've baked over two hundred butter pecan balls and five pounds of peanut brittle. And I made my fruitcakes months ago. They're better if you let them marinate awhile in their own spices."

"My mother was organized like that around her cooking," I say.

Any major holiday—Thanksgiving, say—Mama would decide the exact time we should eat and then she would count the hours back from there, figuring out when the turkey, dressing, sweet potato casserole, green bean casserole, rolls, needed to go into the oven, when the lettuce leaves needed to be washed so they could serve as a base for the cranberry Jell-O salad with walnuts and cream cheese, when she needed to put ice in the glasses, two for each place setting, one for iced tea and one for water. Any detail that had to be tended to, she wrote it down on the schedule. So committed was she to this method of entertaining, she wrote an entire chapter on the art of scheduling in *Gracious Servings.*

"I wouldn't have survived a day working for that fool Augustin without my schedules."

"Our Gus is not big on planning, is he?" I ask.

She presses her lips together. Shakes her head. No. She gives me a sideways smile, as if we are in on a secret together.

We reach the courtyard of the Belthorp. "This is where I live," I say. It still amazes me to get to say that.

"Ooh, I've always loved this building!" Alice says, and I swear she bats her eyes. Gus always insisted Alice was a coquette, and for the first time I know what he is talking about. "From the outside at least. I've never been inside."

"Do you want to come up?" I feel self-conscious asking, as if I am on a first date, but I hope she will say yes. I try to remember whether or not I washed the dishes in the sink or made the bed. "I could fix you a cup of coffee or tea. Warm you up for your walk home."

"I'd really like that, but I'm afraid the delivery boy will arrive before I do. I don't have a doorman."

"Of course, no problem," I say, disappointed. Imagining Alice in my apartment reminds me of how much time I spend alone there.

"Thank you for walking with me," she says. She leans toward me, kisses me on the cheek, her lips soft and dry. She pulls back but remains standing across from me, pressing her lips together, as if contemplating what to say.

"I have always wanted to apologize for being such a pill the day that you cooked lunch for me at the café. I acted terribly. I was jealous, I think, of your talent. Jealous of the attention you were getting. I knew you would become the face of Café Andres, at least for the next generation, and I just let my competitive streak get the best of me. All of my life, I've been bad with transitions, with letting go of the past and moving on to the next thing. It didn't help that I was in between jobs. It didn't help that I was in between relationships, either, and sorting through the messier parts of my life. But that doesn't excuse the fact that I acted like a bitter old woman, and I just want you to know I regret it."

"Thank you for saying that. And surely I was prematurely arrogant, so I can understand why you bristled."

"I heard about the death of your friend, your partner. I am so sorry."

I nod, unable to say anything without starting to cry, which I don't want to do. She kisses me once more on the cheek, before turning to leave.

I walk into the courtyard, passing the empty fountain, passing old candy bar wrappers and soda cans the landlords won't ever clean up because to do so would encourage the tenants with rent control to stay. I am not going to be able to hold on to this place as long as Sebastian did. I find the building's constant state of disarray depressing. And though it was only a moment ago that I felt such a connection to Alice, a cavernous loneliness spreads through my chest, loneliness accompanied by shame. I picture the priest snatching the wafer from my hands, and it makes me shake with embarrassment.

"Bobby! Bobby Banks!"

I turn toward the sound of my name, and there is Alice, waving from across the street. "Why don't you come to my apartment? Help me with my baking?"

"I would, but I've got to . . ." My words taper off. What do I have to do? Nothing. There is nothing I have to do.

"Let me just get a cup of coffee in me and warm up a little. Then I'll head over. What's your address?"

She yells out the building number, and I, committing it to memory, wave good-bye and return to Sebastian's empty apartment, noticing, for the millionth time, how quiet it is when I walk through the door.

As soon as I step into my own kitchen, I remember I have no coffee, having left the beans on the pew of Our Lady of Sorrows. So I fix myself a cup of hot tea instead. Drink it with milk and a little honey, bring it with me into the bathroom, where I study myself in the mirror above the sink. I have been doing this a lot lately, studying my reflection, grooming myself, playing with my curls, rubbing my hands on my facial stubble, trimming the few long hairs that poke out of my nose. Each time I do this I think of the monkeys from Meemaw's nature shows, picking lice off their beloved.

I am no one's beloved but my own.

Same as with Dahlia, grief has painted me with its strange, somber beauty. My dark curly hair, which I now wear short, is beginning to show a few strands of silver. The lines around my eyes are more deeply set. Most startling, my actual eye color has changed, turning so dark it is hard to distinguish the pupil from the iris. I look intense. Weary. And yet, forgive my vanity, handsome. Strange that sissy little Bobby Banks would grow into a handsome man. Though not to be unexpected, I suppose, given how good-looking Daddy always was. I am leaner than I have been in years, with broad shoulders and a cut abdomen. I have an enviable body. The irony, of course, is that I'm not trying for it. Vanity is not my motivator. Escape is. My morning runs and evening sessions at the gym are the only times I can evade thoughts of Sebastian. At the gym I put on my headphones, hit the "play" button on my Walkman, and jump on the stationary bike, pedaling so fast it is as if I'm being chased, pedaling fast enough to stop my thinking. After an hour or so, shirt wet with sweat, I lift weights until my muscles wear out, until I simply cannot lift another thing.

Everything about Alice's building, one of many grand old apartment buildings that grace Riverside Drive, is round instead of angular, including its curved bay windows, which echo the serpentine street below. As I look for her apartment number on the call box outside the building's entryway, a woman in a full-length fox coat rushes out of the building. I hold the door open for her, then walk in myself. There are a few dust bunnies in the corners of the lobby, but otherwise things appear to be fairly orderly. Classic. The floors are laid with black and white tiles, and the brass mailboxes are the old-fashioned kind that open with a key.

Not wanting to arrive at Alice's empty-handed, I brought with me an unopened bottle of Nielsen-Massey vanilla extract and a half-full fifth of Jack Daniel's, left over from a Kentucky Derby party we threw years ago, back when Sebastian was well enough to host such things. Back when Sebastian was well.

Once inside the elevator, I push the button to take me to the fourth floor. On the third, a much older man steps on, wearing a porkpie hat and a striped, skinny tie.

"This is going up," I say.

"I know that, sonny. Believe me, I know."

We stand side by side, each facing the doors, until they open to let me out on Alice's floor. As I step off, the man winks and says, "Lots of nice coeds in this building, sonny. Lots." I wonder if he is going to meet one, possibly in the penthouse. I intend to smile but probably make more of a grimace, and then the elevator doors close and he is gone. I find Alice's door. I can hear music coming from inside her apartment. Nina Simone, whose albums Sebastian introduced me to. (What did Sebastian not introduce me to?) I turn the doorknob and, finding it unlocked, let myself in.

"Hello?" I call, but no one answers.

How can I describe the interior of Alice's apartment as anything but an oasis? I'll start with the smell, which is of oranges, cinnamon, nutmeg, and cloves, reminding me of the Tang tea my mother used to prepare and distribute to our neighbors for Christmas. And then there is the light. Alice's living room faces Riverside Drive, and as this is the last residential street before the park and then the river, there are no neighboring buildings blocking the western light from filtering through the windows, landing in wavy patterns on the wood floors, playing against the patchwork quilt Alice has hung, as if it were a painting, on the ochre wall. "Lilac Wine" plays on the turntable in the living room, the scratch and hiss of the record adding to the sexy sultriness of Nina Simone's voice.

I take a peek into Alice's kitchen, which, though it is only a galley space, looks as if Julia Child designed it. Cabinets are mounted on the left half of the back wall, and on the right is a white pegboard, hung with a full set of cast-iron skillets, from small to large, the outline of each drawn on it, clearly marking where each piece of cooking equipment belongs. There is a metal rack mounted on the ceiling as well, from which hang copper pots. A bumpy strand of garlic hangs from a nail behind the gas stove. The white countertops are remarkably uncluttered for such a small space. There are no gadgets, no microwave, no toaster, no dirty dishes piled by the sink.

Alice emerges from a back room, rubbing lotion into her hands as she walks toward the kitchen, still unaware of my presence. She has changed and is now wearing high-waisted denim pants and a long-sleeved batik print T-shirt, all pinks and blues. She is not wearing a bra, and her breasts move gently beneath her shirt, like slow rolling waves. It occurs to me that even though she is now in her sixties, Alice has the breasts of a thirtysomething woman.

"Miss Alice?"

She looks up, startled, but then smiles. "Lord, you spooked me. I didn't hear you ring."

"Someone was coming out when I arrived."

"Well, welcome. May I get you something to drink? Tea? Irish coffee? A hot buttered rum?"

"You know, as many times as I've heard mention of that drink, I've never actually tasted a hot buttered rum."

"Let me fix you one, then."

It takes her several minutes to prepare. While she fusses with the drink, I further explore her environs, looking at the art on the walls, the framed pictures on the bookshelves and the mantelpiece. Her photographs are impressive. There is Truman Capote, looking straight into the camera, palms outstretched, as if asking for alms. There is Gus Andres when he was a young man, dandyish and dashing, sporting a handlebar mustache, the expression on his face vague and a little sad. There is James Baldwin, his eyes bugging in the picture, not smiling at all. There are several ancient-looking photos, black and white, with perforated edges. One is of a large black family, the men in overalls, the women in loose white dresses, all staring at the camera with a collective look of determination, seeming to say, "We matter."

I recognize Alice in the picture, her posture straight and lovely even as a young girl. Beside her is a boy who looks much like her, only a good six inches taller and with a lighter complexion, noticeable even in the grainy black-and-white print. A chicken perches on his shoulder. The bird's presence does not affect the somber disposition of the family, as if there is nothing unusual about having a chicken be part of a family portrait. And perhaps it *was* natural for that bird to be part of the family portrait, because there is another framed picture of the boy, alone except for the chicken, perched on the same shoulder as before. This picture must have been taken during the winter, for there is snow both on the ground and on the branches of the tree in the background.

"Who's the kid lugging around the rooster?" I ask.

"Hmm?" she asks, walking toward me with a drink in hand. She hands it to me and I take the warm mug gratefully, though when I sip from it I have to force myself not to make a face. I got so carried away by the kitschy name of the drink that I forgot I don't actually care for rum. Or, apparently, hot butter in a cocktail.

"The boy with the chicken," I say, pointing to the photograph.

She looks at the photo, not saying anything, then returns to the kitchen, where she pulls a carton of eggs out of the refrigerator and proceeds to crack them open, one by one, separating them, the whites going in one bowl, the yolks in another.

"She was a hen, not a rooster," she finally says.

"And the boy?"

She removes a bit of egg yolk that got in the bowl of whites, using the cracked edge of a piece of shell to scoop out the errant yellow. "He was my brother," she says.

"He's so handsome," I say softly, not unaware that she said "was" and not "is." "Did chickens just . . . flock to him?"

I roll my eyes at my own unintended pun. She smiles. "Lord, he was something else with animals. Best trapper on the farm. But that chicken. He loved that chicken like a pet. She *was* his pet. Rode around on his shoulder whenever he wasn't working. Hopped off only when she absolutely had to, if James was going to play in a stickball game or something. Waited for him on the sidelines. I don't imagine anyone has ever been as torn up over losing a chicken as James was over that bird."

"What happened?"

"She disappeared one night. Mother told James a wild animal must have taken off with her, but we all knew what really happened when we learned Aunt Sadie served chicken and dumplings for supper that Sunday. Everyone knew Aunt Sadie didn't have any fowl left in her yard and Uncle Sleepy was always getting on James about having a chicken for a pet."

"That's terrible."

Alice shrugs. "Worse things happened."

"To James?" I ask softly.

For a moment Alice doesn't say anything, just keeps cracking eggs, separating the whites from the yolks.

"There was a lynching," she finally says.

"Oh my God. I'm so sorry."

Alice places the final split eggshell, one half pushed inside the other, back into the carton, nestled with the other eleven cracked shells. She grabs a dish towel off the countertop, wipes her hands. "It was a long time ago. Sounds bad to say, I guess, but you move on."

I feel tears push against my eyes, though they aren't for Alice or even her brother. They are for me. One day the memory of Sebastian will fade, and I do not want that to happen. I do not want to move on.

For a moment neither of us says anything.

"What are you making?" I finally ask, needing to change the subject.

"Angel food cake," she says, glancing up at me to smile. "That's what I'm doing with the whites. And then I'll make a big batch of lemon curd with the leftover yolks."

"What a great Christmas gift for somebody."

She shrugs. "I suppose I'll give some jars of the curd away. The angel food cake is for me. I just love having one around. I always add extra vanilla. I'll use some of that wonderful extract you brought. It's such a simple cake; it's a blank slate for whatever you want to add to it."

"What can I help you with?" I ask.

She smiles, lets out a little murmur of pleasure. "It's been a long time since someone asked me that. How nice. Why don't you start by sifting the dry ingredients for the cake onto some waxed paper? The recipe's written on this card here." She taps the stained index card with her finger. "I always double sift the flour for this kind of cake. You want it light as it can be."

I set about scooping flour from the canister and shaking it through the sifter. I love the way it falls in a white snowy drift on the wax paper. I think of the boy in the picture with the chicken, snow all around. I think of how proud he looks. How confident.

"Back when Alpheus was around, he would try to help out in the kitchen, but usually we would just end up getting in a fight. I swear we almost got divorced over the fact that he wouldn't remove the green fibers from inside the garlic cloves he was chopping. We did get divorced, eventually, but not over that."

Right. Alice was married. I learned that at some point, but I forgot, imagining her instead as a solo unit, a trail of discarded lovers in her wake. I must have given her a quizzical look, because she responds as if I spoke my thoughts aloud.

"Don't go being surprised that I was a married woman!"

"No, of course not. It's just, there's so much about you I'd like to know."

She smiles.

"So what happened between you and your husband? I'm sorry, is that rude to ask?"

"Alpheus was what you call a tortured soul. He couldn't help but be angry. And for good reason. Not long after he was discharged from the army, having served two tours of duty, mind you, he was in Midtown, enjoying a cigarette before heading to work. A young officer approached, told Alpheus to 'move it along.' Called Alpheus 'boy.' When Alpheus didn't move fast enough, the officer clubbed him. Split his head right open. This to a war hero."

"That's horrible."

"It was. But my sympathy regarding his past only seemed to make him more agitated. And then he would attack me for what he saw as my complacency. He simply could not understand the ambiguities I lived with. Like how I loved cooking at Café Andres, even though I was uncomfortable being the token Negro. Or how I went to parties even though I knew I got invited just so that white folks could say it was an integrated evening. And the hell he gave me for being engaged to a white man once upon a time—good Lord. Even though I didn't go through with the marriage precisely because my fiancé was white."

I want to ask more but don't want to pry. The music has stopped and a silence permeates the apartment. I walk into the living room, flip the record, and place the needle in the groove. And there is Nina's voice again, filling the air.

The secret to angel food cake, says Alice, is not to let the whites get too stiff, to stop beating them while they are still a little loose and have just turned glossy. The curd is trickier. You have to get it hot enough so that it thickens and turns to custard, yet not so hot that the egg yolks scramble. Alice places a metal cooling rack on top of the stovetop burner to further elevate the custard mixture from the heat, which she stirs constantly. I lean against the counter, glass of wine in hand—Alice quickly deduced that I did not like the hot buttered rum and immediately offered me an alternative—so we can continue talking while she stirs.

This is the best I've felt in a long time. It is like being back in Meemaw's kitchen, except with wine to drink and better music playing in the background. (Meemaw never met a contemporary Christian album she did not love.) While Alice stirs, she, unsolicited, tells me more about her first almost husband, whom she met in 1948, when she was thirty-one and already making a name for herself at the café.

"He was Jewish," she says. "Grew up in Queens. His mother hated me. His whole family hated me. And my family would have hated him, too, if I had ever brought him down to North Carolina. But how could I have? We wouldn't have even been allowed to sit in the same section of the train once we were south of D.C., not to mention the fact that if we had gone through with the marriage it would have been illegal in my home state.

"When we first fell in love, we were so naïve. We met at the café and we tricked ourselves into believing that the world would react to us the same way that Gus and Randall and all of those crazy writers and artists and bohemians did. We made this little world inside Café Andres that didn't match anything going on outside, and then we believed the force of our love could change people's opinions. We believed the force of our love would right all wrongs."

"But sometimes love isn't enough," I say. I wish I did not believe this, but it feels true. I think of the Edenic pleasure with Pete Arnold before my parents exiled us from the Garden, of Sebastian's body, covered with lesions, and how neither my love nor Dahlia's, no matter how strong, could save him. Of my pure yearning that morning at the church and how once again I was refused God's love, this time in the shape of a wafer.

"I tried to take communion at a Catholic church this morning. It was on impulse. I didn't know what I was doing, and the priest, recognizing my ignorance, snatched the wafer from my hand."

"That doesn't surprise me," says Alice.

She dips her wooden spoon into the lemon curd. When she pulls the spoon back up, the curd clings to its back. "This is done," she remarks, moving the pot off the burner.

"What was surprising was how much I wanted to be offered it. I grew up in the Church. Baptist, not Catholic, but still. And sure, looking back I can see how narrow that world was, but . . . I don't know. I loved the way I felt about God when I was a child. The universe was good, and God loved me and I belonged. Like how you speak of the café back in its heyday, how it was this special place where life was elevated somehow. That was how church was for me, and I keep trying to find that place again, and I just—I keep getting smacked down. I'm like Charlie Brown trying to kick the football, and Lucy keeps snatching it away."

She turns to look at me, and I feel a crackling of electricity between us, connection. "I'm not religious," she says. "Not by a long shot. But it seems to me that the priest you encountered believes in a small god, a god that can be shrunk inside a cracker that was produced in a factory somewhere and sold in bulk. It seems to me that you need a God bigger than that, and I don't think you should let your experience today stop you from looking for it. You understand what I'm saying?"

"Yes, ma'am," I say, needing to be a little boy again, comforted by this woman who reminds me of my meemaw, whose God, it occurs to me, was so big as to be uncontainable.

"Now look, Sunday is my bread day. I've got challah dough rising in the refrigerator. Do you know how to braid it?"

"I've never done it, but I'm a quick study."

"Well then, let me show you how it's done."

I learn a lot from Alice that afternoon, but one simple lesson is that, even though it slows down the process, letting bread dough rise in the refrigerator gives a more fully flavored, balanced loaf. But this means that after taking the challah dough out of the fridge we have to let it sit on the kitchen counter for about an hour while it comes to room temperature. In the meantime, I help Alice clean the dishes, pour the curd into little jars with rubberized lids, and pull the angel food cake out of the oven. As soon as it's out she inverts the cake over an empty soda bottle so it will cool evenly.

When the challah dough is ready Alice dusts the countertop with flour, then divides the dough into six pieces and rolls each piece into a strand. She brings all six strands together, then shows me how to braid them, starting with an outside one and crossing it over two inner ones before tucking it underneath, then doing the same thing on the other side. The dough feels so good in my hands, springy and smooth and elastic.

"Did your Jewish fiancé teach you how to make this?" I ask as I tuck the longer strands under the end of a loaf.

"Lord, no. He was an eater, not a cook. That was actually one of the fun things about our romance: I got to cook for him. He did take me to the great New York delis, though, introduced me to all of the classic Eastern European Jewish foods. I can't tell you how many bowls of matzo ball soup I ate when we ended our engagement. Only thing that comforted me."

"God, me too. The month after Sebastian died, matzo ball soup was all I could stomach. I would go to Zabar's every day, sit at the counter, eat the ball with my fork, then lift the bowl to my mouth and just suck down the broth. It got so that the guys behind the counter would know to heat up a bowl for me the moment they saw me come in."

"I have a good matzo ball recipe," Alice says. "I use duck fat instead of chicken fat."

"I can't imagine you cooking anything that's not wonderful," I say.

She smiles. "Cooking is the one thing that has never failed me."

It is late by the time we pull the loaves of challah out of the oven, one dotted with raisins, one sprinkled with poppy seeds. By then the sweet smell of honey and yeast has filled the apartment. By then we are on our second bottle of wine and have played album after album on the turntable. We listen to Miles Davis's *Kind of Blue* as we wait for the bread to cool, just enough to handle. Alice pulls down two small white plates, painted around the periphery with sweet little pink flowers. She keeps her butter in a little pot on the counter, so it is room temperature, spreadable. She sets out a butter knife, and honey stored in a bear-shaped bottle.

She pulls open the challah with her hands. Steam rushes out, and the sweet yeasty smell intensifies. She hands me a strand of the warm loaf, puts it into my cupped palms.

"Here," she says. "Take."

I spread a thick layer of butter on the hot bread, pour honey on top of that. I bring it to my mouth, warm and dripping with sweetness.

I wait to swallow before saying to Alice, "This is divine."

Part Three

Amelia in Connecticut

13

Empty Nest

(Old Greenwich, Connecticut, 1989)

Late last night I returned home from my trip down to Atlanta, where I was helping our older daughter, Lucy, move into her freshman dorm at Emory University. Two weeks earlier my husband, Cam, and I dropped off Mandy, our youngest, at boarding school. Even though I was a boarding school kid myself, I was disheartened when Mandy asked if she could apply to Hotchkiss, then begged to be allowed to attend once she was accepted. While I had *needed* to escape my parents' home, I liked to believe I had created a warm, safe nest for our daughters, a place I might have to give them a gentle push to dislodge them from. But that was not to be. Mandy flew out prematurely, and even our shy Lucy turned and headed back toward her dormitory before I had even pulled the rental car away from the curb.

Despite the melancholy I feel over the absence of our daughters, I decide to approach our first official night as empty nesters as a celebratory occasion. I take a cue from the playbook of Taffy, my southern mother-in-law, setting the table with good china, cloth napkins, the sterling silver that Taffy insisted Cam and I register for when we got engaged, the Baccarat crystal. I light the long white candles in the silver candleholders. I prepare Cam's favorite meal: steak with béarnaise sauce, twice-baked potatoes, green beans sautéed in butter with almond slivers, and vanilla ice cream with homemade chocolate sauce for dessert.

Cam doesn't speak much during dinner, other than to comment that everything is delicious. He wears his pin-striped suit from work, his red tie still on. I keep stealing glances at him, as if we are on a first date and I am trying to discover who he is. He is almost a handsome man. I mean, he is handsome, in that he dresses well and keeps in shape and has green eyes with long lashes. But his forehead is too wide and there is a beefiness to his lips that always makes me think of Vienna sausages. They're strange things, those Vienna sausage lips. They are sexy to kiss, warm and thick and molten. Cam can get me wet just by kissing. But they indicate petulance.

After dinner, as I begin cleaning up, Cam lets our dog, Sadie, into the backyard for her nightly pee. We had another dog, Cleo, who died a few months ago, a reality I have not entirely adjusted to. Sometimes I'll look at the couch and see Cleo lying on the back cushions, or see her little face pressed against the lowest of the windowpanes that frame the back door. It is so natural to see her waiting to be let in that I will head to the door to do so and then, halfway there, realize that what I saw was an illusion, a trick, the brain filling in what it expects to see, creating substance out of nothing at all.

Cam clears the rest of the table while I start rinsing off dishes; then he goes to the door to let in the dog.

"Sadie?" Cam holds the back door open as he calls her name again and again. It is September, and the weather is already turning. The hair on my arms lifts as cold air floats into the kitchen.

"Goddamn it," mutters Cam, and without putting on a jacket

he ventures outside. I hear my husband call Sadie's name once more before the door shuts behind him. By the time Cam and Sadie return I have loaded the dishwasher and am wiping down the countertops with Fantastik.

"Hey, naughty puppy," I say as Sadie darts to her water bowl, taking great gulps from it.

"You left the back gate open," Cam says, his voice devoid of warmth.

I feel my throat tighten as he plants himself in the middle of the kitchen, hands on hips.

"I did?"

"She was all the way down in the Fergusons' yard, Amelia. You have got to be more careful. I mean, good God, was it not enough to kill Cleo?"

It takes a moment for my brain to catch up. Did he actually just say that? Reference the terrible thing that occurred a few months ago, last June, while I was cleaning out the car, parked in the driveway?

It was midmorning, and I had just returned to the house from the gym, where I had signed up for a low-impact aerobics class with the hope that it would help me work off the extra twenty pounds I've put on over the last few years. (Since I hit my forties, everything I eat seems to stick to me, which is particularly aggrieving considering how much I love to cook, how it is the thing that soothes me when I have had a bad day.) My car was pretty junked up, so I decided to take a moment to clean it out, leaving the driver's side door open while I took takeaway boxes from Alpen Pantry, candy wrappers, apple cores, and Diet Coke cans to the trash bin by the side of the house.

Cleo, our little Houdini of a poodle, must have somehow gotten out of the fenced backyard and, while I wasn't looking, jumped into the car.

I didn't realize she was in there. I was distracted. Cam and I had fought the night before, and I could not get some of the things he said out of my mind. That he was tired of our lives. That he was bored. That he wondered if maybe we should call it a day, leave the messy past behind, start over. (I argued with him in my head: *I thought you liked our messy life, the comfort of it, the ease of not having to be perfect all the time, like you were expected to be when you were a child, of letting the dogs get on the couch, of eating ice cream from the carton, of leaving the* Sunday Times *scattered over the couch so you can settle in and read whenever you want.)*

After cleaning out the Volvo I had gone inside, taken a shower, blow-dried my hair, puttered around. Hours later I returned to the car. Mandy had spent the night at a friend's house, and I was running late to pick her up.

The moment I slid into the driver's seat I was overwhelmed by a terrible odor, a smell that reminded me of the time Mandy forgot to take in her container of leftovers from the restaurant and her half-eaten roast chicken stayed in the hot car all the next day. I glanced over my shoulder to see if there were any telltale take-out containers. And just as it occurred to me that there couldn't be, because I would have already cleaned them out, I saw Cleo, my sweet puppy, curled in a semicircle on the floor mat below the backseat. I did not need to touch the animal's body to know that she was dead. She had shrunk and was lying in a shallow pool of water, water from her own desiccated body. I reached out my hand to touch her anyway. She was stiff, her curly hair hard and lacquered.

Oh God. Oh God.

I opened the door of the front seat, jumped from the car, crying, wailing. Oh God, my poor dog. I imagined her bounding into the car, so happy to surprise me—and then becoming confused when she realized I was not coming to get her. Growing hotter and hotter. Starting to pant she was so hot. Jumping to the floor to get out of the awful heat, but the heat would have been unrelenting.

It was June. It was an unusually hot day for Connecticut.

I needed to go pick up my daughter. I was late already. But I could not bring myself to touch Cleo's body again, to remove her from the car. And besides, it would be cruel to pick Mandy up in a car smelling of our animal's death. I could take Lucy's car, the wood-paneled Wagoneer we'd had since she was born. But that would mean leaving Cleo in the Volvo for longer, untended to. And though Cleo was and would remain dead, it seemed wrong to leave her in the spot she had died for any longer than necessary.

But then I remembered: If Lucy's car was there that meant Lucy was home. And if Lucy was home that meant she could pick up Mandy at her friend's house. I felt hysterical for one more moment, but as is often the case when I am in crisis, I went into survival mode. Went inside, dialed the home of Mandy's friend, spoke to her mother. Held back my tears while I explained that I was running a little late, that there was a crisis I had to attend to, that my older daughter, Lucy, was actually coming in my place and would be there as soon as she could.

The woman on the other line simply clicked her tongue and said she hoped everything turned out okay. That's the thing about Daughters of the American Revolution types—they value reserve above all else. A patrician matron will never pester you for personal details. Such reserve has always driven Cam crazy, he who was born and raised in Atlanta by the effusive and gossipy Taffy. (Give my husband one drink and he'll launch into a litany of complaints about living "up north." Connecticut winters top the list, with "Yankee manners and mannerisms" falling close behind.)

I went to Lucy's room, asked my lithe, limpid daughter if she would pick up her sister, gave her twenty dollars so the two of them could stop for a treat, then shut myself in my bedroom, where I watched from the window until I saw Lucy's car turn out of the driveway. Once the car disappeared from view, I sat on the edge of the bed and dialed Cam at his office. The instant his secretary put him through I started crying again, crying hard enough that Cam had to ask me several times to slow down, to take a breath, to repeat myself until he finally understood what it was I was trying to say.

Once he did I heard him take a deep inhale, and then I heard a sudden exhale, and I knew that he was crying, too.

"I'm so sorry," I said, and as the words came out of my mouth it occurred to me that neither of us had apologized for the terrible things we had said to each other the night before.

"Oh, honey," he said. "It's not your fault."

His tenderness rushed over me, a balm that soothed my still open wounds.

"I was careless," I said, starting to cry afresh. "I was not paying attention. I was lost in my head."

"You didn't see her. She jumped in the car when you weren't looking. There's no way you could have predicted that was going to happen. She wasn't supposed to be there."

I thought of Cleo eagerly waiting for me in the car, wagging her tail in anticipation of a ride. I thought of the black leather interior, how it matched her hair, how disguised she was against it. I thought of how hot she must have been, how she must have suffered. I started crying those great, rolling sobs, the ones that take over your body, like when a plane flies through turbulence, only internal. So instead of passing through the rough air, you must let the disturbance pass through you. You must wait until the intensity of the grief lifts.

"Look, it's a fairly light day at the office. I can cut out early. Why don't I come on home?"

"Yes, yes, please. She's still in the car and I just don't know if I can bear to move her. I'm so sorry, Cam."

"Okay, sit tight. I'm coming."

• • •

God bless him, when Cam showed up he took over. Got an old towel, scooped up the dog, rolled her in it like a shroud. He tried to dig a hole in the backyard so we could bury her, but it had been a dry summer and the ground was too hard. So Cam put Cleo's body in a cardboard box, the kind you pack books in, and we taped it up and left it in the outermost area of the backyard while he called around looking for a crematorium that could take her remains. He found one and drove the body there that afternoon. (Later, when I went to pick up the ashes, I was given a squat tin box filled with sticky gray dust, littered with bits of white bone.)

I fixed peanut butter and jelly sandwiches for dinner that night, serving them with milk and Lay's potato chips. As we were finishing our meal I told the girls Cam and I had some news to share that wasn't going to be easy to hear.

"You're getting a divorce, aren't you?" said Mandy. She held her fork in front of her, studying its tines casually, looking bored.

Cam and I looked at each other and I saw the answer clear in his eyes. No. No, we were not.

In bed that night Cam held me tight, and his holding led to us making love, and it was more tender and affectionate and fun than it had been for a very long while. I felt he was present in that room with me, at that moment. I felt that we were connected bone deep, pelvis to pelvis and beyond. I looked down at his soft green eyes while I rocked on top of him, and he murmured my name with such warmth, such openness; it broke my heart. It broke my heart to think of how detached we had become from each other. Afterward I rested my head on his shoulder, and he told me what a good life we had given Cleo, how Cleo enjoyed every minute of her existence, our cute black poodle who loved nothing more than to roll in the warm dirt.

Cam was so tender with me that I came to believe that Cleo had died to save our marriage, that Cleo had become a sort of canine Christ figure. Ridiculous, I know, but because of her death, and Cam's generous reaction to it, our union was renewed. For a long time I had felt so very alone in my marriage. For a long time I had felt unseen, just a middle-aged woman with no one's focus upon her.

But now this: resurrection.

And yet with Cam eventually you pay.

"I'm sorry I left the gate open," I say, burying my own sense of injustice, thinking that if I could unearth all that I've buried I would have something very lethal on hand. "Let's not fight. Please. I just got back in town. Let's find something good to watch on TV. Or if you want, we could go into town, get ice-cream cones."

"Fine," he says, walking into the living room and turning on the television. I am both surprised and relieved that he backed down. We watch junk until *L.A. Law* comes on, a program we both love. We sit side by side on the sofa. At one point I stretch out and put my feet in his lap, as we have done for countless nights of our marriage. During a commercial I make microwave popcorn, splitting the bag between two bowls. I keep glancing at him, smiling, trying to get him to connect with me, but he stares straight ahead, his jaw locked. He doesn't have to say anything to let me know he is still angry. When the show ends I stand to take our empty bowls to the kitchen. He follows me.

"I'm extremely upset with you," he says.

It is now eleven at night. Yesterday I left my older daughter in a city over a thousand miles away.

"Cam. I'm exhausted. I need you to consider that maybe I'm going through a hard time right now with both Lucy and Mandy gone."

"You don't think I go through a hard time every day?"

Oh Jesus. Here we go again. I must have rolled my eyes, because it is as if suddenly someone struck a match and let it drop on the spilled gas all around us. He starts screaming.

"You don't think I miss my daughters, too? And then when I call in my dog, she is on the loose, could have been run over, could have gotten lost."

"You found her!" I yell. "She was at the Fergusons'! She's always at the Fergusons'. She digs up their compost pile; you know that."

"And you know that, too! How could you leave the gate open knowing that? I need better from you, Amelia. I need you to take some responsibility. Notice if the dog jumps in the car. Notice if the back gate is unlocked. Notice when the bills are due, dammit. When I came home tonight I saw a stack of unopened mail on the counter, from days back. It was the electric bill, the water bill, the mortgage. Jesus, Amelia. Keeping up with this shit is part of your job."

"I was away!" I scream, the sound so primal Sadie jumps up and trots out of the room, allowing Cam to give me a look of absolute reprobation. I lower my voice. "I was taking our daughter to college. God, what is wrong with you?"

He lowers his voice. "You want to know what's wrong with me? You want to know what's wrong? When was the last time you looked in the mirror, Amelia? You're twenty-five pounds overweight. You are. You can wear oversized sweaters and scarves all you want, you can bandy about words like 'earth mama' and 'goddess,' but the truth is, you let yourself get fat. It's like, you've given up. You've stopped trying. But you know what? Just because you've stopped trying doesn't change the fact that I'm still a man and I still have needs. Yes, Amelia, you may not want to acknowledge it, but I still have needs. And I'm not ready to sign on for celibacy for the rest of my life just because you've given up. You didn't even look at me when you returned home from Atlanta last night. You just went upstairs and started unpacking your bags, as if I were nothing. As if I were a piece of furniture in the house. But I'm not. I am a man and I need sex. I do! I need it, Amelia. I need sex! I need sex!"

I find myself splitting into two women while he screams, the one crying and overwhelmed, the other separate and analytical, floating above the scene, noting the spit on the sides of this man's mouth, noting how flushed his face is, trying to piece together how this night, which began with such good intentions, disintegrated into something so ugly, so mean. I think of the underwear I carefully put on before dinner, a taupe-colored bra and panty set, made in Paris, expensive and frilly. I had been planning to seduce my husband after dinner. It occurs to me that perhaps I should still attempt to do so, that maybe everything would be all right if we just had sex. (It *has* been a long time.) But the thought of intimacy with this furious man makes me want to cover my most vulnerable parts with my hands.

I do not sleep in our room but instead crawl into Lucy's old bed. I am restless and agitated, but I must finally doze off because I am awoken by loud and incessant noises coming from Cam's and my shared bathroom. I wait for them to cease, but they do not, and so finally I go to investigate, tying my robe around my middle as I make my way to the bathroom where Cam stands in boxers and a white undershirt, opening the medicine cabinet and slamming it shut, over and over again.

"Oh my God, did you take pills?" I ask. I have this vision sometimes of Cam downing a bottle of Tylenol. What I don't know is whether the vision is a fear or a fantasy.

"I'm furious with you, Amelia. I'm just furious."

I bring my hand to my forehead, rub my temples. I breathe in and out, trying to stay calm. "I really need you to calm down. We both need to sleep."

"I need you to apologize," he says.

"For what?" I ask. I am not trying to be petulant, exactly, I just want him to tell me what to apologize for, so I can do it and then go back to Lucy's room, away from him.

He grabs a plastic bottle of Pepto-Bismol out of the medicine cabinet and throws it to the floor, where it lands with a small bounce in the corner of the room. He grabs his razor off the shelf and throws it. The blade pops off as soon as it hits the ground. He follows this by throwing the can of shaving cream, as if the razor blade needs a companion. While I am startled, a small voice in my head says wearily, *Such drama.*

"If you don't know what I'm upset about then we are in real trouble."

I take a deep breath, hold up my hands, surrendering. "Look. I'm sorry I was careless about the dog. I'm sorry I let myself go. I'm sorry we did not have sex when I got back in town last night."

I feel nauseated saying the words, but I need him to calm down. All I want is to return to Lucy's bedroom, to lock the door behind me and burrow under the covers. To allow sleep to take me away from here, away from this house, this man.

"What else?" he asks. His voice is tight and mean, the voice of a stubborn little boy.

"I have to go to bed," I say. My eyes feel sandy I am so tired.

"I'm so upset with you," he says again. "I'm just steaming."

He says this almost as if it is a point of wonder, something the two of us should be very, very interested in, as one might be interested in watching some other natural phenomenon: a solar eclipse, a chick hatching from its soft shell, an autumn moon, round and maternal.

I return to Lucy's room. There is a lock on the door and I turn it. I lie in bed, so tired but unable to relax enough to sleep. Finally I pull a novel from Lucy's bookshelf, *Crossing to Safety* by Wallace Stegner. I read and read and read, losing myself in the sane, quiet lives of good, decent people, people who try to do well by each other despite their innate failings. When I finally fall asleep I dream that Cam enters the room, carrying a wooden hairbrush, much like the one Mother used to spank me with as a child.

"All you have to do is lie there and take it," he says.

And in my dream I think: *I can do that. I can lie here and take it, and nothing will have to change.*

When I wake the next morning Cam has already left for work. I try to imagine that I dreamed the whole fight, but I spot *Crossing to Safety* on the pillow beside me and I know that I did not.

Attempting to go about my morning routine, I make my way down to the kitchen for cereal and coffee. My hand shakes as I try to measure the grinds into the coffeemaker. Is this really my life? I let Sadie out, but not before first walking through the wet, dewy grass and checking the back gate to make sure it is closed, pulling hard on the handle again and again, unsure of my very perception, until a voice much like my own but older, wiser, maternal, speaks to me, saying, *It's closed; it's closed. Just walk away, Amelia, it's closed.* I am spooked. I am fundamentally shaken. I wonder what would have happened had the girls been home. Surely Cam would not have behaved that way, would not have screamed and thrown toiletries in the middle of the night. And then a terrible thought enters my mind: *Now that there's no one else around to witness, he can do whatever he wants.*

I have to talk to someone. I am close with Lucy, but of course I cannot tell my daughter about this. Mother is useless, pickled in our old home in Roxboro, doing God knows what all day (nothing) before beginning her evening cocktails. Daddy is in Palo Alto, in a time zone three hours behind, and besides, he and I never talk about anything personal. Sarah, my best friend from boarding school, lives in Brooklyn. I could call her, but . . . I'm embarrassed. I'm embarrassed to tell her what happened, embarrassed to let her know how much my marriage has deteriorated. Sarah—who never married—would not let a man yell at her the way Cam yells at me. She would knee him in the balls first. I sip my coffee. Try to think of who might best guide me through this. And then the answer comes to me. Of course. I'll call Aunt Kate.

Kate is Mother's sister, younger by over a decade, who lives in Manhattan and works as an editor at Palmer, Long and McIntyre. She was the rogue of Mother's patrician clan, renting an apartment in the West Village when she first moved into the city (later she settled on the Upper East Side), boldly declaring that while she liked children, she had no intention of ever having any, and marrying a boisterous Jewish writer. ("And not one of the good German Jews," my bigoted grandmother was rumored to have said, "but one of those *–skis* from Poland.")

As I girl I vowed to emulate Aunt Kate's enthusiastic approach to life, rather than Mother's bipolar one, Mother who swings from overeager to sullen. And I began by choosing an exuberant man to marry—albeit a backslapping southern boy rather than a Brooklyn Jew. Still, both my husband and Kate's are known for being hotheads. Meaning Kate, more than anyone I know, will understand what I'm going through.

Though it's just a little past nine, I dial Kate at work. I know she likes to get there earlier than everybody else so she can read manuscripts uninterrupted. She picks up the phone on the second ring, and I ask if she has a moment, telling her that Cam and I fought and I need to talk about it. She tells me of course, that she has a 9:45 breakfast, but I'm all hers until then. I try to be thorough but succinct in my telling of last night's events. I am surprisingly unemotional, only tearing up once, when I recount how Cam told me

I had let myself get fat. She murmurs sounds of affirmation, so I know she is listening, so I know she is there. When I finish I hear her exhale, and I know that she is thinking of how to respond. I know that I have been heard. After a moment of silence, she suggests that I come stay with her and Jack for a few days in the city, just until Cam cools down.

"Who would take care of Sadie?" I ask.

"A kennel, maybe?"

"I just can't imagine telling Cam, 'Guess what? I'm locking up your dog at great expense while I go and stay with Kate in the city.'"

"Bring her to the apartment then. She and Lulu can play."

"And take Cam's dog from him?"

"You're awfully concerned about Cam," she says.

"Well, he's clearly in a bad place."

"Yes," she says. "I agree with you on that."

"Look," I say, already feeling calmer just from having told the story aloud, "We all know marriage is hard. We all know that sometimes you burn the house down and have to start all over. Stay married even a year and you know that."

"Forgive my bluntness, dear, but if you are locking your bedroom door at night so that your husband can't get to you, that is not okay."

"You and Jack fight."

"No. Not like that. I'm sure we could if we let ourselves, but we choose not to."

I snort, wanting to say something like "Well, three cheers for you." Instead I try to clean up the mess I have spread before her. "Look. I'm sorry. I'm exhausted. I'm sad about the girls leaving. And Cam's been struggling at work a lot. And I'm thinking that both the girls having left for school is probably affecting him more than he realized. And also, I only got together with Taffy for one night when I was down in Atlanta, and I bet she gave him all sorts of hell for that. I know she was hurt that Lucy and I weren't staying with her and the Judge in Brookwood Hills, that we got a hotel room near the college."

"You do a wonderful job finding excuses for his appalling behavior," she says.

"Kate. This is my life. This is my husband. What am I supposed to do? Divorce Cam after twenty years of marriage? What would I even do?"

"There's an editorial assistant position opening up at PLM. It's yours if you want it."

I let out a little bark of a laugh, though I'm not amused. "Do you think that's realistic? That I'm going to start answering the phones along with the other twenty-two-year-old assistants? That I'm going to move into a converted railroad apartment on Eighty-first and Second and share it with four other girls? Kate, I'm forty-three."

"You can stay with us. For as long as you need, dear."

I start to cry. I might want to leave my husband, but I do not want to leave my comfortable house, my good, loyal dog, my well-equipped kitchen, outfitted with everything I need to make fabulous meals. I do not want to have to depend on the kindness of Kate, who has started lecturing once again, saying things I am only half listening to.

". . . is going through an emotional disturbance that is putting you in danger. I don't think it would have been unreasonable for you to call the police."

Call the police? On Cam? Over a fight? Over a bottle of Pepto thrown in the night? I can just imagine our neighbors coming to their front doors to see about the blue lights flashing in our driveway. I can just imagine the questions I would be fielding today: *Was there a break-in? A theft? Did you hear something? Are the girls alright?*

"Look, I need to go," I say.

"I know you don't want to hear this, but I'm really worried about you."

"I wish you could just listen. Be supportive."

"How supportive is it for me to listen, knowing that you don't recognize the danger you are in?"

"My husband is not dangerous!" I say.

"Listen," says Kate. "I have to get off. I don't want to, but I'm already running late for this breakfast and I simply must be there. My apartment is open to you if you want it. I love you and I'm worried for you and I think you are running hard from the truth of your situation. I think you need to look at how your husband made you feel last night. I think you need to consider how you would feel were he to treat one of your girls this way. I think you should consider being as protective of yourself as you are of your daughters. And now I have got to go. I love you."

She hangs up on her end, and I am alone in my house again. I hold the phone until it starts beeping angrily at me, and then I keep holding it, waiting. By the time the line is dead, I understand the following:

1) Kate always tells the truth.
2) If Kate is telling the truth, I have to leave my husband.
3) I don't want to leave Cam. Not now. Not yet.

And so I resolve to stop speaking to Kate, taking a grim satisfaction in knowing that I'm certainly not the first in my family to come to this decision.

14

Family Tradition

(Old Greenwich, Connecticut, 1989)

Mother is only on speaking terms with Kate about half of the year. The other half she proclaims that her little sister is too much of a judgmental prude to have anything to do with, this because Kate repeatedly tells Mother she drinks too much.

Whereas Mother vacillates between speaking with Kate and giving her The Silent Treatment (a punishment I'm not at all sure Kate minds), when Daddy and Kate had their falling-out—years ago—that was that. At least, I presume that was that. I can't imagine Daddy bothered to reconcile with his estranged wife's little sister after he moved to Northern California.

Before their falling-out, Kate and Daddy were good friends. Indeed, I imagine Mother felt they were too friendly with each other. Daddy was loose around Kate, looser than he was with anyone else. She could tease him, could poke at his pretensions, like how he held a sip of wine in his mouth for what seemed like forever, all the while sucking in, "aerating" it, he said, to bring out its full flavor.

"The full flavor of your saliva," Kate would say. Daddy would arch his left brow at her but smile slightly. Kate also needled Daddy about his refusal to eat a fresh tomato unless it was summertime, and even then he was really picky, insisting it had to be from some nearby garden or farm.

"I hear you, I really do," Kate said. "But c'mon, isn't it *sometimes* okay to buy a supermarket tomato? I mean, one from D'Agostino's if you're craving a BLT?"

"A pale comparison to the real thing," intoned Daddy, and Kate would snort.

Often when Kate and Jack visited she and Daddy would cook dinner while Jack and I played chess and Mother drank cocktails and smoked. It was impossible for Daddy and Kate to actually cook a dish together; their styles were too different and they would have fought. Their strategy was to divide and conquer. Usually Daddy would fix the main course and Kate would make an appetizer and dessert. Daddy approached his kitchen the way a scientist approaches a lab: with careful observation, exact measurements, and fanatical hygiene. (Daddy was always washing up.) Kate had an aversion to washing dishes and was forever finding ways to use fewer and fewer bowls and utensils. Early in her marriage to Jack, she dedicated an entire afternoon to figuring out an accurate way to measure by hand. She would start with a quarter of a teaspoon and go up from there, measuring that amount of salt into her hand, throwing it out, measuring that amount again, throwing it out, doing it again and again and again until her hand was as reliable as a ring of measuring spoons.

Studying Daddy in conversation with Kate at the dinner table, I knew he would have been a happier man had he married someone like her, someone with whom he could discuss recipes, New York opera, gardening. Jack listened, bemused, as Kate and Daddy bantered, playing a verbal game of tennis. Mother listened, too, though I don't think she heard much of anything. Her listening was a performance: She widened her eyes in exaggerated effect, clutched the arm of whoever was seated next to her, threw her head back to laugh at the only mildly funny thing someone said.

When forced to socialize with anyone but Jack and Kate, Daddy would usually rise to the occasion, but like Mother, he was always performing. I never learned anything new about Daddy from any of the stories he shared at the infrequent parties he and Mother hosted for their Connecticut neighbors; instead he trotted out the same half-dozen anecdotes again and again. He was affable but scripted. And then as the guests departed, he retracted his gregariousness, folding his charm up inside himself, the way Mother could shrink the dining room table by removing the extra leaf and pushing together the two ends.

I think Daddy loves me. I am almost sure he does. But he is so cerebral, so private; he does not know how to show it. Growing up I experienced his love through eating his food. Every Sunday Daddy baked, so that we would have bread for the upcoming week. I longed to bake with him, for us to stand side by side in our kitchen, me on a step stool so I could reach the counter as we pressed the springy dough in our hands, exchanging shy smiles while Mother was banished to some far-off room. But for Daddy, baking was a solitary endeavor. He would put on classical music and shut the door to the kitchen. Except in the very coldest months, he would tend his garden while the dough rose, then return inside for a drink and more Beethoven as he kneaded the dough and let it rise again. A monk in his chambers, he was not to be disturbed, no matter how fervently I wished he would invite me in.

I imagine that over the years many women have longed for him in a similarly achy manner, even though, technically, he and Mother are still married, never having secured a legal divorce. I imagine that even when Daddy was still living in Connecticut he had affairs. He was—still is, surely, though it has been years since I last saw him—handsome and brilliant, a Yale-educated MD who studies genetics. He devoted his life to his research lab, a place that remained as distant and mysterious to me as Manhattan, which was only two and a half hours away from Roxboro but could have been in another solar system for all I knew of it as a child. Until Aunt Kate moved to the city after college and insisted I visit her, I was never, ever taken there. Not to see the Rockettes at Christmas, not to ice-skate at Rockefeller Center, not to see the dinosaur bones at the Museum of Natural History. When I pushed on Mother for an explanation she replied that we lived in the country for a reason and it was the same reason we stayed out of New York.

"But you once lived in Manhattan!" I said. "At the Barbizon Hotel."

"Well, that was enough to teach me that the city isn't a place for little girls," Mother replied. End of conversation. She was only slightly less reserved on the subject of how she and Daddy first met, though I begged her to tell me all about it, desperate to imagine that my parents had once been in love.

"We happened to both be on the Metro-North," she would say. "Leaving Grand Central Station. That was back when I was a working girl in the city and your father was in medical school. I stayed with my parents in Roxboro over the weekends, and your father was heading back to Yale. He sat by me, and we got to talking. And I guess I was just so interested in what he had to say that I missed my transfer. Had to take the train all the way to New Haven, where your father bought me a cup of coffee, then drove me back to Mummy and Dad's, over an hour away. From that moment on, I knew he was a gentleman."

Except he wasn't. At least not by the standards of Mother's

hoity-toity clan. Daddy, the orphaned child of Italian emigrants, was an upstart. Daddy's parents entered the country through Ellis Island, but instead of remaining in the city, they made their way across America, having heard rumors of vineyards in California, owned and run by other Italians. And indeed, when they first arrived in the Central Valley they found steady work at a vineyard, but by the time Daddy was a young man the Depression had sunk the country and he and his parents could only find migrant work in the fruit trees. When Daddy was sixteen, his father died of pneumonia. His mother, heartbroken, died shortly after. Daddy, orphaned and alone, decided to hell with California and train-hopped across the country, finally arriving in Manhattan, where he was soon taken in by an Italian family who helped him secure a series of jobs, including working as a busboy at a trattoria in the West Village while he started college at NYU. When the Americans entered the Second World War, Daddy enlisted. When he returned home, he finished college on the GI Bill, then began medical school at Yale.

Impressive, yes, but according to my grandmother, whose New England lineage began with the *Mayflower*, not "our kind of people."

But neither was Mother, not anymore. This was not something Mother liked to talk about, but between her and Aunt Kate I had learned the story of Mother's other life, her life before Daddy. Three days after graduating from high school, Mother married her high school sweetheart. Soon, he was shipped overseas (also to fight the Germans), but not before she became pregnant. The baby, Timmy, was perfect. Mother, living in her parents' home while her husband was away, called Timmy her big, fat, country baby.

I knew from an early age that Timmy died of meningitis when he was six months old and that a week later Mother received a telegraph from overseas stating that her husband had died in combat. But it wasn't until I was in college that I learned the details around Timmy's death. Kate, grim and determined, told me the story one weekend when I was visiting her in Manhattan. I was furious at Mother over something and had declared my hatred of her to Kate.

"Susan drives me crazy, too," Kate said. "But believe me, outward appearances to the contrary, life dealt her a tough hand."

On that day Kate told me the secret shame of Timmy's death, that he had died while Mother was on a picnic at Doolittle Lake with a friend from high school, a male friend kept out of the war for unknown reasons. They were just friends, Kate assured me; in fact, there were rumors that the man was a homosexual. Mother had left the baby with her parents' housekeeper; her own parents were away, at a house party in Litchfield. Mother said she would be back by that afternoon, but it was past dark when she returned. The panicked housekeeper met her at the door. The baby was inconsolable. He wouldn't eat, he had a high fever and a rash, and there was a bulge in his little fontanelle. The housekeeper had waited for Mother's return to take Timmy to the hospital. By the time they got there, it was too late. Timmy died that night.

"Let me tell you," said Kate, "our friends and neighbors did not look too kindly on a woman whose baby died while she was out picnicking with a man other than her husband, innocent though it was. And then for her own husband to die so soon afterward, it was almost as if people thought Susan had conjured the tragedy. So Dad got Susan the position at PLM—he knew one of the founding editors, a connection he used again when I was job hunting—and he secured a room for her at the Barbizon. Dad said he needed to get her out of Connecticut, out of the gossip mill. Plus he thought having a job might distract your mother from her grief. But it didn't. She was so depressed. And then your father appeared on the scene, and it seemed that Susan had a second chance at life. Honestly, we were all so grateful that he came along."

As a girl, I would study the photo Mother kept of herself and Timmy. In the photo, he is fat and rosy cheeked, dressed in a long white baptismal gown, sitting on Mother's lap. Mother looks different than I've ever seen her. Happy. In the photo, Mother glows. I remember studying that picture and fantasizing that Timmy had not died, that he was strong and nimble and fun, always ready with a laugh to talk Mother out of her rigidity. I would compare the picture of Timmy and Mother to the one of Mother and me, taken on the day of *my* Baptism. Mother looks angry behind her smile. Throughout my childhood, much as I tried to appease her, to bring her snacks, to make her laugh, to just be quiet so she could nap, Mother was often angry. Her girl child, born to a man she did not love, had survived, while her fat, cooing baby boy, born to her childhood sweetheart, had not.

Thank God I was headed to boarding school by the time Daddy and Kate had their big falling-out, because I don't think I could have survived my childhood without Kate's presence. All of these years later, I still don't really understand what happened between Daddy and my aunt, except that a cookbook had something to do with the dissolution of their relationship. Yes, a cookbook. How ridiculous. It was one Kate was editing. It hadn't even been released, but Kate had already told me all about the project. At fourteen, I loved getting the "inside scoop" on the publishing world, and I suppose Kate wanted to encourage any career aspirations I might have had, knowing that Mother's sole advice regarding my future was "that it's just as easy to fall in love with a rich man as it is to fall in love with a poor one."

The book was written by Alice Stone, a "Negro woman" (that was the polite term back then) who grew up on a farm in rural North Carolina. Alice went on to be the chef at an eastside café where Kate liked to take authors to lunch, as the restaurant itself had a storied literary past and continued to attract a bohemian clientele.

("Well, fancy bohemians," Kate clarified.) Kate also loved the food at the café and had become curious about the chef's story. After all, it was the early 1960s. For a Negro to be a chef at all was anomalous, let alone a black woman. And so, in typical straightforward fashion, Kate arrived at the café midafternoon, asked if Alice Stone was there, and set up an appointment to talk with her the following week, on Alice's day off. Alice surprised Kate by inviting her to her Riverside apartment for the interview. Kate had been warned that Alice was exceptionally private, but there she was, inviting Kate to her home. When Kate arrived, Alice offered her breakfast: strong coffee, coffee cake made from a sweet yeast dough, and bacon baked on a cookie sheet in the oven. When they finished eating, Alice handed Kate a black-and-white-speckled notebook filled with details about her childhood in North Carolina.

With growing interest Kate read about the gentle slope of land upon which Alice's family built their farm and how in the mornings the dew looked like steam rising from the grass. She read about the pigs Alice's family raised, how they were finished on acorns, making their meat unbelievably silky. Kate read about Alice's mother's cooking, how she could turn the humblest ingredients into something magical: creamy chess pies, tender squirrel stew, butter nut cookies at Christmas time that were both salty and sweet.

Kate was captivated by Alice's story and at that point was high enough on the Palmer, Long and McIntyre totem pole that she was able to get a little bit of advance money for Alice so that she could turn her notes into a book. But when Kate told Alice the good news, that PML was going to publish Alice's memoirs, Alice balked. She did not want just anyone reading about her life. She had wanted to share her story with Kate, specifically. She felt an affinity toward Kate and thought she would appreciate hearing about Emancipation Township. Kate told Alice that a lot of people would appreciate hearing about Emancipation Township, but Alice remained wary. It wasn't until Kate assured Alice that no dirty laundry need be aired that Alice grew enthusiastic, excited to share memories of a simpler time when people relied on the land and closely followed the four seasons. And recipes. There would be lots and lots of recipes, and Kate would help Alice discern which to use. It would be a project they would take on together—the cooking part, at least. Kate was happy to work with Alice in her kitchen, and Alice, whose husband was out of the country, enjoyed the company.

Kate was so proud of how the manuscript came together; she brought it to Connecticut to show off to Mother and Daddy. To Daddy, really. Kate wanted the two of them to cook our Saturday evening meal from it. When she and Jack arrived that Friday evening, after cocktails were poured, Kate pulled the galley out of her L.L.Bean canvas bag. She had wrapped it in one of Jack's clean undershirts to ensure no errant sand or dirt, trapped at the bottom of the bag, got in its pages. She unwrapped the T-shirt from around the book and handed it first to Mother, to be polite, though I'm sure it was Daddy whom she wanted to show it to. He was the intellectual. He was the cook. Plus, Mother was perennially dulled by alcohol.

"I didn't realize she was colored," said Mother. "Do you think that might hurt the book's chances?"

"Oh for God's sake, Susan," said Kate. "In the first place, it's a great American story. And in the second place, I don't really care about its 'chances.' I just love this book."

Daddy was quiet during this exchange. He sat next to Mother on the chintz sofa, reading from Alice's introduction. When he looked up his eyes were glassy.

"It's great, isn't it?" said Kate, smiling shyly.

Daddy looked at her, then rubbed his eyes with his thumb and index finger. He breathed in deeply, the sides of his nose flattening with the great intake of air.

"I don't know what to say."

"Say it's great."

"I don't think it's appropriate that you are publishing this."

"Excuse me?"

"It seems opportunistic. You're idealizing what was clearly a hardscrabble existence. You're publishing this for a largely white audience who will read the book and say, 'Oh, things weren't so bad in the South for Negroes. Look at this. This woman grew up on a lovely farm cooking lovely meals.'"

"We should only publish books about oppression? Alice can't celebrate where she came from? That privilege is only granted to white people? Is that what you're saying?"

"I'm saying this is not a true story. I'm saying there is no way a Negro family living in the South during the 1920s had a happy time of it. I'm saying this minimizes what was a painful time in history for colored people. That is what I'm saying."

"Jesus, what a jackass you're being," said Kate. "This is a beautiful book about the life of an amazing community, an amazing woman. I can't believe you. Do you not understand that I really care about this? Why are you attacking it?"

"I'm not the one calling people jackasses," said Daddy. "And I'd like you to refrain from such crude language in front of my daughter."

Everyone looked at me, scrunched up in the wingback chair, my knees pulled to my chest, trying to pretend I wasn't there so the grown-ups wouldn't send me away.

"Forgive me," Kate said. "I shouldn't talk that way. But I don't think you have any idea how much time and effort Alice put into this. How much effort I put into it."

"You'll have to forgive me that I can't pretend this piece of propaganda is anything short of offensive."

"Has he lost his mind?" Kate said, turning to Mother for backup.

"Oh dear," said Mother. "Jack, we've got two hotheads on our hands, don't we?"

Jack had been silent during this whole exchange between Daddy and Kate. But when pressed, he stood up for his wife.

"I think it's a wonderful book," he said.

"Well, I think it's horseshit," said Daddy.

"Benjamin!" cried Mother as Kate stood.

"We're leaving," Kate said.

"Don't forget your book," said Daddy.

"God, you're a piece of work," she said.

"Now, Kate," said Mother.

"Oh, Susan, go have your eight-hundredth martini and shut up," said Kate.

And then things got even uglier. Daddy stood and told Kate to get out of his house, and Mother, drunkenly, said he had no right to talk that way to her sister. Daddy told her to shut up, that he was defending her, and by that time Kate was already upstairs packing her bag. She and Jack left right then, driving Jack's little MG convertible back to the city, leaving me with a brooding father and a drunk mother. I escaped to boarding school a month later, and Daddy left for Palo Alto the following spring. As far as I know Daddy has never seen Kate again, although after Daddy moved across the country Mother did try to reconcile with her. But when she returned to Roxboro after a lunch in the city with her sister Mother vowed never to speak to Kate again.

"But why not?" I asked, from the shared phone in my dorm's lounge. "She's all the family you have left. You should talk."

Mother sighed dramatically. "You know Kate," she said. "She thinks she understands the world just because she's read a bunch of books."

15

A Question of Scruples

(Old Greenwich, Connecticut, 1989)

The nights all follow the same routine. Cam and I have dinner, clean up, watch television, eat popcorn, and try to pretend things are normal. And then, around 11:00 p.m., he can no longer contain his agitation. Some nights he simply paces. Some nights he lectures, listing the ways that I have failed him. Some nights he screams, and each time he does I think of the bag of Orville Redenbacher I popped earlier that evening. How at first you only hear the steady drone of the microwave. And then, *ping!* A kernel pops. *Ping!* Another. *Ping! Ping! Ping! Ping! Ping!* A sudden fury of explosions.

Once Cam has worn himself out, he goes to our bed and I retreat to our daughter's empty room.

Books comfort me. I pull the ones Lucy was assigned in high school off her shelves: *Anna Karenina, Franny and Zooey, I Know Why the Caged Bird Sings.* I might not be able to leave my physical home, but I can temporarily escape into the world on the page. I read until exhaustion takes over, and when it finally does, usually around four in the morning, I enter vivid and disturbing dreams. In one Cam comes to me, contrite, and we begin kissing. We are in our kitchen, in Greenwich, only it isn't quite our kitchen, in the way that things never match up exactly in dreams. He kisses me urgently with his big, supple lips, and then he turns me around, presses into me from behind. I am hungry for him. I want this. He walks me toward the kitchen table until its edge presses into my abdomen. He lifts my hands above my head, holding them there while he presses deeper into me. I am turned on; I am wet. And then I detect the distinct smell of metal, a dried-blood smell. In an instant I know that I am in danger. I can all but feel a set of metal handcuffs locking around my wrists, allowing him to do what he wants, to hurt me in whatever way he chooses. But the handcuffs do not come. Instead he wraps his arms around me from behind. It is comforting for one second, before he plunges a thick, rusty knife into my chest.

I awake with a gasp.

During the day I walk around in a daze. This is not my life. How can this be my life? I keep waiting for Cam to snap to, to return home from work bearing a bouquet of peonies, a bottle of Veuve Clicquot—my favorite—and a profound apology. I carried peonies at my wedding; ever since they've been Cam's go-to flower for his most egregious fuckups. Like the time he stranded me on our anniversary. I had hired a babysitter, put on a sexy dress, and taken the train into the city to meet him at La Grenouille. I let myself be seated though Cam had not yet arrived. I ordered a glass of Champagne, anticipating the evening to come. Except Cam never showed. After I had been waiting for nearly an hour, the maître d' finally came to my table, saying there was a phone call for me at the bar. It was Cam. An emergency had come up at work. There was nothing he could do. All I could think was, *Why wait an hour to call?* Or the time he allowed an old friend from high school—an attractive, newly divorced, female

friend—to stay overnight at our home while the girls and I were in the city for the weekend visiting Aunt Kate. Or the time he gave me a used set of Jane Fonda workout videos for my birthday, which I am almost positive he bought from a neighborhood garage sale.

I completely forgot about the dinner party we are supposed to attend tonight, even though it's been scheduled for weeks. I've been preoccupied; I've been a little on edge. Of course I will cancel. I cannot imagine presenting ourselves at someone's front door. What a horror for the host. *Surprise! We're here! Your very own traveling performance of* Who's Afraid of Virginia Woolf?

But when I tell Cam I'll get us out of the party, he is emphatic that we go. He has been looking forward to an evening out. It might relieve some stress. And anyway, the hosts are from Atlanta and somehow connected to Taffy, who will be furious if she finds out we backed out on the night of an intimate party, leaving the hostess in a lurch. A mortal sin.

Under normal circumstances I would have questioned why Cam's mother, thousands of miles away in Atlanta, is directing our social life. But right now I only want peace with my husband, and so I get on board, say, "All right then, let's go," thinking that maybe the party will force Cam to get it together. He is a product of the Atlanta elite, after all, and from my observations of that crew, being good-natured and entertaining at a social event is about as sacrosanct as baptizing your child at the Episcopal church and throwing a luncheon afterward at the Piedmont Driving Club.

I dress for the party with care, wanting Cam to be reminded of my attractiveness. If nothing else, I want other men looking at me, affirming my desirability. I may have gained some weight, but I carry much of it in my chest, squeezed into a hundred-dollar double D bra. I wear an emerald green wrap dress—purchased from

Bendel's—that shows off my cleavage nicely. The dress has an almost scandalously low neckline, and the heels I wear are almost scandalously high, making me exactly even with Cam in height. I apply more makeup than usual and spend an hour with a hair dryer and a brush so that my hair hangs straight and silky instead of seizing into the wild curls I inherited from my southern Italian ancestors. (Oh, Daddy. As much as you tried to be the consummate WASP, your humble, immigrant past shows on my head.)

I do not know the couple—the McClouds—whose home we are going to. All I know is that the wife grew up in Brookwood Hills and, like Cam, also attended high school at Coventry Academy. But she's in her midthirties, so she was years behind my husband. The only other thing I know about the McClouds is that Mr. McCloud supposedly paid for their house with cash.

After the McClouds moved in this summer, Taffy phoned every day until I finally sent Cam over there with a welcome basket of wine, cheese, fig preserves, and a baguette. (It was just after Cleo died; I was not up for socializing, and Cam was still being tender with me.) Cam said that the wife, Parrin McCloud, was sweet and enthusiastic about moving up north, but he could not help but feel sorry for her, a southerner about to face a Connecticut winter.

Cam and I don't talk much on the drive over to the McClouds'. The few exchanges we do have are polite and excessively formal: "Do you mind if I turn up the heat?" "Do you think this bottle of Merlot will be good?" "Should I get the car washed tomorrow, or do you think it might rain?"

The exterior of the McClouds' home is stunning. It was built in 1928, during the height of the Robber Baron era, when railroad and oil tycoons were showing off their wealth by building beautiful manors. This one is made of a cool gray stone, Italianate in style.

Two stone eagles perch atop a rock wall at the foot of the driveway, causing me to feel as if we are on our way to visit the Godfather, to kiss the ring and ask a favor. Cam parks, and he and I approach the house side by side, not touching until we get to the three stairs leading up to the front door, at which point Cam holds his arm out for me to steady myself against as I make my way up in my impractical heels. When we ring the bell, Mr. McCloud immediately answers.

He has thick, snowy, patrician hair and a head too large for his body. He wears dress pants and a button-down shirt with the sleeves rolled up to his elbows. No tie, though he looks like the type of man who should be wearing one. He is considerably older than Cam and me (in his early sixties?), and this confuses me for a minute until I remember that he and his wife don't have to be the same age, especially if he is rich enough to buy this stunning house with cash.

"Well, hello!" he bellows. "Bo McCloud. And you must be—"

"Cam and Amelia Brighton," Cam interjects, reaching out his hand for a hearty shake.

"I'm sorry to say you're being greeted by the lesser of the two McClouds, but Parrin says to forgive her, she's just finishing getting ready. Now y'all come on in. Let me fix you a drink!"

Cam shoots me a look of irritation, then immediately returns his attention to Bo McCloud, who, after pulling Cam in by the shoulder, is now slapping him aggressively on the back and beginning a game of "Old Atlanta Geography," throwing out names of people they might know in common.

Cam looked at me with irritation because it was I who insisted that we arrive by 7:30, the time Parrin McCloud called for. Cam always says it's best to show up a few minutes late to a dinner party, allowing the host time to finish up with everything. I say it's rude to arrive late, that the host might have something hot and ready to eat at 7:30 on the dot. In this particular case, I should have listened to Cam, trusting his instincts about the hosting rituals of southerners.

Another fuckup I will surely pay for later.

The McClouds' home is beautiful, stately and established, looking nothing at all like the dwelling of people who moved in only a few months before. It reminds me a lot of the interior of Taffy's house in Brookwood Hills: the same liberal use of color, the same elegance of furnishings, mostly wooden and antique. There are softly faded Oriental rugs on the hardwood floors and lamps everywhere, so we are not assaulted by direct overhead light. The staircase, which curves like a question mark, dominates the foyer, with its wide wooden planks, its curved wooden railing, its wrought-iron balusters. It is archetypal, what you might imagine your daughter descending on her wedding day. I imagine the real estate agent conjured up just that fantasy when she showed the home to the McClouds, who have two young daughters, twins, of whom I see no evidence, save for the portrait I spy in the living room. The portrait is of a beautiful brunette in a white dress with a white lace collar, her arm around two girls, similar in appearance but not identical, also in white dresses with lace collars, oversized white bows clipped to their sandy blond hair.

And then the beautiful woman from the painting, Parrin McCloud, comes gliding down the stairs wearing a simple little beige shift and matching heels. Her jewelry is also simple but substantial: diamond studs in her ears and a stone the size of a skating rink on her ring finger. As she makes her way to us I observe that her makeup is so lightly applied you can still see the freckles across her cheeks. Her eyes are hazel, her nose straight. Looking at her, I see the type of girl I always wished I were, the girl I was able to befriend at Rosemary Hall—more like follow around—but could never quite become. I was too curly, too booby, too uncomfortable in my skin.

But Parrin is the southern WASP ideal: the type whose silver pattern was picked out for her before she was even born, who knows how to make a tomato aspic and owns a deviled-egg plate, who, if called upon, can host a last-minute dinner party for twelve. She's athletic, too, plays a good game of tennis, surely, skis on both water and snow, knows the Charleston and the cha-cha, learned in social dance class, which her mother enrolled her in at age twelve, just as Taffy enrolled Cam. Parrin is elegant as hell, but her minimalist approach to makeup implies a certain tomboyishness underneath, a willingness to slug a shot of bourbon with the boys before donning an old pair of jeans and her bid day T-shirt from Kappa, tissue soft from countless washes, to go on some backwoods adventure.

And now she stands before me, bubbling over with enthusiasm, giving me a great big welcoming smile while touching the sleeve of my dress and remarking on how pretty it is.

"We are just so glad y'all are here! We've been so busy putting the house together we haven't had much time for company, so this is a real treat."

"Thanks for having us," I say.

"No, thank *you* for coming," she says, and I think to myself: *Good God, this woman is Taffy minus thirty years.*

"Okay, y'all need drinks. Cam, do you take Scotch? Bourbon? Something else?"

"I'd love a Scotch," says Cam. Already he's reacquired his good ol' boy accent.

Parrin smiles at me conspiratorially. "Amelia, you don't happen to be a Champagne drinker, do you?"

"Who isn't?"

"Oh good!" Parrin says. "I'm so glad. This means we'll be friends. I try to have a glass every day. Does that make me terribly decadent?"

"Parrin, darling, you are the definition of decadent," says Bo.

"Y'all know what I said to my wife the other day when the AmEx bill came in? I said, 'Honey, I give you an unlimited budget, and you *still* exceed it!'"

"Oh, hush," Parrin says.

Bo throws his arm around her. "Just teasing you, darling."

I shoot a glance at Cam. In a better time he would have caught it, would have known that I was thinking, *Call Dr. Freud; someone married her father.* But Cam is not looking at me. All eyes but mine are on Parrin.

"Now don't worry, Cam, we're not forgetting about your Scotch. Here's what we're going to do. Bo is going to show you his big-game room, where he also happens to have a very old bottle of Glendronach. And Amelia and I will just sneak off to the kitchen and get ourselves a little bubbly. Sound good?"

Bo gives Cam another resounding slap on the back, a display of affection I'm beginning to enjoy because I can't imagine it not stinging. Parrin, meanwhile, loops her arm through mine, steering me first through the living room, then the dining room, and finally into the kitchen, which is a study in white—white floors, white cabinets, white appliances—all except for the stove, which sits like a gun-metal-gray tank in a field of snow. There are trays of food displayed on the center island. Seeing them, I realize that I am hungry.

Parrin opens the refrigerator and pulls out a cold bottle of Moët & Chandon. She unwraps the foil from its top, then removes the hood, standing poised for a moment, a dish towel over the cork, which she eases out with great concentration. The cork discharges quietly into the towel, and she proceeds to fill two flutes already sitting on the island, next to the food.

"Bo says I went a little overboard with appetizers."

I lift my glass, "Cheers," I say, before taking a sip. "It all looks delicious."

In addition to a stack of small white plates, a basket of rolled cloth napkins, and a pile of polished silver forks, there is baked Brie in puff pastry, caviar with blinis (caviar!), a shallow bowl of beautiful purple grapes with a sterling silver pair of scissors placed beside it, poached shrimp with cocktail sauce, and a pale pink mold in the shape of a fish with crackers surrounding it, thin lemon slices and capers on top.

"That's not the salmon mousse from the Silver Palate, is it?" I ask. The salmon mousse from the Silver Palate is perhaps my favorite thing to eat in the world.

"Oh shoot," she says, and I can all but imagine her stomping her little foot. "You found me out. Is it just so tacky I brought in food from the city? I *did* press the mousse into the fish mold myself, and I also fixed the Brie. That is, I put some apricot jam on it and wrapped it in Pepperidge Farm puff pastry dough."

"Parrin, you are about ten steps ahead of the rest of us. This all looks incredible."

"I'm so glad y'all got here first," she says, as if confiding something top secret. She turns and reaches above the refrigerator, patting around for something, then pulls down a pack of Benson & Hedges. "You don't mind, do you?" she asks.

I shake my head, though I kind of do.

"I'll just open the back door and you'll hardly notice. Bo *hates* that I still smoke, but I can't help it. And I've cut down to one cigarette a day. I tell him he simply must tolerate it or else I'll be a devil to live with."

She stands near the opened back door, blowing her smoke outside.

"It's nice to be with people from Atlanta again. It's so different up here. People are just . . . strange."

"I'm actually not from Atlanta."

"Oh my gosh! I'm sorry. I thought you and Cam both were. Where are you from?"

"Connecticut, born and raised."

"Oh Lord. You must think I'm a beast. I'm so sorry. It's just when you sent over that sweet welcome basket I thought you must be southern because I couldn't imagine a Yankee doing such a thing."

She brings her free hand to her mouth, covering it temporarily. "Oh Lord, forgive me. There I go talking about northerners being rude, and look at who the rude one really is."

"Why, just look," I say, mimicking her accent without meaning to. I resist the urge to twist my finger into my cheek and make a dimple.

And then I decide to summon my better angels, realizing it's going to be a long night if we get caught up in a battle of who has most offended the other.

"Tell me about your daughters. What are their names?" I ask.

"Ivy and Olivia." She takes one last inhale, then tosses the remaining stub of cigarette outside and shuts the door. "They're in the playroom with the babysitter. It's the sweetest little space. In the attic, with dormer windows, like a fairy tale. I bribed them with a pizza and a video, told the babysitter I'd give her a bonus if she could keep them upstairs while the guests are here. They're precious, but if I bring them down to meet you they'll be here all night. And frankly, I need a little time off."

I can't stop thinking about Parrin's discarded cigarette butt, still lit. I want to tell her to be careful, that she might burn the house down. But I swallow my anxiety. Parrin is a grown woman and not in need of my advice.

"The portrait of the three of you is beautiful," I say. "I caught a glimpse of it from the hallway."

"Please tell Bo that! It will make his night. He had that painting commissioned for my Christmas present last year. I just love it."

The fact that I will see her children in a painting rather than in the flesh seems very fitting to me and illustrates something about the Atlanta world she and Cam both come from, where surfaces matter—a lot.

"Is Bo's big game room where you keep the Parcheesi set?" I ask, deadpan.

Parrin laughs, delighted by my joke. "I actually *love* board games, but no. The game room is for Bo's 'spoils.' He's been big-game hunting in Africa and India, plus we have a camp in Louisiana, where Bo's from. His most prized possession is his lion, but he's also got a tiger and a bear—he calls it his *Wizard of Oz* collection—and then there's just a bunch of deer heads and stuff. Oh, and some squirrels. Bo hates squirrels. They made a salad bar out of our garden in Atlanta, so Bo shot a bunch of them with these special bullets he buys that have an acorn engraved on the bottom of each one. He took a couple of the squirrels to the taxidermist, and afterward we put the stuffed squirrels in the garden to see if they'd scare away the live ones, but I think they did the opposite and made the rest of the squirrels think we'd thrown them a cocktail party or something."

"Wow," I say, not sure how else to respond. This is certainly outside the bounds of normal Connecticut dinner party conversation, which tends to circle around school issues, library fund-raisers, which play Frank Rich butchered in the *Times,* and what new restaurants we've visited in Manhattan.

"Do Bo and I sound absolutely barbaric?"

I shrug. "Cam hunts. Dove mostly, though occasionally he still goes deer hunting."

"In Connecticut?"

"No, he goes on a boys' retreat every winter. They go to a plantation in South Georgia."

"Bo would *love* that."

There is a pause for a moment while I wonder how rude it would be for me to make a little dent in the salmon mousse. The other couple is still not here, or at least I haven't heard the doorbell ring.

"Did you grow up in Old Greenwich?" she asks.

"I grew up in the country. Litchfield County, in the northwest corner of the state. A town called Roxboro."

"Didn't Alexander Calder live there?"

I look at her, surprised. I forget that pretty southern girls can be intelligent. "He did. My family didn't know him or anything, but we knew his house. There were mobiles in the front yard. It was pretty amazing to drive by."

"I hope I didn't sound too rude earlier about northerners. I think I'm just nervous about having left home. But really, Bo and I think this part of the country is so beautiful."

I nod, but I'm distracted. The salmon mousse is just sitting there. I decide "What the hell," lift the sterling silver serving knife, and glance at her one more time before cutting into the big pink fish.

"Oh, thank you for doing that!" she says. "Now it's a real party." She beams at me like a little girl.

By the time the other couple arrives, Parrin and I have nearly finished the bottle of Champagne and grown very giggly. It is nice to let go after so many nights of holding my breath around my husband. It is nice to get a little tipsy, to let someone cook for me, to be in a home where people are talking in warm and dulcet tones, where Cam is talking in warm and dulcet tones. The dinner Parrin serves—vichyssoise, squab, rice pilaf, green salad, chocolate-orange mousse—is all very "of the moment" and delicious, as I knew it would be. I decide that Parrin is silly but dear, though I continue to be startled every time she puts her hand on her husband's leg. He's fifty-five, Parrin told me, while she is thirty-seven. Even so, he looks older than their eighteen-year age difference, or maybe she, with her Jane Fonda body (she teaches an aerobics class twice a week at the studio in town), looks younger than she actually is.

Observing Bo makes me appreciate what I have in Cam, physically at least. Cam runs five days a week and often lifts weights at his gym in Manhattan before returning home in the evening. No flabby belly presses against me when we make love. Not that the thought of making love to Cam seems very appealing right now. (I no longer even undress around my husband. My clothes have become my armor.) I was right about the party loosening him up, though. He is as charming as he can be in front of these people. He tells funny stories, listens attentively whenever anyone else speaks, and jumps up to help Parrin clear the dishes when we are all finished eating.

After dinner, Parrin claps her hands together, as if she's troop leader of the Scouts, then asks if we might like to adjourn to the living room to play board games and have after-dinner drinks.

"Amelia and I were talking about how much we love playing them," she says, winking at me.

We follow Parrin to the den while Bo goes off in the direction of his office. Parrin pulls A Question of Scruples out of the den closet. We groan, but good-naturedly, as we have all come to expect this. This is the third party I've been to this year where Scruples has come out. It is both awful and fun, but we are all tipsy enough to be titillated instead of nervous. And here comes Bo carrying the bottle of Scotch and another bottle of Champagne.

"This game always gets me in trouble," says Cam.

His accent keeps getting thicker and thicker.

"Well, don't bluff so much," I say. "Because the truth will out."

In Scruples everyone is dealt five "dilemma" cards, each of which asks a morally ambivalent question. For each round played, everyone gets one answer card, which says either "Yes," "No," or "Depends." Depending on which answer card you draw, you have to guess which one of your opponents would answer the same way. If their response matches your answer card, you get to discard your question card without drawing another one. If it doesn't match yours, you have to draw another question card. The first one to run out of question cards wins. The fun part of the game comes when you think someone is bluffing the answer. Then you can challenge them. This is what happened to Cam the last time we played the game at a party, when he answered "Yes" to my question, saying he would leave a note if he were to hit a car in a parking lot and no one else were to witness it.

I knew he was lying. I had been in the car with Cam once when he tried to squeeze into a tight space and ended up scraping the side of a station wagon. I was with him as he backed out of the space and drove right out of the lot. So I called his bluff, brought up his past indiscretion, and everyone voted that his answer was insincere, resulting in me winning the round. Cam had laughed it off at the party but was irritated later that night. "Would it really hurt you to let me be right for once?" he asked.

The thing about Scruples is you aren't really playing to win. You're playing for the questions, to ponder them, to see how your friends will answer. And so Cam, Parrin, Bo, and the other couple—I keep forgetting their names—go round and round, asking strangely intimate questions of each other:

"Your child support payments will be cut in half if you tell your 'ex' about the big raise you got. Do you tell?"

"Your fifteen-year-old daughter needs your permission to get the pill. Do you consent?"

"Your elderly mother-in-law can no longer manage alone in her house and doesn't like nursing homes. Do you take her in?"

It is my turn, and, though I am not supposed to care, I am winning. I only have one question left: "If you could have an affair with no chance of your mate discovering your infidelity, would you do it?"

My true answer fits the response card I have: "No." I would rather leave Cam than cheat. I just don't know how you would do that—live one intimate life beneath another. Even if it were only a one-night dalliance. But here's the thing: I know not to pose the question to Cam, because if he answers "No" I will be tempted to call his bluff. It's not that I am certain he's had an affair. I have no hard evidence, save for the time years ago when he had that woman from Coventry stay at our house while the girls and I were out of town, but honestly, in that case, I don't believe anything untoward actually happened. I met the woman when I returned home early from my trip to New York, and she was a weepy mess about her divorce. In fact, Cam seemed relieved that I had come home, relieved that there was someone else for her to talk to. But if that woman *hadn't* been such a wreck, if she had been looking for a fling, I would not put it past my husband to cheat. It occurs to me that I must accept this awful truth about my husband: when he can get away with bad behavior, he will. Like the way he peeled out of the parking lot instead of leaving his phone number on the car he damaged.

I settle on Parrin as my "No." I don't really know the other couple, and besides, I am pretty sure Parrin is my best bet. She is just so sweet and southern and wifely. Or at least, that's how she presents, how she looks in her portrait. Meaning that even if she wanted to answer another way, I can't imagine her saying anything but "No." And I'm certainly not going to call her on her bluff if she does, because I want to win and I don't need to know her secrets.

"I call on Parrin," I say. "Would you cheat if you knew you wouldn't get caught?"

"Heck no," she says.

I flip over my card, and everyone sees that it matches her answer. She and I smile at each other, woman to woman.

"We've got ourselves some good wives," says Bo, raising his Scotch glass toward Cam's.

Cam does not raise his glass, which is full of amber liquid, having been steadily refreshed by Bo through the night.

"Parrin's bluffing," says Cam.

"Cam," says Parrin, and for the first time that evening she doesn't look in control.

Cam is drunk. This, along with so many other things, I had not fully realized. And as he drawls, "Cause I know there's a naughty girl beneath that sweet exterior," she reddens, and the answer to a question I've been avoiding all night long slides right into place. It is like solving my daughter's Rubik's Cube, when you look and look and look at those mismatched colored squares and suddenly you realize if you turn it like this, then twist it like that, then turn it one more time, all of the colors on all six sides will match up perfectly and the puzzle will be solved.

Cam's fury toward me, his nights of rage, his inability to see anything from my side—I've been looking at it from the wrong perspective. I've been looking at it as if I'm central in this drama. But if I twist and turn myself out of the center and look at the situation from the outside, it all makes a sudden and awful logic: Cam and Parrin are having an affair. This dinner is a setup, a naughty game they are playing, displaying their cuckolded spouses for the other to evaluate. I imagine they have met in the bathroom to grope and to gossip, with neither Bo nor I aware of what they are up to, until this, this (intentionally?) careless move on Cam's part that reveals the exquisite fire these two are playing with, neither of them concerned about whom the flames might lick and burn.

I look around the room. No one but Cam, Parrin, and I seems to realize what is going on here, but clearly Cam wants his affair out in the open, wants to make a scene. And I'll be damned if I give him that pleasure.

"Oh, I don't believe that for a minute," I say, my voice hardy. "Parrin might be naughty, but she's not *nasty*. When you're naughty you wear black lace panties beneath your conservative clothes. When you're nasty you engage in a cheap, cavalier affair. And that's not like Parrin, is it?"

Parrin gives Cam a pleading, desperate look. He looks at her, then looks at me, then looks at her again.

"Of course not," he says. "Challenge withdrawn."

"Amelia, darling," booms Bo, seemingly oblivious to all that just happened. "Looks like you just won!"

16

SEED

(Old Greenwich, Connecticut, 1989)

Fifteen minutes after four and I am halfway out the door, headed for the Old Greenwich train station, where I will catch the 4:33 that will take me through the Connecticut suburbs and into the city. Beneath my heavy down coat I am wearing what I think of as my "fancy pants" (velvet, wide legged, elastic waistband), topped with a luxurious and oversized wraparound cashmere sweater that obscures my thickening middle. The phone rings. I, who am always convinced that *this* call is going to be the one with terrible news about one of my children, turn back inside and answer it.

It is Cam. Of course. On the one day I wasn't thinking about him.

"How ya doing, Ame?" Cam asks, using his old nickname for me, pronouncing it "aim," like what you do with a dart.

I hate that I am excited to hear his voice. "I'm fine," I say. "Just headed to the train station, actually. I'm having dinner with Sarah in the city. That is, if her project manager ever lets her leave the office.

She's working for this crazy boss who thinks an ad campaign is good only if she stays up half the night finishing it. But she promised me she'd find a way to sneak out."

Cam sighs. Our entire married life he has always scolded me about how I need to get to the point faster, to not babble. Our entire married life he has always scolded me.

"I was hoping I could come over," he says. "I'd like for us to talk. But it sounds like tonight's no good."

I have been waiting for this call. It's not that I want to reconcile, at least I don't think I do. It's just that as soon as the girls left for school his anger got so out of hand, and then I realized he was having an affair with Parrin (which he admitted to after we returned home from the McClouds' party), and suddenly he was gone, moved into one of those ticky-tacky new apartment complexes built for divorcés. We never even had the chance to catch our breath. We never had a chance to look at the scorched earth around us and say, "What the hell just happened?"

I glance at my watch. I'm going to miss the 4:33. My plan was to take an early train to the city, then the subway downtown, where I would walk around and maybe have a drink and some of those wonderful spiced cashews at the Union Square Cafe before walking over to Sarah's ad agency, also near Union Square. But I can catch a later train. Hell, I could even ask Sarah for a rain check. It matters that I talk to Cam. He is, after all, still my husband.

"I've got a little time to spare. Do you want to come over?"

"Oh, that's great, just great. Thanks for your flexibility, Ame. I really appreciate it. I'll head out now."

"You know how to find the place?" A joke. Gallows humor.

"I'll manage," he says, trying to sound playful but only managing to sound a little constipated.

• • •

Does Cam want to come home? Has he had his fill of Taffy Two? Surely a thirty-seven-year-old former Buckhead housewife is more demanding than I ever was, plus she's got those two little girls, and I am not at all convinced Cam wants to enter active daddyhood again, especially with another man's children. Surely Cam, who likes his comforts, misses our house, misses our dog, misses my cooking. Were he to come to me truly contrite, were he willing to go to counseling, were he willing to give his entire, broken self to me, could I forgive him?

Funny, it seems easier to forgive his dalliance with Taffy Two than the rage that came before the revelation. I am not sure I will ever forgive him for that. I am not sure I should. And yet the other half of my brain is buzzing with what to offer when he arrives. I have a wedge of Brie and some crackers in the pantry, and I could slice a pear or an apple and drizzle the fruit with some orange blossom honey. That always makes a nice accompaniment for cheese. I've got some olives, too, Lucques. I wonder if I have time to make cheese sticks. I use store-bought puff pastry, roll it out, sprinkle it with salt and red pepper flakes and grated Parmesan, then cut the dough into strips, twist them, and bake. They are particularly delicious with a glass of Champagne, especially when you serve the cheese sticks warm.

But there's no Champagne in the refrigerator. Although there is that bottle of Taittinger I bought last week, marked five dollars off its regular price. I suppose it's a little much to serve, being that Champagne is romantic, but it's so crisp and delicious and would go so nicely with the cheese sticks that I decide to serve it anyway. I walk to the kitchen, take the bottle out from the wine rack beneath the counter, and stick it in the freezer, setting the timer for 45 minutes lest I forget and it explodes.

Since Cam left I have had to be very careful with alcohol. It is easy to let drinking a second glass of wine slip into finishing the whole bottle, and then I become weepy and despondent. My biggest fear is that I might call Taffy Two in such a condition, ask her to please send back my husband, that surely she's had her fun by now and surely he is exhausted.

I return to the freezer, pulling out the package of Pepperidge Farm Puff Pastry dough and placing it in the fridge. It only needs to defrost for a few minutes, just enough time for me to grate some Parmesan and pull seasonings from the cabinet. I find the grater buried beneath a plastic spatula and a pair of poultry shears in the drawer beneath the counter where I have rolled out a thousand piecrusts, scooped endless balls of cookie dough onto metal trays, attempted to knead bread dough—the one culinary art I never quite mastered. I put on an apron to protect my nice clothes. I am an old pro at cooking while dressed for a party. Cam and I used to entertain often.

Cam is half an hour late. Which is not unusual. At least not when he's meeting me. I go ahead and open the Champagne, pour myself a glass. Lift it up and say, "Cheers," ever the ironist, even when alone. The cheese straws are cooling quickly. They are still tasty at room temperature but no longer superb. You can taste the hardened fat, whereas warm they just melt on the tongue. Oh, but who am I kidding? Cam probably won't eat any of this food anyway. What he will do is look at me, then look at the food spread before us, then look at me again, thinking: *This is why you're fat.*

God, do I know that man. You don't spend twenty years married to someone without at least accomplishing that.

I walk through my house as if it is a museum I am visiting. A museum of our old life. I have not yet taken down any of the family photos. Generations fill the walls, from the black-and-white images of my maternal grandparents as newlyweds, about to set sail for Europe, to Mandy's freshman portrait from Hotchkiss. I marvel once again at the fact that there are no photos of Daddy as a child. He told me his family was too poor to ever have any made. "Your mother didn't even have one baby picture taken of you?" I asked. Daddy reminded me that his mother was an illiterate immigrant with no money. And then his parents died when he was only sixteen, one after the other, and he was left an orphan.

Daughter of an orphan, I have displayed my own family with pride. There is the picture of Taffy in the white dress she wore as a debutante back at the Piedmont Driving Club in Atlanta, 1938. The height of the Depression and Taffy's family could still afford for their daughter to come out. Taffy was so beautiful, with her finger curls and her wide, innocent eyes. Mandy looks a lot like her. There is the picture of Mother and Aunt Kate as girls at the lake, in swimsuits down to their knees, Kate still a child, Mother teetering on womanhood. There are framed photos of my beautiful girls all up and down the stairwell, posed school pictures as well as candid shots. Cam must have taken the ones with me and Mandy and Lucy in them. God, look at me in this one: twentysomething years old and effortlessly thin, my hair long and curly, my mouth thrown open in delight as I hold stout Lucy by the waist.

When Cam arrives perhaps I will point to the picture of Lucy and me as if I am a lawyer in court and it is Exhibit A, proof that we were once happy.

Except, of course, Cam is absent from the image. It is only of mother and child.

The bell rings. Finally. I check my reflection in the hallway mirror. It matters that I look good on this of all nights. Matters that Cam recognizes what he is losing. I smile to make sure there are no red pepper flakes stuck in my teeth, twist an errant curl around my finger to make it behave. Without inquiring as to who it is (there is no one else it could be), I open the door. And there is my husband, still handsome in his jowly way, though there are more grays in his dark hair since the last time I saw him. He wears jeans, a green cashmere sweater I bought for him at Brooks Brothers, and a black leather bomber jacket I've never seen before, weathered and formfitting.

"Why, look. It's the Rebel without a Cause," I say, the words flying out of my mouth, unchecked.

He presses his lips together, a sign that he is annoyed.

"Hi, Amelia. You're looking good."

"Oh thanks. It was this or my leather pants."

I'm joking of course, but Cam doesn't smile.

"You look very pretty," he says dutifully.

He could be a teller at the bank, telling me to have a nice day after processing my deposit.

"Well, come in. Let's not let all the warm air out."

(Nag, nag. I sound like a nag.) I try again. "Come in, don't come in, whatever you want! I'm easy." I bark out a nervous laugh, which sounds like I'm coughing up something rather than making any sort of sound of merriment.

Cam steps inside formally, as if he were visiting an unfamiliar house, as if he has not lived here for half of his life.

"I've got some snacks in the kitchen, and I opened a bottle of Champagne." I snap my fingers, remembering. "But you'll want a Scotch, won't you?"

"Guilty as charged."

Why didn't I think to have a glass poured for him at the door? Taffy Two probably greets him each evening with a Scotch. Hell, she probably greets him topless: a Scotch in one hand, a can of whipped cream in the other, a helium balloon tied around each tit.

"Just a splash," he adds.

I go to the liquor cabinet and retrieve the bottle of Dewar's and a cut-glass tumbler, given to us for our wedding. I slosh in a generous pour and bring the glass to the kitchen, where he is waiting for me. I decide, what the hell, I don't have to stick to my one-drink rule tonight. I'm not drinking alone, after all. I take the bottle of Champagne out of the fridge and give myself a refill.

"Cheers," I say, tapping the rim of my flute to his tumbler.

"Cheers."

"Have a cheese stick," I say. "Or just have some Brie. It's delicious with a little of this apricot jam."

"I'm good. I had a late lunch."

"Oh. Well, do you want something sweet? I've got a bag of Mint Milanos."

"No. I'm not hungry. Listen, I have something I have to tell you. It's big. We weren't planning to talk about it yet because, well, it's pretty early. But, well, do you know Gail Ferguson?"

"What do you mean do I know Gail Ferguson? She's been our next-door neighbor for eighteen years."

"Well, this afternoon Parrin ran into her at Alpen Pantry, and, well, she pretty much collided into Gail as she was racing into the bathroom, because, well—"

"Oh my God. Taffy Two is pregnant," I say.

"Who?" he asks.

"Your girlfriend—God, what is her name? Peyton? Peyton is pregnant. And she had to throw up at lunch, and she ran into Gail Ferguson in the process, and Gail guessed what's going on, so now you have to tell me. I'm right, aren't I?"

"*Parrin,* her name is *Parrin.* For Christsakes, Amelia, you need to learn her name. And yes, you are right. Parrin is pregnant."

He looks distinctly disappointed that I guessed his news, that I did not allow him to luxuriate fully in the drama of his revelation.

"Did Gail already call you?" he asks.

"No. But I know you."

He looks at me for a moment, his eyes holding mine, and I am remembering the first time we made love, how quickly he came, how embarrassed he was afterward and how I reassured him that we were going to have a lifetime to practice, to learn each other.

And then we are back in the present and he cannot see me.

"It's terrible timing, I know," he says, his eyes bright and happy again, now that he is once more in control of the news. "And it wasn't planned, I promise you that. Parrin didn't even think she could get pregnant again. They had to do all sorts of test-tube stuff to get those twins, so she just figured she wasn't capable of having a baby au naturel. Honestly, it's kind of a miracle that this happened."

I can't say anything.

He is looking at me with this shit-eating grin on his face, like he wants me to agree with him, like he wants me to celebrate that he and his girlfriend beat the fertility odds.

"So she's going to have an abortion?" I ask, knowing she is not. Only saying it to make him spell out his plan, to make him—he who has always chosen the path of least resistance—take some responsibility for the choice he is making.

He smiles inwardly, as if remembering a joke that he and Parrin shared. "Look, it's really crazy timing, I know. But I hope you can see this is a good thing, Amelia. I want us both to be happy in our next stage of life, and I'm really excited about being a dad again. You know, I could have done it better the first time around. I could have been more present. I know that now. And I'm going to try and do right by this baby, I really am."

I am filled with rage, yet speechless. I want to rain down condemnation, but I find myself having a hard time putting the words together. Nothing makes sense. This thing with Taffy Two, it was supposed to be a dalliance, a temporary acting-out. Now he is linked to her forever. *My God.* Cam was never one for cleaning up messes, was he? And now he's made another before the divorce papers are even drawn. And he expects me to be happy about it. And the thing

is, he's got me trapped. I can't wish ill on this baby who is about to be born. I can't wish anything but for them to have a healthy baby and to raise it well, because any other desire would poison me, would turn my insides black and bitter. There is a baby on the way. Everything has changed. My revved-up fury sputters into exhaustion. Suddenly, I am so exhausted.

I don't break down until after Cam leaves. And then I wilt. Just wilt. I am aware of a great sorrow rooted deep within me. I am aware that I only have access to a tiny bit of it. God, it's going to hurt when I pull it out. God, am I broken. I cry fiercely for about fifteen minutes, and then the tears subside. I walk gingerly to the kitchen, afraid the crying will catch up with me once more. I need to not cry anymore tonight. I need a drink. I need twenty drinks. I need to leave this house. I quickly pour myself another glass of the Taittinger. How nice and dry and cold it is, how perfectly delicious.

After finishing the bottle of Champagne, I decide to take the train into Manhattan after all. For where else but among the tumult of New York might my own heartache, my own sorrow, seem small compared to the rest of the great, wide world?

Sitting in a window seat, my head leaned back, a steady vibration underfoot as the train zips along the track, I try to remember driving from the house to the station. I can't. It's a short distance, less than a mile, and I imagine I drove slowly, but oh God, I shouldn't have driven. Shouldn't have, shouldn't have, shouldn't have. So many things I shouldn't have done. I feel dizzy beneath my closed lids. I drank too much. The night is only beginning and I drank too much, as if I'm a freshman in college, getting drunk to work up the nerve to go to a party.

Taffy Two is pregnant. My God. Taffy Two is pregnant with Cam's child. *Please, please, please, please, God, don't let them send out Christmas cards with pictures of the new baby or, even worse, little inky footprints.* Before Cam left the house this evening he told me that the baby is due in August. *Oh God, make it be a hot summer. Make it one of those drippy, claustrophobic, heat-wave summers during which people in New England rethink their decision not to have air-conditioning. And make Taffy Two's ankles swell.*

So we're not a whole family after all. I wanted that for my girls (my girls, my girls, we are going to have to tell the girls), wanted us to be a complete unit, wanted us to be the type of family that takes no explaining, just Mommy, Daddy, and the kids. So different from the fractured family I grew up with, Mother in a state of perennial grief over her firstborn son, Daddy first emotionally absent and then literally gone.

But surely at one point there was something good between Mother and Daddy. Surely at one point they shared something sweet. Mother spoke most fondly of their brief courtship, before their courthouse marriage. Daddy used to have Mother over to his little garage apartment in New Haven, where he would cook for her. Mother said she had never known a man to cook, other than barbecuing on the grill or serving burnt scrambled eggs on Mother's Day like her own father used to do. But Daddy said in Italy there was no shame in a man cooking. And he was good at it, and he enjoyed it, so he cooked for Mother, and then when I came along he cooked for all of us: bread every Sunday, tomato sauce from the garden, which he canned for the winter. Wonderful tarts filled with fruit from the pick-your-own orchard down the street. Roasts and braises and lasagnas on weekends when Aunt Kate and Jack came up, before everything fell apart between Daddy and them.

But he never taught me. He never showed me his tricks. He never let me lay hands on the springy, elastic bread dough, never let me punch it down after it had risen. I have tried to make bread myself, but it never tastes as good as my father's. It occurs to me that with every loaf I bake, I'm searching for him.

He never shows.

And as I press my forehead against the train's cold glass windowpane, passing through the desolate landscape of a Connecticut winter, I find myself tearing up again and I feel the sorrow that is in me burgeon, like a hardy seed planted in deep, rich dirt, exploding open, pushing through. The dirt rolls and crumbles as the devastating flower of my disappointment pushes up, catching in my throat, making it tighten and ache. I am not thinking of my husband and the life he has gone on to have without me. I will grieve that more, I know, but for now Cam's choices seem . . . almost irrelevant. He is gone, and on some deep level I know that this is as it should be. It is an older desertion I am thinking of. That cold, reticent man who only showed his love through the loaves of bread he baked for us each week. I try to believe it was enough, but in the end, it was only crumbs.

punch it down after it had risen. I have tried to make bread myself, but it never tastes as good as my father's. It occurs to me that with every loaf I bake, I'm searching for him.

He never shows.

And as I press my forehead against the train's cold glass windowpane, passing through the desolate landscape of a Connecticut winter, I find myself tearing up again and I feel the sorrow that is in me burgeon, like a hardy seed planted in deep, rich dirt, exploding open, pushing through. The dirt rolls and crumbles as the devastating flower of my disappointment pushes up, catching in my throat, making it tighten and ache. I am not thinking of my husband and the life he has gone on to have without me. I will grieve that more, I know, but for now Cam's choices seem . . . almost irrelevant. He is gone, and on some deep level I know that this is as it should be. It is an older desertion I am thinking of. That cold, reticent man who only showed his love through the loaves of bread he baked for us each week. I try to believe it was enough, but in the end, it was only crumbs.

Part Four

Bobby and Amelia in New York

17

The Truth Never Hurt Anyone

(New York City, 1990)

I haven't seen Aunt Kate since things blew up between Cam and me, almost six months ago. I didn't even see her over the Christmas holidays, when I, quite frankly, fled, taking Lucy and Mandy down to one of those all-inclusive resorts in the Bahamas with vague promises that their father would try to join us, and then feigned disappointment when I reported he got tied up with work, and then a teary New Year's Eve confession that actually, we had separated, which did not come as news to my daughters at all.

"It's been pretty obvious," said Lucy, pulling on her lower lip with her pinky, same as she did when she was a girl.

Over the past six months Aunt Kate and I *have* spoken on the phone, briefly, but never about anything more significant than which courses Lucy plans to take during her spring semester at Emory, or the fact that Mandy is dating a senior at Hotchkiss, or the cute thing Lulu, Kate's fluffy little lapdog of a mutt, did that morning.

Ever since I phoned Kate, after that first terrible night with Cam, I've carried around a stone of resentment toward her, resentment that she wasn't able to really listen to me when I needed her most, resentment that she made me feel that if I didn't end my marriage that very morning, I was an idiot, deserving of abuse. But maybe that's not what she said at all. Maybe I wasn't able to hear what she was really saying because I wasn't yet ready to hear the truth.

Six months of distance. It occurs to me that I've gone much longer without seeing my father, and I could certainly go that long without seeing my own mother—and be none the worse for it. (Though duty forces me to Roxboro once a month to sip a tepid martini with Mother in the parlor while she goes over her litany of daily grievances: the neighbor who snubbed her, the repairman who overcharged.)

But Kate. I miss Kate. And then, as if she can hear my yearning from her office in Manhattan, she telephones to see if I might take the train into the city tonight, so she can take me to dinner at Café Andres, her old haunt that nearly went out of business in the early eighties, but was brought back to life by Bobby Banks, the energetic young chef from the South who took over the kitchen, introducing Upper East Siders to citified versions of corn grits and cheese biscuits and banana pudding. (I remember him, of course, as the sweet man who offered me a towel when I, in the middle of a Cam crisis, inadvertently interrupted some private event he was having.) I'm excited to go to the restaurant, to taste his cooking, and I'm even more excited to see Kate.

I agree to the dinner with childlike enthusiasm. "Yes, yes, please. Yes!"

God, I love the city. As I make my way up the escalator from the train terminal into the main hall of Grand Central Station, the good mood I've been in all day only intensifies. Here is the bustle; here are the people! Rushing to their commuter trains, rushing to meet a friend, a relative, a loved one. Rushing away from someone they don't want to see. Rushing, rushing, rushing—so many lives, set loose in this mighty space.

I move through the station with the crowd, happy not to be lugging a suitcase behind me, though it occurs to me that perhaps I should have brought one, as I might very well want to stay overnight at Kate's. I feel like staying up late, talking. I feel like sharing a bottle of wine. I feel like not being alone.

Walking east on Fifty-first Street, toward the restaurant, I catch a glimpse of myself in a storefront window, but it is one of those moments when at first you don't recognize *you* and think you are seeing someone else. Of that someone else I think: *I would like to be friends with her.* I am wearing a burgundy-colored wool dress that contains a touch of spandex in the fabric, with three-quarter-length sleeves and a hem that hits just above the knees. It is one of those dresses that looks simple but costs three hundred dollars because it is expertly tailored to hide belly fat and other imperfections. I have on textured stockings and a pair of shoes Lucy gave me for Christmas, Mary Janes with stacked heels, also burgundy, made sparkly with a little glitter. To be honest, they look a bit like what a stripper from the 1940s might have worn, certainly not anything Taffy Two would be caught dead in.

Well, good. Betty Page wouldn't be caught dead in beige, either.

Over the dress, I wear Mother's ancient cashmere coat, black with a fox fur collar. Even though it is February, I wear the coat open and unbuttoned, as I have worked up a sweat walking so fast. God forbid I run into a group of keyed-up animal rights activists while wearing this thing. But really, they should know better than to target vintage fur. I mean, this coat has been around for forty years. This fox has been honored.

The woman I glimpsed in the window (me!) looked fierce with her fur collar and her wild head of curls. She did not look like someone coming into the city from a Connecticut outpost; she looked like someone who belongs here, someone who can walk right into a New York restaurant and assume she will be given a good table simply because of her style, her confidence. And indeed, once I make my way through the long entry hall and into the cavernous, baroque interior of the café, I am given a great table, the one in the rear corner that allows a view of everything and everyone. Granted, it's not me who is given such a prime spot, but Kate, Kate who is already seated.

Kate rises to kiss me, European-style, a peck on each cheek, putting her hand on my shoulder while she does so. Though her hair color has changed from dark brown to silver and there are wrinkles around her eyes and mouth, to me Aunt Kate looks much the same as she did when she was a young woman and I was a girl. Probably because she is careful about what she eats or, rather, careful of the portions she consumes. She'll order a steak anytime she wants but will eat only half of it, boxing up the remainder for lunch at her desk the next day. As always, she wears her hair parted down the middle in a blunt cut that hits just at her shoulders. She is dressed in a sort of kimono-like jacket, the color of poppies, which she wears over a pair of black wool trousers. Her shoes are narrow and sensible.

"I'm awfully glad to see you," she says. "It's a cliché to say, 'It's been too long,' but for us, it really has."

We remain standing, facing each other, and my eyes fill with involuntary tears. "Oh, Kate," I say. "I have so much to tell you."

"Sit," she says. "I've ordered a bottle of wine. I presume that's okay?"

I nod as I seat myself. It's more than okay.

"Have a biscuit," she says, pushing the basket toward me. They are warm. I bite into one. It is delicate and tender and tastes of cheddar and green onion.

"Before we start catching up," Kate says, "I want to apologize. I don't think I did a great job of listening when you called last September. I'm sorry I wasn't able just to hear what you were going through."

Tears push against my eyes again, and I take another bite of the warm biscuit.

"I love you like a daughter, Amelia. You know that."

"Don't set the bar so low," I say, sounding more bitter than I intend.

"Susan had a tough time," she says.

I feel something tighten in my throat. I'm so damned tired of justifying other people's bad behavior—Mother's, Daddy's, Cam's. For the majority of my life, this is what I have done. Justified the adult children peeing in the baby pool. I want to make my way into deeper waters, with adults who can actually swim.

"Cam and I are getting a divorce," I say.

It still feels strange to say those words aloud, accurate as they are.

"Do you have an attorney?" Kate asks.

"I do, but I think I need another one. The one I hired has a pretty good hourly rate, and her retainer was low, but she never returns my phone calls."

"Sweetheart, don't skimp on an attorney. Fire her and get someone good."

Kate is right.

"Do you have a recommendation? I don't want a shark. I don't want a long, protracted fight. But I think I need someone who can stand up to Cam better than I can."

"Almost all of my authors have been through at least one divorce, and half of them live in Connecticut, so I'm sure I can find the numbers of a few for you to check out."

"Thank you."

I love this about Aunt Kate, her eternal competence. By the end of next week she will have called and given me a list with several names of excellent attorneys.

There is a server standing above us with a cold bottle of Pouilly-Fuissé. She opens the wine while asking if we'd like any starters.

I pick up the menu and try to read about the delicious food being offered, but the words blur in front of my eyes. I can't stop tearing up. I place the menu back on the table. "I'm having a hard time making any decisions," I tell Kate. "Could you just order for me?"

She nods, telling the waitress we'll start with an order of fried oysters with a champagne mignonette sauce and a shaved fennel salad, both to share.

"Fried sounds nice," I say.

"You'll have to come in the summer when Bobby puts fried okra back on the menu. It's become one of his signature dishes. He gets it so crispy, and he puts in just the right amount of salt."

"It's hilarious to me that New Yorkers are eating okra. How's Jack?"

"He's good. He's actually in California right now, for work. I miss him."

"Amazing. So many years later, and you're still in love."

"The downside is that I've found myself fixating on the fact that, in the not too distant future, he's going to die. He's almost seventy, you know. We don't have forever."

"But he's healthy," I say.

"We're lucky. Last week I accompanied an author to an event in D.C., and when I got back late that night Jack had made a pot of chili and left it for me on the stove. He had already eaten dinner himself, at the pub down the street, but he knew I'd be hungry when I got home."

"I want that," I say. "To be tended to like that." I start to cry in earnest. Embarrassed, I dab at my eyes with my white cloth napkin.

"Oh, sweetheart, you're closer to having that now that Cam is gone. I'm sorry to say it, but I think it's true."

I nod. I think it's true, too.

"Ever since Cam left, I've been thinking a lot about my dad," I say. "Do you know it's been over ten years since I last saw him?"

Kate exhales audibly, takes a sip of her drink.

The waitress brings our shaved fennel salad, topped with walnuts and ribbons of Parmesan, along with a plate of fried oysters, golden brown, a small dipping sauce filled with chopped scallions in its center. She also brings two empty white plates. Kate takes charge, filling one of the plates with the salad and the fried oysters, then setting it before me. It is lovely to be served. Kate makes a plate for herself, and we tap wineglasses before eating. I dunk an oyster in the mignonette and pop it in my mouth. It is perfect: hot and crunchy on the outside, creamy on the inside, the acid from the sauce balancing it all out. I take a sip of the wine, which is dry enough to cut through the rich flavors.

"There is *nothing* wrong with this," I say, motioning to the food with my fork.

"No, there is not," agrees Kate.

"Did you and Daddy ever talk after your big fight?"

"Which big fight?"

"When you brought that cookbook to Connecticut—the one by that black chef, Alice Stone. And Daddy said, you know, Daddy said that you were exploiting her."

Kate's fork is halfway to her mouth, but she puts her uneaten bite back down on her plate and takes another sip of wine instead.

"It's so odd you should bring up Alice. Did you know that she was the original chef at this restaurant? That's why I used to come here all the time—and why I got the idea that she should write a book about her experiences growing up in North Carolina. And now she's sort of serving as a mentor to the new chef, Bobby Banks. They bonded over their southern roots."

"Oh, of course. I did know that. That's probably why I started thinking about that book once I sat down in here."

"Actually, you met her once, sort of. Though you weren't formally introduced. It was the day you found out Cam had a houseguest in your absence and you came to find me at the restaurant. Do you remember?"

"I don't. I was so absorbed in my crisis with Cam. I only remember meeting Bobby."

I eat another oyster. They are so good. "So why do you think that book made Daddy so mad?"

"How old were you when that happened?"

"Fourteen."

"Hmm," she says. She stares at her plate.

"What?"

She glances at me. "Nothing, nothing. This is all just divine, isn't it? We'll have to get Bobby to come out and say hello." She pours herself more wine from the bottle, though her glass isn't even half empty.

"Why are you acting so weird? What's going on?"

"I'm just surprised you remembered that fight. That's all."

"It was nuclear. You and Jack left. In the middle of cocktails, you two just flew out, Daddy screaming at you from the door. How could I not remember?"

"Of course you would. I'm sorry. I'm naïve to think it would have gone over your head."

"Are you kidding? You and Daddy never spoke again."

She is silent, and when I look at her I see beads of sweat along her hairline.

"What's going on?" I ask. "You and Daddy did speak?"

She takes her napkin and dabs at the sweat. "I swear, I thought I was through with hot flashes, but anytime I get agitated they just come on."

"Why are you agitated? It was so long ago."

"I've held back for so long."

"Oh my God, Kate. Did you and Daddy have an affair?"

I don't know where that idea sprung from, but suddenly it makes sense. His fury toward her (passion gone wrong?), his sudden departure to Palo Alto, the falling-out that Mother and Kate had soon after.

I look at her with wide eyes. She needs to tell me the truth. She is shaking her head, about to speak, but the server returns, asking if we are ready to order. Kate starts to send her away, but I say, "No, let's go ahead. If you'll order for me."

Kate orders the crab cakes and the chicken potpie, though I'm not sure who's getting which. The server, seeing that our bottle of wine is nearly empty, asks if we would like anything else to drink, and Kate says no, but then I surprise myself by ordering a ginger ale. It just sounds comforting. Once the server walks away, Kate speaks.

"No, sweetheart. No affair between your father and me. Nothing like that. It actually wasn't anything I was involved with at all—just something I came upon. A connection your dad had, to Alice Stone. And to be completely frank, Amelia, I wanted to tell you about it back then, but I ran it by your mother first, and she was adamant that I not do so. I was torn. In the end I decided that you were her child, not mine, and I should respect her wishes. I've never known whether or not that was the right decision."

"Whatever it is, I think it's important you tell me now."

Though I speak calmly, I am surprised by how powerful and authoritative my voice is.

"I know," she says. "But I don't know if I can."

I push away my plate, though I haven't touched the fennel salad. I no longer want this food. All I want is the glass of ginger ale and ice the server has silently placed on the table.

"Well, at least tell me what you can. Tell me more about the night of the fight. It never made any sense to me."

"Okay. Okay. Well, at first it didn't make any sense to me, either. And I admit, the whole drive back into the city, all I could do was rail against your father. I was so angry at him, so angry at his elitism, his spurious concern for Negroes, his judgment of me.

"Jack let me rant, but he kept saying, 'I think there's something else going on. Benjamin's reaction just doesn't make sense. There's something we're not seeing.'

"I snapped at Jack, actually, told him to quit trying to excuse Benjamin's horrible behavior, that I was sick of it, sick of how we all accommodated him, sick of how Susan let him do whatever the hell he wanted, leave the house for weeks at a time, run off to his lab anytime something started to bother him."

It was true. Daddy would just leave. Any upset and he simply drove off. We never knew when he might come back.

"At home Jack fixed me a nightcap, and I tried to go to bed. But I was too agitated. Too worked up. I loved Alice's book. I was so proud of it. And I had been so looking forward to showing it to your father. I thought he would love it, he who was so concerned with homegrown tomatoes and homemade bread and eating as close to the land as you could. He who was also the son of humble farmers, who also made something great of himself.

"I got out of bed, made myself a cup of tea, and sat at the kitchen table, Alice's manuscript before me. It was so beautiful, this book. So unexpected. I started talking to your father while I was flipping through its pages, arguing over its merits: *No, Benjamin! Writing about a beautiful experience of a black family in the South does not negate a history of horror! Yes, there was horror. Unbearable horror, not to be diminished, not to be ignored. But there was also love, life, joy—and to ignore that is just as dehumanizing.*

"I got so worked up looking over the pages that I actually telephoned your father in Connecticut. I simply could not understand his reaction. I admit, I didn't think he would actually pick up. I assumed he would have taken off, headed to his lab, or a bar, or wherever it was he went when conflict arose. But he did pick up, on the second ring, as if he were waiting for me.

"When he answered he sounded so tired, so exhausted, that my anger just dissipated. I could not rant against this exhausted man. 'I'm just trying to understand your reaction,' I said. 'I was so excited to show you this book, and I'm just so hurt.' I actually started crying, which you know is rare for me.

"'Oh, Kate,' he said. 'Why did you of all people have to become Alice Stone's editor?'

"I told him I didn't understand.

"'I know her,' he said. 'I love her. I've followed her career all of these years.'"

"How did he know her?" I ask.

"I think you should call your father and ask him that yourself," says Kate. "I don't think I can say anything more."

"So he and Alice were in love?" I ask.

"Call your father."

"Were *they* having an affair? Is that why Daddy disappeared so often? Is that why they always kept me out of the city when I was little? Because he was having a relationship with Alice? Because he wanted to keep the two worlds separate?"

"Call your father. I think it's time he answered these questions."

"My God, Kate. How serious was it?"

"Your father needs to talk to you about this."

"But Daddy was so conservative. I can't imagine him doing anything so bold as to fall in love with a black woman. Not back then."

"We all have our hidden sides," Kate says.

"God, it sounds mean to Mother, but this actually makes me sort of proud of Daddy."

"Sweetie," Kate says. "I can't in good conscience tell you more than I have. But I can tell you this: You don't yet know the full story. I think you should call your father and ask him to tell it to you. Tell him it's time. Tell him it's time for you to know."

Our server stands above us with our main courses.

"Who's having the crab cakes?" she asks.

"Do you mind if I take them?" I ask Kate. I am hungry again, now that I know there is a story to be told, now that I know the questions to ask when I call my father and demand that he tell it.

"They're yours," she says.

The crab cakes are golden brown, each topped with a little salad of sliced avocado, green onion, and grapefruit supremes. I fix myself a bite with all of the dish's components. The sweet crabmeat, the crisp, buttery breading, the citrus and avocado salad, splashed with a fruity vinaigrette—together it's a perfect combination of flavors.

"My God, this is good."

"Bobby is unbelievably talented. Here, try the potpie."

She fixes me a spoonful of the creamy stew, thick with tender chicken and vegetables, topped with crisp, buttery puff pastry.

"Damn."

"Do you want to meet Chef Bobby?" asks Kate. "Or rather, remeet him?"

I do. She calls the server over and asks if Bobby might come out for a minute. A few minutes later a sober-looking man walks out of the kitchen, his face becoming animated the moment he recognizes Kate.

"Darling!" he says. God, he is gorgeous. His hair is nearly as curly as mine, though a lighter shade of brown. His eyes are the color of my slate roof in Connecticut. His body is lean, fit. And he's so young. Even though there are a few streaks of gray in his hair, he looks like a child.

Kate stands, and he bends toward her so she can kiss him on both cheeks.

"This is my niece, Amelia. She was just raving about the food."

Apparently Kate assumes that Bobby will not remember us once having met.

"Everything has been absolutely delicious," I say.

He smiles, but it's the smile of someone used to hearing compliments often. "Thank you. You're so dear. I hope you enjoy."

"I've actually wanted you and Amelia to meet because I think she might be able to assist you with the book."

"Excuse me?" I say.

"Bobby is writing a book tied to Café Andres, illuminating its storied past and his own contribution to its current revival. And he needs help testing recipes."

"I would love that!" I say.

"Well, maybe we can have coffee and chat about it," he says. "Now if you'll forgive me, I've got to get back to the kitchen. I'm making rabbit pâté, and you won't believe how long it takes to debone the bunnies. Amelia, I'm so glad to meet you, and I hope you'll let me treat you to dessert today."

"That would be lovely," I say.

Funny how glib fame has made him. But no matter. No matter at all. For surprisingly, I am filled with an unexpected and buoyant optimism. I am in New York with my aunt, the person, other than my girls, whom I love most. And it is clear to me that the life I know is about to change. Something is coming that is even more drastic than Cam moving out, even more drastic than Cam's announcement of his impending fatherhood. (Do I care, do I even care about that at all? I push on the bruise. Still a little tender, but Cam's desertion is not going to be the thing that defines me for the rest of my life.)

Something solid, substantial, and powerful is on its way.

Suddenly I see a vision of my old life as if it were a Victorian home, once lovely, now decrepit. The floorboards have rotted, there are rats in the walls, the wiring has been chewed through, and the basement is flooded. It's a mercy, really, that a wrecking ball has been set in motion, the force of which will smash the whole goddamn thing right to the ground.

18

Homegrown

(New York City, 1990)

After dinner, Kate suggests she drive us to Connecticut in order for me to fetch Sadie and pack a suitcase, so that I can come stay at her apartment for a few days. "Make a vacation of it," Kate says. It's a spontaneous plan spurred by the fact that her car is not in the covered garage she pays three hundred dollars a month for on the Upper East Side but is instead parked just down the street from the restaurant, as Kate had to drive deep into Queens that day to visit an invalid author whose work she is editing.

Kate assures me that the timing is perfect for me to come visit. Jack won't be back from California until the weekend, so I will have the apartment all to myself during the day, and then she and I can eat together each night "and really catch up." That's as explicit as Kate gets regarding our last six months of semi-estrangement. Nor does she mention the most obvious reason for why I should stay with her: so that after I phone my father (first thing tomorrow morning) she and I can fully debrief.

Without any traffic, it is a short trip to Old Greenwich. Kate waits for me downstairs, sweet Sadie curled on the sofa beside her, while I pack my suitcase. We drag it plus Sadie's bed and food out to Kate's Saab, and then we stuff Sadie in the backseat and head back to the city. It occurs to me that such an impromptu trip would never have happened were Cam around. Cam did not like his schedule interrupted.

It feels right journeying back to Manhattan, dog in tow. I feel oddly calm, though maybe I shouldn't, not after Kate's (partial) revelation. I am gathering energy, I suppose, for tomorrow, when I will phone my father in Palo Alto and tell him that Kate says it's time for him to spill. I try not to think about what all he might tell me, but I find myself working at the knots of my father's past, sticking the fine point of a needle into the most clenched places, loosening the strings. *(What if Daddy and Alice had a child together? What if I have a half-black brother or sister?)*

Kate drops me off in front of her building on East End Avenue—which Jack loves to point out is simply a fancy, uptown name for what is actually Avenue B—and I enlist the night doorman to help me with the dog paraphernalia and luggage. Sadie and I wait in the lobby while Kate takes the car to the garage. Tomorrow I will take Sadie to Carl Schurz Park, the entrance of which is just across the street. For the longest time I mispronounced the park's name, until one day Kate grabbed the front of her button-down and, holding it taut between her pointer finger and thumb, instructed me to say, "Shirts. Carl *Shirts* Park."

Soon Kate returns from the garage and we go up to her apartment. I hear the scratching of her dog Lulu's nails against the floor as Kate turns the key in the lock. Though Sadie is a good head taller than Kate's little dog, it is Lulu who barks and growls. Sadie does her submissive magic, flopping on the ground right there in the hallway, rolling over, and showing Lulu she has nothing to fear. Lulu sniffs Sadie's belly, then turns and clicks her way back through the apartment, and Kate, Sadie, and I all enter.

The apartment is small but charming, with a place for everything and everything in its place. There is a view of the East River from both the living room and Kate and Jack's bedroom. Kate puts me in the tiny "maid's room," which they use as a guest bedroom, blowing me a kiss at my bedroom door. Exhausted, I kick off my shoes and take off my dress, placing it on an old wire hanger in the closet.

I pull a pair of flannel pajamas out of my suitcase, put them on, and stretch out on the twin-size bed, telling myself I will get up in a minute, brush my teeth, and wash my face. I look around the room at all of Jack's vintage Broadway posters tacked to the walls, his boyhood enthusiasms perennially preserved.

Lying in bed, I think about Kate, how she has always been innocent of others' expectations. She has never known how to play a role: not as wife nor as woman. Somehow when Kate started working at Palmer, Long and McIntyre in the late 1950s she never got the memo that she was supposed to, well, type memos rather than edit books. Also lost was the memo mandating that if you *did* make it as a "working girl," it would be at the expense of a happy home and hearth. But Kate has Jack. Jack who can sometimes be difficult, but who loves his Kate specifically and well. Who leaves a pot of chili on the stove when he knows she has to stay late at the office and will be returning home tired and hungry. Who takes needle and thread to her wallet, re-stitching it once the original threads have worn away (Jack and Kate have a propensity for holding on to things *forever*). Who is always willing to accompany Kate on an adventure, be it geographical or culinary.

I often wonder what allows Kate to be so quintessentially herself. It is as if she possesses some gene that precludes her from believing her own bullshit. God, I wish that gene had been passed on to me. I've spent my entire adult life—hell, my entire life—creating narratives that describe how I *want* things to be, rather than how they actually are. Surely one of the reasons I was unable to see the deep holes in my marriage was that doing so would force me to admit its true dynamic: that I was married to a man too invested in surfaces to want to know my core.

That I was lonely for years and years.

I wake up the next morning, the taste of stale wine in my mouth, unsure of where I am. I turn to my side and there is Sadie, standing on the floor by the bed, her wet nose against my face. I glance at the wall, see a poster for *His Girl Friday* and another one for *The Merry Widow*. Right. I'm in the guest room at Kate's house. I go to the bathroom, brush my teeth—I never did last night—then walk to the kitchen. Kate has left a note, telling me that she's heading in early so she can swim laps at the gym before going to the office, but to make myself at home, there's milk and cereal and fruit, and I just need to punch the "on" button on the machine for coffee. She requests that I let Lulu accompany Sadie and me on any walks we might take. Beside the note is the key to Kate's apartment and to her building.

I had planned to call Daddy first thing—well, after a cup of coffee—but I forgot that he is on West Coast time, three hours behind New York. I'm positive he's an early riser, but it's not quite 8:00 a.m. here, meaning it's not even 5:00 a.m. in Palo Alto. I take Sadie and Lulu—now perfectly at ease in each other's company—down to the park so they can pee, fix myself a cup of coffee once I return home, eat a bowl of cereal while reading the *Times*, shower, blow-dry my hair using the new diffuser my stylist gave me—which keeps the curls intact instead of frizzing up—and crunch in some styling mousse to keep them that way. At 10:00 a.m. I try Daddy's house in California but only get the answering machine. I hate the answering machine. I leave a quick message telling him to call me at Kate's, that it's important.

God. When was the last time I called Daddy? I skipped my usual Christmas call this year. I was in the Bahamas with the girls, and I just let it slip by. I guess the last time I phoned was on his birthday, his seventy-fifth, during which we had a brief and awkward discussion about the mileage our respective cars got, before I dutifully told him I loved him ("You too," he replied) and hung up.

I return to the guest room, make the bed, and then lie down on it again, feeling uncertain of what to do with myself. Feeling suspended until I can talk to my father, I stare at the rickety blue bookcase across from the bed, the top shelf housing board games, including Monopoly and Risk. Seeing those games makes me think of Scruples, of what was revealed when we played that night. (Did the creator of that game know the havoc it would wreak on other people's marriages?) The rest of the shelves are crammed with—surprise!—books. I stand to look more closely. Just from scanning the titles, I can tell that many of these are favorite novels of Kate's: *All the King's Men, Kate Vaiden, Portnoy's Complaint, A Mother and Two Daughters, Their Eyes Were Watching God, A Room with a View, Sophie's Choice, Sula, Crossing to Safety.*

I inhale. Seeing *Crossing to Safety* takes me back to that first awful night of Cam's rages, when I huddled under the covers in my daughter's room, trying to escape a terrible situation by entering into the imaginary lives of others. I pull the book out and hold it against my chest, feeling profound gratitude toward Wallace Stegner for having written it.

I'm still on a reading tear, but lately I've been dipping into books I read as a child. I don't need a shrink to tell me I'm trying to regress to simpler times. Not that my childhood was all that simple. Solitary, yes, but not really simple. To Aunt Kate's house I brought my beloved *Harriet the Spy*, which is set in this very neighborhood, a lot of it on the playground at Carl Schurz (Shirts!) Park.

I keep scanning Kate's books, wondering how many she owns in total—thousands, surely—and where she keeps the ones that are not in this apartment. In her office at PLM, maybe, or perhaps in a storage unit somewhere. And then my eye lands on *Homegrown*, and with a start I realize that this is Alice Stone's book, the one Kate edited, the one that made Daddy go apoplectic. I pull the book from the shelf, fingering its textured linen cover, devoid of a dust jacket. God. I don't even remember seeing this in the bookstore. I guess I was already at Rosemary Hall when it was released, sheltered on my bucolic campus. And Kate didn't send me a copy like she usually did with her pet projects.

When I open the book it releases a trapped, musty smell. Usually I avoid old books for this very reason—the mustiness sets off my allergies—but I am too curious about *Homegrown* to put it down. Just reading the names of the recipes makes me hungry: chicken and dumplings, smothered pork chops, fresh trout stuffed with bread crumbs and lemon. There are little line drawings by each recipe, charming and simple. A note at the front of the book says they were drawn by Alice.

(Could patrician, distant Daddy, who aerated his wine, who subscribed to the *National Review*, who never used contractions, really have been in love with the black woman behind these charming, country recipes?)

I keep flipping through the book, having spontaneously decided to prepare something from it for Aunt Kate tonight, to have dinner waiting when she returns from the office. Old habit, I guess. I always had dinner waiting for Cam. Maybe I'll go to Rosedale's, get some really good seafood. Maybe I'll see if there is a recipe in here for shrimp and grits, which Taffy prepared for me whenever I visited

Atlanta, knowing it's my favorite. Whenever I asked my mother-in-law for the recipe she would smile and say, "Oh, it's just a little of this and a little of that."

Except, no, I wouldn't be able to find stone-ground grits in the city and would have to put the shrimp over rice instead. Maybe I'll make the trout stuffed with bread crumbs, shallots, and lemon slices, or the chicken and dumplings, which are simply biscuits made with cream, cooked on top of a chicken stew. I keep turning the pages of the book, thinking I might make dessert, too. Something comforting. Rice pudding, or a fruit cobbler. The first dessert listed is called "Juneteenth Cake." Juneteenth, I read, is a celebration of blacks' emancipation from slavery. The cake is made from fresh coconuts, both the grated meat and the milk from within. Sounds delicious but laborious.

On the page facing the recipe for the Juneteenth Cake is a photograph, a family portrait taken at a Juneteenth celebration. The men wear long-sleeved shirts beneath overalls. The women wear long, white dresses, which appear to be made from flour sacks. I look closely and spot Alice Stone, up front, her hair in two braids, tied at the ends with little white pieces of cloth.

Beside Alice stands a tall boy with something on his shoulder. It takes me a moment to decipher what it is, but then I realize it's a chicken, staring straight at the camera, as if posing. Funny. I look closely at the boy. He is taller than Alice but looks a great deal like her. Same almond-shaped eyes, same sharp cheekbones, same full mouth. For some reason I am drawn to this boy. There is something so familiar about him. It's a little like being at a party and spotting someone you know across the room but not being able to remember his or her name and so spending the entire evening awkwardly avoiding that person out of embarrassment.

Did this boy—Alice's brother or cousin, surely—grow up to be famous? Is that why he looks so familiar?

Perspiration springs to my face, a sudden hot flash. What is it? What am I seeing here? My body is reacting to something I don't yet understand: my heart rate increasing, my mouth going dry. The wild flower of sorrow is growing, reaching toward air, as if on speed release, growing so fast it is coming out of my mouth, pushing itself into the light, pushing itself out of me so that, in order to breathe, in order to breathe at all, I must open my mouth and say aloud the thing my body has already recognized: *Daddy.*

The boy in the photograph is my father.

How the hell is the boy in the photograph my father? Why is my father in this book? Did my father know he was in this book? Yes, surely. Surely that is one of the reasons its publication upset him so. But why is he there, standing beside Alice on a black farm? He should have been in California, standing by his own broken parents, before their sad, short lives ended, back when they worked in the fruit trees. Was the photo taken after Daddy left California? I flip to the back, find the photography credits, which say the picture was taken in 1928. But didn't Daddy's mother die during the Depression, sometime in the 1930s? I should know the exact year, but Daddy was so reticent about his history. So reticent about everything. Maybe he was younger than I realized when his mother died, leaving Daddy an orphan. Maybe Daddy had already started train hopping, making his way across the country to where he would eventually end up, in New York, where he would undergo a quick transformation from farm boy to city slicker.

Could he possibly have stayed at the Stone family farm on his way across the country? Apprenticed there, helped out during harvest in exchange for room and board? But how would he have landed on a black farm? Did they somehow think he was black? Mistake his Italian skin for colored? But why in the world would a white man pretend to be colored in the Jim Crow South?

Maybe if he was starving. Truly starving. Daddy must have been starving. Daddy was starving and so he did whatever he needed to do to get by. And he met Alice on the farm and fell in love with her, all those years ago, in 1928. Daddy would have been thirteen. Can you fall in love when you are thirteen?

I carry the book with me into the kitchen, where the phone is, dial Daddy's number again. Once again I get the goddamn answering machine. "Daddy, it's important; call me," I say, then hang up. I am breathing heavily, pacing around the kitchen, reminding myself of Cam, releasing his pent-up rage.

I consider calling Kate at the office, but something stops me from doing so. Frustration that she did not tell me the full story the night before. Frustration that she has kept this story from me for so very long. My whole life, people have kept things from me. Daddy and his history with Alice Stone, Mother and her alcoholism, Cam and his affair and, before that, all of his little deals and negotiations, investing in companies I did not know about, coming home with a brand-new car before we ever discussed whether we should get one. Am I so much a child? Am I so much a child that difficult things must be kept from me?

I remember something our chaplain at Rosemary Hall used to say, probably when referencing the Honor Code: "The truth never hurt anyone." During assemblies Sarah and I used to snort in derision at his earnestness, but the truth of those words now resonates.

There is nothing more belittling than being lied to.

And just then I notice a bright piece of paper stuck to the refrigerator door with a magnet. I see the word "Alice" printed on it. I pull the invitation off the fridge. It is for an Open House at Bobby Banks and Alice Stone's apartment, dated over a year ago. Yes, that's right. Aunt Kate told me about that when it happened, that it was a strange but fitting alliance. And here is their address, 320 Riverside Drive, an easy one for me to remember because, oddly, it's the month and day of Cam's birthday, March 20.

I will take a cab to the West Side, and I will meet Alice face-to-face. I will bring her book with me. I will point to the boy in the picture beside her, and I will ask her to explain this man to me, to explain my father.

Three-twenty Riverside Drive is between 106th and 107th, a stately if run-down stone building overlooking Riverside Park and the Hudson. It occurs to me that while only a few miles apart, Kate's building watches over one river while Alice's watches over another. Alice's side of the city is messier; there is trash on the street and the buildings look tired.

I ring the bell marked "A. Stone and B. Banks #4D" and wait. A man's voice comes on over the intercom.

"No solicitations, please."

I press the "talk" button. "This is Amelia Brighton, Kate Pennington's niece. Is this Bobby Banks? We spoke last night at the café."

The intercom garbles his voice, but I believe he says, "Are you here about the book?"

"Um, yes," I answer, even though I'm confused. I *am* here to talk about the book, *Homegrown,* but how would he know that? Then I remember what Kate suggested last night, that I help Bobby out with a cookbook he is working on. So he thinks I'm here for another reason. Well, fine. That might even help me gather more information. The door buzzes, I push against it, and I am inside the lobby, its former elegance apparent in the brass mailboxes, the elaborate molding, the curved banister of the stairwell.

There is no doorman, but there is an elevator, thank God. I push the "up" button and wait. I've got so much energy zipping through me that I don't even feel nervous, not really. I'm more keyed up than anything. I am going to meet a woman who can tell me about my father.

Kate says my father loved this woman.

When the elevator arrives, I take it to the fourth floor. The central hallway smells of sulfur, as if someone in one of the apartments is preparing hard-cooked eggs. I find 4D and knock on the door. Almost immediately, it is answered by Bobby. He is even better looking in the daylight, out of his chef's clothes, wearing jeans and a pale blue Shetland sweater.

"Well, hello," he says. "I didn't realize Kate was sending you over today. And to be completely honest, I'm not sure if I'm ready to commit to anything yet. But this is good; it will give us a chance to get to know each other and see if we're a good fit before signing on to work together."

I follow him inside the apartment, which is flooded in light and redolent of cinnamon. Once again I choose not to disabuse him of the notion that I am supposed to be here. In fact, I feel that I am. Supposed to be here, that is. Just not for the same reasons that he thinks I am.

"Is Miss Stone here?" I ask.

"She's at the market, but I imagine she'll be back shortly. May I get you something to drink? A glass of iced tea? Wine?"

It is twenty degrees outside and he is offering me iced tea. How southern. Taffy would ask for a glass of iced tea during a snowstorm. In fact, she once did. While visiting us in Connecticut.

I glance at my watch. It's a little past noon. If it were still morning, I wouldn't allow myself to do it. "Wine would be lovely," I say, adding, "Kate told me you were a southerner, but I forgot, where are you from exactly?"

"I've actually come to think of myself as a New Yorker. I've been here since 1981."

Funny. Only a non–New Yorker would think of himself as a native after living here for *eight whole years*.

"Yes, but where did you move from?" I ask. He has stepped

inside the galley kitchen and is pulling a bottle of wine from the refrigerator.

"Chardonnay okay?"

"Great," I say.

"I grew up in Decatur, Georgia. It's a little town just outside of Atlanta."

"My oldest daughter is at Emory! And my husband is from Atlanta. We visit his family there at least twice a year."

He grimaces while pulling out the cork from the perspiring bottle. "It's been a long time since I've been in Georgia. A very long time."

"Well, we love Emory. Though it's tough having my daughter so far away. Especially now. My husband and I are divorcing, actually."

I don't know why I'm telling him this.

"Should I say 'I'm sorry' or 'congratulations'?" he asks.

"A little from column A, a little from column B," I say.

He walks out of the kitchen carrying our wineglasses and a handful of cocktail napkins. I follow him to the brown velvet couch in the living room. He waits until I sit before handing me my glass and a napkin.

"So, this is terrible. I know that you're Kate's niece, and I know that you're here to discuss potentially helping with the book, but I don't remember your name. Forgive me. I know you told me on the intercom, but my memory is worse than Alice's, and I'm only twenty-nine."

"Oh God, don't apologize. I'm Amelia. Amelia Brighton. Kate is my mother's sister."

I take a sip of my wine, making a conscious effort not to gulp it, though it goes down so easily I am tempted to drain it in one sip.

"How much has Kate told you about the book?"

"Not much," I answer, playing dumb, wanting to find out as much from him as I can.

"It's the recipes I really need help with. They all make sense to me, of course, but that might just be because I've prepared them a million times, both at the café and at home."

The phone rings, but Bobby ignores it, letting the answering machine pick up. When it does, a deep southern drawl fills the room. "Bobby, it's your mother. Listen: Baby Troy is supposed to do a project on New York City for social studies, and I thought it might be fun if you could send down some little trinkets for him to bring to class. You know, just silly stuff—a little Statue of Liberty or Empire State Building, something like that. I'm going to make some candied apples for him to bring for his presentation—which we'll call the Big Candied Apple. He's real excited about it, and I told him to make sure to tell his class that he has an uncle who has turned into a genuine New Yorker who has twice been in *The New York Times*. Anyway, call and let us know if you plan on sending down anything. It's been a while since we've heard from you."

The message ends with a beep. Bobby is staring at the floor, pinching the bridge of his nose. "That's my mama," he says.

I smile. "I gathered. She's still in Decatur?"

"Yes, ma'am."

"She sounds sweet," I say.

"Do you remember Lacy Lovehart?"

"That name is really familiar."

"Save Our Sons? Crusader against the Homosexual Agenda? Spokeswoman for the Central Georgia Peach Growers?"

"Didn't someone throw a vanilla milk shake in her face on national TV? And she said something to the effect of, 'Well, at least they picked my favorite flavor'?"

"You got it. Back in the day my mom helped her organize concerned citizens all over the Southeast against homosexuals, because, you know, we can't procreate, so we recruit!"

Oh. This sweet man is a homosexual. Of course. I don't know why I didn't recognize that immediately.

"I'm so sorry," I say. "That must have been incredibly painful for you."

"Thanks. It was. It is. And then Alice kept pushing me to try and reconcile with them. Told me that it's too easy to lose track of family, to just let people disappear from your life. So last year I wrote them a letter, offered an olive branch. They took it, sort of, on the condition that I not actually tell them anything real about my life. They have embraced the adage 'love the sinner, not the sin,' which is a step up from where they were—Mama at least—but which still means the real me is unacceptable. But as long as we keep our conversations light we can ignore that fact."

He grimaces, shakes his head, and then smiles at me. "I bet you're a good mom. Do you have other kids besides your daughter at Emory?"

"One other daughter, away at boarding school."

"Fancy."

I shrug. "I guess. I'm not sure how fancy my life is going to be after the divorce. We'll see."

"You'll be fine," he says. "I can tell."

I don't really know what to say in response to that. "So what is it like living with Ms. Stone?"

"It's a little unconventional, I suppose, but we enjoy each other's company. I moved in a little over a year ago. I had to move out of my place—long story—and she needed help with her rent. Somehow it works. We cook a lot."

"That sounds lovely."

"And what about you? Kate says you're an excellent cook. Did you train professionally, or did you just pick it up?"

I shrug. "I've read *Mastering the Art* cover to cover, both volumes, and I've cooked pretty much every recipe from *The Silver Palate*, but that's about it for my training."

This is not at all what I came to talk about, and yet I find myself

excited at the prospect of helping Bobby test recipes. It sounds like an adventure.

He studies me for a moment, lips pursed, discerning. And then something shifts and he turns chipper and solicitous. "Would you like some spiced pecans? I made some earlier. I always like a little something to eat with a drink."

"Sounds great," I say.

While he retrieves the nuts from the kitchen, I look more closely around the room. It's a pleasant space, designed for comfort, nice and bright. There's a lovely handmade quilt hanging on the yellow wall, in the wedding ring pattern. And there are brightly colored throw pillows, covered in an ikat print, on the couch. There's a side table with a bunch of framed photos propped on top of it. I scoot to the end of the couch to look at them more closely. And there, framed, is the photo of Alice and her family with my father in it, the same one from the book.

It brings immediate and unexpected tears to my eyes, seeing Daddy in Alice's house.

"Excuse me?" I call. My voice comes out shaky and quivering, and Bobby, who must not have heard me in the kitchen, does not respond.

I pick the framed photo up in my hands and walk to the kitchen with it. "Excuse me, but who is this?" I say, pointing to the boy—Daddy—in the framed photograph.

Bobby is pouring pecans into a small blue bowl. He glances at the photo. "You mean Alice's brother?"

"No. The boy with the chicken on his shoulder."

"Right. Alice's brother. His name was James. Alice doesn't like to talk about him. He died a long time ago."

And as I am trying to figure out how this could be, how Daddy could be both Alice's dead brother James *and* my father who was in love with Alice and who is still very much alive, I hear the turning

of the key, and then the apartment door swings open and Alice, tall, regal, and elegant, makes her way inside, a cloth satchel hanging from one arm, the bright green tops of scallions poking out from it. We look each other up and down, and then our eyes meet. I am staring at her, but also, I am staring at my dad—a female version, and with much darker skin.

There is a framed photo of Aunt Kate and Alice Stone in Kate's living room, both women with their heads thrown back, laughing. I must have looked at that photo a hundred times. How did I not see my father in Alice's face? I am struck by an ugly realization: The darkness of her skin must have stopped me from looking any closer.

And suddenly the knot has loosened and all of the threads are coming undone. I am thinking of the long sleeves Daddy wore while gardening, the oversized hats. I am thinking of the way he used to smear us both in Glacier Creme. I am thinking of the way Mother always despised my curly hair. I am thinking of my maiden name, Brookstone, which contains a "stone" within it.

But Kate said Daddy was in love with Alice.

No.

Kate said he loved her, and I took that to mean he was in love with her. But I was doing what I always do, rearranging the evidence to make it fit the narrative I want to be true.

A voice in my head whispers, *Look, Amelia. Look hard at what is in front of you.*

Oh.

Oh.

Oh. God.

Daddy was not the orphaned child of Italian emigrants. Daddy was James Stone—so close to "Benjamin Brookstone"—born to black farmers in Virginia.

Daddy loved Alice because Daddy was Alice's brother.

Daddy's parents didn't die during the Depression. Daddy's blackness did.

Which means I am not half-Italian. I am half-black. My father was—is—black. And this woman I am facing is blood. This woman I am facing is my other aunt. My aunt Alice.

I reach out to touch her, to lay my hand on her arm, and she jerks back reflexively.

"Alice," I say slowly. "I'm James's daughter, Amelia. I'm your niece."

She flinches, as if stung. "No," she says.

"Yes, yes. I see it now. My father pretended to be a white man with Italian ancestry. But he was your brother, James. That boy"—I put my finger on the photo—"is my dad."

"James is dead. He died sixty years ago."

"No," I say gently. "I don't think so." The tangled knots of my father's past have loosened, and now they are unfurling, rolling me back into the past, where I can see Daddy, a light-skinned young man, arriving in New York with nothing but a suitcase and a lie. Joining the crowds at Grand Central station, realizing that in this great big city he could be whoever he wanted. Thinking he could cut the tie that held him to North Carolina. Thinking he could cut the tie and no longer be vulnerable. I see my father. I see my bright, earnest father, wanting more from life than what he could get with colored skin. Giving up everything. Shedding a history. Slipping into the crowds. Leaving North Carolina behind. Leaving Alice, as if he had died.

"He's alive," I say. "He's a doctor. A geneticist, well known in his field. Oh God, of course. Of course he's a geneticist. Studying how closely we are all related. He lives in Palo Alto, California, has a research lab at Stanford. He's alive and I am his daughter."

"No," Alice says. "I'm sorry, but no. My James is dead. I am no kin to a white man living in Palo Alto. And I'm sorry, but I am no kin to you, whoever you are. No. This I cannot accept. I'm sorry, but no."

"I know this must be hard. Believe me, I'm just figuring it out myself. It's crazy. What Daddy did was crazy—"

"Child, it has been over sixty years since my brother left. You think I want anything to do with him now? You think I want anything to do with his lies, his cowardice, his shame? No. No, I do not. As far as I am concerned, James died a lifetime ago, and I don't need some white ghost showing up and telling me that isn't true."

"Then you're as much a liar as he is," I say.

"You need to get the hell out of my house," she says.

I turn to leave, feeling a fierce and sudden hatred toward this woman, and there stands Bobby, his face contorted in grief. He clutches his arms around his body. He is crying—silently—like an orphan in a crib, like a child who has lost all hope that he might ever be picked up again.

19

The Fragments Left Over

(New York City, 1991)

A partial list of things said to me during my divorce: that I would be better off, that I would lose twenty pounds, that I would be strapped for cash, that I should "make the bastard pay," that Cam had taken a swan dive into the pool of crazy, that I should feel happy for Cam since he is now so obviously happy, that there's no way he and his girlfriend (now wife) are enjoying robust or vigorous or even steady sex now that there's a baby in the picture. That *that* relationship certainly won't last. That it's time to put myself out there: to play the field, to have casual sex, to date younger men, to date older men, especially rich ones who will buy me nice things. That I will probably end up a stepmom to some man's children, and gosh, won't that be trying? That Cam and I always seemed like such a happy couple. That it was obvious all along that ours was a strained marriage. That Cam will be missed, because he always told such entertaining stories and was fun to have at parties. That Cam was an anchor strapped to my body, pulling me down. That I must be wondering what I did to drive him away. That I must be heartbroken. That I must be devastated. That I must not entertain the possibility that the last twenty years of my life were a waste.

Which is to say that some responses were astute, some were cruel, some were funny, and some were simply clueless. But it was Aunt Kate, of course, who provided the best analysis. Who said to me, regarding the *many* changes in my life, "My dear, I have no idea what your future holds, but I guarantee it will be interesting."

My past is more interesting, too, now that I can see my "olive" skin, my curly hair, my full lips, for what they really are: a reflection not of Italian, but of African roots. *Everything* looks different, a twist of the kaleidoscope revealing a changed landscape: fractured, breathtaking.

When I first moved into the city I stayed with Kate and Jack for a few weeks while I looked for a place to live. While at Kate's, I got into the habit of swimming laps at the indoor pool at the 92nd Street Y. Even though I ended up taking an apartment on the West Side, I still go to the Y nearly every day. Today, as I swim up and down my lane, alternately coming up for air and submerging my face in the water, I think of a trip I took with my girls—back when they really *were* girls—to visit Taffy and the Judge in Atlanta. Cam came down with us for the weekend, but returned to Connecticut that Monday, while Lucy, Mandy, and I stayed on for the week. It was summer, and it was hot, and so we remained indoors as much as possible or piled into Taffy's diesel Mercedes wagon, air-conditioning blasting, to drive to the movies or to the pool. One day Taffy's housekeeper brought her daughter, Jasmine, along with her to work. Jasmine and Mandy, both eight, played well together, sliding in sock-covered feet up and down the wooden hallway, brushing out the long blond hair of Mandy's Barbies, making clay out of salt, flour, and water and smashing their palms into it, capturing their handprints. After lunch Taffy suggested we head to the Driving Club for a swim. Mandy asked if Jasmine might come, too.

"Well, that would be lovely, wouldn't it, sweetheart?" said Taffy. "But I doubt Jasmine brought a bathing suit."

"I've got an extra one," said my girl.

A pained look crossed Taffy's face, but then her features relaxed. Sure, she said brightly, Jasmine could come, but Mandy would need to go to the linen closet and bring down towels for us all. I didn't say anything, but I knew the Driving Club kept a seemingly endless supply of plush white towels with blue stripes on hand, the club's name printed on each, so that everyone who swam appeared to be in uniform as they dried off from the water. But apparently Taffy wasn't taking us to the club that afternoon. Instead we went to the Brookwood Hills community pool, where Taffy and I lounged under umbrellas, drinking Frescas while watching the girls splash in the shallow end.

"Amelia, don't judge," Taffy finally said, though I had not articulated one word of critique. "That child would not have felt comfortable there. I promise, I was looking out for her more than anybody. She doesn't need the burden of being the first black body to swim in that pool. Some reactionary old biddy might have made a scene."

"No black person has ever swum in the PDC pool?"

"Not to my knowledge. And certainly not a maid's daughter, I can promise you that."

Today, as I move through the chlorinated water of this indoor, urban pool, it occurs to me that all those years ago, Lucy, Mandy, and I desegregated the Driving Club pool without even realizing it. Assuming we were the only ones there with mixed blood, inadvertently passing. Which might be assuming too much.

Daddy's response, when I finally reached him in Palo Alto to tell him of my newfound knowledge of our family history:

"Don't let anyone tell you you're not as good as they are."

"No one is telling me that," I said.

"Well, no one has to know if you don't want them to."

A pause, while I took slow and deliberate breaths, trying to shrink the lump of anxiety that had swollen in my throat.

"Daddy, I *want* people to know. I want to be known fully."

"Well, sweetheart, you're braver than me."

"It was a different time," I said. "I have no way of understanding what you were going through."

"Thank you," he said. "Thank you for acknowledging that."

We were both quiet for a minute.

"Were you always scared? Of getting caught? Being exposed?"

"I didn't allow myself to give it much thought. I concentrated on my work, my lab. I concentrated on genetic code, patterns beneath the surface. I'm no idiot, Amelia. I see the connection between my work and what I did to be able to pursue it. But I suppose somewhere along the way I decided that it would be easiest to live my life on my own terms if I weren't first and foremost defined by the color of my skin. Frankly, I was right."

"But you left everything. Everybody."

"I'll tell you something. Last year I was given a huge award, arguably the most prestigious one in the field of genetic research. And at the banquet honoring me, just before I gave my speech and accepted my check, I thought to myself, *And all it cost was everything.*"

A week after she kicked me out, Alice invited me back to the apartment she and Bobby Banks share. We sat down at their dining room table, all very solemn. Bobby served hot tea and put out a little pot of Alice's lemon curd and a plate of homemade ginger snaps to spread it on. Alice made it very clear that she was reaching out to me for Bobby's sake and not her own. That Bobby was like a stubborn dog that got ahold of a chew toy and would not let it go. That it was Bobby who insisted she not look away from the truth of her brother's life. That it was Bobby who shamed her for saying she could not accept that I was her kin.

"I told her," Bobby clarified, "that if she refused to accept the truth of who you are, then she's as limited as my mama."

"He scolded me is what he did," said Alice, looking at Bobby with fond annoyance. "Thirty-year-old man scolding an old woman. Lord. What I put up with from that child."

The two of them exchanged a look. I could see the nights of hard conversations behind their locked eyes.

While Alice has come to accept me, albeit grudgingly at first, she has no space in her heart for my father. Alice only speaks of Daddy in the past, as if she is speaking of a dead man. She does not want to contact him, does not want to know what became of his life after he married my mother and had me. I think of Kate and Alice working so closely together on *Homegrown,* and all that time Alice never knew that on the weekends when Kate went to Connecticut to visit her sister and brother-in-law, she was visiting James.

"How could you not tell her?" I asked Kate the night I found out the truth about my father, the night Alice kicked me out of her apartment. I was ready to raise hell with my aunt for withholding so very much from me. Kate said that she had tried to broach the subject with Alice, right after Kate found out my father's secret herself, just before *Homegrown* was published. But Alice turned icy at the mention of her brother. Said he had died a long time ago, said she intended to let the dead rest in peace. Reminded Kate that they had agreed that *Homegrown* would not delve into anything personal, would remain a cookbook and not a memoir, documenting recipes, not lives. Told Kate that in order for the two of them to continue working together, they needed to keep their own relationship strictly professional.

"What could I do but respect her wishes?" asked Kate.

While disinterested in Daddy's life once he eviscerated his black roots, Alice is willing to stretch back in time, to tell of her memories of him from when they were kids, to tell of the mind-reading game she and James used to play, sitting across from each other, one spelling out a word on a chalkboard, the other drawing a picture of that word without ever having seen it written down. She tells me of the night she and James found the lynched body in the woods, which was the same night they learned the truth about their roots, that their great-grandfather was a white man.

Alice says that for a while after Daddy left Emancipation Township she had a sense of him, that he was alive, that he was safe, and that he was lonely. And then she lost him, abruptly, as if he had deliberately cut off the signal. Months later, Alice's mother received a letter with no return address. It was from James. It said everyone should forget about him, should pretend James Stone had never been born.

Impossible. At sixteen, still yearning, Alice headed to Manhattan in hopes of finding her brother, even though many of her cousins had moved to D.C., where they had settled in quickly with relatives who had learned to live off the farm. (Emancipation Township did not survive the Depression. After their grandfather died, after the land was liened because of the overdue tax bill, after yet another year of bad crops, everyone left, scattered to crowded cities, where they lived in apartment buildings, where their feet no longer touched the warm, fertile ground.) In New York, Alice was always on the lookout for James. She was most alert at jazz clubs, in Harlem, at services at Abyssinian Baptist, which she attended not because of any strong religious convictions but because she thought James might show up there.

And then years later, after the soldiers returned home victorious from the Second World War, but before she and Gus opened the café, she saw James, in Manhattan, walking down Fifth Avenue, hand in hand with a pretty, pregnant white woman. Alice was in the middle of helping Gus decorate a store window at Saks, but upon seeing James she walked off the job, told Gus an emergency had come up and that she had to go. She followed Daddy down the street, calling after him, "James! James! It's Alice. Turn around."

He did not turn, but instead walked faster. She, too, picked up her pace. At the next intersection, where James and the pregnant white woman were stopped at a light, Alice caught up with her brother. Tugged at the cuff of his sleeve. He gave her a withering look, still refusing to speak. "If I'd have died on the spot he would have been glad," Alice said.

Alice, wounded and in shock, slunk away. Told herself she was mistaken, that the man she saw walking down Fifth Avenue, hand in hand with a pregnant white woman, was not her brother. Told herself her brother had died a long time ago. Started mixing up the face of the lynched boy she had seen as a girl with the face of her brother. Told herself James was lynched. At first she knew she was making up a story, relying on an untruth to help her move past the pain of her brother's rejection. But eventually she told herself the story of her brother's lynching so many times that she came to believe it as fact. Eventually she came to believe her own lie.

When Alice told me this, I sympathized. Born into the lie of Daddy's fictitious heritage, I continued the family tradition, building my hearth and home around untruths—that Cam and I were happy together, for one—until Cam finally struck a match and burned it all down. I am at a place now where I can say thank God. Thank God it burned to the ground.

I am even beginning to feel grateful Cam left. We both needed out. Our lives have irrevocably split, two vines twisted around our girls, but otherwise growing in opposite directions. I have no claim on his life from this point on, but neither do I feel malice.

Bobby and Alice and I did not linger around the table for too long, talking solemnly. Bobby had a cookbook to put out, and Alice and I helped him test the recipes, to make sure they translated well from restaurant to home kitchen. We did a good job, the essays he wrote to accompany the recipes were dear, and we had a lovely little launch party for it at the café, which Gus decided should double as his farewell party, saying he was tired of being a restaurateur and was ready to close shop.

"It's time for my second act," Gus said, this from an octogenarian. But he made good on his declaration, shutting the restaurant down permanently the week after the launch and purchasing around-the-world airline tickets for himself, Randy, and a young male companion who, Gus said, would be there "to help with the luggage."

The imminent closing of the restaurant certainly made for a teary book launch. Teary and boozy, with everyone concerned about what Bobby would do once the restaurant closed. Bobby assured us that he would be fine, that he was talking to several people about starting his own place, but that he might take some time off before he did, that he needed to figure out if being a chef was what he wanted to do for the rest of his life.

Both of my daughters came to the launch, and Kate and Jack and many others from PML, along with my best friend from boarding school, Sarah. And a whole slew of café regulars, including a group of formidable ladies who lunched back in the 40s, 50s, and early 60s who wore their antiquated—and yellowing—white gloves to wave farewell to their memories of a more elegant time, long since passed but revived for that night. Martinis and Champagne were passed, along with a selection of Bobby's best hors d'oeuvres: potato pillows dotted with crème fraîche and caviar, crawfish spread served in toast cups, miniature crab cakes topped with rémoulade, tiny tuna burgers with fresh grated ginger, served on homemade brioche (Alice's recipe, which I discovered was virtually indistinguishable from what my father used to bake for our family). There were all sorts of desserts, too, mostly southern. But the hit of the evening was, as always, Bobby's banana pudding, made with pound cake instead of Nilla wafers. For the party Bobby fixed individual puddings, served in shot glasses, topped with whipped cream instead of meringue.

The evening had the feel of wedding receptions Cam and I used to attend in the South, back in our twenties, when everyone was getting married and it seemed every other weekend involved a flight down to Atlanta. At those southern receptions, buffets were favored over seated dinners so the guests could mingle. There was lots of mingling at the launch party, plenty of air kisses and bellowing laughter and exclamations of, "My God, it's been ages!" All the while Alice sat like a queen at the far corner table, watched over by one of Gus's alabaster statues while she sipped from a flute of Champagne, observing. I could not read Alice's facial expression, and concerned that she was feeling left out, I went to sit with her. But as soon as I got to her table she flashed me one of her radiant smiles.

"Wonderful, isn't it?" she said. "Takes me back to when I cooked here as a young woman. I used to peek through the kitchen door just to watch the expressions on the customers' faces as they ate my food. Taking delight in their delight."

And then Alice grabbed my forearm, squeezing it as she directed my gaze to a couple just walking in, looking distinctly out of place. It wasn't their style so much as their innocence, a sort of wide-eyed blinkiness, docile as cows in a roomful of foxes. The woman was small boned and petite. In style and physical features she reminded me of none other than Nancy Reagan. She wore a bright red jacket with gold buttons atop a black crepe-wool skirt, black tights, and little black patent-leather loafers, a hard plastic bow decorating each toe. Her hair was short and curly, her blue eyes so bright and twinkly I noticed them from across the restaurant. Beside her was a tall, broad-shouldered man with snowy white hair, wearing a blue blazer, also with brass buttons. Bobby was over by the bar, laughing at something with Kate. Alice and I watched as his eyes darted and he noticed the couple. His laughing mouth froze in place so it looked as if he were making an "O." And suddenly I knew what Alice had already recognized. Bobby's parents had arrived.

Bobby stood and walked to them and I could tell that he was holding himself back from running. I could see the little boy inside him just dying to fling himself upon these people. But instead he was measured, polite. I watched as he shook his father's hand; I watched as he bent down to kiss his mother's rouged cheek. She gave the side of his face a pat.

"Well it's about damn time," said Alice. "Though I hate that it took a good book review in the *New York Times* to get those two to show up for Bobby."

"You don't know that," I said. "Maybe they would have come anyway. It's not the first good review the *Times* has bestowed upon him. Maybe they are finally ready."

"Maybe," said Alice.

And what of myself, a recently divorced woman who discovered at age forty-four that her father was a black man (mixed, actually) passing as white? I think it is fair to say that I no longer have a clear sense of who I am. I think it is fair to say that I have become more interested in observing the world, rather than judging it. I have a lemon-yellow 8-speed bike, an "apartment-warming" present from Bobby, given to me when I first moved into the city, after my divorce was finalized and the Connecticut house had been sold. Weather willing, most days after work I bike the trails through Central Park, just for the fun of it. (A woman my age, biking just for fun.) When I cross town to go swim at the Y or eat dinner with Aunt Kate and Jack, I usually bike there, too. I like passing through the city this way. It's faster than walking but still close to the ground, which is more and more where I feel at home these days.

The eighteen months of alimony I received, plus my share of the profits from the sale of the Connecticut home, make for a small nest egg that won't last long. Finding a full-time job was a necessity, and once again Aunt Kate stepped in, securing a place for me as a junior editor at PML, with a focus on what Kate calls literary cookbooks. Not just recipes, but the stories that go along with them. Like the story that accompanies Bobby's recipe for his grandmother's pound cake, how she sold ten a week for years, tithing the profits and saving the rest, which she eventually gave to Bobby, so he could move to New York and try to be free.

I am lucky to have the job. I enjoy the work. I wish I were paid more.

I think of what Daddy said, in his rueful way, about winning the prestigious award for advances he made in genetic research. That all it cost was everything. I think of how his words apply to me. How there has been a steady burning away of all I once knew: my marriage, my financial stability, even my whiteness. I am no longer white, exactly, but what of being black can I claim? What of being black can my daughters claim? What of being black do we really know? What is it to be black if you were raised white in Connecticut? And yet a part of me always knew. A part of me always knew that something didn't quite add up in our family, that something was off. But the adults all around me whispered, "Shhh, shhh, shhh. Everything is fine." All the while Daddy smeared zinc oxide on me all summer, insisted I wear long-sleeved shirts at the beach. All the while my hair curled and kinked, and a small cut on my arm blossomed into a raised scar, which I now know is a keloid, common to African-Americans, one of the reasons black girls' ears are often pierced early, since keloid scarring is much less likely to occur before puberty.

My own body knew my identity long before I ever did.

I have started going to church with Bobby. Cradle Baptist that he is, he has not been able to give up God completely, which is a blessing for me, as he is watering the small seed of faith that sprouted after my divorce. We attend a small Episcopal church in my upper Upper West Side neighborhood, near the Hungarian Pastry Shop, where we often go after services for coffee and strudel. The priest at Church of the Epiphany, Father Cappey, is an old hippie who still wears his hair in a ponytail, even though it is now completely gray and he has a bald spot on the back of his head. Bobby would prefer we went to the more refined services at St. John the Divine, the grand cathedral only a few blocks away. But I begged for us to commit to this small, raggedy church, and Bobby tolerates it because he likes my company and the bread served at communion—offered to whoever wants to take of it—is homemade and sweet.

I think I might have a little crush on Father Cappey, despite the ponytail. I love his exuberance, love how he will spontaneously shout, "Rejoice!" from the pulpit, in response to nothing more than being alive. How he is out on the streets nearly every morning, talking to the homeless, buying them cups of coffee, handing out sandwiches, directing them to shelters. There is nothing academic or removed about Father Cappey's work, and yet his sermons are intellectually engaging. My favorite was his sermon on living in New York. How living in this teeming city, a city of a multitude of cultures, a city that is constantly shifting in its identity, provides us with a profound opportunity to embrace impermanence. How those of us who are renters are perhaps in a better position to recognize that our time here on earth is a borrowed gift. That it's not ours to own, though it is ours to relish. That it's still worth beautifying, even though it's temporary. So paint the walls, plant tomatoes in pots on the fire escape, but don't cling. Because eventually we will all be asked to move on.

Today Bobby and I arrive late, slipping into a back pew during the first Scripture reading. Bobby and I are both a little hungover, having attended a dinner last night at Aunt Kate's, which included multiple courses and multiple wine pairings. Jack had invited a friend of his to the dinner, a veteran war photographer, rugged and masculine, though twenty years my senior. Kate thought he might be a good match for me. I enjoyed his company but felt no romantic spark. But that doesn't mean I didn't linger through the evening, letting my wineglass be refilled again and again.

And so this morning I have a dull headache and am fighting feelings of nausea. It is no small feat that Bobby and I made it to church at all, but somehow, attending services once a week has become a touchstone for me. It's not about belief exactly. It's about the ritual, the hymns, the communion. I lean my head back on the pew, shut my eyes. And then I notice a particular smell, almost like wet fur. It started drizzling as we arrived at the church. Perhaps Bobby's sports jacket has wool in it and that is what I am smelling. Eyes still closed, I hear a fast panting, almost grotesque in its rapidity. I glance at Bobby, trying to figure out if the panting is coming from him. His eyes are also closed, head leaned back against the pew. He is hungover for sure, but breathing regularly.

Where is the noise coming from? I look down the aisle at the people to the right of us. No one *seems* to be breathing particularly loudly, but somewhere there is panting. Strange. And then I hear a cat's meow, and suddenly I am aware of the different energy all around. An energy that is low and close to the ground. And so I look down, and not a foot away from where my feet rest on the wooden floor is a beautiful golden retriever, head on its paws. I look to my left and the woman sitting in the pew across the aisle has a fat cat, white with gray markings, sitting on her lap, a leash attached to its collar. (A cat on a leash!)

Now that I know what to look for, I realize there are animals everywhere. Up ahead are two parakeets in a wire cage; three pews down is a white bunny quivering in a woman's lap. I lean into the aisle, bending so I can glimpse the bottoms of all of the pews. Dogs abound. And in the laps of fellow congregants are all kinds of creatures: a goldfish in a bowl, a snake in an aquarium, a ferret on a leash, a hamster in a cage, and even, perched on the shoulder of one man up front, a brown-and-white-speckled hen. Like my father's pet chicken when he was a boy.

I lean into Bobby and whisper, "Today must be the Blessing of the Animals!"

"Of course," he says. "They announced it last week."

I must not have been paying attention when the announcement was made. My whole life it seems I have not paid attention.

I have never been to an animal blessing before. I've heard about them but could never quite conceive how all of those different creatures could abide each other's company in such close quarters. Is it the spirit of this place that keeps this menagerie of animals in peaceful proximity to each other? Or perhaps it is simply that the people who bring their animals are responsible and only bring pets that can handle such stimulation.

I am stimulated. I look and look and look, seeing more and more animals within the walls of this holy place. And then I hear a commotion behind me and I turn to see a single woman, a latecomer to the service, her silver hair pulled back by old-fashioned combs, wearing a black-ribbed turtleneck and cat eye glasses, accompanied by a bright blue peacock, a plume of soft feathers undulating behind. When they reach the very front pew, where the only empty seats remain, the bird pauses dead center and spreads his long plume, revealing a glorious fan many times the size of his body. Each outstretched feather is dotted with vibrant green eyes, a thousand eyes filling the church. I feel myself grow still as I take it all in, as I allow myself to feel wonder, awe. I am surrounded by heartbeats, some rapid, some slow. Some inside furry bodies, some inside winged ones, some inside our own imperfect skin.

Acknowledgments

A huge thanks to Claudia Ballard and Suzanne Gluck at William Morris Endeavor. Thanks also to Rebecca Oliver, who helped launch this project. Thank you to the Touchstone imprint at Simon & Schuster, led by the fabulous Stacy Creamer. Touchstone has been championing my books since the beginning of my career, and I am deeply grateful for their rock-solid support. Special thanks to the lovely Sally Kim. And thanks to the amazing and intrepid Marcia Burch. Thank you to my editor, Trish Todd. Trish, thank you for giving me permission to go dark and deep. This is not always something a nice southern lady wants to do, but it was something I *needed* to do. I wrote this book during the most challenging period of my life thus far, and I quite literally couldn't have done it without your steady encouragement and faith in my ability.

While Alice Stone is a fictitious character, the seeds of inspiration for such a formidable woman came from the late, great Edna Lewis, raised in a vibrant community of freed slaves near Charlottesville, Virginia, who later became chef at the now shuttered Café Nicholson, an eastside literary salon legendary for its food and famous clientele. Though Alice and Edna share some biographical details in common, early on in the writing of this novel Alice morphed into an original character with her own story to tell, a story that was born from my imagination, including the story of Alice's relationship with her brother James.

Bobby Banks in turn was inspired by several brave and wonderful men: a friend of my mother's who spoke to me of growing up gay in Georgia in an era before "pride" was ever associated with homosexuality; a friend who came of age in New York City in the late 1970s and early 1980s and had the thrill of watching Balanchine's dancers fly across the stage; and a southern friend who was indeed a Royal Ambassador—not to mention an Eagle Scout—and had to figure out which parts of his background to hold on to and which to jettison once he matured fully into his authentic self. And of course I was also inspired by the cross-generational, cross-racial friendship between Edna Lewis and the inordinately talented chef Scott Peacock. Scott Peacock has his own amazing story to tell about his relationship with Miss Lewis, but I hope my characters Alice and Bobby honor the transformative example that Scott and Edna set.

I read so many books in preparation for writing this one. Hundreds. I want to point to a few that were especially helpful: Isabel Wilkerson's stunning *The Warmth of Other Suns* taught me so much about the Great Migration and the brave souls who fled the Jim Crow South, not because they wanted to leave their homeland but because it was life-threateningly dangerous to stay. Edna Lewis's *The Taste of Country Cooking* is an American treasure, chronicling the farming life of a community of freed slaves in Virginia, as is Scott Peacock and Edna Lewis's collaborative effort, *The Gift of Southern Cooking.* Mary Cantwell's *Manhattan When I Was Young* put me smack dab in the middle of New York at midcentury, as did the stunning collection of photographs by Karl Bissinger, *The Luminous Years.* Judith Jones's *The Tenth Muse* showed me the culinary evolution America has gone through over the past sixty years. Charles Kaiser's *The Gay Metropolis* helped me better understand gay life in the 1980s, especially the devastation wrought by the AIDS epidemic and the pernicious silence surrounding it. There is a short film that has had a long-lasting influence on my life, *Southern Family* by Keith Wilson. *Southern Family* is Keith's tribute to his grandma and great-grandma, both Southern Baptists from Georgia who refused to believe that their gay grandson was anything but precious in God's eyes. I have never forgotten those two women's shining examples of unconditional love, and I tried to pay a small tribute to them through Bobby Banks's meemaw.

I have an incredible community of writers in my life. Thanks to them all, especially Todd Johnson, who read parts of this novel along the way and offered great insight. Thank you to my tireless writing group, Sheri Joseph, Jessica Handler, Beth Gylys, and Peter McDade. Thanks to Patti Callahan Henry for her spirit, her warmth, and her talent. Thank you to Joshilyn Jackson, one of the most remarkable women I know—a damn fine writer with dead-on storytelling instincts who is also in possession of a big, generous, truthful heart. Joshilyn, I'm going to go all Baptist on you here and say that you are truly a blessing in my life.

Alan, our paths have split, but I am grateful for the time we walked together. I am grateful, too, for the friends who stepped in and offered a safety net when I fell from the nest: Ellen Sinaiko in San Francisco; Katharine Roman, Kasey Foster, and Christa Thomas in New York; Peter and Bruce when I returned to Atlanta. Peter and Bruce were truly my guardian angels of divorce, offering me their light-filled carriage house for five months while I regrouped. Their beautiful little girls would visit me nearly every afternoon, insisting we don costume jewelry and have a dance party. Thank you, beautiful girls. You saved me. Thank you, also, to Sarah Enders, wise and wonderful friend. And thanks to Gannon Murphy, fellow seeker.

Thank you to Johnny Nicholson for talking to me about the

golden days of his café, and thank you, the Fales Library at NYU, for access to the Café Nicholson archives. I drafted a lot of this book in the main branch of the New York Public Library. What a beautiful space. Thank you to all who make public libraries happen. Thank you to Greg Johnson for his grandmother's pound cake recipe. Thanks to Steven Soba, Frederick Brooks, and Addie "Louise" Williams for talking to me about their formative experiences—Steven's in New York, Louise's and Frederick's in Georgia. Thank you to Brett Gadsden of Emory University for reading the prologue of this book and giving me invaluable suggestions on how to improve it. All mistakes are mine. Thank you also to my writing students at Emory and SCAD. It is a common trope for each generation to bemoan the one that follows, but working with y'all leads me to the opposite conclusion: The future looks bright.

Thank you to my family, which constitutes a truly diverse mishmash of backgrounds and beliefs, yet can still gather in affection over pizza and beer (Coca-Cola for the teetotalers among us). Special thanks to my parents, Ruth and Tim White. Never have they said, "Shhh, shhh. Don't say that," about anything I've ever written, but instead have responded to my books with love and pride. Thank you to my sister Lauren Myracle for her boundless love and support. Thank you to Wendy Palmer Patterson, my lighthouse in the storm. And finally, thank you to Sam Redburn Reid for gracing me with the Sam-ness of Sam. You make me feel, to quote Kathryn Calder, *safe, safe right here.*

Mittie Cumbie Wade's Sour Cream Pound Cake:

I don't have a meemaw known for her pound cake, but my friend Greg Johnson's grandmother, Mittie Cumbie Wade of Cairo, Georgia, was famous for hers. Greg says his relatives would line up to get a slice of this cake anytime it was served. It makes a cake with a wonderfully moist crumb and a crackly, sugar-cookie-like crust.

2 sticks unsalted butter*
3 cups sugar
6 eggs*
1 teaspoon good quality vanilla extract
Small pinch of salt (I use ¼ teaspoon kosher salt to good effect)
3 cups all-purpose flour (I sift it, though Greg says it's not necessary)
½ teaspoon baking soda
1 cup sour cream*

*Ingredients note: Before you get started, let your eggs and butter come to room temperature. This is crucial. I also premeasure the cup of sour cream and let it come to room temperature, too.

1. Preheat the oven to 325°F.
2. Butter and flour a tube pan.
3. In a stand mixer, cream together the butter and sugar. I do this for a good 3 to 5 minutes, letting the mixture get light in color and fluffy.
4. Add eggs one at a time, beating well after adding each one.
5. Add the vanilla extract and a pinch of salt and mix.
6. Stir together flour and baking soda, then add dry ingredients to wet ingredients just until it is about half mixed.
7. Add sour cream. Mix until all ingredients are combined and batter looks creamy, but don't overmix.
8. Pour into the buttered and floured tube pan and bake on the center rack at 325°F for about 90 minutes. It may need to cook a little longer (5 minutes or so) in a gas oven.

Variations:

1. Add ¼ teaspoon pure almond extract to the batter along with the vanilla.
2. Add 1 teaspoon grated lemon zest to the batter along with the vanilla.
3. Seal cooked cake with a warm lemon-sugar glaze. (Really delicious!)

About the Author

Susan Rebecca White is the author of the critically acclaimed novels *Bound South* and *A Soft Place to Land.* Born and raised in Atlanta, Georgia, Susan earned a BA in English from Brown University and her MFA in creative writing from Hollins University. She currently lives in Atlanta, where she teaches creative writing at Emory University.